SKY
WITHOUT
STARS

SYSTEM DIVINE: BOOK 1

JESSICA BRODY & JOANNE RENDELL

SIMON PULSE

NEW YORK   LONDON   TORONTO   SYDNEY   NEW DELHI

SIMON PULSE

An imprint of Simon & Schuster Children's Publishing Division

1230 Avenue of the Americas, New York, New York 10020

First Simon Pulse hardcover edition March 2019

Text copyright © 2019 by Jessica Brody Entertainment LLC and Joanne Rendell

Jacket illustration copyright © 2019 by Billelis

Map illustrations copyright © 2019 by Francesca Baerald

All rights reserved, including the right of reproduction in whole or in part in any form.

SIMON PULSE and colophon are registered trademarks of Simon & Schuster, Inc.

For information about special discounts for bulk purchases, please contact Simon & Schuster Special Sales at 1-866-506-1949 or business@simonandschuster.com.

The Simon & Schuster Speakers Bureau can bring authors to your live event.

For more information or to book an event contact the Simon & Schuster Speakers Bureau at 1-866-248-3049 or visit our website at www.simonspeakers.com.

Jacket designed by Jessica Handelman

Interior designed by Mike Rosamilia

The text of this book was set in Adobe Caslon Pro.

Manufactured in the United States of America

2 4 6 8 10 9 7 5 3 1

Library of Congress Cataloging-in-Publication Data

Names: Brody, Jessica, author. | Rendell, Joanne, author.

Title: Sky without stars / by Jessica Brody and Joanne Rendell.

Description: First Simon Pulse hardcover edition. | New York : Simon Pulse, 2019. |

Series: System Divine ; 1 | Summary: "This sweeping reimagining of *Les Misérables* tells the story of three teens from very different backgrounds who are thrown together amidst the looming threat of revolution on the French planet-colony of Laterre"—Provided by publisher.

Identifiers: LCCN 2018030021 | ISBN 9781534410633 (hc) | ISBN 9781534410657 (eBook)

Subjects: | CYAC: Space colonies—Fiction. | Criminals—Fiction. |

Revolutions—Fiction. | Science fiction.

Classification: LCC PZ7.B786157 Sky 2019 | DDC [Fic]—dc23

LC record available at https://lccn.loc.gov/2018030021

To our three Sols—
Benny, Brad, and Charlie

L'homme est né libre, et partout il est dans les fers.
(Man is born free, and everywhere he is in chains.)
—Jean-Jacques Rousseau

MED CENTER

POLICIER
PRECINCT

10.000 people/fret

"Honest work for an honest chance."

- PART 1 -
ASCENSION

The System Divine offered hope. Hope to the inhabitants of a dying world. With its three beautiful Sols and twelve habitable planets, the miraculous system would become a new home. A new start. A place where twelve powerful families could begin again. The Paresse family was one of those families and Laterre was their new planet.

High on a hill, the family built their Grand Palais under a vast climate-controlled dome. And in the flatlands below lived their chosen people. The magnificent ships that had once carried these workers across the galaxies became their homes.

They were the lucky ones.

At first.

From *The Chronicles of the Sisterhood*,
Volume 1, Chapter 3

- CHAPTER 1 -
CHATINE

THE RAIN WAS FALLING SIDEWAYS IN THE MARSH. It was never a straight downpour. It was always crooked. Just like the people here. Con artists and hustlers and crocs, the lot of them.

Anyone can be a saint until they're hungry enough.

Chatine Renard was perched high above it all, watching the stream of people churn through the busy marketplace like clotted blood through a vein. She was straddling an exposed metal beam that once connected the old freightship to its roof.

At least, that's what Chatine had been told—that the Frets were once titanic flying vessels that soared across the galaxy, bringing her ancestors to the planet of Laterre, the coldest and wettest of the twelve planets in the System Divine. But years of neglect and crooked rain had corroded the PermaSteel walls and ceilings, turning the staterooms in the passenger freightships into leaky, mold-ridden housing for the poor, and this cargo freightship into an open-air marketplace.

Chatine pulled her hood farther down her forehead in an attempt to block her face. Much to her dismay, she'd noticed over the past few years that her eyelashes had grown longer, her chest had filled out, her cheekbones had become more pronounced, and her nose had slimmed to a dainty point, which she despised.

She had streaked her face with mud before coming to the Marsh today, but every time she caught sight of her reflection in a puddle or the metal of a partially collapsed wall, she cringed at how much she still looked like a girl.

So inconvenient.

The Marsh was far more crowded today than usual. Chatine leaned forward and balanced on her stomach, hugging the beam to her chest as she scanned the countless faces that passed beneath her. They were always the same faces. Poor, downtrodden souls like her trying to find creative ways to stretch their weekly wages.

Or con their neighbor out of a larg or two.

Newcomers were rare to the Marsh. No one outside of the Third Estate bothered with the picked-over cabbages and mangy turnips for sale. With the exception of Inspecteur Limier and his army of Policier droids tasked with keeping the peace, the Frets and the marketplace in its center were normally avoided at all costs by anyone who didn't live here.

Which was why the man in the long coat immediately caught Chatine's eye. His wealth was written all over his groomed black beard, matching hair, pressed clothes, and sparkling adornments.

Second Estate, to be sure.

She'd never known the First Estate to ever venture out of Ledôme. The climate-controlled biodome sat high on the hill on the outskirts of the capital city of Vallonay, shielding the First Estate from Laterre's persistent downpours.

And the slums below.

Chatine's eyes raked over the man, taking in every stitch and every button. Her gaze expertly landed on the gold medallion dangling like bait from his neck. She didn't have to see it up close to know it was a relic from the Last Days, rescued from the burning embers of a dying planet. The Second Estate loved their First World relics.

Five hundred largs easy, Chatine calculated in her head. *Enough money to feed an entire Third Estate family for weeks.*

But it wouldn't be long before the rest of the crocs in the Marsh spotted the treasure too and made their play. Which meant Chatine had to move fast.

Gripping the beam with both hands, she swung her legs over the side and launched her body to the nearby catwalk, landing silently in a crouch. Directly underneath her, the man continued farther into the marketplace, weaving around the loose chickens that roamed the stalls searching for scraps. His gaze swept left and right as though he was taking mental inventory of the space.

For a moment, Chatine wondered what he was doing here. Had he gotten lost on his way back up to Ledôme? Or was he here on some kind of business? But then she remembered the annual Ascension happening later today and reasoned he was probably a foreman of a fabrique, come to round up his workers who were skipping out on their shifts to get jacked up on weed wine, all the while hoping to win a new life.

"Win a new life?" Chatine muttered to herself, and let out a bitter laugh.

Deluded fools, all of them.

She crept across the grid of overhead walkways and ramps, skillfully ducking to avoid broken water pipes and leaping over giant chasms in the grated floor. All the while, she kept a close watch on the man, making sure she was never more than a few steps behind him.

He finally slowed near Madame Dufour's stall, pulled an apricot from his pocket, and took a large bite, the juice dripping into his beard. Chatine's mouth started to water. She'd only ever tasted an apricot once, when a crate had fallen off the back of a cargo transporteur delivering fruit from the hothouses to Ledôme.

Chatine watched Madame Dufour size the man up with sinister fascination. The old croc was practically licking her lips at the sight of such an easy mark.

It was now or never.

Ducking under the broken railing, Chatine grabbed onto the raised rim of the walkway floor and somersaulted over the edge. She whipped her body forward, fell three mètres down, and adeptly caught the beam below her. She circled around until it rested against her hips and she could balance there.

She was now only a mètre above the man's head. Yet with the buzz of the busy marketplace, no one even bothered to look up.

"What a pitiful sight," the man said, taking another bite of his apricot. He didn't even bother to hide his disgust. The Second Estate rarely did. It was something about being stuck in the middle, Chatine had always noticed—not quite rulers and yet far from being one of the wretched like her—that gave the Second Estate their shameless sense of arrogance.

They were almost more intolerable than the First Estate.

Almost.

Chatine's gaze cut to the left, taking in the tower of empty crates stacked up next to Madame Dufour's stall. She shimmied along the beam until she was directly above them. Then, she tipped forward, rotated around, and kicked both feet out in front of her.

The crash was louder than she anticipated. The crates toppled to the ground, avalanching around the man as he fell to his knees with a grunt.

Chatine moved quickly. She landed in a squat, then crawled through the wreckage until she found the man and graciously helped him back onto his feet. He was so busy brushing dust and cabbage leaves from his coat, he didn't even feel the medallion being lifted from his neck.

"Are you all right, monsieur?" Chatine asked in her friendliest tone, slipping the pendant into her pocket.

The man barely looked at her as he straightened his hat. "Quite all right, boy."

"You must be careful in the Marsh, monsieur. It isn't safe for someone of your rank."

"Merci," he said dismissively as he tossed the apricot he'd been eating toward Chatine.

She caught it and flashed him an appreciative smile. "Vive Laterre."

"Vive Laterre," he echoed before turning away.

Chatine grinned at the man's back as she turned on her heel and slipped the half-eaten apricot into her pocket. It took all her strength not to consume the entire thing here and now.

She knew the man would hardly even miss that gold medallion from his neck. He probably had ten just like it back in his manoir in Ledôme. But to her, it was everything.

It would *change* everything.

The wind picked up, howling through the stalls and biting viciously at Chatine's skin. She pulled her tattered black coat tighter around her, trying in vain to stave off the chill. But the holes and ripped lining of her clothes weren't the problem. It was the hunger—the ribs poking through her skin. There wasn't a single shred of insulation left on her body.

But after that score, she was finding it hard to care.

As Chatine headed toward the south exit of the Marsh, weaving through stalls selling moldy potatoes, slimy leeks, and pungent seaweed dragged in from the nearby docks, there was a new lightness to her gait. A new hopefulness in her step.

But just before passing through what used to be the old cargo ship's loading bay, Chatine felt a large hand clamp down on her shoulder and she stopped dead in her tracks, a shiver running through her.

"So nice of you to help out a member of the Second Estate," a cold, robotic voice said. "I've never seen such chivalry from a *Renard*."

The emphasis he placed on her last name made Chatine squirm.

She closed her eyes, mustering strength, and painted on a blithe smile before slowly turning around.

"Inspecteur Limier," she said. "Always a pleasure."

His stony expression didn't change. It hardly ever did. The circuitry implants on the left side of his face made it nearly impossible for the inspecteur to express any emotion. Chatine often wondered if the man was even *capable* of smiling.

"I wish I could say the same for you, Théo." His tone was flat.

Only her parents called her Chatine. Everyone in the Frets knew her as Théo. It was the name she'd given herself ten years ago, when they'd first moved to the capital city of Vallonay and Chatine had decided that life as a boy would be much less complicated than life as a girl.

Chatine clucked her tongue. "I'm sorry you feel that way, Inspecteur."

"What did you take from the kind monsieur?" Limier asked, his half-human, half-robot voice clicking on the hard consonants.

Chatine refreshed her smile. "Whatever do you mean, Inspecteur? I know better than to steal from the hand that feeds me."

She nearly gagged on the words. But if they saved her from a one-way ticket to Bastille—the price you paid for stealing from an upper estate—then she could choke her way through them.

Chatine held her breath as the inspecteur's circuitry flickered on his face. He was computing the information, analyzing her words, searching for hints of perjury. Over the past ten years of living in the Frets, Chatine had learned how to lie. But lying to a human being was one thing. Lying to a cyborg inspecteur, programmed to seek the truth, was quite another.

She waited, keeping her smile taut until the circuits stopped flashing.

"Will that be all, Inspecteur?" Chatine asked, smiling sweetly while pressing her hands against her tattered black pants. Her palms were starting to sweat, and she didn't want his heat sensors to pick up on it.

Then, slowly, Chatine watched the inspecteur's gloved hand extend toward her. With a soft touch that chilled her to the bone, he pushed up her black hood to reveal more of her face. His electric orange eye blinked to life, scanning her features. It seemed to linger a beat too long on her high, feminine cheekbones.

Panic bloomed in her chest. *Can it see who I really am?*

Chatine hastily took a step back, out of the inspecteur's reach, and yanked her hood back down. "My maman is expecting me home," she said. "So, if you don't mind, I'll be going now."

"Of course," the inspecteur replied.

"Thank you, Inspecteur. Vive Laterre."

As Chatine turned to leave, she felt her entire body collapse with relief. She had done it. She had fooled his sensors. She was a better liar than even she had come to believe.

"I'll just need to check your pockets first."

Chatine froze. She quickly surveyed her surroundings. She spotted five Policier droids in her vicinity. More than usually roamed the Marsh, due to the annual Ascension ceremony today. The droids—or bashers, as they were referred to around here—stood at almost twice the size of an average man, and their slate-gray exoskeletons crunched and whirred as they walked.

Chatine wasn't afraid of them, though. She'd escaped Policier droids plenty of times. They were fast and stronger than ten men, but they still had their limitations. For instance, they couldn't climb.

Careful not to move her head, Chatine glanced up, thanking her lucky Sols that there was an old pipe running directly over her head. She refused to get flown off to Bastille. A neighbor was currently serving three years for stealing a measly sac of turnips. A First World relic lifted off a Second Estater? She'd be looking at ten years minimum. And hardly anyone lived that long on the moon.

She slowly spun back around to face Limier. "Of course, Inspecteur. I have nothing to hide."

Flashing another smile, Chatine stuffed her hand into her pocket and felt the medallion cool and smooth against her skin. The inspecteur once again reached a hand in her direction. Then, before he could react, Chatine hurled the apricot the monsieur had given her straight at the inspecteur's face. His circuitry sparked as his brain tried to make sense of the incoming object. Chatine bolted, scrambling onto a table full of fabric scraps before leaping toward the pipe.

For a second, she was flying, soaring above the inspecteur, the shoppers in the Marsh, and the Policier droids who were just starting to take notice of the disturbance. As she caught the pipe, she used her momentum to circle her legs around until she was straddling the rusty metal pole.

"Paralyze him!" Inspecteur Limier shouted to his droids, peering up at Chatine. His circuitry was going haywire, like someone had hacked the signal. "Now!"

The bashers maneuvered their bulky PermaSteel bodies around one another, assembling into attack formation. Chatine knew she had to move quickly. One rayonette pulse she could dodge, but five? That would be rough.

The pipe was too narrow to walk on, so Chatine shimmied across it on her stomach, weighing her options. The north exit was out of the question. It backed up to the Vallonay Policier Precinct, where she would certainly run into more droids. There was a catwalk about three mètres ahead of her. If she could reach it without getting shot, she could crawl the rest of the way to the east exit, back near Madame Dufour's stall.

A split second later, she felt the heat of the first rayonette pulse whiz by the side of her face. She sucked in a sharp breath and shimmied faster. A second droid took aim below her, its shot perfectly aligned at her left knee. She braced herself for the impact. But just then, a group of drunk exploit workers stumbled through the fray, arguing about who among them had the most Ascension points stored up. One of them crashed right into the droid, and the pulse barely missed her leg.

"Oh, excuse me, monsieur," the drunk worker slurred to the droid, bowing ceremoniously. His friends broke out into hoots of laughter while Chatine took the opportunity to slide the rest of the way across the rusted pipe.

Thank the Sols for strong weed wine, she thought as she launched herself toward the catwalk. She caught the railing with both hands just as a third pulse was fired from below. This one glanced her left shoulder.

It wasn't a direct hit, but it was enough. The pain was instant. Like someone had scraped her skin with a blazing-hot knife. She bit her lip to keep from crying out. The sound would only improve the droids' aim.

Within seconds, her left arm started to lose sensation from the paralyzeur now pumping through her blood. She scrambled to swing her feet up over the ledge of the walkway but was unsuccessful. Now she was just dangling there, her feet paddling against the air.

The droids shoved people aside as they zeroed in on her location. More rayonette pulses tore past her, rippling and bending the air. It was only a matter of time before another one found its target.

Chatine knew she needed a distraction. She spotted a crate packed with chickens directly in front of her. She shook out her left arm, trying to chase away the numbness that was spreading toward her fingers, but it was no use. The paralyzeur was quickly working its way through her muscles.

Favoring her right hand, she gripped the railing as tightly as she could and pumped her legs until she'd built up enough momentum to reach the crate. She arched her body and kicked her legs out hard. The crate crashed to the ground and busted open. The chickens squawked and tried to fly away, but their useless wings barely allowed them to get off the ground.

The commotion was enough, though.

People were screaming, the stall owner was desperately trying to wrangle the loose birds, and the Policier droids fought to barrel through it all. But their efforts only managed to rile up the birds even more. They fluttered about, scraping people with their sharp claws.

The droids started firing with abandon. But with all the chaos below, their aim was poor. They hit more chickens than anything else. The birds absorbed the stun of the rayonettes and fell limp to the ground. They wouldn't be able to move again for a few hours.

With the droids distracted, Chatine was finally able to pull herself onto the catwalk and crawl, one-handed, across the rusty metal plank before shimmying down a support beam next to Madame Dufour's stall.

She glanced back to see the bashers still trying to push their way through the crowd to reach her. But with the number of people in the Marsh today and the riled-up chickens, it wasn't an easy task.

Madame Dufour glared at Chatine, her wrinkled arms folded across her chest. "Like father, like son," she said, making a *tsk* sound with her teeth. "Mark my words, boy, you'll be rotting on the moon before the end of this year."

Chatine flashed her a goading grin before swiping a loaf of chou bread from one of Madame Dufour's crates and darting toward the exit.

"Arrête!" The old woman's command sounded like a croak. "Get back here, you wretched croc!"

"Thanks for breakfast!" Chatine called back in a singsong voice.

And then, before the droids could track her or Madame Dufour could catch her, Chatine was gone.

Once she'd put a good distance between herself and the marketplace, she slowed to a walk and massaged her dead arm with the opposite hand. It wasn't the first time she'd been shot by a rayonette. And it probably wouldn't be the last. The sensation would return soon enough.

Chatine reached into her pocket and pulled out the pendant she had lifted from the Second Estater. She sucked off the sweet apricot juice and held the medallion in her open palm, studying it. For the first time, Chatine noticed the ornate golden Sol carved into the surface. It was unlike any of the three Sols that hung in the sky of the System Divine. This was a First World Sol. Its brilliant, fiery rays flared out to the edge of the medallion. Chatine reverently clasped the pendant around her neck, a rare genuine smile creeping across her face.

She hadn't seen the light of a Sol in nine years.

This was definitely a sign of good things to come.

- CHAPTER 2 -
CHATINE

AS CHATINE WALKED THE MUSTY, COLD HALLWAY that led to her family's couchette, she was bombarded by the familiar sounds of the Frets: people fighting over scraps of food, children's footsteps scrambling across the grated metal floors as they played games of hide-and-seek and crocs-and-bashers, the sporadic cluck of a lost chicken that had wandered away from the Marsh.

She called this eighth-floor corridor of Fret 7 the "No Way Out hallway." Partially because every time she walked under its low, rusty ceiling, she was reminded of how trapped everyone was here. But mostly because of the various corroded signs on the wall that said, NO WAY OUT.

At least, that's what Chatine had convinced herself the signs said. The truth was, she had no idea. She couldn't read them. No one could. They were written in the Forgotten Word. A cryptic code of slanted sticks and swirling lines that had gradually vanished from the minds of Laterrians shortly after the settlers arrived from the First World.

Along with their hopes for a better life.

Chatine slowed, tucked a wayward strand of light brown hair back under her hood, and pulled the loaf of chou bread she'd stolen from Madame Dufour out of her pocket. She tore it in half and immediately stuffed the second half into her boot so she wouldn't be tempted to eat it.

She supposed she could always tell her parents she'd had no luck in the Marsh today. But she knew if she wanted to keep her *other* score a secret—the First World medallion—she'd have to have something to distract them with. Her mother would never believe that Chatine would leave the Marsh empty-handed. Unless she had something to show for her morning, her mother would immediately grow suspicious. And if her mother was suspicious, then her father would start snooping. And nothing good ever came from Monsieur Renard's snooping.

She stared down at the paltry half loaf in her hand, her stomach growling at the mere sight of it. She took a single bite, forcing herself to go slowly, make it last, *chew*. But her hunger instantly took over. She swallowed the partially chewed lump, feeling the disgusting cauliflower dough pushing its way down her throat, and immediately lunged for another bite.

But before she could sink her teeth into the bread's tough exterior, she heard a piercing wail cut through the dark hallway. Chatine glanced up to see a woman seated on the floor outside one of the couchettes, trying unsuccessfully to coax a fussing baby to her breast. The baby squirmed and let out another shrill cry that tore through Chatine like a dull knife through stale, overcooked meat.

Would she *ever* be able to hear a baby cry and not feel like she was being ripped apart from the inside?

She attempted to block out the sound, but it was as if the harder she tried, the louder that baby screamed.

"Argh!" Chatine groaned. "Can't you shut him up?"

She expected the woman to explode right back at her. That was just how things worked around here. Anger in the Frets bounced around like light in an endless corridor of mirrors.

But she didn't. The woman looked up at Chatine with dark, hopeless eyes, and she started to cry.

"I'm sorry," she whimpered, burying her face in the baby's tuft of black hair. "He won't eat because there's nothing left. The milk is all gone. My body's too hungry."

Shame warmed Chatine's cheeks. She turned her back on the woman and child, preparing to flee, to find another route to her couchette so she wouldn't have to walk past them. But her legs refused to move. It was as though the paralyzeur had somehow spread from her shoulder, all the way down her body, settling into her feet.

"My husband works in the potato ferme," the woman went on, sniffling, "and makes a good wage, but he's been injured. My tokens from the fabrique just aren't enough."

The remainder of the half loaf was heavy in Chatine's hand. She stared down at it.

Stolen.

Because she, too, was starving.

Because this woman was proof that even when you played by the rules, you still starved.

And the baby was still screaming.

With a frustrated growl, Chatine spun around and stalked toward the mother and child. She didn't stop as she approached them. She simply tossed the chou bread at the woman and kept going.

Chatine could hear the woman calling out to her. "Oh, merci! Merci, ma chérie! You are sent from the Sols!"

But Chatine didn't stop. In fact, she quickened her pace until she was running. The sounds of the baby's hungry wails followed her down the hall, chasing after her, reminding her far too much of the past she'd been trying to escape for twelve years.

Chatine didn't stop running until she reached the door of her family's couchette. She was breathing heavily, and her stomach growled again.

She couldn't believe what she had just done.

That bread would have been the most she'd had to eat in days. And she'd just given it away like she had food to spare. Like she had *anything* to spare.

Chatine shook out her left hand, her fingers just starting to tingle with sensation again. She reached toward the lock on the door of the couchette but froze when she heard the unmistakable sound of her mother's voice thundering through the wall, shaking the crumbling corridors and threatening to bring down what was left of the doors.

"Thirty-five percent?! You're out of your mind if you think I'm stupid enough to give that old croc more than a tenth!"

Fantastique, Chatine thought. *She's in one of her moods.*

From the sound of it, Chatine's father had just returned from his latest job and her parents were arguing over the cuts. They were always arguing over the cuts.

Chatine reached into her boot and pulled out the other half of the chou bread. She nibbled at the edges until they looked clean-cut and not torn. As the tiny morsels of bread touched her tongue, it took all of her willpower not to cram the entire thing into her mouth and pretend it never existed.

It wasn't until she bent over to return the loaf to her boot that she noticed the tear in the fabric of her black pants, right over her knee. She must have done it when she was crawling around on the catwalk, trying to escape the droids.

Chatine sighed. Her pants were already patched with so many metal wires, chain links, and whatever other random scraps she could find around the Frets, there wasn't much fabric left to patch.

She straightened up and listened at the door. Her mother's tirade seemed to have subsided. She waved her left arm in front of the lock.

"Access granted." The latch hissed and Chatine quietly pushed the door open and slipped inside.

Chatine imagined that the couchettes must have once been clean, shiny staterooms with proper doors and running water and a stove that didn't sound like a sheep in labor. Before they turned into the decrepit slums they were now.

The Renards' couchette, however, was still one of the nicest in the Frets. Her father's position as the leader of the Délabré gang had awarded Chatine and her family some extra comforts, like their own kitchen, a location on a high floor, and two bedrooms instead of one. Most of the Third Estate didn't even have couchettes of their own. They slept in old cargo holds on the ground floor, tightly packed into shoddy bunks stacked all the way to the ceiling.

None of the couchettes had their own bathrooms. And only every other communal lavatory worked properly, making for a highly unpleasant smell that had become a constant fixture for life in the Frets.

When the Renards had first moved across the planet to Vallonay from their inn in Montfer, Chatine had spent her days outside in the semi-fresh air and her nights trying not to vomit from the stench. But since then, she'd grown accustomed to it.

It was amazing what conditions a person could get used to.

As suspected, when Chatine entered the couchette, she found her father sitting at the table in the living room, counting a large pile of shiny, Sol-shaped buttons. She remembered him talking about a job he was planning to pull at the garment fabrique. This was clearly the result. Chatine knew, based on their shape, that the buttons were supposed to go on the uniforms of Ministère officers. They were made of pure titan, which her father would undoubtedly melt down so he could use the precious silvery metal as currency.

Typically, only the First and Second Estates had access to titan. Members of the Third Estate were paid in digital tokens—or largs, as they were called around here—deposited into their profile accounts each week. That is, if you actually showed up for your assigned job, which Chatine and her parents never did.

SKY WITHOUT STARS   21

Chatine's mother was standing over Monsieur Renard, monitoring the count.

"I can't believe that greedy woman wanted thirty-five percent for flashing a tette! I could have flashed a tette for thirty-five percent!"

"Trust me. Your old tettes aren't worth thirty-five percent," Monsieur Renard said under his breath.

But her mother heard it. And so did Chatine. She attempted to stifle a chuckle but was unsuccessful. Madame Renard jerked her head up, noticing Chatine for the first time since she'd walked in. Before Chatine could see what was coming, her mother reared her hand back and slapped Chatine hard across the face.

She stumbled from the blow, slamming against the couchette door.

"What the fric?" Chatine held her throbbing cheek. "He's the one who said it!"

"These old tettes have made more money around here than both of you combined!" Madame Renard was screeching now. She turned and glared hard at Chatine. "Because I know how to use what the Sols gave me to my advantage."

Chatine bit down hard on her lip.

It had been over two years since since she'd turned sixteen, and there wasn't a day that passed when her mother didn't less-than-subtly mention how many largs a healthy young girl such as Chatine could make in Vallonay. The blood bordels paid almost double for girls her age. Once you turned twenty-five, the price started dropping.

But Chatine preferred *her* methods. They were working. And as long as she continued to bring in more largs as a boy named Théo than she ever could as a girl named Chatine, she was able to convince her parents to keep up the charade that they'd given birth to a son eighteen years ago, instead of a daughter.

And Chatine would rather empty her veins into the Secana Sea than sell her blood to the First Estate.

"What did you bring me?" Madame Renard asked, dragging

her hard gray eyes up and down Chatine's black coat, searching for extra bulk.

Chatine pulled the half loaf of chou bread from her boot and tossed it at her mother. Madame Renard caught it deftly with one hand and started to examine it, running her dirty fingernails over the edge where Chatine had torn it in half.

"Where's the rest?" Madame Renard asked. "You better not be trying to steal from me too, you worthless clochard."

Chatine returned her mother's challenging stare with one of her own, refusing to show any fear. "It came that way," she stated evenly.

Her mother's eyes narrowed. She clearly didn't believe Chatine.

"I lifted it from Dufour's stall," Chatine went on. "You know that old croc can't be trusted."

This seemed to do the trick. Her mother let out a grunt and tossed the loaf onto the table. It crashed into the pile of titan buttons that Monsieur Renard was counting, causing them to scatter.

"Fric!" Monsieur Renard swore. "Now I have to start over."

"Good." Madame Renard spat out the word. "Maybe this time you'll magically find the missing hundred you still owe me from the last job." Then she reeled back on Chatine. "Guillaume told me new bodies were delivered to the morgue this morning. Cavs ripe for the picking. You better get your dirty face over there before their profile accounts are emptied."

Chatine shivered at the thought of going to the morgue again. She hated everything about that place. The ghostly quiet hallways. The smell of rotting flesh. But mostly, she hated the cavs themselves. Those empty, unseeing eyes always seemed to be staring right into Chatine's soul.

She wanted to argue. She wanted to refuse to go, but she knew better than to disobey her mother. Her father may have been the leader of the most formidable gang in the Frets, but Madame Renard was definitely the master of the house.

Chatine clenched her fists tight and stalked into her bedroom, closing the door behind her and collapsing against it. She shut her eyes and took a moment to try to restore her angry, ragged breathing to normal.

Keep it together, she told herself. *You're almost out of here.*

She touched the small lump under the collar of her jacket—the gold Sol medallion—and could practically taste the freedom on her tongue.

It tasted *nothing* like chou bread.

"Hey," a soft voice interrupted her thoughts, and Chatine opened her eyes to see her older sister, Azelle, lying on the bed they shared, staring at the small screen embedded in the inside of her left arm.

"Why aren't you at work?" Chatine asked.

"Night shift," Azelle replied without looking up.

Unlike Chatine, Azelle never missed a day of work at her Ministère-assigned job. She worked in the TéléSkin fabrique, processing the zyttrium metal that arrived by the shipload from Bastille and manufacturing it into new Skins to be implanted in the arms of the thousands of children born each year. When Azelle wasn't dutifully logging hours at the fabrique, she could usually be found here, in the couchette.

Chatine was supposed to work in the fabriques too. The textile fabrique. At least that's what her Skin told her. But she rarely listened to anything her Skin had to say. She was convinced the Ministère had those things rigged, which was why she'd rigged hers right back. She'd paid a pretty larg to have her Skin hacked so that her profile said Théo Renard and so that the Ministère could no longer track her whereabouts or send her reminders to check in at work each morning. But there were certain notifications—like Universal Alerts, curfew warnings, and the reminder for her monthly Vitamin D injection— that she simply couldn't deactivate.

"Where you been?" Azelle asked.

"In the Marsh," Chatine replied, opening a tin box next to their bed and riffling around until she found a stray piece of steel wire. She bent down and hastily threaded the metal through the fabric of her pants, stitching the tear back together. It wasn't her finest patch-up job, but she couldn't be bothered to care at this point.

"I was just AirLinking with Noemie down the hall," Azelle said, her light gray eyes never leaving her arm. "She said there's a woman in her fabrique who's trying to organize a protest for more wages."

Chatine snorted. She didn't have time for murmurings of protests. They never worked. The last major rebellion was in 488, seventeen years earlier, instigated by the Vangarde, a group led by a woman who called herself Citizen Rousseau. Thousands of Third Estaters lost their lives for that woman, who was now locked away on Bastille. And for what? What did they have to show for it?

Nothing but a pile of ashes.

There were always rumors of unrest floating around the city of Vallonay. Hopeful fools trying to rally supporters, just as Citizen Rousseau had done back in 488.

"I don't know why anyone would be stupid enough to protest," Azelle said.

Chatine moved to the foot of their bed and popped up the metal floor grate, pulling out the wool sac that she kept hidden underneath. She wasn't worried about Azelle noticing. The Ascension was starting in a few hours. The girl would be glued to her Skin for the rest of the morning.

"If you're caught, you'll be immediately flown off to Bastille and the Ministère will delete *all* your Ascension points," Azelle went on. "I can't think of anything more horrible than that!"

Chatine fought the urge to argue that she could think of punishments much worse than losing Ascension points. The last thing she needed right now was a fight with Azelle over the credibility of the all-powerful Ministère. Her sister lived and died by their laws and broadcasts. In Azelle's eyes, the Second Estate—and the Ministère especially—were as powerful as Sols.

In Chatine's eyes, the Second Estate were nothing but gullible marks to steal from.

She reached into the sac and started transferring items to her pockets. As she did, she took a mental inventory of each object in her collection, making sure nothing had disappeared in the night. In a family of thieves and con artists, you could never be too safe with your secret possessions.

Some of the First World relics she knew the names and purposes of—like watch, pencil, and Sol-glasses. But for others, she'd had to resort to her own interpretations. Like the bound pile of papers with scribblings of the Forgotten Word on them. Or the thin black rectangle with the metal backing that Chatine thought looked like an external Skin.

Chatine stuffed the last of the items into her pockets. She put the empty sac back into the hole in the floor and replaced the grate. After patting down the pockets of her long black coat and making sure none of her clothing looked suspiciously bulky, she headed toward the door.

"Where are you going?" In her shock, Azelle actually looked up. "The Ascension is starting at 14.30! Don't you want to watch it with me? What if they call your name?"

"They're not going to call my name," Chatine replied. If there was anything on this wretched, Sol-less planet she could be sure of, it was that they would *never* call her name.

"But they could!" Azelle said. "Everyone is equal in the eyes of the Ascension. Anyone can be chosen. That's the beauty of it. Your luck could change just that fast. Honest work for an honest chance."

Chatine's sister was parroting the party line of the Ministère word for word. It was the reason Azelle checked in at the Skin fabrique two minutes early every day. The reason she worked until her hands were raw and her feet grew blisters. Azelle was the only one in the family who played by the rules, because she was the only one who bought into the "honest work for an honest chance" philosophy that the Ministère tried to brainwash into everyone from birth. Chatine knew the truth, though. The only chances you got around here were the ones you took for yourself.

"I think I have a good shot this year," Azelle continued, returning her attention to her Skin. "I've been checking in every day, watching all the Ministère broadcasts, and logging all my hours. I even put in overtime at the fabrique the last few months. I have almost twenty-five hundred points stored up." Azelle gasped and gestured excitedly toward her arm. "Oh my Sols, look! They're showing footage of Marcellus Bonnefaçon! I saw him in the Marsh the other day. He's just as dreamy in person as he is on the Skin."

Chatine glanced over at her sister's arm and caught a glimpse at the familiar face of one of the Second Estate's most famous members: the grandson of the powerful General Bonnefaçon, and an officer. The Ministère loved broadcasting Marcellus's pretty face on the Skins whenever they got the chance. They'd been doing it ever since he came of age, turning him into a regular Laterre celebrity. He was almost as famous as the Patriarche and Matrone themselves.

In the clip, Marcellus was sporting that ridiculous shiny dark hair, flawless Second Estate skin, and gleaming smile.

Fric, Chatine thought. *Does the boy clean his teeth with soap? Who has teeth that white?*

Azelle jabbed at the screen, maxing out the volume of the implanted audio chip in her ear. "Oh," she sighed at whatever Officer Bonnefaçon was saying in the clip. "He's so charming!"

Chatine knew that all the girls in the Frets had a hopeless crush on Marcellus, including her sister. Another unobtainable thing for them to dream about. But Chatine honestly couldn't understand why. He was one of the highest-ranking members of the Second Estate, which automatically meant he was stuck-up, pretentious, and despicable.

"Did you know General Bonnefaçon is grooming Marcellus to be the next commandeur of the Ministère?" Azelle asked wistfully. "That's what everyone in the Frets is saying. They think that's why he's been seen around the Marsh lately. He's been training with Inspecteur Limier."

Chatine shuddered at the memory of her earlier encounter with the creepy cyborg inspecteur.

"He'll probably be there today for the Ascension. Are you going back to the Marsh? Maybe you'll bump into him!" Azelle said with sudden excitement. "Wouldn't that be amazing?"

"Yes," Chatine replied. And she meant it. Marcellus Bonnefaçon was extremely wealthy. The thought of the things she could cop off that boy if she ever got the chance to *bump* into him made her head spin.

But she would not be returning to the Marsh today. Not if she could help it. With the Ascension happening, that place would be a mess and she wanted to stay as far away as possible. Even Azelle was smart enough to watch the ceremony from home.

Her sister sat up in bed, leaning her back against the wall and tucking her legs in while she kept her gaze trained on her Skin. "Oh Sols, please pick me this time. *Please* pick me."

Chatine watched her with a mixture of pity and annoyance. If Azelle spent half as much time and energy conning as she did collecting points for the Ascension, their family would probably be rich by now.

Chatine checked the messy knot of hair at the back of her head, making sure it was properly hidden behind her hood. It wouldn't be much longer now until she could sell it all to Madame Seezau. The croc paid well, and it was a nice side income for Chatine. She just hated this in-between phase, when her hair was long enough to give her away as a girl, but not yet long enough to get the full two hundred largs.

Azelle sighed dramatically, cupping her chin in her hand as she watched more pre-Ascension footage on her Skin. "I mean, how fantastique would it be to live inside Ledôme? Where the Sols shine four hundred and eight days a year."

"*Fake* Sols," Chatine corrected.

But it was as though Azelle hadn't even heard her. "There's never any rain. And you get to live right next to the Grand Palais. I bet you'd even get to see the Patriarche and Matrone every once in a while. I like this one so much better than the last Patriarche. He was so serious and boring all the time. This one looks like he'd actually be fun to hang out with. And his Premier Enfant is so cute! Did you see the special they ran on her yesterday? She's turning three next week and is finally speaking full sentences. She still can't pronounce 'Third Estate,' though. She calls it the 'Terd Estate.' Isn't that beyond adorable? I think she looks like the Matrone, but Noemie was saying yesterday that . . ."

Chatine rolled her eyes and left the room without bothering to hear the rest of the story. She knew it would probably be minutes before Azelle even realized she was gone.

Her parents were still arguing over the Ministère buttons on the table when Chatine re-emerged into the living room of the couchette. Her mother glanced up long enough to shoot Chatine a nasty glare and toss her the leveler.

"I'll be checking it as soon as you get back," her mother sneered. "So don't even think of trying to steal from me."

Chatine grimaced down at the device in her hands and felt a chill at the task that lay ahead of her. She told herself she'd just do it quickly. If she skipped it, her parents might grow suspicious and interfere with her plans. She'd just have to get it over with. Get in the morgue and get out. Then she could move on to her more pressing errand of the day: a visit to the Capitaine. She couldn't wait to show him what she'd snagged in the Marsh today.

Chatine murmured something that resembled a good-bye, shuffled out of the couchette, and headed down the No Way Out hallway of Fret 7.

As soon as she was outside and alone, she patted her chest again, feeling the weight of the gold medallion hanging from her neck. Her heart raced at the thought of what it meant. What it represented.

It was her one-way ticket off this miserable planet.

It was literally her salvation.

Azelle was more than welcome to sit around all day waiting for the greedy pomps in the Second Estate to help her. But Chatine was much more inclined to help herself.

- CHAPTER 3 -
MARCELLUS

"YOUR FATHER IS DEAD."

Marcellus Bonnefaçon heard his grandfather's words but could not seem to process them.

Dead?

Father?

It had been years since Julien Bonnefaçon had even been mentioned inside these walls. And now the sentence came so coolly from his grandfather's lips, it was as if the death of Marcellus's father was just some minor detail, barely worth mentioning.

Although Marcellus knew, after what his father had done, it probably *wasn't* worth mentioning.

Marcellus kept his gaze straight ahead. His grandfather's words might have turned his blood to ice, just for a second, but he knew better than to stop walking. He knew better than to *react*.

Instead, he made sure to keep his stride in sync with his grandfather's. Orderly and methodical. Just as he'd been taught since childhood. They walked in silence down the long corridor of the Grand Palais's south wing. Chandeliers with thousands of handcrafted crystals dangled above them, and the polished marble floor beneath their feet winked and flashed in the morning Sol-light.

There were so many questions fighting for space in Marcellus's mind, but he shoved them back one by one. This was all part of his training. He knew that. Command your emotions. Stabilize your breath. Keep your mind clear at all times. If there were more details about his father's death worth giving, his grandfather would give them. But, as they entered the banquet hall, Marcellus couldn't help but steal a quick glimpse at his grandfather. Firmness lined his features, nothing to hint that the man's only son had died. Marcellus honestly wasn't sure why he'd expected otherwise. In the seventeen years that he had lived with his grandfather, he'd rarely ever seen a trace of grief on the man's face.

And his grandfather had known plenty of grief.

A moment later, the double doors on the opposite side of the banquet hall flung open and the Patriarche, dressed in his usual late-morning robes of dark silk, blustered into the room, followed by the Matrone, swathed in a purple satin gown, and their two-year-old daughter, Marie.

"Good morning, General," the Patriarche grumbled with barely a glance at Marcellus's grandfather.

"Good morning, Monsieur Patriarche," his grandfather replied evenly.

"Let's get this over with." The Patriarche sat down in one of the plush velvet chairs and immediately started to shovel food onto his plate. As always, the banquet table was overflowing with titan dishes piled high with smoked Novayan salmon, roasted quail, and duck pâté imported straight from planet Usonia. There were baskets of freshly baked brioche, a tray holding the finest sausages from planet Reichenstat, and every imaginable fruit, picked that morning from the hothouses that stretched across the flatlands below Ledôme.

Marcellus, at eighteen years old and still growing, could usually eat his own body weight in food, especially during brunch.

But not today. Not now.

Instead, he just sat at the table and stared numbly at the brioche on the plate in front of him.

"Your father is dead."

He couldn't stop his grandfather's words from cycling through his mind. Although he knew he should stop them. Immediately. They were dangerous words. Dangerous thoughts.

But his mind was a traitor.

Just like his father.

Marcellus finally picked up his brioche and spread blackberry jam over the top, fighting to keep his face neutral as he took a small bite and chewed. He knew this was a test. His grandfather would be analyzing how he handled this news. Every reaction, every seemingly innocent facial twitch—they all had meaning in the eyes of General Bonnefaçon. And rightly so. If Marcellus had any hope of being promoted to commandeur in the coming year, he couldn't be seen as anything less than unwaveringly allegiant to the Regime.

"Production is up at the aerospace fabrique," his grandfather was saying, his voice firm and his back straight. His gaze flitted from his TéléCom on the table to the Patriarche, to whom he was giving his weekly update.

Dead.

The word continued to flutter around in Marcellus's brain like a flock of quails frightened by the sound of a shot from one of the Patriarche's antique hunting guns.

Marcellus took another bite as he silently reminded himself to look focused. Interested. Like a commandeur would. Like he was sure Commandeur Vernay used to do.

"But production is down in the garment fabrique," his grandfather continued.

The Patriarche stuffed a piece of salmon into his mouth, wiped his lips with an embroidered napkin, and set down his fork. "And why is that, General? Is there a problem?"

"The foreman claims there's been a shortage in supply of titan from planet Usonia, holding up the production of buttons for the Ministère uniforms—" General Bonnefaçon started to explain, but was interrupted.

"That's unacceptable," the Patriarche grunted. "The whole reason we helped Usonia win their independence from Albion was so our access to titan would no longer be hindered by that mad queen."

Marcellus noticed a slight pulse in his grandfather's jaw, just under one of his neatly trimmed sideburns. It was a rare chink in his usually impenetrable armor. But Marcellus knew the Usonian War of Independence was a sore spot for the general. The only reason Marcellus was sitting in this briefing instead of the more qualified Commandeur Vernay was because of that war.

But a moment later, his grandfather resumed his usual countenance: calm but firm, cool with a hint of a polite smile. Marcellus found himself adjusting his own face, wondering if he could ever achieve that look. A look that gave nothing away.

He dreamed of being able to give nothing away.

"Are you sure that's not just an excuse?" the Patriarche asked, picking up his fork and digging into a pile of pâté. "Maybe the workers are just being lazy again."

"Oh dear, mon chéri," the Matrone said, pausing to take a sip from her flute of champagne. "You must not be so harsh on the poor workers. Perhaps they're just tired. Or maybe they're in need of a nice little treat from us, to boost their morale and let them know that we support them." She blew at a ringlet of dark hair, which had escaped the tower of carefully entwined curls atop her head. "We must send them a crate of this beautiful gâteau." She dug her spoon into the giant, three-layered, pink-and-green-frosted dessert in front of her and scooped out a large piece. "Don't you think, Marcellus?"

Surprised to be spoken to, Marcellus almost choked on his mouthful of brioche. "Very good, Madame Matrone," he sputtered.

The Matrone leaned over and fed the spoonful of gâteau to Marie, the Premier Enfant, who was sitting on the chair next to her mother. The little girl's dark curls, held up with silk ribbons, glinted in the Sol-light streaming through the banquet hall's vast windows.

"Don't be ridiculous, chérie," the Patriarche admonished. "If you sent gâteau to one fabrique, you'd have to send gâteau to them all. Lest you want to start a riot. As my late father would say, 'That's just basic politics.'" He shared a conspiratorial look with Marcellus's grandfather. "This is why women should never run a planet, am I right, General?"

Marcellus saw the Matrone shoot a disdainful look at her husband before downing another gulp of her drink. Her brunch—and the majority of her meals, Marcellus speculated—seemed to consist mostly of champagne.

Oblivious of his wife's reaction, the Patriarche turned and cooed at his daughter. "Except my little darling, Marie, who is the cleverest girl on all of Laterre and who will be an excellent ruler one day." He blew a loud, wet kiss, which the child ignored.

Marcellus had been coming to these meals for only a few months, but already he dreaded them. Not just because he had to sit here watching the Patriarche shovel food into his mouth and the Matrone drink herself into a melancholy stupor, but because he never knew quite how to behave. How to sit. What to do with his hands. This room made him feel like a fidgety child forced to sit still in a scratchy uniform. As the future (but not yet) commandeur of the Ministère, Marcellus wasn't supposed to voice his opinion on matters. He was supposed to just sit there looking impervious and paying close attention so that, one day, he could contribute. But he always found his mind wandering. Today even more so than usual.

"Your father is dead."

"Oh, you little imp!" The Matrone's voice brought Marcellus back to the banquet hall. The Premier Enfant was now standing on her chair, stamping her feet. "Now, why are you standing up there? You know Maman doesn't like you climbing. We wouldn't want you to get hurt."

The Matrone reached for her daughter, but the little girl jumped off her chair, grabbed two titan serving spoons from the table, and started to bang them together. The Matrone sighed a deep, loud sigh and drained the last of her champagne.

General Bonnefaçon cleared his throat and focused back on his screen. "The bread fabrique has also seen a dip in production, but it should be rectified when—"

"Oh, fabrique *this*, fabrique *that*," the Matrone said, interrupting the general yet again. "All we seem to talk about these days are the fabriques. It is impossibly boring. Boring, boring, boring. And you"—she waved a finger at the general and then the table in front of him—"always poking and prodding at that silly TéléCom. I hate having these awful gadgets at my dining table. So disruptive. So hideous. So . . . *inferior*. Technology is for the weak minded. Those who cannot occupy their own thoughts turn to devices to do it for them."

Marcellus gazed out one of the windows of the banquet hall. As the head of the Ministère and the Patriarche's chief counsel, General Bonnefaçon, and his grandson, by extension, were awarded special privileges. Like their own dedicated south wing in the Grand Palais. Meanwhile, the rest of the Second Estate lived in smaller, less lavish manoirs throughout Ledôme.

Marcellus had grown up with this beautiful view of the Grand Palais gardens. But today, despite the artificial Sol-light streaming down from the TéléSky, the landscape seemed darker somehow.

"Ma chérie," the Patriarche was now saying. "Leave the poor general alone. He needs the TéléCom to deliver his reports, that's all. You know he wouldn't bring his ugly tech into the banquet hall if he didn't have to."

"Madame Matrone," Marcellus's grandfather said in a low, gentle tone. "I must inform you that due to these delays at the fabrique there may not be enough sweet breads for the Premier Enfant's third birthday fête next week."

Suddenly, it was as if a black cloud from outside Ledôme had drifted into the Palais and across the Matrone's face. Her dark eyes narrowed, her brows dipped, and her nostrils flared. "What on Laterre do you mean?" She didn't wait for a reply. She shook her head fiercely, knocking her curl tower askew. "This must not be tolerated. You get out there right now, General, and you tell those lazy workers that—"

"Now, now, ma chérie. Don't work yourself into a tizzy. You'll get wrinkles. You wouldn't want to undo the effects of those youth injections, would you?" The Patriarche patted his wife's hand. "There *will* be enough sweet breads for the birthday fête. General Bonnefaçon will see to it personally."

Hearing the word "birthday," the Premier Enfant began to beat her spoons together again. "Bur-day, bur-day, bur-day!" she shrieked.

The Matrone raised the back of her hand to her forehead and said in a strong whisper, "Please, ma petite. Be quiet now."

But the little girl was already too excited to stop. She raised the spoons above her head and clapped them together again and again, stomping in time with the beat.

"Nadette!" the Matrone and Patriarche shouted at the exact same moment.

A few seconds later, Marie's governess came bustling into the banquet hall carrying a plate of sliced fruit. Her face was flushed and her auburn hair was unkempt.

"I'm sorry, Madame Matrone. I was fetching the mademoiselle a peach from the kitchen. She's been asking for one all morn—"

But the servant's words were cut short when the Matrone raised a hand and waved toward her daughter, her numerous titan rings clattering with the gesture. Nadette fell silent, bowed, and immediately started toward the child in an attempt to quiet her.

Marie, however, evidently thought it was a game. She let out a squeal and began to run around the banquet hall, all the while still banging her spoons.

"Oh, my head," the Matrone said, looking like she might faint. "This is too much, too early in the day."

"Here." The Patriarche passed his wife his own flute of champagne. "Have some more sparkles." He then turned to the general. "Have you checked with the gamekeeper yet about the hunt this afternoon? I want to make sure the gardens are fully stocked with game. Last time I went out, there was barely so much as a squawk to be heard."

Marcellus let out a long breath and allowed his mind to wander, just for a few seconds.

"Your father is dead."

How did he die?

Did he suffer?

"Monsieur Patriarche," his grandfather replied. His tone was cool, patient. "Perhaps if the quail population is dwindling, you'd be best to hold off hunting until more can be bred in the menageries. Your father always limited his hunting to—"

The Patriarche sat bolt upright in his chair. "Hold off?!" He spat out the words, as if it was the most ludicrous suggestion his chief counsel had ever made. "On a hunt? What on Laterre do you presume I do all day? Sit around polishing my guns?"

His anger seemed to rile up the child even more. She dropped her spoons and started chanting, "Bang! Bang! Bang!" as she formed guns with her chubby fists and fired them into the air.

"Nadette!" the Matrone cried. "Please. My aching head! Can't you do something?"

Nadette, looking terrified, finally caught the girl and tried to shush her by stroking her hair and feeding her pieces of fruit.

"No!" Marie pushed her governess's hand away and started to cry. She appeared to be thinking about running again, but just then, Marcellus caught her gaze and cocked an eyebrow. Without a word, he pulled a fresh napkin onto his lap.

The Premier Enfant saw his signal, sniffled, and rubbed her teary face. She dropped to her knees and crawled under the table toward Marcellus. When Marcellus felt the silk of her gown brush against his legs, he started folding the napkin.

One fold, two folds, three, and four.

He'd done it so many times, he didn't have to look anymore. The swan's neck, wings, and beak soon materialized in his hands. It took only a minute to complete. When he was done, he felt Marie's fingers on his. She took the napkin-bird and crawled away. Even though the Patriarche was still chattering about his upcoming hunt, Marcellus could hear the girl cooing to her swan under the table.

"Finally, Nadette," the Matrone said. "It took you long enough to quiet her." She turned to Marcellus. "You would think, given it's her *only* job, she'd be better at it."

Suddenly there was a loud *bang*, and everyone startled and looked over at the Patriarche, who had just pounded his fist on the table, causing the Matrone's champagne flute to tip over.

"This simply will not do!" He banged his fist again as a servant came in to mop up the spilled drink. "Dwindling quail population?" He snorted. "What nonsense! If you won't speak to the gamekeeper, General, I might just have to find a general who will."

Marcellus tensed at the comment. He hated when the Patriarche threatened his grandfather. General Bonnefaçon had devoted his life to the Regime. He was the most loyal servant of Laterre that Marcellus had ever known. His grandfather had been practically running this planet for the past thirty years. The former Patriarche, Claude Paresse, had promoted Bonnefaçon to general when he first inherited the Regime. He'd passed away only two years ago, and now his son, Lyon, the current Patriarche, would be positively lost without Marcellus's grandfather. And yet he acted like the general was as replaceable as a faulty droid.

Marcellus opened his mouth to say something—even though he had no idea what *to* say—but the general silenced him with a subtle shake of his head.

"I will speak to the gamekeeper this afternoon," the general said cordially.

"Forget it," the Patriarche spat. "I'll speak to him myself. Apparently if you want anything done right around this place, you have to do it yourself." And with that, he rose from his chair and stalked out of the room, promptly ending the meal.

General Bonnefaçon rose too, which was Marcellus's cue to wipe his mouth and push back his chair.

"Please excuse us, Madame Matrone," the general said. "Officer Bonnefaçon and I have much to do to prepare for today's Ascension ceremony."

The Matrone slouched in her seat. "Oh, not another dreadful Ascension! If you keep letting Third Estaters into Ledôme, we'll be positively overrun."

"I assure you there is plenty of room in Ledôme," General Bonnefaçon said. "And the Ascension manoirs are a long way from the Palais."

The Matrone waved a dismissive wave, sending her rings clacking together once again. Then she stood up, teetering somewhat on her feet. "Come, Marie. Come walk with Maman in the gardens."

Marie let out a wail and burst into tears. "No! Birdy! Birdy!"

The governess immediately ducked under the table and scooped the child up into her arms, cooing into her ear. "Yes, yes. We're going to see the birdies right now in the gardens."

"If my husband hasn't shot them all," the Matrone said under her breath.

"No!" The little girl's voice was almost muffled by sobs now. "Birdy! Birdy!"

Nadette attempted to shush the child again as she followed the Matrone out of the banquet hall. Marcellus's gaze fell to the floor next to the edge of the tablecloth, and he noticed his white swan lying abandoned under a chair.

For some reason, he felt a strong urge to pick it up and run after the little girl, but then he saw that his grandfather was already halfway out the opposite door. Marcellus turned and followed behind him, grateful that the meal was finally over and he wouldn't be expected to sit through another one for an entire week.

As Marcellus and his grandfather walked back to the south wing, Marcellus's mind filled with more questions about his dead father that he longed to ask.

What were his last words?

Was he all alone?

But he knew there was no way he could ask such things. Curiosity could easily be misconstrued as concern, and concern could just as easily be misconstrued as grief.

And you don't grieve traitors.

So he continued down the corridor in silence, following the general into his large, oak-paneled study. The walls were covered with First World paintings and relics, including the head of an antlered beast (never successfully bred on Laterre), which hung above the fireplace with its dead eyes watching over the room. Marcellus's grandfather took a seat behind his vast, imposing desk and immediately began to watch the many AirLink messages that had appeared on his TéléCom since they'd left for brunch.

"Will that be all?" Marcellus asked.

He knew he'd be expected in the Marsh soon for the Ascension, but he secretly longed for a few moments alone before then, so he could process the news about his father in private.

"No, actually," his grandfather replied, still staring at his TéléCom. "Your father's body is in the morgue at the Vallonay Med Center. They've requested that you go to sign off on the disposal."

A wave of nausea instantly passed over Marcellus. "Me?"

His grandfather looked up from his screen, a knowing smile dancing on his lips. "First time seeing a dead body?"

Marcellus knew his grandfather was teasing him, the way everyone at the Ministère liked to tease him. He had a reputation for having a weak stomach—something he was working hard to overcome. He straightened up, reprimanding himself for losing control. "Yes. But I'm fine. Obviously, I have no connection to my father. His body will be like any other . . . body."

He swallowed down the bile rising in his throat. He needed to stop saying "body."

His grandfather set down his TéléCom and flashed Marcellus a sympathetic look. "It's perfectly normal to feel uneasy. I remember my first. Sols, I damn near fainted."

Marcellus perked up. "You did?"

His grandfather chuckled at the memory. "Yes. I was working in the Policier, and my inspecteur had sent me to Montfer to investigate the murder of an exploit foreman. It was dreadful. The man had been ripped open with a mining pick. His insides were spilled out all over the ground. I took one look at him and I swear every planet in the System realigned."

Marcellus felt himself grow woozy at the image and quickly sat down across the desk from his grandfather. "What did you do?"

His grandfather leaned forward conspiratorially, as if sharing a long-kept secret. "I clenched my teeth so hard to keep from passing out, my back molar cracked right down to the gum. Spent the rest of the day in the Med Center. Told them it was a piece of overcooked sheep bacon I'd bitten down on at lunch."

Marcellus let out a laugh, instantly feeling lighter.

"But it gets easier," his grandfather went on. "Eventually you see enough dead people that they stop being people and start being . . . bodies."

A memory from earlier this year—almost three months ago—suddenly drifted into Marcellus's mind. He could still see his grandfather's vacant eyes as he'd returned from claiming the remains of the twelve men and women who'd come back from their mission to assassinate the Albion queen. The rebels on Usonia had eventually won the war, but that particular mission had failed.

He knew those soldiers were not just bodies to his grandfather.

One in particular.

"But, Grand-père," Marcellus began with a shaky breath. "What about when it's someone you know? Maybe even someone you're close to?"

The general's eyes narrowed, and Marcellus knew he was treading on uneven ground. But he pressed forward anyway. His grandfather had to talk about what had happened at some point. Didn't he?

Marcellus tried to wet his lips, but his tongue was as dry as sand. "Not my father, obviously. I barely even remember him. But when you saw the body of Commandeur Vernay . . ."

Marcellus saw the shift in his grandfather's expression immediately. Like a curtain being drawn.

"It's already after 13.30," his grandfather said, picking up his TéléCom again and swiping at the screen. "You should get on your way to the morgue. I'll message Inspecteur Limier and let him know you'll be late for your Ascension duties in the marketplace."

Marcellus searched his grandfather's eyes for a hint of the levity and openness he'd glimpsed just moments ago. But it was gone. Stamped out. Like a planet passing in front of a Sol.

Since childhood, Marcellus had trained himself on the complex workings of his grandfather's worn and weathered face. Like an explorer mapping out rugged, uncharted terrain, he'd memorized every wrinkle, every muscle, every subtle movement and what it meant. He'd learned to recognize the rare moments when his grandfather was open and exposed, and more importantly, the all-too-frequent moments when his grandfather was closed. Locked. Bolted.

And right now, the bolt was as heavy and unrelenting as PermaSteel.

He should never have mentioned her name.

"Of course, sir," Marcellus said, rising from his chair. "I'll go now, on my way to the Marsh." He swallowed as he walked to the door, glancing back long enough to say, "And I'm sorry."

The general's head whipped up and his gaze landed on Marcellus. It was cold and dark. "For what?"

But Marcellus didn't answer. He just left.

- CHAPTER 4 -
CHATINE

"ONE THOUSAND EIGHT HUNDRED THIRTY-TWO Ascension points. Fourteen tokens."

The computerized voice of the leveler echoed off the decrepit walls of the Vallonay Med Center morgue as Chatine scanned the Skin of the first body. It was a woman, possibly late thirties, probably a fabrique worker. She had clearly died of rot, from the looks of her blackened stump of a leg. Rot was the most common cause of death in the Frets. Médicaments were in such short supply in Vallonay that even the smallest cuts or nicks could eventually fester and turn black. And once the rot invaded your bloodstream, there was really no hope.

The leveler emitted a beep, alerting Chatine that the points and tokens had been successfully lifted from the woman's profile account, and she moved on, ducking under the gurney to avoid the motion sensors that activated the morgue security microcams. Chatine had performed this morbid task enough times to know exactly where they were stationed. All thirty-seven of them.

Holding her breath as she passed by what was left of the poor woman's leg, Chatine glanced up at the rows and rows of cavs that stretched out before her—all of them waiting to be frozen and ground to dust. This was going to take forever. There were so many bodies, some had been placed two to a gurney. Chatine spotted a man who was missing all ten of his toes and knew right away that it was the work of the Délabré, her father's gang. This was someone who clearly hadn't paid his debts. All the bodies were in varying states of decay— rotting flesh, sores around the mouth, sunken eyes—even though Chatine knew they'd only been dead less than a day.

Ascension points and tokens were normally emptied from accounts within thirty hours of death—the time it usually took for the Ministère to register the death and for the profile to be wiped from the Communiqué. Chatine's father had discovered years ago that those points and largs could be lifted beforehand and "redistrib-uted" to the highest bidder, and so the unpleasant task of retrieving them had fallen to Chatine.

She just really wished the Med Center workers would close the eyes before bringing the cavs in here. This job would be so much eas-ier if the dead weren't staring back at her, begging her to save them.

Chatine moved on to the next corpse—a younger woman, a *girl*— and placed the leveler flush against the inside of her arm, directly over her darkened Skin. The device rapidly flashed as it analyzed the data.

"Fifty-two Ascension points, four hundred twelve tokens."

Chatine blinked at the amount and studied the girl, careful to avoid her open, unseeing eyes. She was thin—like almost everyone in the Third Estate—but her feet and ankles were puffy and swollen, as though all the fat on her body had drained downward. Her arms and legs were covered in bluish-purple splotches, and rough scales enveloped her neck as though attempting to strangle her.

Chatine pressed her lips together to keep from being sick. She recognized the symptoms. She'd seen the same ones on the girls standing outside the blood bordels.

The girl on the gurney had low Ascension points, which probably meant that, like Chatine, she had ignored her job assignment and vowed to make her own way in the world. She'd chosen to defy the Ministère's "honest work for an honest chance" propaganda. But instead of stealing and pulling cons like Chatine, she'd decided to sell the nutrients in her blood. Chatine could understand the reasoning behind the decision. Extra largs meant extra food. Extra food meant you and your family could live to see another day. Unfortunately, however, most girls—like this one—took it too far. Sold too much to the blood bordels. Got addicted to the feel of all those extra tokens in their profile account.

Dishonest work for a dishonest death.

Chatine felt a shiver ripple through her, and she glanced away from the girl's young face. Mercifully, the leveler beeped just then, and she moved on to the next cav.

Chatine ran a hand down the side of her coat, feeling the weight of her stolen trinkets lining her pockets. That was all she needed to assure herself that she would never end up like that girl, lying in this run-down building while vultures stole her precious largs.

The next cav was a man, much older than the previous two corpses. The skin around his eyes had wrinkled and sagged years ago. His long dark hair and beard were streaked with silver. And his fingertips were blackened and calloused. An exploit worker perhaps? Someone who had spent practically his entire life underground, mining precious metals and minerals to send to the fabriques for processing?

His clothing was tattered and caked with a fine dust. Chatine had to pull up the sleeve of his shirt in order to access his Skin. She hated when she had to actually touch the bodies.

She placed the leveler against the Skin and waited, turning her face to the wall so she wouldn't have to look at him. The leveler seemed to be taking an unusually long time, and Chatine glanced back to make sure it was making proper contact with his Skin. Then it let out a series of soft, rapid beeps.

"Error message. Zero points. Zero tokens."

Chatine jumped back, nearly dropping the leveler. She told herself not to look. She urged herself to just keep going, move on, finish this job and be done with it, but she couldn't help it. Her gaze was pulled back toward the man.

Toward the *prisoner.*

He had to be. Only those arrested and sent to the moon had their accounts completely emptied. And it was only now that she took note of the color of his ripped and tattered clothes. Bastille blue. This man had died on the moon. He'd died a convict.

But what was he doing *here*?

Plenty of prisoners died on the moon, which was why it had its own Med Center and morgue. The bodies were normally disposed of there. Everyone knew life sentences were short on Bastille. Living conditions were even worse there than they were in the Frets.

Keeping close to the edge of the gurney, she skirted around to the man's other side.

Don't do it, she told herself, but her hands seemed to move on their own. She had to see it with her own eyes. She had to know for sure.

Chatine slowly peeled back the man's other sleeve, sucking in a sharp breath when the neat row of metallic silver bumps came into view.

His prisoner tattoo.

A lifelong brand. Even those who did their time, who survived the harsh conditions of Bastille, were forever marked.

Chatine suddenly felt a longing to touch the markings. To feel the raised surface under her fingertips. To imagine what it must feel like to have those metallic bumps seared into your flesh. Was it similar to having the Skin implanted? But of course, Chatine couldn't remember that. Just like everyone else in the Third Estate, she'd been a small child when the médecins had implanted the Skin into her left arm and the connected audio chip into her ear.

With shaking hands, she slowly reached out. Her fingertip had barely brushed the surface of the first bump when she heard the doors of the morgue hiss open and footsteps echo down the corridor.

Chatine glanced around the crowded morgue, searching for a place to hide. But there was nothing. No curtains, no closets, no supply cabinets. And anywhere she tried to go would certainly trigger the microcams.

The footsteps grew louder.

Chatine's pulse raced. If she was caught in here stealing from the dead, she'd most certainly end up with a prisoner tattoo of her own.

She had only one option.

She hopped onto the neighboring gurney, scooted the blood-bordel girl aside, and lay down next to her, hiding the leveler inside the sleeve of her coat. Her skin crawled and bile rose in her throat as she felt the girl's cold, scaly flesh brush up against the back of her hand. She kept her eyes open, staring at the ceiling as she held her body perfectly still, trying to emulate the frozen expression of terror that was on all these faces.

Out of the corner of her eye, she saw two men enter the morgue. One was dressed in green scrubs. A médecin, judging from the cyborg circuitry implanted in his face. The other was wearing a crisp, bright white military uniform with silvery titan buttons, marking him an officer of the Ministère.

What is a member of the Second Estate doing in a Third Estate morgue?

"My records state that he died of frostbite," the médecin stated with an emptiness in his voice that mirrored the eyes of the cavs. "I'm very sorry for your loss."

"Don't be," the second man replied flatly. "This loss is a gift to Laterre."

Chatine fought to keep the surprise from her face. *Who is he talking about?*

She held her breath as the two men walked down the row of gurneys, stopping at the one just next to Chatine. The prisoner.

"Were you close to your father?" the médecin asked.

"No," the other man replied, and Chatine thought his voice sounded vaguely familiar. "I never even knew him."

His father? Chatine thought. *This man—this officer—has a father who was in prison?* She didn't think Second Estaters were even sent to Bastille. They were hardly ever convicted of crimes. She was desperate to turn her head, flick her gaze to the side for just a moment. She wanted so badly to find out who this officer was.

"I'll leave you alone with him," the médecin said, and then Chatine heard the clacking of footsteps receding back down the hallway.

The man in uniform walked around the gurney, standing between Chatine and the prisoner. Chatine saw the twinkle of something shiny on his finger. A ring. Definitely valuable. Maybe even titan. She contemplated leaping up from the gurney now and using the element of surprise to swipe the ring and run. But she worried about the aftermath. The motion-sensor microcams had most definitely been activated as soon as this man entered the morgue. She simply couldn't risk getting caught. Not when she was this close to freedom.

The man stood motionless next to the body, staring down at it. She could see his hands curl into fists, as though he were angry about something. Then, a moment later, his hands relaxed and Chatine heard him speak.

"Why did you do it?"

There was something soft and fragile in his voice. Broken, even. Chatine was almost certain he was speaking *to* the dead prisoner. But before she could begin to fathom why, out of the corner of her vision, she saw the man touch the fabric of the prisoner's sleeve. The one Chatine had peeled back to reveal his prisoner tattoo.

"What is this?" he asked, and it wasn't until right then, seeing the shirt from this awkward angle, that Chatine noticed what had evidently caught the man's eye.

There was something stitched into the inside of the prisoner's shirt.

Could that be what I think it is? Chatine wondered.

The man quickly grabbed something from a nearby tray and started to cut away at the convict's shirt.

Chatine flicked her eyes to the side, trying to take in as much information as she could in a single glance, but it wasn't enough. She still couldn't make out what was stitched into the fabric.

Careful not to make the gurney creak, Chatine slowly turned her head a millimètre to the right, letting her gaze fall upon the man gripping the tattered shirt in his hands. She had to fight back the gasp that sprang up in her throat.

She recognized him.

How could she not?

Nearly everyone on Laterre would recognize him. That shiny dark hair with just a hint of a curl; those sharp, handsome features; that tall, slender build. In her shock, Chatine must have completely forgotten about the leveler shoved into the sleeve of her coat, because suddenly she heard a loud crash as the device slipped off the gurney and fell to the floor.

- CHAPTER 5 -
MARCELLUS

HISS.

The doors of the morgue sealed shut and Marcellus was finally alone with his father. A man he'd never met. Never spoken to. Barely even remembered.

His hands trembled. He tried to remind himself that the man on *this* gurney meant nothing more to him than any of the other lifeless faces in the room. He swallowed hard and cast his gaze downward.

At the infamous traitor, Julien Bonnefaçon.

Marcellus studied the deep, jagged lines of his face, his cracked purple lips, the vacant dead stare of his hazel eyes.

And yet, Marcellus felt nothing.

Or, at least, that's what he told himself. He *had* to feel nothing. Feeling anything at all would only confirm the suspicions that Marcellus was sure everyone had about him.

That had always been his punishment for his father's crime, ever since he was a little boy. When you're born the son of a traitor, you are forever a suspect. Forever guilty of a possible future crime. Forever your father's son.

Marcellus had spent his entire life fighting against those suspicions, trying to prove to everyone in the Ministère—everyone on Laterre—that he wasn't anything like his father, and he would never betray his planet, his estate, his family.

So why were his hands still shaking?

A body. Not a person.

Just as his grandfather had said.

He balled his hands into fists, willing them to stop trembling. As Marcellus gazed into his father's open, unseeing eyes, he felt at once frustration, shame, revulsion, and most of all, anger.

This was the man who'd abandoned Marcellus when he was just a baby. This was the man who'd chosen to join the Vangarde, an unruly group of known terrorists, instead of being a father. When Julien had betrayed his family, Marcellus's mother had died soon after of a broken heart and his grandfather had had to raise him as his own. But most important, this was the man single-handedly responsible for the biggest tragedy of the Rebellion of 488: the bombing of the copper exploit that killed six hundred people. Poor people. Innocent people.

What kind of man does that? What kind of man brings such shame on his family?

The man laid out on the gurney in front of him.

That kind of man.

Marcellus thought back to the first time he'd seen the footage. He remembered it so clearly: The insanity in his father's eyes as he was captured and loaded into a voyageur bound for Bastille. The babble spewing from his lips as they took him away. They were the rantings of a madman. A fanatic. A terrorist.

That was seventeen years ago, and ever since then, Marcellus had been trained to hate this man, to despise him and loathe everything he stood for. But now, standing here, in front of his frail, frostbitten body, Marcellus felt something else tugging at him.

This was his father.

His *father.*

A man who had loved and married his mother. A man whose blood he shared.

He'd come from one of the most reputable families on Laterre. And yet he'd joined the Vangarde and killed so many people.

"Why did you do it?" Marcellus didn't realize he'd asked the question aloud until it was out of his mouth. Now it was too late to take it back. And it was far too late to answer.

But the reason shouldn't matter. Marcellus knew that. He shouldn't wonder about these things. He shouldn't try to get into the head of a madman. He should just turn and walk out of here, give his permission to dispose of the body, and go on with his life, become the next commandeur of the Ministère.

And yet, Marcellus couldn't bring himself to move. While one part of him tried to push down these dangerous questions, another part of him, the painfully curious part—the *involuntary* part—slowly reached out and touched the back of his father's hand. It was cold and rigid in death, its fingertips scarred from years mining zyttrium on Bastille.

Marcellus wondered how often these hands of his father's had bled. How often they'd shivered in the freezing cells of the prison. How often . . .

His thoughts came to a halt when his finger snagged on the sleeve of his father's blue prison shirt. A piece of loose gray stitching inside the cuff caught his eye, and he pushed back the torn sleeve.

"What is this?" he said aloud as his gaze fell upon a series of crooked lines and rounded loops of what could only be described as letters.

Letters?

But that couldn't be. The Forgotten Word wasn't used anymore. It was lost several centuries ago, shortly after the early settlers had come to Laterre. No one could even read it. Let alone *write* it.

But you did once, a voice in the back of his head reminded him.

"M is for Marcellus. . . ."

Marcellus hastily shoved the voice away, back to the far, dark corners of his mind where it belonged. He didn't think of that anymore. Those thoughts were strictly forbidden.

His fingers were trembling again as he pushed back the sleeve a little more. The stitching continued on and on, up the arm of the shirt. Marcellus glanced around the crowded morgue, spotting a scalpel on a nearby table. But then his gaze snapped up to the corner of the room, where he knew the security microcam hung like an invisible eye.

Of course, he thought.

He was never *really* alone. The Vallonay Med Center—like most Ministère buildings—was under constant surveillance. There were very few places on this planet where Marcellus could escape the eyes watching him, analyzing his every move.

Careful to keep his back to the microcam the whole time, Marcellus snatched up the scalpel and began cutting away at the fabric of the shirt. His father's body was rigid, though, and Marcellus had to tug hard at the garment to pull it free.

He turned the shirt inside out and laid it across his father's chest, using his body to block the microcam's view.

That's when he knew for sure what he was looking at.

The Forgotten Word stretched out across the lining of the shirt, sewn right into the fabric with thread. The letters traveled up the sleeve, across the shoulder, and down the back. The sight of them made Marcellus nauseous. It had been so many years since he'd set eyes on those cryptic symbols. And yet every loop and line seemed so familiar. Familiar and revolting.

Did his father write this? But that was absurd. A prisoner who could write the Forgotten Word? It was as preposterous an idea as a droid who could dance.

And yet, Marcellus couldn't shake the unsettling suspicion that somehow his father had left that message. For *him*.

Crash!

The sound yanked Marcellus from his thoughts as something hit the floor beside his feet. He jumped back, stumbling into the gurney behind him. Shaky and spooked, he picked up the fallen object, realizing it was a device he'd never seen before.

Marcellus felt movement at his back and spun around to see two bodies shoved side by side onto the same gurney: a girl with blemished, flaking skin, and a young boy in a tattered black coat.

Except the boy wasn't dead.

He was very much alive.

And he was watching him.

- CHAPTER 6 -
CHATINE

CHATINE HAD ONLY ONE THOUGHT IN HER MIND AS she gazed into the hazel eyes of Marcellus Bonnefaçon: *Get the leveler.*

If her father found out Chatine had let his precious larg-stealing device fall into the hands of a Second Estater—an *officer* of the Ministère no less—he would have her strung up and yanked to pieces. Thousands of tiny painful pieces.

She knew she had to act fast. The security microcams had already captured her face and most likely scanned her Skin. Now she just needed to get out of there. She sprang up from the gurney and lunged for the device clutched in Officer Bonnefaçon's hand, certain he was no match for her speed and dexterity. After all, Chatine had grown up in the Frets—in the slums of society—while this coddled pretty boy had grown up sleeping in titan-colored sheets and having his satin slippers delivered to him by servants every morning.

But Chatine felt her hand grab empty air as the officer pulled the leveler up and out of her reach. Chatine recomposed herself and made another attempt. She had to jump because the officer was tall, and holding the leveler high above his head appeared to be a game to him.

Of course it was a game to him. This was Marcellus Bonnefaçon! The grandson of the general. This whole miserable planet was their playground, and Chatine and the rest of the Third Estate were just game pieces to them. Objects put forth for their amusement.

Chatine let out a low growl and jumped for the device again. "Give that back, you rotten pomp!"

"Whoa, whoa. Calm down," Marcellus said, looking surprised by her efforts, but still not lowering the device. Then, after a moment, he asked, "Wait, what did you call me?"

Chatine ignored him and kept jumping. She knew it was foolish to insult an officer of the Ministère and a member of the Second Estate. It would only add time to her sentence if she was caught. But she didn't care. She needed to get that leveler.

"A *pomp*?" Marcellus asked. Except he didn't sound angry. He sounded amused. Chatine swore she could hear a hint of laughter in his voice.

And that's when she punched him.

Hard, in the gut.

He buckled forward, but only for a second. She'd clearly surprised him more than winded him, and he still kept a firm grip on the leveler, which was now thankfully within Chatine's reach. She leapt forward and attempted to pry his fingers from the handle. But as hard as she tried, she couldn't loosen his grip.

Defeated, she stepped back to catch her breath.

"You really want this thing, don't you?" Marcellus asked, holding his stomach and looking at the leveler. "What is it, anyway?"

"None of your Sol-damn business." The words puffed out of her, hard and angry.

The corners of the officer's mouth tweaked up, like he might be about to smile, and Chatine's hands balled into fists once more. She couldn't stop herself. Her rage got the better of her. She lunged at him again, but this time he saw it coming and was ready for her. He jumped back, away from her punch. Then, with a firm but careful hand, he grasped the top of her head—right over her hood—and pushed her an arm's length away from him. For a few seconds, she flailed beneath his hand, punching and kicking at the air.

She hated how strong he was, how tall he was. She hated even more that he still had the leveler.

"You're a feisty kid, you know that?" Marcellus said as she began to lose energy and her thrashing slowed. "The Ministère should sign you up for informant duty."

Now it was Chatine's turn to laugh. It came out strong and bitter, like the weed wine her father's gang illegally brewed from unwanted plants and sold to people in the Frets.

"I would *never* spy for the Ministère!" Chatine spat out the words.

"Too bad." Marcellus shrugged. "My grandfather always needs fearless new recruits. Boys like you, who aren't afraid to fight for their Regime."

"You mean like you?"

Chatine noticed a slight twitch on Marcellus's face before he slowly released her. She jumped back, out of his reach, but the sudden movement caused her dark hood to begin to slip from her head, threatening to reveal her long hair tied up underneath and the whole of her face—eyelashes, cheekbones, and all. She yanked the hood back into place.

"They would need to feed you up, though," Marcellus added after a moment, cocking his head to the side to study Chatine. *All* of Chatine.

Heat rose, instantly and surprisingly, to her cheeks. She was blushing. Something that *never* happened to her. But no one had ever stared at her for this long before. Not her parents. Not her sister. No one. Her heart did a quick double beat behind her ribs.

Had he noticed something when her hood slipped?

She decided the best thing to do was to stare back at him, firm and fierce.

"What?" he said, raising his arms in mock surrender. "I was just saying you could do with some meat on your bones." He ducked his head slightly. "Are you hungry?"

"I don't want food," she snarled, but even as she said it, she felt her empty stomach clench. She pointed at the leveler still in his hand. "I want what belongs to me."

Marcellus looked from Chatine to the device and then back again. He was clearly thinking. But Chatine didn't have the time nor the patience for his thinking.

"It's mine!" she shouted. "Give it back!"

"Okay, okay," Marcellus said in a tone that almost sounded *kind*. "Listen, I'll offer you a deal."

Chatine crossed her arms over her chest. "I don't do deals."

Marcellus smirked and glanced down at the leveler again. "Something tells me you're the kind of kid who *does* do deals."

"Just give it back to me."

Chatine was growing more and more agitated. How dare this guy swagger in here, wearing his dazzling white uniform, smirking his annoying smirk, and steal *her* stuff? He might be the grandson of General Bonnefaçon, but that didn't give him the right to be such a pretentious, arrogant—

"If you come with me and let me get you something to eat, I'll give this back to you." He waved the leveler, taunting her. "That's the deal."

Chatine narrowed her eyes. It had to be a trap. He clearly thought she was a gullible sot. Typical arrogant Second Estate, thinking they could fool anyone with empty promises. Well, they couldn't fool her.

"Go with you?" she asked skeptically.

"Yes."

"And get food?"

He nodded. "Anything you want. Cheese. Salmon. Fresh-baked brioche. The Matrone has some gâteau she's trying to get rid of."

Chatine heard her stomach growl. She was so, *so* hungry.

Traitor, she reprimanded her gut.

But she couldn't deny the fact that she was tempted by his offer. Very tempted. And for a moment—just a moment—she allowed herself to imagine what it would be like to eat all those amazing foods. To taste real sugar on her tongue. To feel full for the first time in her life.

Then the moment passed, and she remembered who she was and, more important, whom she was dealing with.

Chatine let her hardened expression fall away and released a deep, grateful sigh. "Oh, monsieur," she cooed. "Do you really mean it? You'd really feed me and take care of me and help me?"

Marcellus looked momentarily stunned by Chatine's change of heart, but he quickly cleared his throat and replied. "Yes. Of course."

"That is so kind of you, monsieur. So terribly kind. How would I ever repay your kindness?"

Marcellus fumbled for a response. "No need to repay me. I just want to help."

Chatine took a small step forward and lowered her gaze. "I just . . . ," she began to say, and then her voice broke and her next words were muffled by quiet sobs. "I just can't believe anyone would do that. I can't believe that *you*, an officer of the Ministère, would be so charitable and generous to such a poor, wretched boy like me."

Marcellus chuckled uneasily. "Well, I'd like to think I'm different from my fellow officers."

"Yes, monsieur," Chatine said, sniffling, taking another step forward. "You most certainly are." She lifted her head to meet Marcellus's gaze with clear, focused eyes. "I've never met an officer as gullible as you."

Then, before he could react, she snatched the leveler from Marcellus's grip, spun quickly on her heel, and ran from the morgue as fast as her scrawny legs could carry her.

"Hey!" she heard Marcellus call after her, but she was quick. Too quick.

A moment later, she burst out of the Med Center and sprinted headlong toward Fret 17—the Capitaine's territory. She had no doubt that pomp Marcellus would soon be calling for reinforcements, and she didn't feel like dealing with any more droids today. She'd been waiting for this moment for too long.

This visit to the Capitaine would be her last. She was sure of it this time.

As Chatine ran, she thought about how easy that had been. How quickly the officer had believed she would actually fall for his pitiful little trap.

But more than anything, Chatine reprimanded herself for not taking advantage of the opportunity to steal something more valuable, like that titan ring she'd seen on his finger. It was a mistake she would be sure to remedy if she were ever to come face-to-face with Officer Bonnefaçon again.

- CHAPTER 7 -
CHATINE

BREATHLESS AND FATIGUED, CHATINE REACHED THE top floor of Fret 17, the northwestern-most building in the Frets, and pulled her hood farther down her forehead. There were no couchettes up here. This was Capitaine Cravatte's turf. She headed down the long corridor and knocked on the thick PermaSteel door at the end.

A moment later, the door screeched open and a tall, menacing figure stepped out of the shadows. Chatine lowered her gaze but kept her voice steady. "I'd like to see the Capitaine, please."

"Again?" The guard sneered, revealing a checkerboard of missing teeth. "You don't give up, do you, boy? What makes you think the Capitaine will want to see you again so soon?"

Chatine pressed her shoulders back, trying to appear taller and more muscular than she was. "I have enough this time. I swear."

The guard looked skeptical. "That's what you said last time. And yet . . ." He let the sentence hang but Chatine knew exactly what he was saying.

She wiggled her toes inside her boots. The leather had worn thin as her feet had continued to grow. Soon she'd be able to see her toenails poking through the black tips.

"Please," she said, cringing at the high squeak of her voice.

The guard guffawed. "When are those tiny balls of yours going to drop?" He opened the door wider and motioned her inside.

Chatine followed the guard down the dimly lit corridor, avoiding the puddles of rain that had gathered beneath the cracks in the decaying roof. When they reached the Bridge, the guard remained in the hallway as Chatine stepped inside.

She always loved the view from the Bridge. Fret 17 was the tallest of the old freightships. Even on the rainiest of days, you could see almost all of Vallonay from up here. The rolling hills and the low, wet valleys. The Secana Sea and rusty docklands to the left and the rows of fabriques, fermes, and hothouses to the right. And of course, Ledôme, sitting high and regal atop the largest hill in the city, illuminated with that eerie glow of artificial Sol-light. Chatine tried to imagine what this view would have looked like 505 years ago, when Freightship 17 was barreling through space at hypervoyage speed, leaving behind the wreckage of a destroyed planet. When the stars were nothing but a vast glow of light. When her ancestors sat in their couchettes, dreaming of a promised better life on Laterre.

At what point did they realize they'd been tricked? Chatine always wondered.

Was it when they'd first arrived on Laterre only to find a rainy, gray planet that almost never saw the light of the Sols? Was it when they were put to work in the exploits and the fabriques while the Patriarche and Matrone and their First and Second Estates disappeared behind the walls of Ledôme to enjoy the fruits of *their* hard labor?

"I didn't expect you back so soon." The Capitaine's voice interrupted Chatine's reverie, and she blinked and stared at the throne-like chair that sat in the center of the Bridge, facing out the panoramic windows. The original glass, from when the freightship had been built on the First World, was long gone. Capitaine Cravatte had replaced it with sheets of plastique. The thin material kept out most of the rain but none of the cold.

Chatine shivered. "I have what you asked for, Capitaine. I have enough this time."

The chair swiveled and Chatine kept her gaze fixed on the Capitaine's disfigured features. She'd learned a long time ago not to look away, and it had become easier with time.

There were rumors about how the Capitaine had received his scars. Some said he fought in the failed Rebellion of 488 seventeen years ago and was burned by poisonous gases released by the Ministère. Some said he cut up his own face in order to extract a higher price for his services. Some said he was just born that way.

Chatine happened to believe he was betrayed by one of his comrades, and that was why he worked alone now and why he was guarded thirty hours a day. He'd lost his trust in people.

But it didn't matter how the Capitaine came to be the way he was, just as long as he gave Chatine what she wanted.

"Let me see," the Capitaine said.

Chatine pulled the collection of trinkets and relics from her pocket and spread the items out on the broken console in front of the Capitaine's chair.

The man diligently studied each piece, running his fingers over the pair of solid titan cuff links she'd snatched off a Policier sergent a few weeks back.

When he reached the end of the collection, his face fell into a frown that exaggerated his sagging left eye. "This is exactly what you brought me last time. What makes you think it would suddenly be enough this time?"

Chatine fought to hide the triumphant smile that was forcing its way onto her face as she reached under her coat and unclasped the Sol medallion. "Because last time, I didn't have this."

She dropped the pendant onto the console, feeling satisfaction in the *clink* it made against the corroded metal.

The Capitaine's frown vanished as he leaned forward to examine the new addition.

"A genuine First World artifact, rescued from the Last Days," Chatine said, doing her best to up sell the value of her latest acquisition.

"It *is* beautiful."

"But more important," Chatine added, "it's enough to pay for transport on the next trade voyageur to Usonia."

The Capitaine cocked a dark eyebrow. "Are you still quite sure that's where you want to go? You want to spend the rest of your life in a plastique bubble, billions of kilomètres from the Sols?"

"At least they can see the Sols."

"It's a very unstable planet these days," the Capitaine said, sounding infuriatingly cryptic. "They signed their own death warrant when they broke free from the Albion queen. I don't care how mad they claim her to be, people simply cannot be trusted to rule themselves."

Chatine gritted her teeth. Why was he stalling? "I'll take my chances."

The Capitaine regarded her with what could only be described as curiosity. "Oh, don't tell me you're one of *those*. Idolizing republics will only lead you to trouble, boy. They didn't work on the First World, and they especially won't work here in the System Divine. If your head is in the clouds with the rest of these idiots, I suggest you—"

"My head is soaked with rain. It's too heavy to float in clouds," Chatine interjected. She resented the implication that she would ever sympathize with revolutionaries. Here or on Usonia. She'd been dreaming of going to the farthest planet in the System long before they'd ever declared war against the mad queen of Albion. "I'm going to Usonia," she maintained. "And you promised to save me a spot on the next trade voyageur."

The Capitaine nodded, steepling his hands under his chin. "I did indeed promise you. *If* you brought me sufficient largs for passage."

Chatine gestured to the assortment of stolen relics. "There is over eight thousand largs' worth of trade here."

"Which is not enough."

Chatine scoffed. "What do you mean it's not enough? That was our arrangement. Eight thousand largs to sneak me onto a trade voyageur to Usonia."

The Capitaine pressed his lips together and slowly pushed the Sol necklace back toward Chatine with the tip of his crooked finger. "I'm afraid the price of passage has gone up."

Chatine could feel her heart thundering in her chest. She fought to keep her temper in check. To keep from screaming at the top of her lungs like a spoiled little Fret rat. "How can that be?" she asked through gritted teeth. "I was here only three weeks ago. How could the price have gone up that fast?"

The Capitaine leaned back in his chair and folded his hands across his lap. "Supply and demand, mon ami."

"Supply and what?" She was starting to feel itchy, fidgety. She scratched at her arms, which were covered in tiny bumps from the cold air.

"Demand," he repeated. "Apparently the Usonians have elected their first leader." The Capitaine rolled his good eye. "Foolish sots."

"What does that have to do with me or my transport?"

The Capitaine smiled an eerie, unsettling smile. "Some people might see this advancement as promising. Which means you're not the only one who's going to be asking for transport to Usonia in the days to come. Therefore, I have no choice but to raise the price. Regardless of my own opinion of what's happening out there, I am a businessman, first and foremost."

Chatine clenched her fists inside the sleeves of her coat. Three years she had been saving up for this. It had felt like a lifetime.

She had thought that medallion was her ticket off this Sol-forsaken planet. She had thought she had finally made it. But now her dream of leaving Laterre and her miserable family behind had never felt farther away.

"How much?" she asked, struggling to keep her voice from cracking.

"Fifteen thousand largs." The Capitaine shrugged, clearly unapologetic.

Chatine drew in a sharp breath. "Fifteen thousand?" Tears formed in her eyes and she rapidly blinked them away. "But that's nearly double what I have. It'll take me years to steal that much! How am I ever supposed to—"

The Capitaine's hand shot up. "This is not a negotiation. It's fifteen thousand largs or a life in the slums of Laterre." He let out a low chuckle and tapped on his Skin. "Or, of course, there's always the Ascension. Who knows? You might get lucky today."

Chatine glared at the Capitaine. His distorted features made it virtually impossible to gauge anything from his expression. But his next words sent a new chill through her already-chilled bones.

"The next trade voyageur to Usonia is scheduled to pass through in ten days," the Capitaine said. "If you want on it, I suggest you don't waste any more time."

- CHAPTER 8 -
MARCELLUS

"IF YOU'LL JUST AUTHENTICATE HERE." THE MÉDECIN
pointed at his TéléCom. "We can dispose of the body."

Marcellus was standing in the foyer of the Vallonay Med Center,
just outside the doors to the morgue. He glanced down at the device
in the médecin's hand. An image of his father's face stared back at
him from the screen.

Dispose. The word was so cold. So clinical. But Marcellus reminded
himself that this was not a person. This was a traitor. A dead one.
Disposal was the perfect end for Julien Bonnefaçon.

Marcellus waited for the TéléCom to scan him.

"Marcellus Bonnefaçon," the computerized voice confirmed his
identity. "Disposal authorized on day twelve of month seven, 505
ALD. Profile name: Julien Bonnefaçon, prisoner number 39874."

And that was it.

His father—prisoner 3.9.8.7.4.—was gone.

By the time Marcellus left the Med Center, the rain was coming
down in droves. In his seventeen years of life, he had yet to identify

any pattern in the weather on Laterre. The rain seemed to come and go on a whim, which made Marcellus very grateful for his warm, *dry* residence in Ledôme.

He buttoned up his long silver raincoat and started on foot toward the Marsh. The Med Center was one of the farthest buildings from the center of the Frets, but today, he didn't mind the walk. Even in the rain. It gave him time to think about what he'd just done.

Not only the disposal of his father's body, but before that as well.

He pressed his hand to the front of his coat, feeling the bulk of the fabric under the jacket of his uniform.

His father's prisoner shirt.

He wasn't sure what had prompted him to take it. One moment he was staring at it, spread out across his father's chest, and the next he was scooping it up, turning his back to the security microcam once again, and stuffing the shirt down the front of his uniform.

He just couldn't shake the feeling that the message sewn into the fabric had been meant for him.

Not that he had any hope of reading it. Marcellus hadn't been able to read the Forgotten Word for years.

When he arrived in the vast and chaotic marketplace, Marcellus quickly located Inspecteur Limier near the statue of Thibault Paresse, the founding Patriarche of Laterre. The inspecteur was standing on top of a narrow platform, flanked by a small army of droids. The platform had been erected as a makeshift watchtower, to survey the crowd during the broadcasting of the Ascension.

Marcellus had never witnessed an Ascension before. Of course, he knew what they were, how they worked, how much they tended to rile people up, but he'd always been safely tucked away up in Ledôme when they were happening. Now that he was on course to be named the next commandeur, his training had been moved to the Frets. His grandfather wanted him to experience all of Laterre. The good *and* the bad.

"Officer Bonnefaçon." Inspecteur Limier greeted Marcellus with a subtle nod.

"Inspecteur," Marcellus said, returning the cold greeting.

"I see your maid has wrapped you up nicely for the weather." The inspecteur peered down at Marcellus's glossy silver raincoat, and Marcellus could swear he saw the hint of a smirk break through the cyborg's impermeable façade. "How went your business in the Med Center?"

Marcellus tensed at the question, knowing it was an extension of his grandfather's test. There was no one on Laterre more loyal to General Bonnefaçon than Inspecteur Limier, and whatever Marcellus did and said now would undoubtedly be reported back to his grandfather.

Marcellus searched for the perfect one-word answer. "Uneventful."

The inspecteur's head clicked toward Marcellus, and Marcellus could feel the heat of the cyborg's orange eye roving across his face, searching for weaknesses, scanning his body temperature for spikes. Marcellus kept his eyes trained on the masses of people gathering in the Marsh, knowing that if he peered out of the corner of his vision, he would see the inspecteur's circuitry flashing.

Marcellus had known plenty of cyborgs. A tenth of the Second Estate had some kind of neurological enhancements, but there was something about Inspecteur Limier that unnerved him. A brutal coldness that sent shivers down his spine whenever he looked at him. It was as if something had gone wrong during Limier's operation, and the médecins had accidentally nicked something vital to his humanity.

"I despise Ascension day," the inspecteur said, thankfully changing topics.

Marcellus didn't respond. Instead he glanced out from the platform, taking in the Marsh in all of its misery. The decrepit market stalls and the piles of sorrowful vegetables for sale. He could see the mud, the squalor, the filth. He could smell the scent of rotting seaweed that was brought in daily from the nearby docks. A pitiful replacement for food. And then there was the giant crowd assembled. They were all there to watch the Ascension together. They'd turned it into a celebration of sorts. Stall owners dropped prices. Homemade weed wine was passed around in shared cups. Third Estaters who'd skipped their shifts at the fabriques played music by banging on kitchen pots and whistling through pieces of broken pipe. Minute after minute, they checked their Skins, wide-eyed and hopeful, waiting for the broadcast to begin. Some of them were close enough for Marcellus to see their shabby, wet clothes, their missing teeth, their sunken cheeks streaked with rain.

"The whole thing is pathetic," Limier went on, raising his voice over the noise of the crowd. "They trade in the last of their tokens for more points, keeping themselves hungry for a lottery they'll never win. Some of this lot will be dead from starvation before the next Ascension rolls around. These déchets have about as much chance of winning as I have of becoming Patriarche."

Marcellus bristled at the vulgar word for the Third Estate. *Déchets.* Although Marcellus himself was counting the days until his training in the Frets was complete and he no longer had to step foot in this foul, filthy marketplace, he still couldn't bring himself to see these people as garbage. He couldn't look upon them the way he knew Inspecteur Limier did. The way most of the First and Second Estates did. His grandfather seemed to be the only person Marcellus knew who had any respect for them.

"Every estate has its place and purpose," General Bonnefaçon always said. "The First Estate rules us, like the brain governing the body. We, the Second Estate, are the heart, providing the power and pulse. While the Third Estate are the legs on which we all stand." He would always add with a gruff laugh, "Laterre is the envy of the System Divine because of how well our beautiful body functions."

Looking out now at the crowd, Marcellus wondered how these sodden and sorry *legs* could ever hold up the body of Laterre.

The crowd gasped in collective excitement, interrupting Marcellus's thoughts, and he noticed the flickering of images on the insides of their arms.

"Get ready," Limier warned. "They tend to get rowdy when they don't win."

Marcellus pulled out his TéléCom and tapped on the Ministère's feed to watch the proceedings. Music and energizing sound effects burst through the audio patch secured behind his ear, indicating the beginning of the broadcast. It started with a highlight reel. An amped-up, poignant montage of former Third Estaters who had Ascended and who were now living the life of luxury in Ledôme: selecting fine furniture for their brand-new manoirs, trying on clothes made of handspun cloth, dining at massive tables lined with gourmet meats and cheeses, lounging in the faux Sol-light that was projected onto Ledôme's TéléSky.

It never rained in Ledôme. Not like here, where there was nothing to protect people from Laterre's natural elements. In Ledôme, it was bright and luminous 408 days a year.

Then the montage came to a close and the Ascension's familiar animated logo played: a pair of hands reaching toward Laterre's three Sols. The music dimmed and a commanding, accented male voice spoke the motto that every member of the Third Estate had had drilled into them from the day they were born:

"Honest work for an honest chance."

The crowd roared with enthusiasm, keeping their gazes glued to their Skins as their faces lit up with hope and optimism. They all wanted it so badly. A chance to live high on the hill, inside Ledôme. A chance to get out of their pathetic existence in these lowland slums.

The voice spoke again. "Someone's life is about to change. Someone has put in their honest work for an honest chance, and that chance is now here. Someone is about to *Ascend* to the Second Estate."

The crowd cheered louder. If they were cold, they barely noticed now. Their hope was keeping them warm.

"Just like the Ascendants before them," the voice continued, "the chosen one will receive a brand-new manoir in Ledôme, where the Sols shine all year long! And, in just a few days, the lucky Ascendant will have the honor of meeting our beloved Patriarche and Matrone Paresse at the Grand Palais for the Ascension banquet."

The image on the Skins changed, causing another ripple of excitement to move through the Marsh. This was the moment they'd all been waiting for. This was it.

A spinning wheel of faces flickered across the screens. Real Third Estaters from all over Laterre who had dutifully checked in to their Skins every day, clocked in at work on time, logged their hours, and did everything else the Ministère had asked of them. Dramatic music swelled as the faces spun, fast at first and then gradually slowing down. Soon it would come to a stop at the final one. The face of the next Ascendant.

Marcellus gazed out over the silent crowd. Everyone was transfixed, staring at their inner arms. Hooked on the idea that this time—this year—it could be *their* face that rolled into the winning spot.

As he watched their hopeful expressions, Marcellus found himself searching the crowd for the boy—the one who had so easily conned him in the morgue. He still couldn't believe it had happened. No one had ever conned Marcellus in his life. No one had ever dared. It was a certain unspoken advantage of being the grandson of the mighty General Bonnefaçon. Third Estaters didn't mess with you.

Surprisingly, however, the boy hadn't actually stolen anything from Marcellus. That was what confused Marcellus the most. Limier had warned him on his first day of training in the Frets that many of the Third Estaters were thieves. Especially the children. They distract you with one thing and then promptly steal something else. But when Marcellus had checked his pockets after the boy had left the morgue, he'd found nothing missing.

He knew he still should have felt angry at the boy for conning him, but all he'd managed to feel in that moment was fascination. With just an ounce of respect.

And now, for some odd reason, Marcellus found himself hoping right along with the rest of these people in the Marsh. Hoping that the boy would be the one selected.

Marcellus didn't even notice that his mind had wandered off until he heard the murmurings.

"The faces!"

"Where did they go?"

"Who won?"

"Who will Ascend?"

Marcellus glanced down at the TéléCom in his hand and suddenly understood their confusion and frustration. The Ministère's feed had gone dark. The faces had stopped spinning.

No winner had been chosen.

Marcellus turned toward Inspecteur Limier, who, for once, looked baffled. He immediately began murmuring something into his TéléCom, no doubt calling in to the Ministère for an explanation.

The crowd started to grow restless. The murmurs slowly turned to shouts of rage. Marcellus noticed the circuitry on Inspecteur Limier's face blink to life as he analyzed the potential threat. The Policier droids stiffened, straightening up to their full height and arming their rayonettes.

A lightning bolt of dread shot through Marcellus. He turned toward Limier, waiting for orders. Waiting for information. But the inspecteur had fallen silent. And now all Marcellus could hear was the growing unrest of the crowd.

Then three sharp beeps echoed in Marcellus's audio patch, signaling the commencement of a Universal Alert.

Everyone's eyes returned to their inner arms, to the official Ministère seal glowing on their Skins: a silhouette of Laterre behind a pair of crisscrossed rayonettes.

Marcellus glanced down at his handheld device. His throat squeezed as the seal vanished and his grandfather's face appeared on the screen.

"Fellow Laterrians. It is with great sorrow that I interrupt today's Ascension ceremony with the most distressing of news."

Marcellus looked to Inspecteur Limier to see if he knew what was coming, but the inspecteur gave nothing away. He glanced back into the crowd. A hush had fallen over the Marsh. The city. The planet.

"The Premier Enfant, two-year-old Marie Paresse, was found dead in the Grand Palais gardens earlier today."

Marcellus suddenly heard a loud ringing in his ears. For a moment, he swore his audio patch had malfunctioned, causing him to misunderstand what his grandfather had said.

The Premier Enfant was found dead?

But that couldn't be true. Marcellus had just seen her a few hours ago. She'd been in the banquet hall with them at brunch. He'd made her a napkin swan. There had to be some mistake.

He quickly peeled off his audio patch and reattached it behind his ear, making sure it was securely in place.

"The Chief Médecin has concluded that she died from an apparent poisoning," the general continued, his voice crisp and clear. Marcellus's stomach rolled.

Poisoning? Who would poison a two-year-old child? A sweet, innocent little girl?

"An investigation into this unspeakable crime is already under way," the general went on. "But until we can ascertain who exactly is responsible and bring this criminal to justice, the Ascension will be canceled."

Suddenly, the gruesome thoughts of poor little Marie choking among the rosebushes vanished from Marcellus's mind, and he felt the breath hitch in his lungs. He glanced over again at the inspecteur and noticed him visibly stiffen. His circuits were flashing so rapidly, it looked like they were malfunctioning.

Marcellus didn't need to be a cyborg to feel the shift in the air, to sense the instant change in the energy around him. The fear that pulsed through him was enough.

Anger rippled through the crowd. It was a coiled snake preparing to attack.

The first person lunged toward the platform. And Marcellus knew this would not end well.

Then, like a reply to his thoughts, there was a sudden flash of metal. And a thud.

A searing, sharp pain splintered through his skull as his vision blurred. He pressed a hand to his forehead, feeling sticky, warm liquid pooling between his fingers. But he barely had time to assess the wound before he heard Inspecteur Limier shouting beside him.

"Rayonettes armed! Paralyze mode only! I want no casualties."

Casualties?

Marcellus's murky brain fought to comprehend what was happening.

Then he saw it. The angry crowd surging toward the platform, carrying rusting pieces of pipe ripped from the walls of the Frets and secondhand pots and pans grabbed from market stalls.

Marcellus reached for the rayonette strapped to his belt, only to realize a moment later that it was buried under his raincoat. He fumbled with the buttons, trying to unfasten them one by one, but his hands were shaking too hard and his fingers kept slipping on the blood.

Blood . . .

It was everywhere. Dribbling down his face and onto his coat. Dripping into his eyes, turning everything red. He wavered on his feet, feeling light-headed.

Do not pass out, he commanded himself. *DO NOT PASS OUT.*

Someone let out a roar, and Marcellus looked up just in time to see a man barreling toward him, a broken plank raised in his hand. Marcellus scurried backward, stumbling off the platform and into the fray.

He pushed through hundreds of bodies, his feet fumbling for traction. He kept pressing onward, fighting to stay awake, stay conscious. Through his blurry vision he could make out dark, musty hallways, an endless maze. The planet was spinning under his feet, and he could feel the blood still oozing from the cut on his head. He could taste it, the warm iron taste, dripping into his mouth. He tried to staunch the flow with his fingers, but it was coming too fast, and without both hands to steady himself, he was slipping, swaying.

Falling.

For a moment, it seemed he was suspended in time and space. The darkness creeping in like a black hole consuming a broken star. He was collapsing, his legs buckling beneath him. He crashed to the ground, trying desperately to hold on to his consciousness. Behind him, he heard voices. Some were screaming in terror, others in anger. Somewhere far in the distance, he swore he heard the whirring sound of a Policier transporteur arriving, bringing in reinforcements. More droids. He'd never thought he'd ever welcome the sound of more droids.

Get up, he commanded himself. But the pain in his head was too strong, his legs too weak. And his eyelids were so, so heavy.

"Bonnefaçon!" someone shouted in his audio patch. "Where are you?"

And that was the last thing Marcellus remembered before everything went black.

- PART 2 -
THREE SOLS

Three layers formed on Laterre, firm and unwavering like strata of rock. On the very top, the wealthy descendants of the Paresse family became the First Estate, the royalty of the land. Then came the Second Estate, serving and protecting and managing the planet. Finally, the vast Third Estate stretched out beneath, tilling the fermes, mining ore in the exploits, and crafting goods in the fabriques.

The Regime was steadfast and strong.

Until Laterre's constant rain seeped into the cracks.

From *The Chronicles of the Sisterhood*,
Volume 3, Chapter 1

CHAPTER 9

ALOUETTE

MEALS IN THE REFUGE WERE ALWAYS EATEN IN
silence.

"Grateful Silence," the sisters called it.

And Alouette Taureau *was* grateful today. Truly, she was. She
knew it was a blessing to have a bowl of steaming potato soup for
lunch when, elsewhere on Laterre, tiny children cried from hunger
and parents fought with their fists over scraps of stale chou bread.
Sister Jacqui said that some children in the Frets didn't even have
parents to fight for them. Alouette was grateful that she lived here
in the Refuge of the Sisterhood, where they were safe and warm and
where she never needed to beg or steal.

Or worse.

But it wasn't the gratefulness that Alouette found difficult.

It was the speed.

Grateful Silence at mealtimes not only meant eating with no
talking, it also meant eating with mindfulness and gratitude. In
short, it meant eating very, *very* slowly. Old Sister Muriel was the
expert at this. Under her halo of bright white curls, Sister Muriel

always chewed each bite of her food twenty-five times. Twenty-five joyful and thankful times. Alouette struggled to get to four or five chews on a good day. And with soup?

Who could chew on soup?

Alouette knew that, like Muriel, she should be slowly enjoying every bite of the food her father had prepared for them. She knew that if she wanted to become a sister one day, she had to follow all the rules, pay attention in her lessons, study the Chronicles, help care for the books, and complete her chores with mindfulness and diligence.

And normally, she *was* mindful and diligent.

Today, however, it was more difficult than ever.

Because today, she had the transmitteur.

Alouette glanced around the Refuge dining room, taking in the ten sisters who were all quiet and focused on their soup. She slipped her free hand into the deep pocket of her tunic and felt for the small square of silicon. It was still there, nestled in the handkerchief she'd used to protect it.

So tiny. And yet so significant at the same time.

She fought the smile that threatened to break free on her lips.

Two months. That's how long it had taken Alouette to build the transmitteur. A hundred and two days secretly toiling away at Sister Denise's workbench, while Denise and the other sisters were locked away in the Assemblée room for their daily Quiet Contemplation. Two whole months.

And today was the day she would finally see if her hard work had paid off.

Alouette brushed her fingertips lightly around the edge of the transmitteur, thinking of all the potential this little device held. It was a key. A key to unlocking another piece of a world she didn't know.

A world she barely remembered.

A world she hadn't seen in person for over twelve years.

Even though it existed only ten mètres above her head.

Alouette felt a sharp nudge on her right arm that almost sent the spoon in her hand flying. She yanked her fingers out of her pocket and looked up to see Principale Francine, the head sister and the director of the Refuge, peering at her with steely gray eyes. She patted the air with a downward-faced palm and then glanced purposefully at Alouette's bowl of soup. Alouette was eating too fast.

Slow down, she reminded herself. *Slow down or they'll know. . . .*

As she lowered her gaze back to her soup, Alouette caught the eye of Sister Jacqui, her favorite of the sisters, who flashed Alouette one of her reassuring smiles. Jacqui's short brown hair was sticking out at chaotic angles, and her free hand fidgeted with her devotion beads. Every sister wore a string of them around her neck, and Alouette couldn't wait for the day she received her own. The day her own name would be engraved on one of those small metal tags that hung from the end.

She glanced at the clock on the wall. Only five minutes to go.

As the seconds ticked on, the only sounds in the dining room were the clink of spoons on soup bowls and the clicking of Jacqui's beads. Until finally—*finally*—the silence was broken by the sound of the bell, signaling the end of lunch. Alouette was the first on her feet. She grabbed her bowl and darted to the kitchen, where she found her father drying out a large cooking pot with a dishcloth.

"Merci, Papa," she called as she threw her bowl down next to the sink and turned on her heel to fetch two pails from the hook on the wall.

"What's the rush?" her father called over to her. "Your papa doesn't get a thank-you kiss anymore? Too old for that now, I suppose."

Alouette grinned, turned, and hurried back toward him. She was tall these days, so tall she had to dip her head to go through the Refuge's low doorways, yet she still had to stand on tiptoe to kiss her father's cheek.

He leaned over, his coarse white hair glowing in the dim light of the kitchen, and returned a kiss on the top of her forehead.

"Remember to get those floors scrubbed in time, Little Lark," he whispered. "Principale Francine won't be happy if they don't get done."

Alouette frowned a little. "Principale Francine is not very happy with me *most* of the time."

Hugo Taureau was a huge man with hands as large as the metal dinner plates on which he served the Refuge's meals. But those hands were gentle, too. He lifted one now and tweaked a springy coil of his daughter's dark hair.

"She's a good woman, Alouette. She has been kind to us. She gave me this job." He waved the dishcloth around the kitchen. "And she gave us this home for the last twelve years. Her heart is good." He grinned, the lines around his eyes forming little darts under his thick white eyebrows, and dipped his voice again. "But yes, she does have some sharp edges."

Then, with one hand, he effortlessly lifted the cooking pot he'd been drying over their heads and onto a high shelf. It was as if the giant pot weighed as little as the dishcloth in his other hand. As he pushed it into place, his short sleeve slid back, revealing the five silver bumps on his muscular right arm. Her father had never told her what the markings meant or how he'd gotten them. But when she was younger, Alouette used to trace those metallic bumps on his skin, counting the number of dimples in their raised surfaces, and ask him why she didn't have them on her arm too. He would laugh his tender laugh, and his answer would simply be, "You will never have these, ma petite. *Never.*" One time she asked if those strange, glittering marks had been on her mother's skin. He'd said nothing in reply.

Hugo Taureau gave Alouette love—more than she probably deserved. He gave her food—more than a Third Estater could probably afford on Laterre. But he rarely ever gave her answers.

She'd almost given up asking the questions.

Almost.

"Papa, I have to go now," Alouette said, finally grabbing the two metal pails from the hook on the wall. "But I will help you with the dishes after supper."

"Sure, sure," he laughed as he flicked the dishcloth gently in her direction. "Shoo, Little Lark."

Alouette carried the pails to the kitchen sink and turned on the faucet. The water was running painfully slowly today.

Come on, come on, she silently urged the stream.

When the pails were finally full, Alouette heaved them from the sink, out of the kitchen, and down the dingy hallway. The buckets were heavy in her hands, and the water sloshed a little against her long gray tunic. But she moved quickly. Years of scrubbing floors and carrying water had made her strong. Not like her father, of course. But still strong.

Once she reached the vestibule, she carefully positioned the two pails just outside the small alcove where the Refuge's only entrance was located. The sisters would be heading in the opposite direction to the Assemblée room. There they would stay, locked up for at least two hours in Quiet Contemplation. But if any of them were to wander this way, they would see the pails and think Alouette was scrubbing the vestibule.

She *would* clean the floors eventually. Of course she would.

But first she had to see if the transmitteur worked.

Alouette ducked under the doorway. Most rooms in the Refuge were small and dark, with ceilings so low they could be touched with an outstretched hand. But the vestibule was the tiniest and dingiest room of them all. It was just big enough to open the Refuge's heavy PermaSteel door. Alouette had walked through this door only once in her life, when she was four years old and first came to the Refuge with her father. It was after her mother had gotten sick and died, and her father came to the sisters for help because he couldn't possibly care for a little girl all on his own. After Alouette had passed through the door, it had clanged shut, sealing them inside for the next twelve years. She had no memory of that day or any other day before they'd arrived here. Now the only people who went through the door and up the ladder to the above-world were Sister Jacqui and Sister Laurel, who were tasked with the weekly supply runs to the Marsh.

But Alouette's attention wasn't on the door right now. Instead, she stood in front of a thin screen embedded into the wall. The image on the security monitor was obscured today because of yet another leak. Water droplets were splattering, one after another, right in front of the monitor's external microcam. The tiny device watched over the Refuge's entrance, which was hidden inside a mechanical room of one of the old Vallonay freightships.

The monitor didn't show much of the above-world. The image was grainy and always in black and white. All it revealed were some corroding PermaSteel walls, a few rusting machines, and the big puddle of water that was always in the center of the floor. Alouette didn't care, though. Ever since she was little, she loved to sneak into the vestibule and study the view. This little slice of the world she didn't know. It was like peeking through a keyhole. The range of what she could see was limited, but the possibilities were endless.

Alouette's gaze slipped down to the control panel under the monitor. After checking that the hallway was empty, she ran her fingers around the rim of the panel until she found the little depression where her fingernail fit. The plastique covering popped off easily.

Alouette knew the sisters wouldn't approve of what she was doing. Not even Sister Jacqui, who had always taught Alouette to question everything.

The whole point of the Refuge was to be cut off from the rest of the world. The sisters were the protectors of the First World books and the keepers of the Chronicles. Their sacred job was to maintain and preserve not only the histories of Laterre, but the library of books that had been rescued from the old planet and smuggled onto the freight-ships bound for the System Divine. Ever since the year 362 ALD—After Last Days—when the Refuge was built, the Sisterhood had been the ones to protect these treasures. They valued a "life of the mind," as they called it, which meant retreating from the harsh and dangerous world above. People outside the Refuge valued different things than the Sisterhood. The above-world didn't care for books, careful thought, or silence. Even the written word had been long forgotten up there.

If the Ministère were ever to find the Refuge, they would surely destroy the books and the Chronicles. And everything the Sisterhood had accomplished in the past 143 years would be gone.

"We are the protectors of knowledge and the history keepers," Francine had once said when Alouette was rereading one of the vol-umes of the Chronicles during her history lesson. "Recording the world and its events is a blessed and vital task." She'd then wagged a fountain pen at Alouette. "And the only trustworthy and long-lasting way to do this is by hand. It is for this reason that we must keep the written word alive. Lest we forget the mistakes of our ancestors."

For as long as Alouette could remember, all she'd wanted was to become Sister Alouette, an official contributing member of the Refuge. Someone who could attend Assemblée every single day. Someone who could help maintain and update the Chronicles. Someone who would be called on not only to dust the priceless books in the library as part of her chores, but to pledge her life to protect them.

And she still wanted all of that. Truly, she did. She just didn't understand why she couldn't lead a life of the mind *and* get a better look at the above-world.

Just one glimpse, she told herself. And then she'd be satisfied.

The motherboard inside the control panel was tiny and old, yet its components were still in good shape. Alouette set the plastique cover to one side, reached into a pocket of her tunic, and pulled out a small pair of pliers. Blowing a dark curl from her face, Alouette peered closely into the motherboard until she located the old transmitteur. She gripped the edge of it with her pliers and carefully eased it out of the component connection slot. The monitor screen flickered and then went dark. She slipped the old transmitteur, which was dusty and corroded, into her pocket. It clearly hadn't been updated in years.

Alouette always thought of the Refuge when she looked at a classic motherboard. Like the components of an electronic circuit, all the sisters had their own specific function. Sister Jacqui maintained the library and catalogued and cared for the books. Sister Laurel kept everyone healthy with her herbs and homemade salves. Sister Denise made sure the Refuge's devices ran smoothly. And Principale Francine, the head of the Refuge and the chief record keeper of the Chronicles, was like their central memory chip.

From her other pocket, Alouette removed the handkerchief with the new transmitteur tucked inside. Not long after Sister Denise had started teaching her the basics of electronics in her science lessons, Alouette had come up with the idea of crafting a new component for the monitor. Now her 102-day project sat in her palm, sparkling and winking in the dim light.

Alouette grasped the transmitteur between the tips of her pliers and gently eased it into the now-empty connection port.

"Easy and steady," she whispered.

The device slipped into its slot.

Alouette held her breath and looked at the monitor. But nothing happened—the screen remained dark. She felt panic flutter in her stomach. What if she'd just wasted two months of the year on something that didn't work?

She nudged the transmitteur in harder.

"Come on," Alouette murmured, her gaze sliding back and forth between the motherboard and the screen. But still, the monitor was black.

She glared at the new transmitteur sitting idle in the connection slot. She had to get it to work. She simply had to. Gripping her pliers, Alouette steadied her hand and reached in to remove the new component. Perhaps if she took it back to Sister Denise's workbench and re-soldered the—

Alouette's gaze snagged on something as she carefully pulled the transmitteur from the slot. The connectors weren't lining up with the motherboard. Had she built the device backward?

Suddenly, Alouette let out a snort of laughter and slapped her palm against her forehead. "Silly Lark," she scolded herself. She hadn't built the transmitteur backward. She'd inserted it upside down!

With a renewed rush of anticipation, Alouette carefully flipped the pliers around, keeping the tips gripped firmly around the component, and slid the transmitteur back into the slot.

And then . . .

Boom!

Color flooded the screen. Alouette almost dropped her pliers in shock as her eyes darted greedily over the monitor's view, taking it all in. She'd done it! Her new transmitteur worked! Where there were once just black-and-white images, there was now every color imaginable. The bright reds, greens, and blues of the wires snaking into an old machine in the left corner. The rust of the PermaSteel, a deep brown like the crusts on the bread her father baked in the mornings. The slither of golden light streaming in from some unseen source just outside the monitor's view. A doorway? A light fixture?

And then there was the puddle.

She'd seen it a thousand times before. But back then it was gray and silver on the monochrome screen. A simple pool of water. Now it was a pool of rainbows. The light was hitting the puddle at just the right angle, and it blinked and dazzled with color. Streaks of blue and green, and droplets of red.

Red?

Alouette leaned in closer to the monitor as something unseen dripped again into the puddle. But it didn't look like rain. It was dark and crimson. Like . . .

Blood.

As soon as the realization barreled into her mind, someone crashed into view.

A man.

His tall body filled nearly the whole screen. Alouette gasped aloud at the sight and instantly reeled backward, away from the monitor.

"What?" The word came out in a disbelieving rush of air. "Who . . . ?"

She'd never seen anyone on the monitor screen before. *Ever.* Not in all the years she'd been sneaking into the vestibule and stealing glances at this view. She figured it was just because there wasn't much use for a mechanical room now that the giant freightships no longer flew. Which was why it was the perfect hiding place for the Refuge's entrance.

The man was wobbling now. He seemed to be on the verge of falling, or at least buckling at the knees. Alouette blinked once, then again, making sure her eyes weren't deceiving her.

But he was still there.

Alouette moved back toward the monitor. Her heart thudded against her rib cage when she saw his hand pressing against his forehead and the blood seeping out between his fingers, splattering down onto his long silver raincoat. He was hurt. Really hurt.

"No!" The word escaped Alouette, loud and sharp.

She reached out, touching the cold surface of the monitor. The man staggered a few more steps and then stopped. She spread her fingers out over him. What was she even trying to do? Protect him? Help him? But of course she could do none of these things, stuck down here, ten mètres belowground.

She might as well be a whole galaxy away.

Alouette dropped her hand and whispered, "Come on. You're okay. You must be okay. Go. Find someone to help you."

But he seemed to do the opposite of what she was instructing him to do. He limped forward, deeper into the mechanical room, and grabbed for a rusty pipe on the wall. But the pipe broke in his hand, and he collapsed to the floor.

"No!" she said again, this time in a hoarse, panicked whisper. "Get up."

But he didn't move. He seemed to be drifting in and out of consciousness, his eyes closing, then dragging open, then closing again. His hand fell from his forehead, revealing a gash across his flesh. It was bleeding profusely.

Suddenly, all Alouette could think about were the instructions she'd read in the medical textbooks during her wellness lessons with Sister Laurel.

"Open wounds . . . apply direct pressure immediately . . . clean the area . . . sterile dressing or bandage . . . elevation . . . check for signs of concussion."

He was passing out.

He was all alone.

In a forgotten mechanical room, lying in a dirty puddle.

Someone has to help him, Alouette thought, the desperation building in her chest. *Someone has to go up there.*

Then, with a shot of fear and adrenaline, an alarm bell started to ring in her mind as she realized that that someone had to be *her*.

- CHAPTER 10 -
CHATINE

CHATINE STALKED DOWN THE HALLWAY TO HER family's couchette and angrily swiped her Skin in front of the lock.

"Access granted."

She flung the door open and slammed it closed behind her. She pulled the leveler from her pocket and tossed it down on the table. She fully expected to see her mother standing there, hands on hips, red-stained lips pulled into a scowl, demanding to know how much Chatine had managed to lift from the morgue. But the couchette seemed empty. She glanced around, marveling at this rare moment of quiet. Then she heard a soft sob coming from the direction of her bedroom.

Of course she's still here, Chatine thought bitterly. *She never leaves except to go to work.*

When she walked into her bedroom, she noticed that Azelle hadn't moved a millimètre since Chatine had left, although her expression had changed drastically. She was still staring at the Skin on the inside of her arm, but where there had formerly been a look of anticipation and excitement for the upcoming Ascension, there was now a pitiful, tearstained face.

"They canceled it!" Azelle blubbered without looking up. "Chatine, how could they do that to me? I worked so hard this year. I stored up so many points. How could they just cancel it?"

Chatine ignored her sister. She didn't have the patience to deal with her pathetic little problems right now. She had too many problems of her own. She suddenly had to come up with a way to make seven thousand more largs in only ten days. It was impossible. It couldn't be done. She was stuck on this dreadful planet until she died.

And now the people were rioting.

Fantastique.

"And the Premier Enfant is dead!" Azelle continued her lament. "This is the worst day ever. She was just a little girl. Who would kill a little girl?"

"Where's Maman and Papa?" Chatine asked gruffly.

Azelle sniffled, rubbing at her cheeks. "They went to the Marsh."

Chatine nodded. Of course they went to the Marsh. A riot would be a prime time to steal. Paralyzed bodies unable to fight back. Stall owners distracted by the blur of rayonette pulses. As long as her father could stay away from Inspecteur Limier, they'd come home with plenty of loot.

By the time Chatine had arrived back home in Fret 7, the disturbance in the Marsh had already started to spill out into the Frets, spreading through the hallways like a virus through a body. Chatine had never seen so many bashers in her life. The droids had all been marching in perfect unison, their rayonettes armed and ready to paralyze anyone showing signs of disobedience.

Chatine had watched the Universal Alert. She knew why people were yelling and ranting and throwing things like children having a tantrum. Canceling the Ascension was an act of war to these people. The pathetic fools were rioting because they couldn't deal with the disappointment of losing something they already lost every single year.

Did they even care that an innocent child was dead? Or were they too busy lamenting their lost Ascension?

Idiots, Chatine thought as she trampled over to the floor grate, bent down, and ripped it up, no longer caring about how much noise she was making in the process. She was fuming, raging, on the brink of rioting herself. She grabbed the empty sac from the gap in the floor and started pulling objects from her various pockets and stuffing them angrily back into the bag. With each useless item she returned, she recounted the hours and hours she'd spent conning and scheming, just to end up right back where she started. Trapped.

"Now they're saying the Ascension might never come back," Azelle whined, her eyes still locked on her Skin for updates. "They won't reschedule it until Marie's murderer is discovered. But that could take years! And what if they're never found? What if they manage to escape to Reichenstat and are never heard from again? We'll be doomed to live here forever."

"We're already doomed to live here forever," Chatine replied bitterly as she continued to unload her collection.

She should have stolen that ring off Marcellus Bonnefaçon when she had the chance. She should have smacked him over the head with the leveler, searched his pockets, and taken everything he owned. The grandson of the general would certainly have enough valuables on him to buy a passage to Usonia. The titan buttons on his uniform alone were worth more than a week's wages at the fabriques.

If she hadn't been so distracted by the pomp, she wouldn't be in this predicament in the first place.

"But I was going to win this year," Azelle went on, her voice breaking. "I know I was! I could have taken us all to Ledôme. We would have had a nice house to live in and food to eat, and Sol-light. Chatine, we haven't seen the light of the Sols in nine years."

Chatine definitely didn't need to be reminded of *that*. She reached down the front of her coat and pulled out the Sol pendant she'd stolen in the Marsh this morning. The one that had given her so much hope. Now, holding it, watching it dangle in front of her, she felt like a sot for hoping. A fool for believing she ever had a chance of getting off this planet. For thinking the Sol engraved on this pendant was some kind of sign. There were no signs. There was no escape.

Once again, the Sols had failed her.

"I hate whoever did this to us!" Azelle went on. "I hate the person who killed the Premier Enfant. This is all *their* fault. I hope that whenever they find them, they get sent to the deepest exploits on Bastille and never come back!"

It might have been the first time ever that Chatine actually agreed with her sister. She, too, hoped they caught the idiot responsible for this uprising. It was undoubtedly going to make it even more difficult for her to get off this planet. If the Capitaine claimed the election of a new Usonian leader would raise the demand for transport, she couldn't imagine what a riot on Laterre would do.

Chatine stuffed the pendant into the bag, vowing not to put her faith in useless things like stars ever again. But, in her haste, the pendant missed the edge of the sac, and a moment later she heard a clatter as the necklace disappeared into the hole in the floor.

"Fric." She lowered herself to her belly so she could extend her arm under the floor. She felt around for the pendant, trying not to cringe as her fingertips brushed against all manner of disgusting dead things. When she finally managed to grasp the pendant and pull it toward her, she noticed the chain was pulling something along with it.

Something small.

Something smooth.

Something . . . *familiar.*

As soon as Chatine detached the little plastique doll arm from the necklace's chain, the memory hit her like a transporteur. She was suddenly back in Montfer, at the old inn her parents used to own.

Back when life was somewhat bearable and Chatine didn't have to con and steal to get a half a loaf of chou bread. Before her parents were chased out of town for being crocs. Chased over the Secana Sea to these miserable Frets in Vallonay.

"What's that?" Azelle's voice barreled into her thoughts, and Chatine looked up to see her sister staring at the plastique arm still clutched in Chatine's hand. Azelle's eyes suddenly widened with recognition. "Oh my Sols! Is that what I think it is?"

"No," Chatine replied hastily. She was about to drop the arm back into the hole in the floor, but Azelle reached out and snatched it.

"It is," Azelle said, turning the arm around in her hands. "This is the arm from Madeline's doll. I didn't know you still had it."

Madeline.

Even the memory of that name made Chatine's blood boil and her muscles clench.

Azelle chuckled. "Remember how we used to call her 'Ugly Madeline'?"

Chatine nodded dazedly but didn't speak. From the day that little girl first arrived at the inn, she had been a stain on Chatine's entire existence. A leech who ate their food and stole their toys.

"You were so angry about that doll," Azelle went on, running her fingertips over the smooth plastique of the arm. "I remember the look in your eyes when that man gave it to her. It was kind of scary."

Chatine could still see the man so clearly in her memory. Madeline's father. His cropped hair was as white as ice. His stature was almost as tall and as menacing as a Policier droid. His hands were so large they looked like they could strangle a man with one twist.

And in one of those hands, the man held the most beautiful doll Chatine had ever seen. It looked like something First Estate children received at their birthday fêtes. Long, curly black hair that looked real, a silky yellow dress with titan buttons and lace. It even had leather shoes with heels and straps.

Chatine had felt herself instinctively reaching for the doll, hands outstretched, heart beating wildly at the thought of holding such a beautiful thing. But Chatine might as well have been a ghost for the amount of attention the white-haired man paid her. Instead, the man knelt down in front of Madeline. He reached out and stroked her thick black curls. He called her "ma petite."

He gave *her* the doll.

Madeline had immediately cradled it to her chest. And as Chatine watched her rock it back and forth, something inside of her snapped.

With a growl, she lunged for the doll, her fingers outstretched, her lips twisted in a nasty snarl. But Madeline was too quick; she swung the doll out of reach, and all Chatine could grab onto was one of its tiny arms. She gave it a tug and it popped out immediately.

Madeline had started to cry. The white-haired man immediately scooped her into his arms and left.

She was gone.

They both were.

And all that Chatine had left was that sad little plastique arm.

"Do you ever wonder what happened to her?" Azelle asked.

Chatine felt the rage welling up inside of her again. She snatched the arm back from Azelle and tossed it into the hole in the floor. "No."

Azelle studied her for a painfully long time. "Chatine," she said softly, a somber expression crossing her face. "She was only a little girl. She didn't know what she was—"

"Enough!" Chatine said, cutting her off. The last thing she wanted to do was sit around reminiscing about Madeline. Azelle might have been able to forgive the girl for what she'd done to them—to their family—but Chatine never would. Ever.

She kicked the grate back into place and stood up.

"Where are you going?" Azelle asked, and Chatine couldn't help but hear the tenderness in her sister's voice. The pity. It made Chatine pulse with anger. She would *not* be pitied by anyone. Especially not Azelle.

"Out," was all she said in response before slamming the couchette door behind her again.

- CHAPTER 11 -
MARCELLUS

THE VOICE WAS SOFT LIKE A BREEZE, SWEET LIKE A
bell. Almost melodic.

"Come on, wake up. Please, wake up."

Marcellus heaved his eyes open. But as soon as his vision started
to focus, he knew he must still be unconscious. He *must* be dreaming.

The person, the *girl*, who crouched in front of him was unlike
anything—or any*one*—he'd ever seen before.

"Can you see?" The girl held up two fingers in front of Marcellus's
face. "How many?"

Marcellus said nothing. His lips were frozen, his tongue stuck
to the roof of his mouth. His mind was fuzzy. Disconnected words
trickled into his thoughts: "Ascension," "canceled," "Premier Enfant,"
"poisoning."

Where am I?

He tried to glance around, but everything was blurring in and out
of focus. He was lying on his side, his cheek pressed against a cold
metal floor, and his head throbbed like the weight of a transporteur

was pushing down on it. It appeared he was in the hallway of one of the Frets. But which one? And how did he get here?

"Where am I?" he asked again. This time his mouth managed to say the words aloud.

"You're in Fret 7," the girl said in that same sweet voice. Her large, dark brown eyes darted up and looked around. "In one of the hall-ways. You collapsed, but when I came to find you, you weren't there. You must have stumbled out here."

She was beautiful. Too beautiful to be real. He had to be imag-ining her. Because no one looked like her. *No one.* Her eyes were so wide, not only could he see himself reflected in them, it seemed the whole hallway was reflected back at him too. If the girl had been outside—instead of in this dingy, foul-smelling Fret—Marcellus had no doubt that Laterre's endless clouds would have been mirrored in those huge eyes.

And she was so clean. Unlike anyone else in the Frets. Her skin was as unblemished as her spotless gray tunic. And her curls, dark and tightly coiled, radiated every which way.

A chorus of shouts somewhere off in the distance wrenched him from his thoughts. Wrenched his gaze from the girl and back to the grimy hallway where he was lying.

"The riot," he murmured.

He needed to get back to the Marsh. Back to Limier. He had to help calm the crowds. Do his job. Act like the commandeur he was supposed to become.

Get up! he scolded himself. *Don't be weak. Get back out there. Do you think Commandeur Vernay would have just lain down here and given up? No.*

Marcellus let out a low, painful groan as he tried to push himself up, but the girl's hands were suddenly on his shoulders, forcing him down.

"Stay still," she said. "Your head is a mess. I just need to find something clean. . . ." She trailed off as her gaze darted around, land-ing on his coat. "What's this?"

She reached under his chin and Marcellus felt her pull something out from under his raincoat, and then she was pushing it against his forehead. He winced, not just from the pain, but from the shock of her touch. A touch that was somehow both gentle and firm at the same time.

She's real.

"I'm sorry," she whispered, clearly feeling him flinch.

"'S okay," he managed to croak out.

This made her smile a smile so bright and white, it seemed to illu-minate the entire hallway.

"We need to get this cleaned up," she said, and then started to mutter to herself. "Staunch the flow. Clean to reduce risk of bacteria. Streptococcus or staphylococcus. Apply antibiotic prophylaxis."

Marcellus stared up at her. Who *was* she? Who spoke like that? Was she a médecin? But she didn't look like a cyborg. She had no cir-cuitry implanted in her face, at least none that he could see. And she didn't seem removed and clinical like every other médecin he'd ever met. She seemed just the opposite: compassionate and kind.

"You probably have a concussion," she continued. "Do you hear ringing in your ears? Are you nauseated? Dizzy?"

"I think I'm okay."

With the girl's help, he finally managed to push himself up to sitting. She pulled her hand away from his head and rocked back on her heels, giving him another smile. Marcellus's heart thumped just at the sight of it. There was something ethereal about that smile.

Maybe the bump to his head *had* done some real damage. What was happening to him? No girl had ever looked at him like that before. But then again, Marcellus hadn't actually spoken to many girls in his life. The First and Second Estate girls he knew had always seemed like flowers to him. Like the roses or orchids or sweet-smelling lavender in the Palais gardens. Skin gleaming and lips vibrant from their expensive youth injections and creams. They were bright and colorful, but something to be left well alone.

"How do you feel?" she asked. "Do you think you can get up? You should go somewhere to get help. The wound needs proper cleaning and probably biosutures, so it can heal without infection. Maybe you should go to a . . ." She paused, seeming to search for the right word. "A med center?"

He waved this away. A sense of urgency was beginning to bubble up inside him. He didn't want to go to a med center. He didn't want to leave here.

He didn't want to leave *her*.

"Who are you? Where are you from? How did you find me?" The questions fired out of him, fast and furious like pulses from a rayonette.

The girl looked away from Marcellus to the dingy hallway around them. Her eyes suddenly grew wide, as if she were just now noticing where they were.

"How did you find me?" Marcellus repeated.

The girl reached out and touched the nearby wall, as if testing to see if it was real. "I saw the blood," she said, somewhat dazedly. "I followed the drops and found you here." She finally pulled her gaze from the wall and peered down at her lap, where she was holding something. "I'm sorry, this was all I could find. I saw it tucked into your raincoat. I needed something to stop the bleeding."

Marcellus glanced at the object in her hand—a tattered, torn piece of cloth, now stained with his blood—and he drew in a sharp breath at the sight of it.

His father's shirt.

Suddenly the memory of the morgue came barreling back into his mind. The stitching. The letters. The Forgotten Word. A message sewn right into the fabric.

"I'm sure it's not ruined," the girl went on, seemingly misinterpreting the panic in his eyes. "A little baking soda and water will get that stain right out."

But Marcellus was barely listening to her now. All he could do was stare at the garment in her hands. The crooked, shaky letters stitched in thread felt like they were beacons calling out to all of Laterre. *Look! Look what Marcellus has.* If anyone saw that shirt— if anyone suspected him of receiving messages from a Vangarde prisoner—his life would be over. His grandfather would surely . . .

"Sister Muriel says baking soda and water can get out most anything," the girl went on. "She says—" but she stopped herself, biting down on her lip.

Marcellus struggled to move his arms, to grab the shirt, but just then the girl pulled the cloth away from his reach, shaking it out as if she were one of the Palais maids on laundry day. She held it between pinched thumbs and forefingers, and for a moment, he could no longer see her face. The old, tattered, and now bloodied shirt formed a curtain between them.

"Is that your name?" she asked from behind the curtain. "Marcellou?"

In that instant, the blood in every vein and artery of Marcellus's body seemed to halt. He no longer thought of the shirt. He no longer thought of the cryptic forbidden message stitched painstakingly with thread. He no longer even thought of his traitorous father.

All he could hear and see and think about was that word.

That *name.*

He hadn't heard it in seven years.

"Marcellou! Help! Please! You must stop them!"

Marcellus shut his eyes tight against the memory, forcing it back to the dark corners of his mind where it lived. He would not think of such things. He would not remember such nights.

"Wait." His eyes snapped open. She was no longer looking at him. "How did you know that name?"

"It says it right here." She lowered the shirt and pointed to the mysterious stitching in the fabric. "'My dear Marcellou.'"

Once again, the blood in his veins seemed to skitter and then stop. He looked in amazement from the girl to the stained cloth, then back to the girl again.

"You can *read*?"

- CHAPTER 12 -
ALOUETTE

FOR THE FIRST TIME IN TWELVE YEARS, ALOUETTE Taureau was above the ground instead of below it.

No longer was she sneaking glimpses at a grainy view on an old security monitor.

Now she was *in* that view.

Beyond that view.

She was inside the Frets. Breathing real air. Touching real walls.

She couldn't stop staring. At everything. The floors. The ceilings. The intricately interwoven pipes that lined the hallways. It was all so . . .

New.

Alouette had always known the passcode to get in and out of the Refuge. Principale Francine had made her memorize it in case of emergency. But Alouette had never used it. She'd never needed to until now.

"How did you know that name?"

The question snapped Alouette out of her daze and she turned to study the man in front of her. He was the first man she could ever remember seeing in person, apart from her father.

Except the person in front of her wasn't really a man, was he? His face looked nothing like her father's, which was shadowed by thick gray stubble and crisscrossed by deep crevices and lines that held stories he would never tell.

But this man—this *boy*—was so different. There was something fresh about his face, like it was newly formed. Unmarked and unscathed by time.

In answer to his question, she pointed to the shirt in her hand. "It says it right here. 'My dear Marcellou.'"

"You can *read*?" he asked in surprise.

Alouette was suddenly speechless, distracted by his gaze. It was so intense. So probing. His brown eyes—with their hints of green—seemed like they were trying to figure Alouette out, inspect her, assess her. He seemed as curious about her as she was about him.

"Yes, I can read." Alouette finally found her words, and then, to avoid his inquisitive gaze, she dipped her eyes back down to the bloodied shirt in her hands and to the message so crudely but painstakingly stitched into the fabric. Each stitch seemed so tiny, so intricate. It reminded Alouette of Sister Muriel's handiwork on the sisters' tunics in the Refuge.

"Where did you get this?" Alouette asked, but when she looked up again, his gaze was no longer probing. It was now downcast. Avoiding.

"I . . ." He seemed to struggle with his response. "It came from a prisoner."

Alouette's thoughts spun. "A prisoner? But why would you—"

"What does the rest of it say?" he cut her off, as though he was in a hurry to redirect her line of questioning.

She glanced back down at the shirt in her hands. "It says, 'My dear Marcellou, Mabelle is in Montfer. Go to her.'"

His eyes darkened. "No. You must be mistaken. It can't possibly say that."

Confused, Alouette smoothed out the fabric so she could reread the words stitched into it. But they didn't change. She wasn't mistaken. "That's what it says."

"Mabelle is in prison," he said dismissively. "For life."

"Who is she?"

"No one. She's nothing. Just a governess I once had."

A governess? People in the Frets can't afford governesses.

Her eyes shifted down to his sleek silver raincoat, covered in blood, as he fiddled with one of its shiny titan buttons.

Definitely not Third Estate.

Maybe Second Estate? Maybe he was a foreman of a fabrique. Or a superviseur of an exploit. A médecin, perhaps? *No.* He didn't have the cyborg circuitry implanted in his face.

Sensing the shift in him, Alouette searched for something else to say. "So is that really your name? Marcellou?"

But this question didn't bring the warmth back to his eyes. "It was just a nickname," he said with a flick of his hand. "My real name is Marcellus."

She smiled a little. *Marcellus.* That suited him better. There was something noble about it. Like a god, or a hero, or a warrior in those really old books Sister Jacqui read to her when she was little—the warriors who fought strange one-eyed monsters and women with snakes for hair, who could lift mountains and throw thunderbolts.

Marcellus.

"Where did you learn to read the Forgotten Word?" he asked urgently, interrupting her thoughts. His examining gaze was on her once again.

Alouette opened her mouth, but then clamped it shut again. Her gaze darted from Marcellus back up the hallway. She took in the rusting walls, the strange dank smell, and the moist air. Her chest suddenly tightened. What was she still doing here? She was supposed to just tend to his wound and then get back to the Refuge. Quickly. Before Assemblée was over and the sisters ever knew she'd left.

But instead, she'd gotten distracted and here she still was. And now this boy—this stranger—was asking her questions. Questions she could never answer. She couldn't tell him about how the sisters had taught her to read so that one day she could maintain the Chronicles and help protect the library. Because if she told him, it would mean breaking the sisters' vow of secrecy.

Long ago, Sister Jacqui had explained to Alouette why the Ministère could never know about the Refuge and the books that had been smuggled off the First World. If they were ever to find the sisters' hiding place under the Frets, they'd surely shut the Refuge down and destroy the library. Alouette had promised to keep the vow to never reveal the Sisterhood's existence or location. And it had always been easy to do so. Because she'd never had anyone to keep the secret from.

"I should go now," she blurted out. "I need to get home."

Marcellus's eyes grew wide. "No, wait. Don't—"

But his words were cut off by a noise. The stomping of feet somewhere nearby.

Alouette and Marcellus froze.

The footfalls grew louder, and soon a shrill, whooping siren filled the air.

Alouette peered into the maze of rusting hallways, searching for the source. She tried to ask what could possibly be making a noise like that, but all that came out was a strangled cry as her gaze fell upon the most ghastly and terrifying sight.

It was at least three mètres tall—much bigger than any man—with a face straight out of a nightmare. Part human and part machine, it marched toward her, its joints whirring and clicking.

It was a monster!

No, her rational mind corrected. *A Policier droid.*

Alouette had learned about them in the Chronicles. She'd even seen a hand-drawn picture of one, but she never imagined how frightening they would be in person. Their massive chests looked like the bodies of the insects she'd read about in Sister Laurel's nature journals. Except these bodies were crafted from dull gray PermaSteel. Where the creature's eyes should have been, there were two blinking orange lights, which shone like faltering flashlights. Sister Jacqui once told Alouette that a single droid could lift four men at once.

"Don't worry," Marcellus said with a small laugh, clearly sensing her panic. "It's just a Policier droid. It's rounding up rioters."

But Alouette barely heard him. All she could hear was that horrible whirring and clanking. Metal grinding against metal. And those terrifying eyes, scanning the hallways; they made her feel alone and helpless.

Everything about this situation felt wrong. So very wrong. The world was upside down. For the first time since she'd found Marcellus, Alouette felt cold again. Freezing, in fact. She began to shiver inside her tunic, and suddenly all Alouette could think about was home. The Refuge. The warm and safe Refuge.

"I really have to go." The words shot out of her. She tried to stand up, but something tugged on the side of her tunic. Panicked, she looked back at the boy and blinked.

"Wait," he said. "It won't bother us. Look! It's leaving." He pointed to the droid turning left down another hallway and rapidly moving away from them.

But that didn't matter to Alouette. Her body was trembling— from cold or fear, she wasn't sure. She just knew she couldn't stay here. The sisters had been right all along. The above-world *was* dangerous. It was no place for Alouette.

"I have to."

"Can I AirLink you, at least?" he asked.

Alouette's brow furrowed. "What?"

He tapped a finger to the inside of his arm. "Can I message you?" he clarified.

Before she could reply, Marcellus gently took her hand and pushed up the sleeve of her gray tunic. Alouette felt a curious tingle travel up her arm and down her spine.

"I'll message you. On your—" But Marcellus halted when his intense eyes fell on her scar. The long ridge of raised flesh that formed a perfect rectangle on the inside of her arm.

Marcellus yanked his hands away as though her scar had bitten him. "What on Laterre . . ."

Alouette didn't like the expression she was seeing on Marcellus's face. It was too questioning. Too suspicious. Too distrustful. She quickly pulled the sleeve of her tunic back down and pushed herself to her feet.

"Stop! Please!" Marcellus called out again. "Wait. Don't go."

But she was already running, the soft soles of her canvas shoes slapping the grated metal floor beneath her feet.

"I don't even know your name!"

She halted, just for a moment, and looked back. Marcellus had pushed himself up from the floor, steadying himself against the rusting wall.

"Tell me your name." The suspicion was no longer in his eyes. Now, all that she could see there was desperation.

Her world was tilting.

Should I tell him?

Nothing made sense.

Is it dangerous to tell him?

Everything was too confusing, too perplexing, too much.

It isn't technically breaking the vow of secrecy. . . .

She took a breath and then shouted, "Alouette," before ducking around a corner and leaving the boy behind her.

CHAPTER 13

CHATINE

"DO YOU SEE? THAT LIGHT RIGHT THERE? THAT'S Sol 1."

Chatine closed her eyes, letting the memory rush over her, trying to hold on to it, but it was like trying to hold on to mist.

"Isn't it pretty? Look how it's trying so hard to shine for you."

His tiny face was fading with each passing day as she grew older, and his body—which was now no more than frozen dust—crumbled further into nothing.

"There are three Sols in the sky. Yes, three! Sol 1 is the white one, Sol 2 is the red one, and Sol 3 . . ."

She saw him now only in splintered pieces—cracked moments of time. A curl of light brown hair, the same shade as her own. A dribble of spit-up on his chin. A piercing cry in the night. A thin, bony thigh, pink and angry from their mother's unforgiving palm.

On some days, she couldn't even see his face anymore.

"Aren't we lucky to live under so many stars?"

When she was little, she used to rock him to sleep and point to a streetlamp outside the window of the inn in Montfer. She would tell him that it was one of the Sols. And that the light was dim because it was trying to break through the clouds. Of course, he was less than a year old and unable to understand anything she was saying. But even then, she never wanted to tell him that they lived on a planet that hardly ever saw the light of the Sols. She wanted him to grow up in a different kind of world. A better world. Where the Sols shone brightly every day. Where everyone had enough to eat. Where the upper estates didn't treat the people like vermin to be swept up under the rug.

A world like Usonia.

Which now felt farther away than ever.

At only six years old, she'd wanted all of this for baby Henri, even though she knew he'd probably never see it.

"When we're big, we can go up there. We can zoom off in a big space voyageur and we can see all the stars really close."

Chatine leaned her head back against the railing. She sat in the old, collapsed stairwell of Fret 7, staring up through the giant gash in the ceiling. No one ever came here. Most of the residents in the Frets were terrified of this place after the stairs collapsed three years ago, killing eight people. But Chatine liked coming here. It was quiet. And, in the middle of the day, when the sky was the lightest shade of gray, she liked to look up through the giant tear in the ceiling and imagine that she could see the bright white rays of Sol 1 shining above her head.

But mostly, Chatine came here because it was the one place in the Frets where she allowed herself to think about Henri.

"Give him back! You're holding him all wrong! Maman, tell Madeline she can't hold him."

"Shut up, both of you! Chatine, go buy me some vegetables for the stew. Your father has special guests coming for dinner tonight."

"Don't send me. Send her. Send Madeline."

"GO! Now, Chatine. Get out of my sight."

Chatine's eyes fluttered open. No matter how hard she tried to think about the good moments with Henri—his hand pressed against her cheek, her lips kissing the raindrop-shaped birthmark on the back of his shoulder—it always ended here. She always saw him the way she'd seen him for the final time: cradled in Madeline's arms. She could still remember the way the little girl had held him. Like he was a doll. Like he was her own personal plaything. Like his life meant nothing.

And apparently, to her, it didn't.

The memory squeezed her chest so tightly, she felt as though she couldn't breathe. But even so, she still knew, deep in her heart, that her little brother was better off dead. If he'd lived to be a man, he'd undoubtedly have ended up on Bastille. Third Estate boys born into families like the Renards had little hope of living an honest life.

"Stop! Please!"

The voice crashed into Chatine's mind, and for a moment, she couldn't tell if it was real, or just another hazy piece of that horrible day she'd come home to find Henri dead.

She leapt to her feet.

"Wait. Don't go."

Chatine froze. The voice was real. And she recognized it. She hated that she knew it, but she knew it.

Marcellus Bonnefaçon.

Was he speaking to her? Had he found her? Had he somehow tracked her here from the morgue? Panicked, Chatine checked the display on her Skin. The tracker was still disabled. Chatine let out a quiet sigh of relief.

But that still didn't change the fact that Officer Bonnefaçon had somehow found her and was calling out to her, possibly wanting his revenge for the little stunt she'd pulled in the morgue.

Silently, Chatine pushed her back against the wall, trying to calm her pounding heart.

"I don't even know your name!" he shouted. "Tell me your name."

Of course he'd want to know her name. She'd outsmarted him. She'd conned him into giving her the leveler back. Not to mention she'd punched him in the stomach. He obviously wanted to know her name so he could report her to Limier and ship her off to Bastille for the rest of her life.

But there was something strange in his voice. Something that wasn't there before. It almost sounded like pain. It was enough to rouse her curiosity and lure her away from her hiding spot. Chatine grabbed on to the broken railing and swung herself over the giant open shaft that used to be the stairwell. She tentatively stepped into the hallway and, careful to stay close to the wall, peered through the slats in the metal flooring.

And that's when she saw him, slumped and bleeding in the corridor one floor below.

Injured, her mind calculated at once. *Incapacitated. An easy target.*

Chatine also noticed he wasn't looking back up at her, as she'd suspected. He was looking at something unseen in the distance, farther down the corridor.

"Alouette," a female voice called out, light and melodic, like a song.

Chatine bent forward, straining to see whom the voice belonged to. She caught a glimpse of dark, curly hair and unnaturally clean skin. Second Estate, perhaps? But what was she doing in the Frets? And her clothes were definitely *not* Second Estate. Chatine could make out a billow of drab gray fabric as the girl vanished around a corner.

The officer let out a painful moan, pulling Chatine's attention back to the hallway directly beneath her. She peered between the slats just in time to see his body slump farther down the wall.

Chatine crouched lower, pushing her face against the grate, trying to make out whether or not he was still conscious. His eyes were closed and a small trickle of blood dripped from a wound on his forehead. Her gaze zeroed in on the ring around his finger. The one she had failed to nick earlier today.

Go, her mind urged her. *Take everything you can.*

Chatine knew this was her chance. *This* was the other option she'd been looking for. The officer could have enough on him right now to secure her passage to Usonia. She could take the lot and head straight back to the Capitaine.

Her eyes roved the hallway, searching for signs of life. In the distance she could hear the whirring and clicking of Policier droids on the move, but she couldn't determine which way they were heading. Was the sound getting closer or farther away? Were they coming for him or going after some foolish protester on the run?

Chatine focused back on Officer Bonnefaçon, whose eyelids were drooping. She'd been around the Frets long enough to know that he shouldn't be closing his eyes after a head injury. She remembered when old Massay from her father's gang had hit his head on the underside of a Policier patroleur during one of their jobs. The other members of the Délabré had dragged him back to the Frets and let him sleep it off. He never woke up.

Someone had to keep the officer awake. Someone had to ask him questions, make him talk. Otherwise . . .

"Damn the Sols," Chatine whispered, and pulled herself to her feet. She couldn't believe she was going to do this. She, Chatine Renard, rescuing a Ministère officer?

But there was just something about how helpless he looked. Something about the memory of his eyes, in the morgue, as he offered to get her something to eat. Despite her conviction that he'd been luring her into a trap, there was also something genuine there. Something that told her, if the situation were reversed, he would be rushing down to save her, too.

You're wrong, a voice inside her head warned. *He would never save you. You are worthless to him.*

She knew the voice was right. The voice was always right. It was this skeptical yet shrewd intuition of hers that had kept her alive and out of Bastille for the past eighteen years, despite all the odds stacked against her.

And yet, for the first time in her life, Chatine defiantly chose to ignore it.

It was a choice she would surely come to regret.

- CHAPTER 14 -
ALOUETTE

"HALT!"

The robotic voice ricocheted off the rusting walls of the hallway as a beam of bright orange light cut through the murky air.

But Alouette did not halt. She kept running, her long gray tunic snapping and twisting around her legs. She glanced over her shoulder and could just barely make out the terrifying, gargantuan monster in the distance.

A droid.

Still there. Still pursuing her.

And she still had no idea *why* it was chasing her. After she'd left Marcellus, she'd tried to run straight back to the mechanical room, only to discover the mechanical room wasn't where she thought it was. Somehow she'd gotten entirely turned around. That's when she'd heard the voice.

"Halt!"

There it was again.

Alouette shrieked and spurred her body onward. She'd never run so hard or so fast in her life. Her muscles burned, and her breathing was coming out in quick, ragged gasps.

She came to another crossroads in the corridors and slowed. She tried to catch her breath as she surveyed her options, squinting into the dim light in each direction, trying to make out something—anything—familiar. But every passageway looked the same. The poorly lit hallways of the Frets were an endless maze, and she was lost. Completely lost.

The sound of metal pounding against metal grew louder. The droid was getting closer. What would happen if it caught her? What would it do to her? Where would it take her?

She didn't want to know.

She could never know.

In a split-second decision, Alouette turned left, sprinting down another hopelessly long hallway. She had no idea if she was getting closer to the mechanical room or farther away. But she couldn't stop. She had to get back to the Refuge.

Back to safety.

As she ran, she kept her gaze trained on the ground, trying to find some trace of those droplets of blood. The ones that had first led her to the boy—Marcellus. But only grime and mud coated the floor. She couldn't make out one single drop.

For the first time in her life, Alouette wished she still had a Skin to guide her. She'd read in the Chronicles about Skins—or TéléSkins, as they were formally called—and how they could be used to track people and locate destinations. But all she had now was this useless scar.

"By the order of the Patriarche, you are commanded to halt." The droid's voice boomed out again.

Alouette braved another glance behind her and that's when she saw it. All of it. Its terrifying silver body seemed to fill the entire hallway. Its head clicked toward her, two menacing orange eyes zeroing in on her. Then, a weapon extended from its arm.

A rayonette.

"Sols!" she cried aloud. Her knees buckled and she nearly crashed to the ground. But she managed to fling herself around another corner.

Up ahead, she noticed an open doorway. She had no other choice. She flew toward it and ducked inside to find a stairwell. She crouched into a dark crevice under the stairs as she tried desperately to remember everything she'd read about droids in the Chronicles. Were they programmed to follow movement or sound? Or both?

Regardless, she sucked in a breath and held it, keeping her body as still and as quiet as possible. Outside, she could hear the thud and clank of the droid's footsteps. The floor vibrated as it got closer and closer. She shut her eyes tight.

And then, suddenly, she was no longer in the stairwell.

She was somewhere else. Somewhere cold and dark. Somewhere in the deep recesses of her memory.

And yet she could hear the same terrifying footsteps moving closer. Shaking the ground.

Something was looming over her head. A tree? No, a rock. It was enormous. Threatening to press down on her. On *them*.

She wasn't alone. Her father was with her. Next to her. They were huddled together on the cold, damp ground. She could just make him out in the gloomy light. He was holding his finger to his lips.

"Hush, ma petite. Hush."

Alouette gasped and opened her eyes. What was that? A memory from before she came to the Refuge? But she knew nothing about *before*. Everything *before* was a murky darkness. Her memories stretched back no further than the Refuge and the sisters and her father cooking in the small kitchen.

But those footsteps. The sound of the clanking droid. It was so familiar.

"Go! Don't look back! The bashers are right on us!"

Alouette startled out of her reverie and listened to the voice coming from outside the stairwell. It wasn't the robotic monotone of a droid. That was a *human* voice.

Alouette steeled herself, crept out from her hiding place, and peered around the doorway just in time to see two men rounding a corner, breathing hard. Their clothes were shabby and their foreheads glistened with sweat.

What on Laterre?

Before she even had time to process what was happening, a droid rounded the corner. The same one? Or a second? She couldn't be sure. They all looked the same. Alouette scrabbled back into the darkness of the stairwell, pressing herself against the wall.

"By the order of the Patriarche, you are commanded to halt." The same command reverberated through the hallway. Alouette held her breath again.

Had it seen her?

"Halt!" the droid thundered again. "Or I have permission to paralyze you."

Then Alouette heard a commotion, a scuffling of feet, someone yelling, followed by two muffled thumps. With her heart still racing, she took a tentative step forward and stole another peek around the doorframe.

Two droids now stood in the hallway, looming over two crumpled bodies that were lying lifeless on the ground.

Dead?

Alouette bit her lip.

One droid extended a long, bionic arm and picked up one of the men by the back of his neck. The man twitched slightly, and Alouette swallowed with relief. *Not dead.* But there was definitely something wrong with him. The man hung in the droid's grasp, his useless legs dangling beneath him. His eyes were open, but they seemed sleepy, confused.

The droid's orange gaze flashed across the inside of the man's arm—right over his Skin. But Alouette was barely paying attention. Because she was momentarily distracted by something on the ground. She had to squint in the low light, but she could definitely make out three tiny droplets of crimson.

Marcellus's blood?

Her gaze darted up and landed on a rusty sign on the opposite wall. The words were scratched and faded with time, but she could just make out the letters spelling out, "Mec anic 1 R m" with an arrow pointing right.

Thank the Sols!

The entrance to the Refuge was only a few mètres away.

"Clement Dinard," the droid's voice announced. "Third Estate. Residence in Fret 10. Prisoner number 48590. Previous incarcerations: two."

Prisoner?

Alouette's attention was pulled back to the droid in the hallway. She stared at the man dangling from its metal fist with sudden fascination.

He'd served time. He'd survived the harsh climate of Laterre's moon . . . *twice*. She knew from reading the Chronicles that Bastille was a hostile, unforgiving place. Even more so than the Frets.

The other droid reached for the second man, scanning him in the same way. "Gaspard Nevers. Third Estate. Residence in Fret 17. Previous incarcerations: zero."

But Alouette couldn't stop staring at the first man, still clutched in the grasp of the droid. His ripped shirt sleeve had ridden all the way up, revealing five silver bumps embedded into the flesh of his right arm.

Alouette felt the air seep out of her lungs.

As the droids carried the two men away, Alouette stood motionless in the stairwell. She was finally alone. The mechanical room was just a few paces away. And yet she couldn't bring herself to move. She couldn't tear her thoughts from what she had just seen.

She knew those bumps. She'd spent countless nights when she was little tracing them with her small fingers as she fell asleep. She'd memorized every dimple in their surfaces.

She just never thought she'd see them on another man.

A man who wasn't her father.

- CHAPTER 15 -
MARCELLUS

THE GIRL WAS GONE. AS SUDDENLY AND GHOSTLIKE as she'd appeared. There one minute, tending to the wound on his head and reading messages in the Forgotten Word, and disappeared the next.

"Search person," Marcellus instructed his TéléCom.

He was still sitting in the musty hallway of Fret 7. Water dripped from the ceiling, puddling near his feet, and steam was hissing from a broken pipe nearby.

The TéléCom beeped, signaling for him to proceed.

"Alouette," Marcellus pronounced.

He just wished he knew her last name. It would make tracking her down so much easier.

"Searching . . . ," the friendly voice of the TéléCom replied through his audio patch. Faces began to flash rapidly across the screen as the search function cycled through every profile in the Communiqué, the Ministère's central database. First, Second, and Third Estates. Living *and* dead.

Countless eyes, noses, and lips blurred and morphed into one unrecognizable jumble, until finally a handful of images populated on his screen.

"Forty-two results found," the TéléCom announced, concluding its search.

Marcellus quickly scanned the profile images. None of them looked like the girl he had just met. None of them had her wide eyes with that otherworldly gaze.

He tossed the TéléCom aside.

Who was this girl? Where did she come from? Why was she not in the Communiqué?

As Marcellus sat in the now-empty hallway, he could almost believe the whole encounter with Alouette had been a vision, dreamed up inside of his bruised and battered head. But then his gaze fell upon the prisoner shirt in his lap, and he knew it couldn't have been a dream. The garment was soaked with his blood from when *she* had dabbed it against his forehead. The crooked letters and words that *she* had read to him were still stitched into the fabric.

A message written . . . for him.

There was no other explanation. His father had somehow learned to write on Bastille, and he had sent him this message. But how did he know that nickname? That was Mabelle's nickname for Marcellus when he was a child.

Her special nickname.

My dear Marcellou . . .

Mabelle had been Marcellus's governess for almost his entire childhood. She had come to take care of him when he was six months old, after his mother died and his father was disowned for joining the Vangarde. It was shortly before his father bombed the copper exploit, killing those hundreds of workers. The only good thing to come out of that explosion was that it eventually put an end to the Rebellion of 488. Citizen Rousseau's followers were finally able to see her precious Vangarde for what it really was: a terrorist organization.

Her numbers plummeted, and the Ministère was able to squash the rebellion once and for all.

Mabelle had raised Marcellus, fed him, taught him to speak, to walk, even to read and write the Forgotten Word.

Growing up in the Frets, Mabelle had cleverly taught herself the language by piecing together the cryptic symbols on old signs in the hallways and on the rusting freightship machinery.

Marcellus had loved Mabelle like she was his own mother.

Until she was discovered to be a spy for the Vangarde.

Until she was dragged from their wing in the Grand Palais, screaming and begging for Marcellus to stop them.

Until Marcellus learned she was a traitor. Just like his father.

The day she was taken away was the day the Forgotten Word became forgotten to Marcellus, too. After she was gone, the words and letters slowly disappeared. There was no one else to practice with. No one to write secret notes to anymore. No one to leave him a trail of written clues where, at the end, he'd find a little prize.

Now, sitting in the cold, dark hallway of the Frets, holding his father's shirt, Marcellus ran his fingers over the stitching, remembering what the girl had read.

My dear Marcellou, Mabelle is in Montfer. Go to her.

He leaned forward, trying desperately to see what the mysterious girl had seen, to try to make sense of the swirling loops and lines. Some of the letters seemed impossibly unfamiliar to him. Unreachable memories tucked into the corners of his mind. And yet, surprisingly, some of the letters came back to him easily. The crescent-moon curve of the *C*, the deep valley of the *U*, the mountainous peaks of the *M*.

"M is for Marcellus . . . and mountain. See how it looks like the top of a mountain?"

Marcellus felt his weak hands tighten around the shirt. He'd tried so hard to forget—so hard to erase her from his mind—and yet the memories kept creeping back in, like shadows that never fully went away, even when the lights were turned on.

The girl must have been wrong. There was no other explanation. She'd misread the message. She'd mistaken the letters. Mabelle wasn't in Montfer. She was on Bastille. He couldn't go to her. No humans went to the moon unless they were convicted. The prison was run by droids and supervised by Warden Gallant from a safe office in Ledôme.

The whole thing had been one giant misunderstanding.

And Marcellus would prove it to himself.

Still shaky, he pulled the TéléCom back onto his lap. "New search," he instructed the device, and after another soft beep, he pronounced the name he never thought he would ever say aloud again, "Mabelle Dubois."

"Searching . . . ," the TéléCom repeated, and once again, countless faces spun across his screen.

Finally, the wheel slowed as, this time, the Communiqué came up with an exact match. The image of his governess filled the screen. The picture had obviously been taken in her younger days because she looked exactly as he remembered her. Smooth skin. Long neck. Soft brown waves framing her face. Marcellus had to look away, unable to peer into her soulful eyes, even through the thin plastique of the TéléCom.

"Mabelle Dubois," the TéléCom recited the highlights of the profile. "Third Estate. Former employee of General Bonnefaçon. Convicted of treason against the Laterrian Regime in 498 ALD. Prisoner number 47161. Current location unknown."

The breath caught in Marcellus's throat, making him feel as though he were being strangled.

Current location unknown? How could that be? She had been given a prisoner number. Marcellus himself had seen her being arrested by the droids.

"Marcellou! Help! Please! You must stop them!"

"More information," Marcellus commanded the TéléCom. "Filter: postarrest."

"Mabelle Dubois," the TéléCom continued, "served seven years on Bastille before escaping in the sixth month of 505 ALD."

Escaped? In the sixth month of 505? That was just last month. Why was Marcellus never told? He didn't even know anyone *could* escape from Bastille.

The sound of approaching footsteps crashed into Marcellus's thoughts. He blinked and glanced down the hallway, squinting into the low light to try to make out who was coming.

Droids? Inspecteur Limier?

Then he remembered what was lying on his lap.

The shirt.

The message.

From a traitor.

About a traitor.

Marcellus scrambled to bunch up the fabric and stuff it back down the front of his uniform. He forced himself to stand up again—to act like a commandeur and not a weak little boy—but as soon as he was on his feet, his forehead throbbed and the blackness started to curtain his vision again. His knees buckled, and he reached for the wall to steady himself.

A moment later, a figure rounded the corner. Marcellus let out a sigh, relieved to see it was not Inspecteur Limier but rather a young boy in an oversized black coat and pants. His clothes were so old they were held together with strange clips and wires.

"It's you," Marcellus said, recognizing the boy he'd met in the morgue earlier.

The boy rushed forward, and Marcellus's hand went instinctively to the shirt stuffed inside his jacket. The boy ducked under Marcellus's arm, taking some of the weight off Marcellus's feet.

"Easy there, Officer," the boy said with that same mocking tone Marcellus remembered from the morgue. "I don't think you should be standing. We wouldn't want you to mess up that glossy hair of yours." He snorted. "Although it looks like that bateau has already sailed on your fancy coat."

Marcellus glanced down, just now noticing how dirty his silver raincoat was.

When he looked up again, he saw the smirk on the boy's face.

"I was—" Marcellus started to defend himself. "There was a riot. Someone threw something at my head."

"Awww," the boy cooed as he helped Marcellus back down to the ground. "Poor bébé. Was it something really hard? Like a loaf of bread?"

Marcellus huffed and tried to think of something to say in response, but the lack of blood to his brain was making all words difficult. Instead, he felt his eyes start to close again. He was so sleepy.

"Hey!" The boy was shaking him. "You can't go to sleep right now. It's not safe."

"Because you'll rob me?" Marcellus asked, his words slurring slightly.

The boy laughed. "Well, that too. But mostly because—"

Flash!

The boy's words were cut off as a troop of four Policier droids clanked around the corner. The bright orange light from their robotic eyes momentarily blinded Marcellus.

Panic flashed across the boy's dirty face. He scrambled to his feet and tried to take off at a run, but it was no use. The droids immediately surrounded him. The boy fought, shoving himself hard against the droids' PermaSteel bodies, but he may as well have been ramming himself against a wall for how much good it did.

"Ah, Théo Renard," came a chilling voice. Marcellus glanced up to see Inspecteur Limier approaching them. "Just the boy I've been sent to find. How nice of you to make my job easier for me."

"Théo," Marcellus repeated the name, silently remarking that it somehow didn't seem to fit the boy.

From beneath his low-hanging dark hood, the boy's clear gray eyes cut to Marcellus, a look of betrayal flashing on his face. "Did you do this?" he cried. "Did you send for them?"

"W-w-what?" Marcellus stammered, trying to make sense of the accusation. But before he could negate it, or even think how to intervene, a paralyzeur pulse shot out of one of the droids' rayonettes, rippling through the air and finding its target in the boy's left leg. As the boy—Théo—collapsed to the ground in pain, he caught Marcellus's eye once again, and this time, there was nothing but fury in the boy's eyes. The look hit Marcellus even harder than Théo's earlier punch to the gut.

"Wait." Marcellus finally found his voice and turned toward the inspecteur. "Stop. What are you doing to him?"

"This business doesn't concern you, Officer," Limier said. "This is a Policier matter."

"The Ministère oversees the Policier, which means it *is* my business."

Limier cut his gaze to Marcellus. "I'm afraid not this time." He snapped his fingers and pointed at the boy, who was trying to crawl away. One of the droids easily seized him and carried him down the corridor with Limier. The boy fought the entire way, one leg kicking the air, the other dragging uselessly behind him.

Marcellus felt anger course through him. Anger at Limier for dismissing him so callously. But mostly anger at himself for not fighting harder, pulling rank, and demanding they release the boy. Even though Marcellus had only met him once, he felt oddly protective of him.

But then the three remaining droids turned their attention to Marcellus, and he suddenly remembered the shirt tucked into his uniform. It felt heavier than it did ten minutes ago.

As one of the droids scanned his body to assess his injuries, Marcellus was certain the shirt would be discovered, and Marcellus would end up occupying his father's now-vacant cell.

Or Mabelle's.

"Contusion. Left frontal lobe. Med cruiseur requested," the droid announced its findings.

No mention of the shirt.

Marcellus breathed out a sigh of relief. That is, until Inspecteur Limier stalked back down the corridor toward him, and his chilling robotic gaze raked up and down Marcellus's body, as though he, too, were performing a scan of his own. A secondary check.

Marcellus felt himself stiffen, which he knew would only make the situation worse. Cyborgs were designed to interpret body language. He reminded himself to relax. As a Ministère officer, he was ranked above the inspecteur. He shouldn't be afraid of him. And yet, at this very instant, his heart was beating faster than a voyageur engine preparing to launch into space.

"We have been looking for you, Officer. Pity you couldn't be bothered to join us in the Marsh."

Marcellus winced at the jab. He knew the inspecteur was referring to the fact that Marcellus had fled the scene the moment he'd been injured. Like a coward. He had done exactly the opposite of what a commandeur of the Ministère should have done. Exactly the opposite of what Commandeur Vernay would have done.

Injured or not, Vernay would have stayed and fought. She would have made the general proud.

Like she always did.

Until she was shipped off to Albion to fight for Usonia's independence and returned in a box, leaving Marcellus to try to fill her very unfillable shoes.

Marcellus steeled himself. "I apologize for leaving my post, Inspecteur, but I—"

The inspecteur's hand suddenly jutted into the air, silencing Marcellus.

Marcellus watched the circuitry in Limier's face flash as his sensors processed some new piece of information. Marcellus swallowed, the lump in the front of his uniform suddenly feeling like a lump in his throat.

The inspecteur lifted his large, aquiline nose into the air and sniffed a long, curious sniff. If it weren't for his circuitry, which was blinking even more furiously now, Limier would have looked just like one of the Patriarche's hunting dogs when they'd caught the scent of fresh game.

Marcellus had never seen anything quite like it. It chilled him to the bone.

"What is it?" he asked Limier, fighting to keep his voice from cracking.

The inspecteur didn't move and seemed, at first, not to hear Marcellus's question. But then, after a few more sniffs at the air, he shook his head and muttered, "Nothing. Just an old scent I lost a while back. I thought I caught a trace of it again, but I must have been mistaken."

"The med cruiseur has arrived," one of the droids announced, cutting through the tension in the air.

Limier's gaze slid to Marcellus again, and his orange eye zeroed in on the wound on Marcellus's forehead. "Med cruiseur?" he asked curiously. "For such a small scratch?"

Marcellus opened his mouth to defend himself—even though he hadn't the slightest clue how he was going to do it—when three médecins arrived and lifted Marcellus onto a stretcher. That's when Marcellus remembered he had bigger things to worry about. Like the fact that he was carrying a secret message from a sworn enemy of the Regime.

- CHAPTER 16 -
CHATINE

THIS IS WHAT YOU GET, CHATINE SAID TO HERSELF as she was loaded into the patroleur parked outside of Fret 7. *This is what happens when you forget your place. When you forget how the Regime works. When you're foolish enough to try to help an officer of the Ministère.*

She pounded her fist against her numb leg, trying to urge the blood to flow and the feeling to return. It was no use. She knew that. The paralyzeur wouldn't fully wear off for at least another two hours. And by then she'd probably already be halfway to the moon.

She had no doubt the inspecteur was taking her to the Vallonay Policier Precinct, where she would await her passage to Bastille. They'd clearly reviewed the footage from the morgue security microcams. They knew about the leveler. Marcellus Bonnefaçon had probably turned her in himself. That's why his hand had immediately reached inside his jacket the moment he'd seen her. He'd been calling for backup on his TéléCom.

And no doubt Inspecteur Limier was overjoyed by the turn of events. If he was even capable of feeling joy. The fritzer had been after her and her family ever since they'd first stepped off that bateau from Montfer. Chatine was a big score for the head of the Vallonay Policier. Something to brag about to his friends back at the Precinct. *Today, I bagged a Renard.*

She glanced across the seating area of the Policier patroleur, where Inspecteur Limier sat. His head clicked toward her and his icy orange eye met hers. Chatine felt the urge to look away, but she held her ground.

"So, what will you charge me with?" she asked. "Theft? Breaking and entering? Insubordination? Lack of hygiene? The options are plentiful."

The inspecteur didn't respond. He just continued to stare at her, his circuitry hard at work.

"I'm just trying to figure out how long I'll be gone. I have some appointments I'll need to reschedule."

More silence followed.

Chatine tried again. "Are we talking months? Years? Life?"

The inspecteur still said nothing. She gave up and turned her gaze out the window. They were whizzing alongside the edge of the Frets and past the huge transportation fabrique where patroleurs like this one were made. It would have been much quicker to pass straight through the Marsh, but Chatine wondered if maybe the inspecteur wasn't even taking her to the Policier Precinct. Maybe he was taking her straight to the prisoner transport center.

As she stared up at the dull gray sky, Chatine tried to picture the giant prison of Bastille, somewhere up there beyond the clouds. Her future home.

She thought about all the men and women up there right now, tirelessly digging in the freezing exploits, their bodies heavy with fatigue and decay. Their fingers black with rot. Just like the man she'd seen in the morgue today.

The prisoner.

The one Marcellus Bonnefaçon had come to see.

Was that man really his father?

Angrily, she pushed thoughts of Officer Bonnefaçon from her mind. The man had betrayed her. She would not allow him to also occupy her thoughts.

She refocused on the scenery outside the window, quickly noticing that none of it looked familiar. She'd assumed they were circling around the Frets to get to the prisoner transport center, but it suddenly occurred to her that they were no longer anywhere near the Frets. They were now racing past rows of hothouses. Chatine could just make out the colorful glow of fresh peaches, apricots, and oranges growing on trees behind the endless plastique windows.

She flashed an accusing look at Limier. Where was he taking her? Maybe he had simply decided to bypass punishment altogether and take matters into his own hands. Maybe he planned to activate the kill setting on his rayonette and dump her body in the icy tundra of the Terrain Perdu where it would never be found. She certainly wouldn't put it past him.

"Where are we going?" Chatine asked, feeling prickles of fear cover her body.

Once again, the inspecteur didn't respond. Chatine noticed something that looked like annoyance pass over his face.

She was just about to ask the question again when she felt the patroleur tilt backward and start a fast climb up a steep hill. Then, a few moments later, a flood of bright, dazzling light blinded Chatine. She whipped her gaze back toward the window, and suddenly she couldn't breathe. Her whole body seemed to feel the effects of the paralyzeur in her leg. She was completely numb at the sight that lay in front of her.

It was brilliant. It was breathtaking. It was more beautiful than she'd ever imagined.

A luminous blue sky spread out before her, as far as the eye could see. Blue! Chatine had never experienced such a color. Her entire life had been a constant canvas of gloomy grays and murky blacks. And now it was as though she were swimming in color. She pressed her nose to the window and strained to see all around her. The patroleur turned right, and suddenly Chatine was shrouded in a delicious golden glow.

She looked up and her heart stopped. For the first time in nine years, her body felt warm. Her skin felt alive.

There, in the distance, hanging in the azure sky like priceless medallions, she saw them.

All three of them.

A giant shimmering white orb, flanked by two much smaller and dimmer spheres on either side—one a reddish gold, the other a pale blue.

The Sols.

They were magnificent. They were radiant. They were . . .

"Fake," the inspecteur spoke for the very first time since they'd boarded the patroleur. Chatine cut her eyes to him and noticed he was watching her with an amused, mocking expression. "You do know that, right?" he asked, as though he could read her very thoughts.

The realization of the truth collided into her, and she suddenly felt foolish and naïve. Like a child. She silently berated herself for her unguarded reaction. For letting *any* emotion show in front of the inspecteur.

Of course they were fake.

She knew that. She wasn't staring at the Sols. She was staring at the infamous TéléSky. They had obviously entered Ledôme, where the artificial Sols shone over the First and Second Estates 408 days a year.

But why? she immediately wondered. Why had the inspecteur taken her way up here of all places? If there was anywhere on Laterre where Chatine Renard did *not* belong, it was inside Ledôme.

The vehicle drifted to a stop, and Chatine noticed they had paused in front of an enormous pair of ornately sculpted gates, which were swinging open to let them in. As they glided through, the solid titan shimmered silver and white and almost blue in the fake Sol-light.

The patroleur swept down a wide avenue, flanked on both sides by grass so green that it almost hurt Chatine's eyes. Spread among the grass were statues carved in bright white stone and fountains thrusting litres and litres of bubbling turquoise water high into the air. And everywhere along the avenue—and down the countless paths that jutted out from it—there were flowers. Crazy and ridiculous in their colorfulness.

Just when it seemed the gardens had no end, a vast building came into view, looming large in the distance. It was easily the size of five Frets pushed together. The walls were gleaming white, punctuated by a hundred windows, each of them tall and arched and reflecting perfectly the sky above and the flowers and grass below.

The patroleur finally pulled to a stop in front of a huge door, capped by an elaborate crest. Chatine squinted up, trying to make out the shapes carved into the polished stone. She could swear she saw two lions facing toward each other, claws outstretched. But she knew she must be mistaken. That was the crest of the Paresse family. The First Estate. The Patriarche and Matrone themselves. She couldn't possibly be looking at their coat of arms. That would mean that they were at the . . .

Once again, the inspecteur seemed to be seeing her thoughts as though they were being broadcast right onto her Skin.

"Welcome to the Grand Palais," he said with a sneer.

- CHAPTER 17 -
MARCELLUS

THE REARING LIONS OF THE PARESSE FAMILY CREST greeted Marcellus as the med cruiseur swept toward the Grand Palais. Marcellus felt his chest squeeze at the sight of them. He still had his father's shirt tucked into his uniform. Incredibly, none of the médecins had taken note of it as they cleaned the wound on his head, patched it up with biosutures, and gave him a strong injection that had instantly eased the throbbing in his temples. But Marcellus knew he couldn't count on his luck to last much longer. He was about to enter the heart of the First Estate carrying a message sent to him by a traitor.

Mabelle is in Montfer. Go to her.

All the way back from the Marsh, Marcellus had fought against his feelings of relief in learning that Mabelle had escaped from Bastille. He still had regular nightmares about her rotting away in that cell.

He would not go to her, though. That much was obvious. Mabelle was still a Vangarde spy. Still an enemy of the Regime. Her escape from prison confirmed that.

The cruiseur pulled to a stop in front of the entrance to the Grand Palais, and Marcellus immediately jumped out and hurried into the foyer. He had to get to his rooms and hide the shirt until he could figure out what to do with it. He could not be caught with it on his person. If he was fast, he could make it to his rooms in the south wing in just a few minutes. He headed across the vast foyer to the imperial staircase, but he halted when he saw two men in dark green robes rushing down the steps toward him, one on each of the two curving stairways.

Marcellus sucked in a sharp breath as the titan medallions hanging from their necks flashed in the light of the chandeliers.

Advisors to the Patriarche looking for him?

That can't be good.

"Officer Bonnefaçon," announced one of the robed men when they reached the bottom of the stairs. "You are needed in the Imperial Salon."

The Patriarche's advisors weren't droids, not even cyborgs. But sometimes they seemed so cool and impassive, so starched and coiffed, that Marcellus wondered if they were fully human.

"I will be there as soon as I have freshened up," Marcellus said, gesturing toward his raincoat, which was still bloodied, wet, and dirty from the Frets. He tried to squeeze between the advisors, but they each took one step closer together, blocking his path.

"You are needed *now*, Officer."

"I will take your coat, monsieur," said a servant who'd just appeared from the hallway.

He should have known it was a lost cause. The Patriarche didn't wait for anyone.

"Of course." Marcellus forced a smile to hide the panic that bloomed in his chest as he stripped off his coat and handed it to the servant, making sure his uniform jacket was still buttoned all the way up. Even though he knew there were no microcams in here—the First Estate would never allow it—it still seemed as if the Grand Palais was full of eyes. Always looking, always assessing, always probing.

He followed the two advisors out of the foyer and into the Hall of Reflections, with its three hundred titan-trimmed mirrors. As he walked, Marcellus snuck glances at himself. Dirt from the Frets still covered his face, and his uniform looked bulkier than normal. He wiped at his cheeks and smoothed down the front of his jacket. The shirt stuffed inside suddenly felt like a boulder as opposed to just a threadbare piece of cloth.

When they finally reached the east wing and entered the Imperial Salon, Marcellus froze in the entryway, taking in the chaotic state of the room. He'd never witnessed such a scene inside these walls.

The Matrone lay sprawled across a sateen chaise, the silk of her dark gown billowed up around her like a giant rain cloud. Utterly silent, she stared at the ceiling. An empty champagne flute dangled in her limp hand, while a dozen attendants surrounded her like a gaggle of exotic birds, whispering and fluttering and weeping into their embroidered handkerchiefs.

At the other end of the salon, the Patriarche was pacing and ranting seeming nonsense to the pack of green-robed advisors who flurried behind him, trying to keep up. "Traitors! Murderers! Find them! Now, I tell you, now! Didn't I say this would happen? No one listens! And now my child is gone."

Marcellus suddenly felt as though he'd been punched. Somehow, in the midst of the riots and the mysterious girl in the Frets, and the message from his father, he'd managed to forget about poor little Marie. But now the grief flooded back over him.

"Marcellus!" The Patriarche's booming voice made Marcellus jump and clutch his chest. "It's about time one of you *Bonnefaçons* showed your face around here." The bitter way he pronounced his last name made Marcellus's throat tighten.

"I'm sorry," Marcellus began, his voice shaky and his words stilted. "I was on duty in the Marsh when the news of the poisoning . . . my deepest condolences, Monsieur Patriarche. Your daughter was . . . it's just so awful and . . ."

Marcellus cringed and gave up. He was babbling like a Third Estater drunk on weed wine. At this rate, he would never be named commandeur. He could barely even speak a complete sentence to the Patriarche; how was he ever supposed to lead the entire Ministère?

But the Patriarche didn't seem to be listening. He waved away Marcellus's words as if they were an irritating fly. "Where is your grandfather?" he demanded. "We need him here. *Now*."

"I . . . ," Marcellus fumbled again. "I don't know. . . ."

Marcellus immediately noticed the look of irritation on the Patriarche's face. It was no wonder the Patriarche rarely ever spoke to Marcellus. He clearly saw Marcellus as the incompetent child that he was. The *lesser* Bonnefaçon.

Marcellus swallowed, trying to organize his thoughts and think like a leader. Like Commandeur Vernay. "I will message him right now," Marcellus said, clear and decisive. He reached into his pocket for his TéléCom.

"Don't you think I already had Chaumont try that?" the Patriarche roared, flinging his hand toward one of his advisors, a small man with protruding eyes and a well-groomed moustache, who was buzzing around the Patriarche like an insect.

Marcellus's hand fell from his pocket, heat flooding to his cheeks. "Of course, yes, right."

The Patriarche narrowed his watery gray eyes. "What on Laterre is the general good for, if he can't be here when I need him?"

Marcellus could think of a lot of things his grandfather was good for, but of course he didn't respond. Everyone knew, despite the Patriarche being the official head of state, that General Bonnefaçon and the Ministère were the real rulers of Laterre. They were the ones who maintained the peace, managed the Regime, and most importantly, kept the Third Estate in line. The Third Estate made up 95 percent of the population, which meant if they were ever to rebel—*really* rebel—the First and Second Estates wouldn't stand a chance.

"Mon chéri." The sudden sound of the Matrone's words silenced everyone in the room. Her voice was ragged and breathless, barely more than a whisper. "Where is he? Where is the general? He has to catch the monster who did this to our Marie."

"Oh, he will, ma chérie, he will," the Patriarche growled over his shoulder before grabbing Marcellus by the lapels and pulling him so close, Marcellus could feel the Patriarche's breath on his face.

"Citizen Rousseau is behind this," the Patriarche said in a harsh whisper. "She is responsible."

"Citizen Rousseau?" Marcellus could barely get the words out. All he could think about was how close the Patriarche was to his chest. How, with just one misplaced hand, he would find the shirt still stuffed down the front of his uniform.

"Yes, Citizen Rousseau, you imbécile!" the Patriarche growled. "The vile woman my father put behind bars! Don't tell me you're so incompetent you don't even know who Citizen Rousseau is."

"No, of course I know—"

The Patriarche pulled Marcellus even closer. "The Vangarde is making a comeback. I am certain of it. And Citizen Rousseau is behind this . . . this"—he stuttered and fumed—"*murder*. I need to know where she is. And I need to know *now*."

Marcellus swallowed hard and fought the urge to glance down at the Patriarche's hands, which he knew were only centimètres away from his father's shirt. Why hadn't he stashed it somewhere in the Frets? The rough fabric scratched at his skin, chastising him, reminding him how close he was to being caught.

"Citizen Rousseau remains in solitary confinement on Bastille," Marcellus said, instilling his voice with as much confidence as he could muster. "Five droids surround her cell every hour of every day."

Marcellus knew this for a fact. During his training, he'd learned about the high-security measures in place to secure Laterre's most dangerous enemy.

"That woman could take down five droids with her eyes closed," the Patriarche spat. "How do we know she's still there?"

Marcellus fought back a groan. Over the years, Citizen Rousseau's reputation had reached the status of legendary. Since Marcellus was a child, he'd heard her described as being larger than a giant, stronger than ten droids, and even capable of shooting lasers from her eyeballs. But he knew better than to argue with the Patriarche.

Plus, if Mabelle had managed to escape, who's to say Citizen Rousseau couldn't escape too?

Then again, Mabelle hadn't been in maximum-security lockdown thirty hours a day.

"I'll contact the warden right away," Marcellus said. "We'll get proof that she is still secure in her cell."

The Patriarche considered this solution and eventually released his grasp on Marcellus, backing away. Marcellus tried not to let his relief show as he reached into his pocket, pulled out his TéléCom, and unfolded it across his palm. He spoke clearly into the screen. "AirLink request for Warden Gallant."

The Patriarche huffed and started to pace again, as though the logistics of the communication process bored him immensely.

Within a few seconds, the warden of Bastille appeared on the screen, sitting behind a desk in his oak-paneled office at the Ministère headquarters. He was a small, compact man with crisp silver hair and a cool, unreadable gaze.

"Officer Bonnefaçon," he greeted Marcellus.

Marcellus wasted no time with pleasantries. "The Patriarche requests visual access to Citizen Rousseau's cell."

The warden nodded. "Yes, Officer. Right away."

The image dissolved, replaced with a high-angle shot of a woman curled up on the floor of a dirty cell, her knees drawn to her chest, her head lolling on the bare stones beneath her. She looked so small, so shrunken, so emaciated, so harmless. In her vulnerable fetal position, it was hard to believe that this was the woman who'd caused so much death and destruction seventeen years ago. Who'd rallied legions to her cause with her charismatic rhetoric and promises of change. This crumpled, tiny shell of a woman, in her sullied blue prison uniform, had once been the architect of mayhem and carnage. Now she stared unblinking at the nothingness of her cell.

As Marcellus watched her—her shallow breathing, her shivering limbs—he found himself thinking of his father. Of his last days curled up in a cell like this one. Of his withered body lying on that gurney in the morgue.

But then he felt the Patriarche by his side and hastily shoved the thoughts from his mind.

"Sol-damn woman," the Patriarche said with a snarl.

Marcellus cleared his throat and spoke into the TéléCom, struggling to keep his voice steady and assertive. "Warden Gallant, has there been any . . . uh . . . breach in security of this cell in the recent weeks?" Marcellus almost laughed at his own question. This woman was barely able to stand up, let alone plot an assassination.

The warden's face reappeared in a small frame in the bottom right corner of the screen. Marcellus turned on the TéléCom's speakers so the Patriarche could hear. "No, Officer."

The Patriarche grabbed the TéléCom from Marcellus. "Has she spoken to anyone?" he demanded. "Has she received or sent any messages?"

"No, Monsieur Patriarche," the warden replied, without a moment's hesitation. "Citizen Rousseau is on full lockdown and in complete isolation. Her security status has not changed."

The Patriarche grunted and thrust the TéléCom back at Marcellus.

"Would you like me to request archived footage of the cell?" Marcellus asked.

"No," the Patriarche barked. "That won't be necessary."

As Marcellus disconnected the AirLink and returned the device to his pocket, he couldn't help feeling a small rush of pride. He'd done it. He'd handled the situation, assuaged the Patriarche. And without his grandfather's help.

The Patriarche collapsed onto a nearby chaise, holding his hand over his eyes. Marcellus wondered if this was his cue to leave. He was desperate to get to the safety and privacy of his own quarters, wash away the dirt and blood, and steal a moment for himself to think. And most important, he was desperate to rid himself of this anchor weighing down the front of his uniform.

It was making him feel more like a traitor—like his father—by the second.

But before he could contemplate his escape any further, a *ping* echoed through his audio patch, informing him of an incoming alert. He reached for his TéléCom again before noticing that Chaumont already had his out and was staring wide-eyed at the screen.

"What is it?" the Patriarche demanded, clearly having noticed the advisor's reaction. He was back out of his chair, stomping over to Chaumont.

Chaumont lowered the TéléCom and spoke somberly to the entire room. "An update from the Ministère headquarters. On the status of the investigation."

The Matrone turned her distraught face toward the advisor. Her gaggle of handmaids stopped fluttering to listen as well.

"A suspect has been identified and detained," the advisor announced.

Marcellus drew in a breath. The room remained deathly quiet. When the advisor did not continue right away, the Matrone whispered in her hoarse, despairing voice, "Who? Who is it?"

Chaumont shared a look with a fellow advisor, as though trying to summon strength from his colleague. "It's Nadette Epernay."

Marcellus felt the room spin. He reached behind him for the top of a chair and gripped it tightly to keep from falling over, trying to assure himself it was his recent head wound—not the name—that had shaken him. He hadn't known Nadette well, but he'd seen her with the child. He knew how much she cared for Marie.

"Nadette?" the Patriarche roared, clearly as disbelieving of the news as Marcellus was.

"Affirmative," Chaumont replied, his voice impressively steady given the circumstances. "It would seem your daughter was poisoned by her own governess."

- CHAPTER 18 -
CHATINE

THE GRAND PALAIS.

One of the richest, most lavish, most expensive buildings in all of the System Divine. Built to show Laterre's friends—and enemies alike—just how powerful and successful this Regime had become in its 505 short years of existence. This was where heads of state from Reichenstat, Novaya, Usonia, Kaishi, Samsara, and all the other major allies of Laterre were brought together to be wined and dined and impressed.

The only members of the Third Estate who were *ever* allowed into the Grand Palais were servants and, once a year, Ascension winners, who were invited to a banquet with the Patriarche and Matrone. Never in her eighteen years of life did Chatine ever expect to find herself inside Ledôme, let alone inside the Grand Palais.

And yet there she was, being guided by Inspecteur Limier himself through a door adorned with titan that could easily feed a hundred families in the Frets for an entire year. Her leg, still numb from the paralyzeur, dragged slightly behind her as they traveled across a grand foyer and down a long, lavish corridor with purple silk carpeting and titan-framed paintings on every wall. Chatine tried hard not to stare. She tried not to outwardly *gawk*, but it was impossible. Her eyes couldn't process what she was seeing. Her mind couldn't add it up, couldn't calculate the worth fast enough. She had seen parts of the Grand Palais on her Skin. But it was something else entirely to be standing in the middle of it.

The paintings on the walls were certainly all First World relics, cherished works of art from another time, another planet.

She turned to the painting to her left and slowed to a stop. It appeared to be a portrait of a young woman in a blue and yellow head scarf, glancing back over her shoulder. She had a glowing white orb hanging from her ear, which reminded Chatine of a star set against the dark sky.

Chatine wondered how much a painting like this would fetch. A thousand tokens? A hundred thousand? Probably more, but Chatine didn't even know any numbers higher than that. She doubted Third Estate accounts could even hold that many largs.

"Don't even think about it," Inspecteur Limier's sharp voice clicked from behind her. "You'd never even get one foot out the door."

Chatine felt her teeth clench at being so easily marked by the insufferable cyborg. Yet, she still forced herself to turn around and flash him the breeziest, most innocent of smiles. "Whatever do you mean, Inspecteur? I was simply admiring the beautiful artwork."

She walked over to the next painting. If you could even call it that. It looked more like someone had thrown buckets of paint on the wall and then smeared it with frenzied hands.

Chatine clucked her tongue approvingly, trying to conjure up her best impression of the Matrone with her long vowels and lilting cadence. "Would you look at this one! Isn't it fantastique? Simply *deeevine*. Is it your work, Inspecteur? Or did one of your droids paint this?"

The inspecteur kicked her in the back of her dead leg, almost causing her to fall *into* the painting. "Go," he commanded.

Chatine continued her parody of the Matrone, letting out a buoyant laugh as she tossed an invisible strand of hair. "Oh, Inspecteur, how easily you anger! You must have some more smoked salmon to calm your poor nerves!"

"Walk, déchet!" he scolded, using the word for the Third Estate that Chatine despised. She suddenly felt anger boil up inside of her again. How dare he call her garbage? At least *she* still had human emotion, which was more than she could say for him.

"Silly Inspecteur," she said, turning around to continue her charade. But she was so busy prancing and acting like the lunatic Matrone that she didn't even notice she had reached the end of the corridor. That is, until she pranced right into something hard and imposing. She staggered slightly from the impact, took a step back, and glanced up into the stark hazel eyes of a face she knew all too well. A face she'd seen often on the screen of her Skin, but prayed she'd never *ever* meet in person. It was the face she feared more than Inspecteur Limier, more than the Policier droids, more than Bastille itself.

A chill ran down her spine as she took in his height, frame, and immaculate white uniform. She swallowed hard and immediately lowered her eyes to show respect. And through her dry, scorched throat and jagged breaths, she finally managed to squeak out, "Good evening, General Bonnefaçon."

- CHAPTER 19 -
CHATINE

"ARE YOU ALWAYS THIS QUIET?" THE GENERAL ASKED.

Chatine sat in the imposing, wood-paneled office with her heart in her throat and her hands tucked between her knees. She hadn't looked up nor made eye contact with the general since she'd walked in here a few minutes ago. She was still too mortified about what had happened in the hallway, when she'd literally pranced right into him. And Chatine was *never* mortified.

Then again, Chatine never pranced, either.

She had no idea what had come over her.

"Yes, monsieur," Chatine replied softly.

"And such good manners," the general remarked, clearly mocking her.

Chatine simply nodded.

"Not exactly the report I got from Inspecteur Limier. He seemed to imply you had somewhat of a problem with authority. He's told me much about you and your parents, and your unorthodox . . . *means*." The general clucked his tongue against the roof of his mouth. "Not exactly the kind of 'honest work' we endorse at the Ministère."

Chatine bit the inside of her cheek to keep herself from lashing out. Was that what this was about? Did he drag her all the way in here just to tell her to check in to her Skin more often? Collect more Ascension points? Pay into a sham of a system that could easily erase all your hard-earned tokens with the push of a button?

"Your sister, however," he continued. "Now, *she* is a model of immaculate Third Estate behavior."

"My sister is delusional," Chatine muttered hotly under her breath, unable to keep her frustration inside any longer.

The general let out a small bark of a laugh. "I might say the same thing about you."

Chatine grunted, although after the events of the day, she was starting to wonder if the general was right. *Was* she as delusional as her sister?

"I think you'll find I know pretty much everything there is to know about you, Théo." The general's smile turned sinister. "Or, shall I say, *Chatine*?"

Chatine's head whipped up, and she locked eyes with the general. She fought hard to keep her expression neutral, but she was certain the shock was written all over her face. The general stood up and began to walk slowly around the desk, coming dangerously close to Chatine.

She squeezed her thighs tighter together, until she could no longer feel the blood in her fingers.

"For instance, I know your parents were chased out of Montfer ten years ago for being con artists and crooks. I know that your father is the head of the Délabré gang, who specialize in conning and terrorizing people in the Frets. I know that you haven't shown up for a single day of honest work since you arrived in Vallonay, despite your very generous job assignment in the textile fabrique."

The general vanished momentarily behind her chair before reappearing on her other side. As he walked, he seemed to be deep in thought, as though he were trying to figure out what exactly he was going to do about her family's long list of crimes.

He reached for the TéléCom on his desk and swiveled it around. "I also know," he said as he pressed play and Chatine's own face appeared on the screen, "that you steal from the dead."

Chatine swallowed as she watched the footage play out on the screen. It was taken from that same morning, at the morgue. The sound was off and all she could see was herself fighting to get the leveler back from Marcellus, and Marcellus holding it out of her reach with an amused expression on his face.

Chatine's whole body clenched. She was right. She *was* here because of the morgue. Because of *him*. That pomp officer had turned her in.

"It's not my fault," she pleaded, immediately launching into her pitiful I'm-the-daughter-of-crooks charade. It was usually a safe bet. "I was only doing what my father bid me to do. The leveler was his idea from the start. I don't even like using it. But he forces me to. I swear I—"

The general let out a hearty laugh, stopping Chatine midsentence. "You think I brought you all the way up here for *that*?" He paused the playback and pointed at the leveler still in Marcellus's hand on the screen.

Chatine closed her mouth, confused. If this wasn't about the leveler, then why in the name of the Sols was she here?

"I brought you here because of *that*." He dragged his finger a centimètre across the screen from Marcellus's hand to his face. Then, in one swift motion, he zoomed in to the frozen image, filling the entire screen with Marcellus's gleaming smile.

Chatine wasn't following.

"That," the general went on, "is not the look of someone who is distrustful of a Third Estate crook. *That* is the look of someone who is amused. Intrigued. *Charmed*, even."

He punched his finger against the screen, linking to the audio chip implanted in Chatine's ear, before resuming playback. Now Chatine could hear her own conversation with the officer.

"It's mine!" her gruff voice shouted. "Give it back!"

"Okay, okay," on-screen Marcellus replied. "Listen, I'll offer you a deal."

"I don't do deals."

"Something tells me you're the kind of kid who *does* do deals."

"Just give it back to me."

Chatine cringed as she watched herself be so forward toward an upper estater. The Marcellus on screen smiled another smile. This one, Chatine immediately noticed, was not amused or intrigued. It was warm. It was frustratingly genuine. It was exactly as the general said—lacking any trace of the usual distrust she had come to expect from Second Estaters, especially Ministère officers.

"If you come with me and let me get you something to eat, I'll give this back to you," on-screen Marcellus said, waving the leveler. "That's the deal."

The general paused the video again and looked expectantly at Chatine.

"Yeah? So?" she asked. Despite her confusion about the surprising look on Marcellus's face, she still wasn't following.

"He trusts you."

She snorted. "No, he doesn't."

"Yes, he does," the general confirmed. "I know my grandson, and I can tell from this footage that he *likes* you."

Chatine bowed her head and pulled her hood over her burning cheeks, cursing the blood pumping in her own veins. "Whatever. I don't care."

"You should care."

Chatine glared at him. "Why? Why should I care if some stupid Second Estate pomp trusts me? That's his problem."

The general turned his back on Chatine and stared out the picture window behind his desk. For a moment, Chatine worried she'd been too bold. Said too much. It probably wasn't the best idea on Laterre to outwardly insult the general's grandson *to* the general himself.

But when he spoke, he didn't sound angry or even offended. He sounded tormented. Almost tortured. "We, at the Ministère, believe that the Vangarde is planning another rebellion."

"I have nothing to do with the Vangarde," Chatine fired back. It was a gut reaction. She had no idea why the general was suddenly mentioning the Vangarde, but she refused to let him think—for even a second—that she was at all wrapped up in any rebellion nonsense. There were a lot of things Chatine was—crook, con artist, Fret rat—but revolutionary was not one of them.

The general turned to flash her a wry smile. "I know. And we appreciate your loyalty to Laterre."

Chatine felt herself smirking. They both knew he was being sarcastic.

"I have certain intel that the Vangarde has contacted my grandson and may be in the process of attempting to recruit him."

Chatine fought and failed to keep her reaction contained. "*What? Why?*"

The general sighed. "Because of who his father was."

Chatine's mind spun as she thought about the dead, withered man she saw in the morgue today. The father of Marcellus Bonnefaçon. A former prisoner of Bastille. "A criminal?"

Chatine watched the general's shoulders drop a millimètre. "A traitor," he corrected. "He was one of Citizen Rousseau's most trusted operatives during the Rebellion of 488. He betrayed his planet, his family, and his Regime."

Chatine shrank back a little in her seat. "Oh."

The general returned to his chair and rested his hands on the desk. He was suddenly all business again. That little glimpse she'd gotten into his mind, his past, his pain, was gone. "With Citizen Rousseau still locked up on Bastille, the Vangarde need a new face for their cause. Someone who can rally the people. Marcellus is the perfect choice. He has ties to the last rebellion, through his father. He is high up in the Second Estate. He's already a visible figure. They need him. And I need you."

Chatine blinked in surprise. "Me?"

"I want you to befriend Marcellus. Gain his trust. Become his confidante. When the Vangarde attempts to recruit him, I want you right there with him."

Chatine stared at him in disbelief. "You want me to *spy* for you? On your own grandson?"

A flicker of something passed over the general's face but it was gone just as quickly as it had appeared. "The Vangarde are regrouping, preparing to rise up again. If we're going to stop these terrorists from launching another strike against the Regime, we need to gather as much information about them as we can. I'm exhausting all resources on this matter. That's where you come in. When the Vangarde makes contact with Marcellus, I want you to report back on everything: what is said, where the meeting takes place, who is involved."

Chatine shook her head, confused. "But if the Vangarde is attempting to recruit Officer Bonnefaçon, why not just ask him to report back to you himself? Why do you even need me?"

The general glanced down at his hands. "Marcellus is . . . ," he faltered, looking unsettled. "He has many commendable qualities. Several attributes that will make him a great leader one day. But he still has a lot to learn."

Chatine suddenly remembered something Azelle had said to her earlier. "But isn't he supposed to be promoted to commandeur soon?"

The general stared at her with a stern expression but didn't answer.

Chatine squinted at the man, trying to decipher his cryptic gaze. "Are you saying you don't trust him?"

"I'm saying he's not ready to take on such a significant task."

A shiver passed through Chatine as realization slowly dawned on her. "He hasn't told you that the Vangarde contacted him, has he?"

The anguish that flashed in the general's eyes was all Chatine needed to see to know she was right.

He let out a weary sigh. "I worry about him sometimes." Chatine was surprised to hear what sounded like genuine tenderness in the general's voice. "I worry that his father's spirit runs too deep in his veins. But mostly, I worry for his safety. He has no idea what he's getting himself into. The Vangarde are dangerous. They're volatile and unpredictable and . . . desperate. He might think he has all of this under control, but he doesn't. He's still so naïve about so many things. I need someone who can look out for him." The general locked eyes on Chatine, and in that moment, she felt just the slightest bit sorry for him.

"Why me?" she asked.

The general straightened in his chair, resuming his stern countenance. "Like I said, he trusts you. He's more likely to open up to you than to anyone from the Ministère. And I've been studying your profile. You're very . . ." He paused, as though searching for the right word. "Crafty."

Chatine narrowed her eyes. She could smell a trap. "What's in it for me?"

The general smirked. "Marcellus was right. You *are* the kind of kid who does deals."

"But you already knew that," Chatine fired back. "Or else I wouldn't be here."

"Clever girl."

Chatine bristled at the word "girl." She still didn't like that the head of the Ministère knew her secret. It made her feel exposed and vulnerable.

The general swiveled in his chair and pointed at the scene outside the giant window behind his desk. "If you were anyone else, I would offer you all of this in exchange for your services. A manoir in Ledôme. An Ascension to the Second Estate. The kind of life someone of your status can only dream about."

Chatine narrowed her eyes, unsure where the general was going with this.

"But you're *not* anyone else," he continued. "Given your lack of Ascension points, I would venture to guess that you have no interest in living out your life here with us in Ledôme."

"You're right," Chatine replied guardedly. "I don't."

"And I know that threatening your family probably wouldn't work, since you don't seem to care about them, either."

Chatine snorted. "Right again, monsieur."

"Which is why I have another offer for you."

Chatine leaned forward in her chair. She couldn't imagine the general offering her anything that might actually interest her, but that didn't mean she wasn't just a little bit curious.

The general folded his hands across his lap. "The Patriarche has a very special relationship with the newly formed government on Usonia. Let's just say they owe us *several* favors."

Chatine froze.

The general *knew*.

How did he know?

He smiled, clearly enjoying her reaction. "Deliver me the information I need, and I'll deliver you a whole new life on Usonia."

- CHAPTER 20 -
ALOUETTE

ALOUETTE'S FINGERS MOVED QUICKLY OVER THE hand-sewn spines of the Chronicles.

"Three . . . four . . . five . . . ," she whispered urgently.

Each volume bore a slick, clear jacket, which protected the cloth-bound cover and delicate pages inside. Alouette had dusted these histories of Laterre a thousand times. She knew them—their varying heights and thicknesses—like she knew every nook, cranny, and recess in the Refuge's library.

"Six . . . seven . . . eight . . ."

The thick volumes were packed tightly together on the shelf, and when she finally reached the tenth volume, Alouette had to yank hard to pull it out. As soon as it was in her hands, she scurried over to a small table in the back corner of the Refuge's library, between two bookcases. She pushed aside a pot of ink and a scattering of Principale Francine's fountain pens, and she set down the volume.

Alouette stood in front of the table and drew in a ragged breath, inhaling the reassuring scent of the thousands of old books surrounding her. She hadn't taken a full, proper breath since she'd returned to the Refuge just a short while ago.

When she'd climbed back down the ladder, punched in the passcode, and entered through the thick PermaSteel door, thankfully no one had been waiting for her. No one, it seemed, even knew she'd been gone. The sisters were still in Assemblée; her father was still in the kitchen preparing the evening meal.

Although she probably should have gone straight back to her chores to avoid any questions or suspicion, Alouette couldn't help herself. She'd come straight here instead. To her favorite place in the world.

The library.

It was by far the largest and most important room in the Refuge. And for good reason. It was, after all, why the Refuge had been built in the first place. To store the thousands and thousands of books that were rescued from the Last Days. They were the Sisterhood's most prized and sacred possessions.

The library was a cluttered maze of hand-built shelves stacked to the ceiling with these books from the First World. When Alouette was little, Sister Jacqui used to tell her incredible stories about the brave women who smuggled all the books aboard the original freightships. The written word had already been dying out on the old planet. Books were deemed unnecessary for a new life, and too heavy to transport across galaxies. But these women defied the rules and risked everything to keep the written word alive and preserve the First World knowledge.

It wasn't until many years later, a long time after the first settlers arrived on Laterre, that all the books were gathered together again, and the Sisterhood and the Refuge were founded to protect them.

The library also stored the Chronicles. Every volume that had ever been written. One of the first residents of the Refuge, Sister Bethany, had started writing the history of Laterre in her beautiful, looping handwriting nearly 150 years ago. But today it was Principale Francine who maintained and updated the Chronicles.

"Volume Ten," Alouette whispered as she ran her fingertips over the plastique covering of the book on the table in front of her.

Alouette's hands still trembled from everything that had happened in the hallways of the Frets earlier. As she glanced down at them, she noticed a small stain of blood on her little finger. The boy's blood. Marcellus's blood.

But she couldn't let that distract her now. She had to find what she was looking for before the sisters came out of Assemblée.

Carefully, she eased open the cover of Volume 10, her heart pounding in anticipation of the answers she so desperately sought. This had to be it. This was the volume that recounted everything there was to know about the Ministère, the Policier, and Bastille.

"Little Lark? Are you in here?"

Startled, Alouette immediately snapped the cover shut again and grabbed a book from the shelf next to her, placing it on top of the volume so the title was hidden. When she looked up to see her father appearing around the corner of the tall bookcase, she realized how silly she'd been to try to hide it from him. Hugo Taureau was the only person in the Refuge who couldn't read. He'd never had any interest in learning the Forgotten Word.

"Yes, Papa." Alouette's voice was high and strained.

Her father's vast frame just about filled this little alcove of the library. And for the first time in Alouette's life, his height, his enormous shoulders and huge arms, seemed unfamiliar. Puzzling. Frightening, even.

Of course, it was ridiculous to be scared of her father, this man who'd never dream of hurting her. Yet Alouette found herself shrinking back into her chair.

"Dinner's ready," he said with a wink.

Alouette let out a sharp breath of relief. Suddenly, he was her father again. His enormous shoulders, his kind smile, it all assembled back together into something familiar. Something she knew and loved. Something that made sense.

Her father cocked his head. "Are you okay?"

She nodded quickly and smiled. "Yes, yes. I'm just . . . you know . . ." She looked down at the table, searching for words, and almost laughed when she noticed which book she'd randomly snatched from the shelf to conceal Volume 10 of the Sisterhood's Chronicles. It was the story of the little girl who stole books during one of the big wars on the First World. She pointed to its plastique-wrapped cover. "Catching up on some reading."

Her father beamed. "Always reading." His warm brown eyes sparkled under the library's light. "I remember when you were little, and you used to hide from Principale Francine back here. She would be ready to lock up the library for the night, and you would beg for just five more minutes. One more chapter."

Alouette laughed and studied her father for a long moment. He had this wistful, faraway look on his face. The look he sometimes got when she suspected he was thinking about the past.

A past so shrouded in mystery.

"Prisoner number 48590."

A shiver traced down Alouette's spine as she suddenly remembered the jarring robotic voice from the Fret hallway. And the man dangling from the droid's grasp.

Maybe it meant nothing. Maybe the metallic dots on the man's arm were a coincidence. Besides, how could her father have been a prisoner? Hugo Taureau was a good man, an honest man, and a gentle man.

He couldn't have ever been a prisoner.

He was nothing like that man she saw in the Frets.

"Are you sure you're okay?" her father asked, startling her back to the present.

She nodded. "I'm fine."

"Okay, I'll see you in the dining room, then."

But as her father turned to leave the library, Alouette heard herself call out, "Papa!"

"Ma petite?" He looked surprised at her sudden and frantic tone.

"I . . . ," she began, but the words stuck in her throat. "Did you . . . ," she tried again. "Were you always a chef? Even before you came here?" She waved around at the walls and walls of books. "Before you came to the Refuge, I mean."

There was a flash of something on her father's face. Alouette flinched at the sight of it. Was it anger? Or fear? Or both? She couldn't tell. And just as quickly as the unreadable look had appeared, a frown swiftly replaced it.

"Little Lark," he said with a sigh.

Alouette opened her mouth as more questions began to bubble up from deep within her. But she stopped herself. There was no point. Her father would never answer her questions. He never had, and he never would.

And how could she really demand the truth from him, when she'd just done something she could never tell him about? She'd left the Refuge, their home for the past twelve years, and she'd gone up to the Frets to help a stranger—a boy—who was in trouble. She'd been chased by droids! She'd put herself in danger. A lot of danger.

Now, Alouette realized, they both had secrets.

"Dinner is ready, and the sisters are waiting," her father said with an air of finality.

Alouette glanced down at the plastique-covered volume of the Chronicles peeking out from under the book on the table. Volume 10 would have to wait. *She* would have to wait.

Her father cleared his throat. "Are you coming?"

She grabbed the book and the volume and returned them both to their correct places on the shelves. When she turned around, her father was already on his way out of the library. The lightness he'd come in with earlier was now gone.

It made her sad.

And frustrated.

"Papa," she called again.

He stopped in the doorway. "Yes, ma petite?"

Alouette slowly approached her father and looked up at him, letting her gaze settle on his for a moment before she reached up and wrapped her arms around him. She squeezed him tightly.

"I'm sorry," she whispered.

He kissed the top of her head and chuckled. "What on Laterre do *you* have to be sorry for, Little Lark?"

But Alouette didn't respond. She pulled away, letting her hand linger on her father's upper arm. She felt the five silver bumps rough under her palm, each dimpled with a different number of dots. She'd traced them so often when she was little, she knew each of them by heart.

Two dots, then four dots, then six dots, a smooth surface, followed by one lonely dot at the end.

Now, suddenly, in the blink of an eye, these dimpled silver bumps had become something else. They formed a very different picture of her father. Alouette now realized that the markings spelled out a sequence. A number.

His number.

2.4.6.0.1.

CHAPTER 21

MARCELLUS

"THE PREMIER ENFANT'S GOVERNESS, NADETTE
Epernay, has confessed to the murder."

General Bonnefaçon's hands gripped the podium, while his
steady gaze roved over the Ministère's situation room. Six rows of
high-ranking officers sat in front of him, resembling droids with their
stiff backs, stern faces, and identical ice-white uniforms. Beside the
podium, the head of the Vallonay Policier, Inspecteur Limier, stood
erect with his chin tilted upward and his hands behind his back. The
circuitry in his face flickered and hummed.

"We believe that Mademoiselle Epernay did not work alone," the
general went on.

Sitting near the back of the room, trying to remain rigid like his
fellow officers, Marcellus swallowed hard. He felt sick. Sick that little Marie was dead. Sick that Nadette had confessed to the murder.

Sick that his mind kept returning to his own governess.

"The poisoning was a clever piece of work," Marcellus's grandfather continued, pulling Marcellus back into the situation room.
"Not the efforts of some brainless young girl." The general motioned

to a cyborg in green scrubs who flanked him on the other side of the podium. "Médecin Vichy, explain your findings."

The Chief Médecin stepped forward; the circuitry in her forehead and cheek winked and glistened under the harsh lights of the situation room.

"Postmortem analyses show that the Premier Enfant was killed by a lethal dose of cyanide," she began. "The poison caused immediate internal asphyxia, which resulted in rapid breathing, severe cerebral convulsions, vomiting, unconsciousness, and death within fifteen minutes."

Bile rose up from Marcellus's stomach, and he had to swallow hard again. *This* was what had happened to little Marie? This horrible and painful death? How could the médecin sound so cold and stark delivering these facts? It was as if she were talking about a defective TéléCom, not a little girl.

Marcellus wondered, not for the first time, whether some of these cyborgs really did have a piece of their humanity plucked out when their circuitry was put in. Perhaps that's what enabled them to do their jobs so well.

"We believe the cyanide was ingested via a piece of fruit, probably a peach, that the child ate this morning," the médecin continued. "Cyanide occurs naturally in pitted or seeded fruits such as apples, cherries, and peaches. However, the level of cyanide in the Premier Enfant's blood far exceeded any naturally occurring doses. My colleagues are running further tests, but our working hypothesis is that the cyanide came from the jewelry fabrique, where it is commonly used for gilding and cleaning."

The médecin prepared to speak again, but the general cut her off, taking back control of the podium. "The murder of the Premier Enfant was *not* the work of an amateur. Industrial-grade cyanide is not something a nineteen-year-old governess would have access to. This plot required planning and strategy." The general scanned the situation room again, his face grave as he delivered his next words. "We are certain this was the work of the Vangarde."

Marcellus sucked in a sharp breath as whispers broke out among the officers in the room.

"The Vangarde?"

"They're back?"

"What does this mean?"

Marcellus was asking himself the exact same questions. The Vangarde had been little more than ghosts for the past seventeen years, ever since Citizen Rousseau was arrested, bringing an end to the failed Rebellion of 488. However, every so often, one or two of their supporters would pop up somewhere—like Mabelle—just to remind Laterre that they had not fully disappeared. That they would always be lurking in the shadows, biding their time.

But Marcellus had always felt comforted in knowing that the Vangarde had little hope of fully regrouping without their charismatic leader. She had been the strategic mind and rallying force behind the former rebellion. And as long as she remained behind bars on the moon, Marcellus felt safe from another uprising. Which was why he'd put no stock in the Patriarche's paranoid insistence that the Vangarde were behind this murder.

But now, as he listened to his grandfather's briefing, he wondered how safe they really were. If the Vangarde could penetrate the Grand Palais, could *murder* a member of the Paresse family, what else were they capable of doing without Citizen Rousseau? Was it possible they were rising from the dead without her?

"Nadette did not act alone," the general went on. "Officers LaPorte and Meudon are continuing their interrogation of the governess, as well as every worker in the jewelry fabrique, in an attempt to identify any accomplices."

Accomplices.

Marcellus's mind raced as he thought back to the search he had performed on his TéléCom earlier. The search that revealed Mabelle had escaped from prison in the sixth month of this year. What had she been doing since then?

Was *she* the accomplice his grandfather was referring to?

Marcellus simply couldn't bring himself to believe that his beloved governess would ever be capable of murder. Let alone the murder of a *child*. Marcellus wanted so badly to shove the idea from his brain, but it seemed too big of a coincidence to just ignore.

Mabelle escapes from prison, and less than a month later, Marie Paresse, the only heir to the Paresse family, is dead?

"From here on out, we will focus all our resources on rooting out this terrorist group before they can rise up against us again," the general announced.

Inspecteur Limier, still standing rigidly beside the general, lifted his chin higher. His orange eye glowed fiercely and his circuitry flashed, as if the general's directive had pushed the cyborg into a new gear.

"Everyone—I repeat, *everyone*—in this room is tasked with gathering intel on the Vangarde," General Bonnefaçon continued. "We want to know *who* they are, *where* they are, and *what* they are planning next."

Beads of sweat began to trickle down the back of Marcellus's neck as he thought about his father's prisoner shirt. He'd thankfully been able to stash it in his bedroom before he'd been called to the briefing. But now, standing here, surrounded by nearly every high-ranking member of the Ministère, it was as though he could still feel the shirt blazing against his skin. He still felt like a fraud.

My dear Marcellou, Mabelle is in Montfer. Go to her.

He should turn the shirt over to his grandfather. He knew this. It was exactly the kind of "intel" his grandfather was referring to. It pointed directly to a Vangarde operative. If Mabelle was in Montfer, perhaps there was a Vangarde cell operating out of there. Perhaps *she* was leading it.

But how would he ever explain his possession of the shirt to his grandfather without causing suspicion?

"All our efforts will be redirected to this new objective," the general continued. "You will all be assigned a region and will have full authority to arrest anyone suspected of Vangarde activities or affiliations. Anyone who resists arrest will be sent directly to Bastille." The general pushed a fist onto the podium. "The assassination of our Premier Enfant is an act of treason. Mademoiselle Epernay and anyone found to have been working with her will be punished accordingly."

Murmurs of assent percolated the room.

"We cannot have any more lives lost to cruel and senseless terrorism. The Vangarde promise freedom, yet all they offer is destruction and bloodshed and chaos." He pounded his fist on the podium. "The safety of Laterre depends upon these terrorists being found and eliminated. It depends on *you*."

Hearing these words, Marcellus felt as though every cloud on Laterre had gathered above his head, threatening to descend. As Laterre's most brilliant strategist, General Bonnefaçon was obsessed with order and obedience. Not just on Laterre, but in his own family. Ever since Marcellus's father had bombed that exploit in the name of the Vangarde, Marcellus had become a suspect. A potential criminal. Even though he had been only a year old at the time.

And now, with the Premier Enfant dead, the Vangarde possibly on the rise again, and the fate of the entire planet resting on the general's shoulders, Marcellus knew he could not—*would* not—give his grandfather any reason to doubt him.

He'd taken that shirt off his father's body in a moment of weakness. He'd hidden it in his uniform in a moment of stupidity. And now, in a moment of clarity, he knew exactly what he had to do.

The shirt—and the message contained within it—must be destroyed.

- CHAPTER 22 -
CHATINE

AS CHATINE WALKED THE DARK STREETS OF
Vallonay, avoiding the pleading eyes of starving children and the
begging hands of their parents, she thought about everything that
had just happened.

Could she really do it? Work for General Bonnefaçon? Spy for the
leader of the Second Estate? She hadn't given the general an answer,
and she really didn't know what answer to give.

What if the general didn't keep his word? What if she followed
Marcellus and was able to deliver the information the general wanted,
and he still shipped her off to Bastille? Then what? She'd be even
worse off than she was now.

Or would she?

She shivered and pulled her tattered coat tighter around her,
glancing up at the starless sky, inky black like a never-ending abyss.
It was at this time of the day that Chatine could make believe that
she was seeing straight into space. All the way to the end of the
System Divine. And not at the constant clouds that hovered over
Laterre like a dark omen.

Laterre was currently in the season of the Darkest Night. But as far as Chatine was concerned, it was *always* the Darkest Night. She'd never known any other season. She'd heard some older people in the Frets tell stories about the season of the Red Twilight, when the faded crimson light of Sol 2 illuminated the cloudy sky thirty hours a day, even at night. And once, when she was a little girl living in Montfer, a very old woman had come into the inn who swore she was alive during the last White Night, when it was never dark. When the light of Sol 2 and Sol 3 shone all through the night. The idea was almost unfathomable to Chatine. Night was night. And it was always dark.

Hardly anyone in the Third Estate lived long enough to see more than two seasons. And Chatine often wondered if the White Night was just a myth that people told to give one another hope. A promise of lighter days to come.

Chatine turned down the dank alleyway behind Fret 19 and continued into the Fabrique District. She didn't want to go home. Not yet. She needed to clear her mind. Weaving between buildings, she eventually made her way into the dimly lit square of the Planque: the small, hidden area of Vallonay behind the lumber fabrique. For the right price, one could buy the kinds of things here that were never available for sale in the Marsh—a jug of weed wine, a Skin hack, a few extra Ascension points. This was Délabré territory. Very little went on around here that her father's gang didn't have a hand in.

Chatine paused when she reached Madame Marion's blood bordel. Outside the building, three girls huddled together to stave off the cold. All of them looked younger than Chatine. Even in the low light, Chatine could see their bruises. Dark welts stamped across their skin. It was a common side effect of the procedure.

Her gaze was immediately drawn to the girl on the far left of the group, the one dressed in what looked like a shiny new coat, red like the color of Sol 2. Purchased with blood money, no doubt. The more blood nutrients you sold to the bordels, the more money you made, and the more your body deteriorated.

This girl was, by far, the frailest of the three. Her hair had already started to fall out in patches. Her limbs were as skinny and brittle as fallen twigs. And in among the bruises on her face, an angry red rash covered her skin. The girl's fingernails were broken off and her teeth were brown and crumbling too.

All so the First Estate could have their fancy face creams and injections to make them look young.

Trading in blood nutrients was supposed to be illegal, but Chatine was pretty sure the Ministère just overlooked the whole operation. She'd never seen a Ministère officer ever step foot in the Planque, let alone come near a blood bordel. And she doubted anyone in the First or Second Estate knew what was *really* in those face creams.

The blood of girls under the age of twenty-five was the most valuable. Apparently it was rich in the right kinds of nutrients.

Chatine laughed aloud at the idea of a Fret girl like herself being rich in anything.

"What are you laughing at?"

Chatine startled when she realized the girl in the red coat was looking at her, *talking* to her. She quickly lowered her gaze and muttered, "Nothing."

"I've seen you around here before," the girl said, a bitterness in her words. "Watching us. And now *laughing* at us. You think you're better than us, don't you?"

Chatine hastily shook her head.

"We're making more than ten times what they pay at the fabriques," the girl continued, sounding defensive. "Which means we're feeding our families. And buying new clothes. Something you *clearly* can't afford to do."

The other two girls snickered, and Chatine glanced down at her ratty black pants, the seams barely being held together with wire and mismatched pieces of metal. She told herself she didn't care what those girls thought. She *was* better than them. She'd managed to make her way on this planet *without* selling her blood to the First Estate. And yet, she still felt like she wanted to shrivel right up into her coat and disappear.

Chatine pulled her hood farther around her face and was about to keep walking when the girl said, "You should get started now while you're still young."

Chatine nearly stumbled over her own feet. "What?"

"Madame Marion pays good money for girls your age."

"I—I—" Chatine stammered, "I can't sell my blood. I'm not a . . . I'm a boy."

The girl barked out a laugh, causing her two companions to laugh again too. "Who do you think you're kidding? You're not fooling me with that stupide hood."

A chill slithered its way up Chatine's spine. She told herself to keep calm. Don't let her emotions show. She attempted to lower her voice to a deep grumble. "You don't know what you're talking about."

But the girl in the red coat clearly wasn't buying any of it. "Like I said, I've seen you around here. I've seen the way you stare at us. Boys look at us like they're afraid we might touch them. You look at us like you're afraid you might become us."

Chatine knew she should walk away. Get out of there before the girl's big mouth caused her any trouble. But for some reason, she couldn't bring herself to move. Her gaze raked over the girl in the red coat before she finally found the courage to look into her hollow eyes.

The girl stared back. Hard and chilling and broken.

Chatine flinched as she felt something pass between them. A somber energy. An understanding of sorts. It was if they each somehow recognized that they were both human. Both struggling. Both victims of a corrupt planet.

When the girl spoke again, her voice was noticeably softer. More fragile. As though that one look had brought down all her defenses. "You might as well join us. It's either your choice or theirs. And if you're going to end up here anyway, why not make sure it's yours?"

Chatine swallowed hard as another shiver racked her body. She finally managed to tear her gaze from the girl in red and turned and walked away. As she pulled her coat tighter around her, Chatine tried to imagine what her life would be like if she were to push back her hood, let down her hair, wash the camouflage of dirt from her face.

Be who she truly was.

Was the girl right? Was this where she would end up? Was it inevitable that she would eventually find herself on the front steps of a blood bordel, next in line to be hooked up to some horrible machine that sucked and spun your blood until every last drop of nutrients was scraped out?

When Chatine braved another glance at the girl, she was back to talking with her friends, their three frail and wrecked bodies crammed together to keep warm.

And in that moment, Chatine knew. They would *all* soon end up in that morgue. They would all eventually be lying on a gurney just like the young girl she had seen today. Frostbite, rot, starvation—Chatine's destiny on this planet was clear. It had always been clear. Since the day she was born into this Regime, she was fated to die young. She would never see the stars. She would never feel the warmth of real Sol-light on her face. She would never escape.

Because *no one* escaped.

Chatine dropped her gaze to her Skin and tapped on the screen.

"Recipient?" the voice echoed in her audio chip.

"General Bonnefaçon."

Chatine waited, counting her breaths until she heard the AirLink access confirmed. "Please record your message."

The little red light on the corner of her Skin illuminated, and she spoke to her outstretched arm. She kept her message short. There weren't many words required to convey her decision.

"I'm in."

Even if it was a trap, even if the general had no intention of letting her leave this planet, this was still her best chance. Her *only* chance.

She had to take it.

She watched the message vanish from her Skin, disappearing into space to find its way across the decaying Frets, up the hill, through the walls of Ledôme, and onto the TéléCom screen of General Bonnefaçon. Up until today, he'd represented Chatine's greatest enemy, and now he was her only hope.

Oh, how the Sols liked to tease her.

As Chatine walked away from the Planque, back to the Frets, she swore she could feel the eyes of the girl in the red coat following her. But she didn't dare look back, for fear of facing what she'd left behind.

- PART 3 -
MONTFER

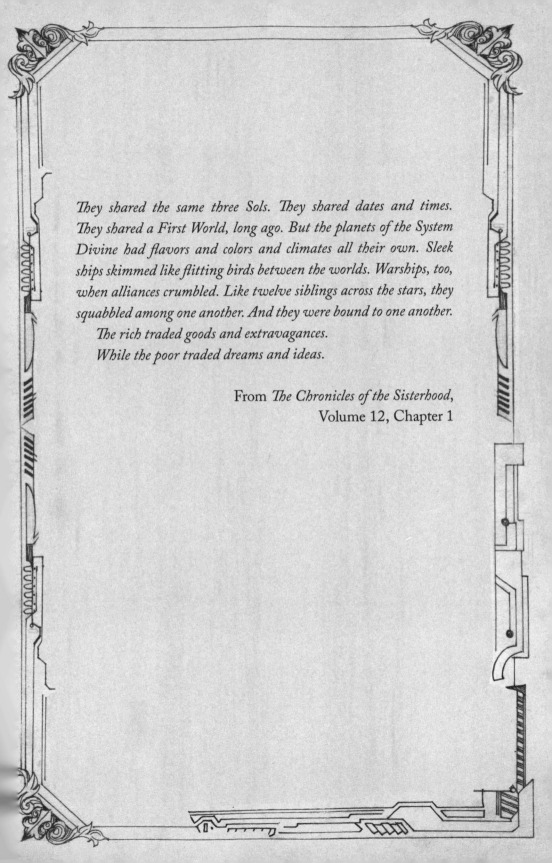

They shared the same three Sols. They shared dates and times. They shared a First World, long ago. But the planets of the System Divine had flavors and colors and climates all their own. Sleek ships skimmed like flitting birds between the worlds. Warships, too, when alliances crumbled. Like twelve siblings across the stars, they squabbled among one another. And they were bound to one another.

The rich traded goods and extravagances.

While the poor traded dreams and ideas.

From *The Chronicles of the Sisterhood,*
Volume 12, Chapter 1

- CHAPTER 23 -
MARCELLUS

MARCELLUS GRIPPED THE HANDLES OF HIS MOTO AS it skimmed and weaved through the trees. The single high-density headlight cut through the early-morning mist rising from the forest floor. There was no rain today, just a sticky dew that seemed to cling to everything. Traveling through the woods without guidance was difficult. But he didn't dare connect his TéléCom until he was back within Vallonay city limits. He couldn't risk being tracked.

The Forest Verdure stretched for thousands of kilomètres south of Vallonay, all the way to the bottom of Laterre. Few people ever braved the darkness of the dense woods; the huge trees were endless and tightly packed. Cruiseurs didn't stand a chance here. Only someone nimble on a moto could get through.

It took Marcellus longer than usual, but he finally found the clearing and pulled his bike to a halt. The old Défecteur camp was just as he remembered it from last time. The circle of huts—crudely made from sticks, mud, and old vines—sat huddled in a circle. Completely deserted. Eerily quiet.

Years ago, groups of people had tried to escape the laws of

the Regime by setting up camps in remote places around Laterre, like the Forest Verdure. But the camps didn't last long. General Bonnefaçon had launched the initiative to have all the Défecteurs captured, Skinned, and logged into the Ministère Communiqué. Most were sent back to work in the fabriques and exploits, while the rest, the more rebellious ones, went straight to Bastille.

His grandfather would certainly not approve of Marcellus sneaking out of the Palais before dawn to come here. The general hated the Défecteurs nearly as much as he hated the Vangarde. "They're foolish and misguided," his grandfather often said. "Obsessed with the old ways of the First World. They don't appreciate the beauty and order of our Regime."

Marcellus had found this particular camp earlier this year, in the fourth month, on one of the long moto rides that he sometimes took through the forest. There was nothing better for clearing his head than the splatter of mist against his helmet's visor and the brush of vines and fallen branches on the underbelly of his moto. Despite the fact that he shared his grandfather's disapproval of the Défecteurs, he could understand why someone might want to live out here, at least for a while, enveloped in trees and fog—unwatched and unchained and unknown.

This was a place to be truly alone. A place to think. It was a place where, for once, Marcellus couldn't be seen or questioned or expected.

And it was the only place he could bring his father's shirt.

As the Sols rose behind the clouds, turning the sky from a murky black to soupy gray, Marcellus paced around the perimeter of camp, picking up the driest sticks he could find and tucking them under his arm. Five minutes later, he sat down in the center of the camp by the fire pit and arranged the sticks into a pile.

No one built fires on Laterre, except the Défecteurs. But, by his second visit here, Marcellus had taught himself how. He'd figured out the purpose of the shallow hole, filled with the remains of charred wood, in the center of the camp, and eventually he'd discovered a box of handmade matches in one of the huts.

Today his fire ignited with only one match, and within a few minutes, he was watching the roaring flames. He loved how they danced, weaved, and kicked at one another and how the small sparks spat and sizzled into the wet air. He could watch the fire and its twirling, twisting, battling flames for hours.

Except, today something bigger was on his mind.

He pulled his father's shirt out from inside his uniform, where he'd tucked it again this morning. Then, in the warmth and glow of the fire, he fidgeted and fussed with the shirt in his hands. He'd come here to destroy it. He *had* to destroy it. He had to prove to himself, once and for all, that he was *not* his father's son. He was a loyal grandson and a proud member of the Second Estate. He would soon become a competent and faithful commandeur of the Ministère. He had nothing to do with the Vangarde. Nor would he ever.

"The Vangarde promise freedom, yet all they offer is destruction and bloodshed and chaos."

That's what his grandfather had said at last night's briefing. And he was right. What kind of cruel and senseless group of people would blow up exploits and kill innocent workers in the name of freedom? What kind of people would subject a two-year-old girl to the most painful and horrible death? No wonder Marcellus's grandfather was so single-minded about rooting out the Vangarde. They'd been nearly invisible for seventeen years. Phantoms living among them. But now they were clearly regrouping, rising up, and most definitely getting ready to strike again. If killing Marie Paresse was their first act, what would they do next?

Marcellus shook out the shirt in his hands so it unfurled in front of him. The glow from the fire lit up the crude lettering stitched into the fabric.

The message.

The Forgotten Word.

Mabelle is in Montfer. Go to her.

He roughly balled up the shirt again. He didn't want to see it anymore. Mabelle was dead to him. She had been for seven years. There was no reason to talk to her. No reason to see her. And definitely no reason to go to her.

He must burn his father's words. Render them as meaningless as smoke disappearing into nothingness.

Marcellus shook out the shirt one more time and then, slowly, held it over the fire. A stiff cuff alighted first, and next a shabby sleeve. In a few more seconds, almost half the fabric was ablaze, and Marcellus dropped the shirt into the fire so his fingers wouldn't burn.

He watched the flames, transfixed. They leapt and coiled around one another, the smoke rising above them like a gray, spiraling ghost. It was as if the fire were eating everything. The sight of his father's dead body in the morgue. The message. The memory of his governess being dragged from the Palais, screaming for his help. For a few moments, Marcellus felt like a great, heavy weight had been lifted off his shoulders. For the first time since he'd pulled the shirt from his dead father's body, he felt like he could breathe again.

"Adieu," he muttered, not sure if he was talking to the shirt or to his father.

The flames continued to lick and devour the fabric, until almost the entire shirt was black.

Except for a single letter.

M.

There it was. The gray thread forming the twin peaks and the dipping valley in the center.

"M is for Marcellus. . . ."

And then something snapped inside him. He lunged forward and tried to pull the remains of the shirt from the fire with his bare hands. But the flames were too hot and it was already too late.

The message was gone.

The shirt was gone. As forgotten as the words that were stitched into it. The only thing his father would ever say to him was now just a pile of ashes.

Marcellus shook his head and stared at the trees above. They seemed taller, thicker, more dense. Only moments ago, he'd wanted the trees to hide him, shield him from the probing eyes of his grandfather and the Ministère. But now it felt like the trees were closing in. Suffocating him. Making everything more unclear.

CHAPTER 24

ALOUETTE

AFTER BREAKFAST, ALOUETTE HURRIED TO THE library so she would be early for her lesson with Sister Jacqui. She needed only a few minutes. Just enough time to look at Volume 10 of the Chronicles. Principale Francine locked the Refuge's library every evening to protect the books, so Alouette hadn't been able to return after dinner last night.

The volume was exactly where she'd left it yesterday. Alouette grabbed it from the shelf and sat down at the table. She'd barely cracked open the clothbound cover when she heard footsteps approaching from the hallway. With a sharp breath, she shut the book and scooped it off the table, into her lap.

"Little Lark!" Sister Jacqui called out as she swept around a nearby bookcase. "Early again, I see. Just like the lark." She grinned down at Alouette. "Always my best and favorite student."

Alouette tried to smile back, but it was a struggle. She worried her guilty face would give her away.

Jacqui paced the library's small alcove, a book clutched under her arm while her fingers fiddled with the metal name tag on the devotion beads that hung loosely around her neck. Her bright red, nonregulation canvas shoes—which Principale Francine always complained about—gently slapped the stone tiles under her feet. Alouette couldn't remember a single time when her favorite sister had conducted one of her lessons from a chair.

Sister Jacqui was always moving.

Always thinking.

"Oh happy Sols!" the sister exclaimed, letting out an accompanying whoop and setting her book down on the table. In a matter of seconds, her expression changed from deep thought to delight. "The time has finally come. In today's lesson we get to dive into the question of knowledge! This is one of the most exciting questions in all of philosophy. And, as you know, a subject dear to our hearts here in the Refuge." The sister ran in place, pedaling her fists in the air to emphasize her excitement.

She paused, looked at Alouette, and waited for a response.

But all Alouette could muster was a half smile. "Great."

"Great?!" Jacqui threw up her hands. "Come on, Little Lark. This is a big moment."

Alouette tried to smile again. But her thoughts were too chaotic. Too cluttered. She'd barely slept a wink last night. She lay in bed for hours, thinking about her father's tattoo.

His *prisoner* tattoo.

2.4.6.0.1.

Her fingertips brushed the cover of the book in her lap. She should have come to the library even earlier and given herself more time. But breakfast had dragged on forever, and Principale Francine had given Alouette two stern looks for rushing through her food.

"Think about it, Little Lark," Sister Jacqui was now saying. "We get to explore the question of where our knowledge comes from! Do we acquire knowledge from simply experiencing the world? Do we find out what we know from touching and seeing and smelling things?"

Sister Jacqui started to pat the table, her books, her own legs, then she comically sniffed under her arms to demonstrate her point. "Or are we born with knowledge already stored in here?" Jacqui tapped her forehead and then reached over and tapped Alouette's head too.

But Alouette was so deep in thought, she barely felt the sister's touch.

It still made no sense. What could her father have possibly done? What crime had he committed? A crime so bad he'd been sent away to the cold, terrible prison on the moon?

"But how can we really physically experience something like space or time?" Sister Jacqui turned toward the chalkboard that hung amid a gap in the bookshelves on the opposite wall. She began scribbling notes in her big, messy handwriting.

Alouette immediately saw her chance.

Her fingers crept inside the book on her lap and pushed back the cover.

"You can't just learn these more abstract concepts from the real world," Jacqui went on, still scribbling. "It's not like we can feel or touch or see these abstract things like we would with, say, a table or a human or a piece of paper. . . ."

Quietly, very quietly, Alouette began to flick through the pages.

"Maybe what we *think* is reality is actually shaped by our own minds," Sister Jacqui continued, her chalk tapping and squeaking on the board.

Alouette's fingers kept working their way speedily through the book, while her gaze flitted up and down the pages.

"Think about it this way," Jacqui went on, "perhaps our minds form and create our reality."

The Bastille Prison.

Yes! This was it!

This was the chapter she was looking for.

After checking to make sure Sister Jacqui's back was still turned,

Alouette skimmed the first pages quickly. Yes, she'd definitely read this before. She'd read about the droids that stood guard over the prison thirty hours a day. She'd read about the Minstère and how they'd chosen to move the prison to Laterre's moon after it was discovered that zyttrium—a mineral vital to the fabrication of TéléSkins—was plentiful there.

But she couldn't—for the life of her—remember reading anything about prisoners being marked with silver bumps. Maybe she'd missed something. Perhaps there was a description of the Bastille tattoo in a footnote.

Her eyes moved frantically over the pages, over the tiny footnotes, searching for any mention of tattoos, metallic bumps, or prisoner numbers.

But there was nothing.

"And this raises an interesting question," Sister Jacqui chattered on, still scrawling on the chalkboard. "Back on the First World . . ."

Alouette flicked back and forth through the pages, but still she couldn't find a single reference to the tattoos. Or the prisoner numbers.

She let out an involuntarily huff of frustration and, a moment later, heard the scratching of chalk come to a halt.

"Little Lark?"

Sister Jacqui began to turn around and Alouette quickly shut the book, keeping her finger wedged into the page to mark her spot.

"Are you okay?"

"Yes . . . I . . . ," Alouette stammered, while her cheeks flamed with heat. She cleared her throat. "Just a tickle."

The sister cocked her head and stared at Alouette. As though she knew something. Or was trying to figure something out.

Alouette forced a smile, digging her finger anxiously into the soft, hand-sewn spine of the book.

And that's when she felt it.

Something rough and prickly against her fingertip. Like a piece of paper. A *ripped* piece of paper.

Has someone torn a page out of the Chronicles?

But that's forbidden!

"You're not coming down with anything, are you?" Jacqui asked, still studying her. "Because if you're not feeling well, you should head straight to the plant propagation room after lessons and ask Sister Laurel for some of her elderberry lozenges."

Alouette shook her head. "No. I'm fine. It was just dust, I think."

She held her breath, counting the seconds until Sister Jacqui finally turned back toward the chalkboard. "So who forms knowledge? This area of philosophy is called epistemology. *E-P-I-S . . .*"

As soon as the sister's back was turned, Alouette flung open the book again and bent down a little to get a better look at the rough edge in the seam.

There definitely used to be another page here.

Her mind whirled with questions.

Who would have torn a page from the Chronicles? And why?

Suddenly, Alouette's tunic felt tight at her neck, and the ceiling seemed to loom lower than usual.

Principale Francine? she wondered. *Sister Jacqui?*

But they'd always shared everything with Alouette. They'd taught her all there was to know about the above-world.

At least, she'd thought they had.

"The central questions are: How do we know what we know?" Sister Jacqui was now saying and writing, "What does it mean to know . . ."

Alouette's breath snagged in her chest as another thought occurred to her.

If this page was torn out, are there others?

Other secrets, other stories, other facts about her father, or even about herself, that she didn't know? That someone didn't *want* her to know?

"Why are we here?" The question shot out of Alouette almost by itself.

Sister Jacqui stopped scribbling and turned around. "Oh, right, well, *that* is a good question too and one of the biggest questions in philosophy. But we will get into that later when we look at metaphysical philos—"

"No, I mean, why am *I* here? Why is Papa here?"

"Again, that would be a question we will cover—"

"No, no!" Alouette let out a huff of air. "I mean, why do Papa and I live here? In the Refuge? With all of you?"

Jacqui was silent for a few moments, as if she was pondering the right way to proceed. "Little Lark, you know why," she said finally. "Your mother died when you were very young, and Hugo couldn't take care of you alone. He brought you to the Refuge, where you would be safe and cared for, free from hunger and disease and poverty. . . ."

Alouette almost sighed aloud as she heard the words recited to her. It was as if Jacqui were reading from a script.

Jacqui gave a small laugh. "And, of course, to receive a deep, philosophical education so you will be a wise and thoughtful sister one day. Speaking of which, let's get back to—"

"But what else? Is there more? Where did we live before? Before the Refuge? Where was Papa from?" Alouette felt breathless and frustrated, the questions streaming out faster than she herself could even make sense of them.

Sister Jacqui sat down in the chair across from Alouette, and Alouette gripped tighter around the edges of the book hidden in her lap. "Little Lark. These are not my questions to answer." She smiled an inscrutable smile. "We should get back to the lesson—"

"NO!" Alouette shouted, and then quickly recoiled, surprised by her own outburst. She'd never raised her voice to any of the sisters before, especially not to Sister Jacqui. But nothing felt the same now.

Everything had seemingly changed since she saw that man in the Frets. That convict with the silver bumps. "You're the one who told me to ask questions."

"I know," Jacqui replied, her golden eyes dark and troubled. "I know I say that. And it's true. You should ask questions. It's just that . . ." Her voice drifted off as she lowered her gaze, clearly struggling with her next words. "Think about today's lesson, Alouette. Think about—"

"But—" Alouette tried to interject.

Jacqui held up a hand. "Think about how we acquire knowledge. Perhaps knowledge is in us from the very start, but it's *also* out there to be found."

Then, as if nothing had happened, Jacqui smiled, stood up, and in her usual upbeat tone, said, "Let's finish there for today. We'll continue with this topic in the next lesson. Take some time for yourself before Tranquil Forme."

And before Alouette could even comprehend what had just happened, Sister Jacqui sauntered out of the library, leaving her alone with her racing mind. She glanced down at Volume 10 of the Chronicles in her lap, one of the thousands of books that Alouette had come to rely on for information. For answers to all of her questions.

But now, it seemed, her questions had grown too big, too deep, too complicated for even this vast library. She could no longer rely only on books.

- CHAPTER 25 -
MARCELLUS

THE FRETS COULD BE SEEN FROM ALMOST ANYWHERE in the city, making it difficult to get lost. As Marcellus emerged from the Forest Verdure on his moto, the massive metal monstrosities appeared to rise up from the ground like fallen giants. The former freightships were an eyesore on the capital, but the Patriarche insisted they served some kind of purpose. "Give a rat a new home, and he's going to start demanding furniture," he was fond of saying.

Five minutes later, Marcellus pulled his moto to a stop in the center of the Frets. He reconnected his TéléCom, attached his audio patch behind his ear, and took a deep breath, attempting to prepare himself for what he was about to do.

But nothing could quite prepare him for what he encountered when he stepped into the Marsh.

Marcellus had never seen the marketplace in such an uproar. The walkways between stands churned like overflowing rivers. Third Estaters shoved against one another, stall owners shouted to be heard, and the mud-covered ground was a soup of rotting vegetables, discarded planks, and broken pipes from yesterday's riot over the aborted Ascension. Hundreds of sergents and deputies in their crisp white uniforms patrolled the scene like bright Sols amid a filthy fog, shouting, shunting, and cuffing people as they went. It was as though every member of the Vallonay Policier had been called in to act upon his grandfather's orders.

"*. . . arrest anyone suspected of Vangarde activities or affiliations.*"

Marcellus jumped out of the way as a Policier sergent dragged a gray-haired man across Marcellus's path.

"I swear, I don't know anything!" the man protested. "Please, have mercy. I have a family at home. I do honest work for my honest chance!"

Marcellus actually recognized the man pleading for his life. He sold turnips. He had offered Marcellus one on his very first day of training in the Marsh. Marcellus remembered the kind smile on the man's face as he'd peeled the blackened outer layer from the rotting vegetable and offered it to Marcellus. *"See, Officer? Good as the Sols on the inside."*

Marcellus would have sworn that that man was as far from Vangarde as one could get. But apparently, that didn't matter anymore. Apparently, *everyone* was a suspect now.

And as he made his way through the crowd, Marcellus could hear the whispers of conversation following him.

"The Vangarde. They're resurfacing!"

"Ghosts—back from the dead."

"Is that who killed the Premier Enfant?"

"Don't know. They won't tell us anything!"

Marcellus pushed through a particularly jammed walkway, only to be cut off by three droids blocking the path. One of them had a woman dangling from its metallic fist, its orange eyes clicking and glowing as it scanned the woman's Skin.

At the sight of them, Marcellus couldn't help but think of *her*. Alouette. And how she'd fled from the droids yesterday. How she'd fled from him. He hadn't really been able to stop thinking about her since then. Her dark, round eyes had danced in his memory as he'd tried to fall asleep last night.

Where is she now? he wondered as he backtracked to find another way through the marketplace. Did she even live in the Frets? Was Fret 7 her home? She certainly hadn't acted like any Fret girl he'd ever met. Plus, she didn't have a Skin. The only people Marcellus knew of who didn't have Skins were First and Second Estaters and—

Marcellus stopped dead in his tracks.

He thought again about how fast the girl had scurried away when the droids appeared. Then he thought about the camp he'd just left. The one buried deep inside the Forest Verdure. Hidden from view. Hidden from the Ministère.

Is she a Défecteur?

The idea immediately made Marcellus's breath quicken.

There were always rumors floating around Laterre that some of the Défecteurs had managed to get away when the camps were raided. But Marcellus had never believed those rumors.

But what other explanation was there for a girl without a Skin who didn't have a profile in the Communiqué? Unless, of course, she'd given him a fake name. Which sounded exactly like something a Défecteur would do. But then, if she really was a Défecteur, what was she doing wandering around the Frets?

"You're late."

Marcellus startled and looked up to see Inspecteur Limier striding toward him.

"You were expected at 09.00."

Marcellus cursed the heat rising in his cheeks. He hated how Limier always made him feel like a five-year-old dressed up in a uniform, pretending to be an officer.

"I was just making some initial inquiries," Marcellus said.

The inspecteur stood before him with his usual broad stance and imperious stare. "Inquiries?"

Marcellus tried to hold the inspecteur's gaze, but it made his stomach roll. He looked away. "Yes, inquiries."

The circuitry in the inspecteur's face flashed in a cool, steady rhythm like the fireflies in the Palais gardens. Marcellus held his breath as he watched the inspecteur's orange eye rove the hectic marketplace.

"Well, now that you've made your *inquiries*," the inspecteur said, returning his enhanced gaze to Marcellus. "You can proceed to Fret 16 and commence door-to-door interrogations at the couchettes."

Marcellus knew this was his opportunity. He stood up straighter, steeling himself to say the words he had rehearsed the entire way back from the Forest Verdure.

"Actually, I will be traveling to Montfer this morning," he announced with all the authority and confidence he could muster.

"Montfer?" the inspecteur shot back. "You are not needed in Montfer. You will proceed to Fret 16."

Marcellus's stomach clenched, but he pressed on. "I have leads on Vangarde activity in Montfer. I have only come to the Marsh to report for duty, after which I will be hiring a cruiseur to take me across the Terrain Perdu."

Limier's circuitry flashed furiously as his mechanical eye scanned Marcellus's face, searching for signs of weakness. Marcellus clenched his jaw until it hurt, but he did not back down. He returned the inspecteur's harsh stare with one of his own.

For a few long seconds, no words passed between the two men. There was no need. Both of them knew what the other was thinking.

Marcellus was a boy. An officer who'd barely had a chance to get his uniform dirty in the field. Who was probably being promoted to commandeur only because his grandfather was General Bonnefaçon. Limier, on the other hand, was the most respected and most feared inspecteur in the whole of the Ministère.

But Limier was an inspecteur and Marcellus was an officer.

Limier was outranked.

They both knew it.

It was Limier who finally broke the standoff. "Fine," he snapped. "But you will take Sergent Chacal with you."

"What? No. I don't require any help."

The last person Marcellus needed with him when he was trudging around Montfer searching for a convicted Vangarde spy was Sergent Chacal. Chacal had the persistence, cruelty, and personality of a droid. If Marcellus made one move that wasn't regulation, the bullheaded sergent would be on his TéléCom to Limier.

Perhaps even to the general himself.

Limier flashed a sinister snarl of a smile. "Oh, but I insist, *Officer.*" His circuitry slowed to an even flicker. "It's for your own protection. We can't have you wandering around a foreign city by yourself in these dangerous times."

Marcellus considered his options. It wasn't protocol for anyone to cross the barren, ice-cold lands of the Terrain Perdu alone. If Marcellus pulled rank again, insisting he not be accompanied to Montfer, the inspecteur would surely get even more suspicious. He'd just have to find a way to distract Chacal once they'd arrived.

Marcellus painted on a smile. "Yes. Good thinking, Inspecteur. Please tell Chacal to meet me at the cruiseur port."

"Very well." Limier got on his TéléCom to relay the directive, and Marcellus headed in the direction of the Vallonay Policier Precinct.

Only Ministère personnel had use for them in the Frets. Cruiseur transport was expensive and the Third Estate lacked the funds. When they did travel, they usually went by sea. It took days for a bateau to travel the Secana Sea from Vallonay, on the west coast of Laterre's single landmass, to Montfer on the east. Marcellus's grandfather had always said it was better this way. A working class that can easily move around quickly becomes an *un*working class. It's best to keep your laborers in one place: close to their jobs.

After ordering his cruiseur, Marcellus disconnected his TéléCom again. Having Sergent Chacal with him was inconvenience enough. He didn't need anyone tracking his location around Montfer as well.

The Marsh was still thick with Policier and commotion, and it took Marcellus longer than usual to reach the Precinct—a huge, windowless black cube of a building just north of the Marsh.

He hated this place. It was a warren of endless claustrophobic hallways filled with sterile white interrogation rooms, over-crowded holding cells, and ever-vigilant security microcams. In the Precinct's artillery vaults, rows and rows of Policier droids hung like slabs of meat as they recharged, their robotic eyes dead and ghostly.

Thankfully, today, Marcellus didn't have to go inside. The cruiseur station was just outside the Precinct, and as soon as he arrived, he saw the gleaming silver vehicle waiting for him, hovering just a few mètres off the ground.

But he stopped walking when he noticed someone sitting on the hood, head down, legs dangling in front of the cruiseur's headlights.

Dressed in black with a hood pulled up to hide their face, the figure was slight, almost wispy, like the slightest breeze might blow them right away. A young girl, perhaps?

Marcellus slowed his approach, resting his hand on the rayonette strapped to his belt. He hated using the weapon. The sticky sound the pulse made when it entered a human body had always sickened him. And that was just on paralyzeur mode. Marcellus prayed he'd never have to hear the sound it made when it was set to kill.

Upon hearing him approach, the hooded figure lifted their head, and two stone-gray eyes blinked back at Marcellus from beneath a layer of grime. He felt himself relax and his hand drop from his weapon when he recognized the boy. The one he'd met in the morgue yesterday, whom he'd *sworn* Limier arrested during the fray of the canceled Ascension.

Théo. Marcellus remembered the ill-fitting name that Limier had called him.

"I hear you're going to Montfer," the boy said, his words crisp and direct.

Marcellus stopped walking. "How did you know that?" There was something about this boy—the steeliness of his eyes, or the raw conviction in his posture—that made Marcellus feel both safe and on guard.

Théo shrugged. "I know things."

Marcellus cocked his head and studied the boy's face, remembering how hard he had fought in the morgue for that strange device. And then remembering how betrayed the boy had looked when Limier's droids came for him in the Fret hallway. "Look, I didn't call Limier on you yesterday. I swear, I—"

"It's fine," the boy snapped, refusing to meet Marcellus's eye.

Marcellus could tell it was clearly *not* fine, but he got the hint to drop it. "So, how did you get away from Limier?"

Théo scoffed. "The same way I always get away from that flic."

"What did you call him?"

The boy averted his eyes, as though caught doing something wrong. "'Flic,'" he repeated. "It's what we call your kind. Anyone who works for the Policier or the Ministère."

Marcellus couldn't help but smile. It seemed he was always learning new words from this kid. "I thought I was a pomp."

"Oh, you're that, too."

"So, I'm a PompFlic?" Marcellus said with a snuffle of laughter.

Théo looked almost annoyed. "Nobody says that."

Marcellus wiped the amusement from his face. "Oh. Sorry."

The boy's impassive expression didn't shift. "You're gonna need a guide."

"Excuse me?"

"In Montfer. You can't just walk into an exploit town in a uniform and expect people to talk to you. You need someone who knows the town. Speaks the language."

"They speak a different language in Montfer?"

Once again, the boy looked annoyed, as though Marcellus were a waste of his time. "Someone who speaks Third Estate, I mean." He leveled his gaze at Marcellus. "Someone who knows what 'flic' means."

Marcellus blinked. "You want to come with me to Montfer?"

He shrugged again. "I'm just saying I can help."

"So you know the town?"

"Yep. Used to live there."

Marcellus felt the urge to agree. What the boy was saying was true. He barely knew Montfer. And he'd certainly never rooted out a suspected terrorist before. How would he even know where to start? The only thing the message from his father had said was that Mabelle was in Montfer. But how would he ever find her? Montfer was the second-largest city on the planet.

He needed all the help he could get.

Marcellus narrowed his eyes. "What's in it for you?"

The boy's deadpan expression slowly morphed into a smirk. "A few largs will do it."

Marcellus nodded. It seemed like a fair trade. The boy slid from the hood of the cruiseur and scurried around to the door. Marcellus reached for the panel to open it but stopped and turned back toward the Marsh. "Actually, I have to wait."

Théo looked confused. "For what?"

"For another"—Marcellus paused, trying to remember the right word—"flic," he finished, proud of himself.

The boy laughed and shook his head. "Just . . ."

"What?"

"Don't."

Marcellus's shoulders slouched in defeat. "Fine. But I do need to wait for him. His name is Sergent Chacal."

Marcellus noticed the boy bristle at the name, and he wondered what kind of run-ins Théo had had with Chacal and his metal baton in the past. But he seemed to shake off his trepidation quickly. "Why is he coming with you?"

"Inspecteur Limier ordered it."

The boy's face twisted in confusion. "I don't get it. Don't you out-rank both of them?"

Marcellus couldn't help but sigh. Even this Third Estate boy could tell he was a coward. "Technically yes, but—"

"Then what are we waiting for?"

Marcellus considered the question. Théo was right. What *was* he waiting for? He needed to start acting like the commandeur he was destined to be. He glanced between the boy and the cruiseur, its sleek silver body humming gently as the engine idled. Quickly, he activated the door panel and the cruiseur hissed open. "Nothing," he finally replied. "Let's go."

CHAPTER 26

ALOUETTE

WITH HER HEART IN HER THROAT, ALOUETTE GENTLY turned the knob and nudged at the door. It squeaked open a crack. She'd been inside her father's room countless times. But never like this.

Never in secret.

Never without his permission.

After glancing over her shoulder to make sure the hallway was empty, Alouette gave the door another nudge until it was open wide enough for her to squeeze through. She peered back into the hallway one more time. Tranquil Forme was beginning soon, which meant the sisters would be gathering in the common room and her father would be starting to prepare lunch.

She had only a few minutes.

Alouette sucked in a breath and tiptoed inside.

Hugo Taureau's room was sparse. Only a narrow bed, neatly made with one coarse blanket, a straight-backed chair, and a small nightstand with nothing on it except a single lamp. He had no shelves, no books, and only a tiny closet for his clothes.

But maybe, just maybe, she thought, there was more hiding in this sparse room. Something. Anything. A clue to who her father was.

An answer to why he had that number tattooed on his arm.

2.4.6.0.1.

Alouette moved farther into the room and knelt on the floor, peering under the bed. But she found nothing except a faint smattering of dust. She slid her fingers under the mattress and heaved it up, revealing the springs of the old metal frame. Nothing there, either. Her gaze traveled to the nightstand and its cupboard under the lamp. Still on her knees, she turned the small handle and pulled the door open.

An old plastique doll sat upright inside the cupboard.

Alouette tilted her head slightly. "Katrina?" she whispered in surprise.

She hadn't seen the doll since she was a child. She always assumed her father had thrown it away after she'd outgrown it. But here it was.

"Katrina," Alouette said again, reaching for the doll and entwining her fingers in its thick nylon curls. Almost instantly, Alouette felt some of her anxiety melt away. Just like when she was a child and she would wake up from a horrible nightmare and Katrina would be there waiting to calm her.

Alouette held the doll out in front of her and let her gaze wander over its delicate face and faded yellow dress. Her eyes settled on the empty sleeve where one of Katrina's arms used to be. She tried to remember how the doll had lost its arm, but the memory was too vague. Too thin and wispy to grasp on to. And the harder she tried to do so, the farther away it receded into the back of her mind, like an itch she could never scratch.

With the doll still clutched in her arms, Alouette pushed back onto her feet and circled slowly around the small room, peering into crevices and shadows. Finally, she came to the closet and pulled back the curtain. As always, Hugo's clothes and aprons were neatly folded on the three shelves inside, above an extra pair of canvas shoes. Alouette pulled out sweaters and pants and ran her fingertips along the surfaces of the shelves. But there was nothing different. Nothing unusual.

She sighed.

This was completely futile. There were no answers to be found. No strange things lurking. She was almost ready to give up.

But then Alouette saw it.

A shimmer, a glint, at the back of the closet, on the top shelf.

All the closets in the Refuge were carved directly into the bedrock, so their backs and sides looked much like the rest of the walls—uneven and very dark. Except there was something at the back of her father's closet that was smooth enough to shine under the dim light of his room.

After setting Katrina down, Alouette pushed aside the clothes on the top shelf and reached her hand to the back of the closet.

"What on Laterre?" she whispered, shocked by what she felt beneath her fingertips.

The back wall of the closet felt nothing like rock. It was smooth and soft, almost warm. It felt like the leather seat covers on the chairs in the Refuge's library.

Without a moment's hesitation, Alouette grabbed the chair from the corner of her father's room. She positioned it in front of the closet and hopped up. From her new vantage point, she could see that the mysterious object on the top shelf was a case. An old leather valise with a shiny metal handle.

She tugged it from its hiding place and gently carried it down from the closet over to the bed.

The leather on the surface was worn and scratched, and two latches fastened the valise on either side. Alouette quickly popped them open and began to lift the lid, but she stopped herself. A wave of guilt suddenly surged inside her. Should she really be doing this? Snooping through her father's things? It seemed like a betrayal.

A betrayal of her father's trust.

A betrayal of his deep and clear love for her.

But then she reminded herself of the convict in the Frets yesterday and the bumps on her father's arm. There were clearly things her father didn't trust *her* with.

Alouette lifted the lid of the valise.

And her hopes sank.

It was full of clothes. Old clothes, faded and musty. Most likely garments her father used to wear before he ever came to the Refuge. Alouette quickly sifted through the neatly folded stacks of clothes, her disappointment growing with every boring shirt, wool sweater, and pair of trousers. With another sigh, she carefully started to restack the garments. She was just refolding a long, hooded coat, trying to position it exactly as she had found it, when she heard a *clatter* on the floor.

Something had fallen out of the pocket of the coat. Alouette glanced down to see a small rectangular box made of titan. It glittered under the dim light of her father's room.

Gently, reverently, Alouette picked it up and studied its intricate design. She wasn't sure if she'd ever seen anything so lovely. Ever. Engraved on the lid was an ornate image. A pair of majestic First World creatures sitting with their front paws raised atop a glistening planet. Alouette searched her memory for the name of the animals.

Tigers?

No, they didn't have stripes. Instead, shaggy manes framed their faces almost like the rays of a Sol.

Lions. She finally found the right word. *King of the Beasts*, she remembered reading once. The etching captured them so beautifully.

She tried to open the lid, but unlike with the valise, it wouldn't budge. The box stayed locked tight like a fist.

She turned the box over in her hands, inspecting it. It was surprisingly heavy. As her fingers brushed over the engraved surface, her palms began to tingle with a strange and unexpected warmth. Like someone had wrapped a cozy, thick blanket around her.

"Maman." The word seemed to come from nowhere. Almost as though someone else had whispered it.

Alouette startled at the sound exhaling from her own lips. She had no memories of ever saying that word. To anyone. Yet the two syllables felt familiar and reassuring on her tongue, as though they belonged there. She blinked and swallowed as she stared at the box. If this really had belonged to her mother, then why hadn't her father ever shared it with her?

Throughout the years, Alouette must have asked over a thousand questions about her mother. What did she look like? How did she speak? Where did she live? How did she get sick? But he'd given her so little in reply.

"She loved you more than the three Sols, Little Lark. That's all you need to know."

Alouette had heard that same answer so many times, she'd eventually stopped asking the questions. But at the sight of this beautiful box, Alouette's chest suddenly ached. Ached like she'd lost something. Ached with guilt that she so rarely thought about her mother these days.

Alouette wrapped her fingers around the box and squeezed. Hard. So hard that its corners dug into her palm. Suddenly, the ache in her chest had been replaced by something new. Something hot and burning and angry.

She was so sick of it.

The secrets.

The mysteries.

The torn-out pages.

The hidden boxes.

She needed answers. And she needed them now.

Alouette tossed the box aside and grabbed for her father's valise. She flipped it over, dumping all the contents out onto the bed. She ran her hands roughly through the various fabrics, her fingers searching pockets and folds and crevices.

What else are you keeping from me? she wanted to cry aloud to her father. *What other secrets are you hiding?*

Before long, Hugo Taureau's bed looked like a windstorm had blown across it. There were clothes strewn everywhere. But Alouette no longer cared. She kept searching, kept rummaging, kept picking up garments and running her hands over every square millimètre of them.

Until she stumbled upon something cold and hard and metallic. Something wrapped up in one of the old shirts.

Alouette pulled out the long, tapered object and gripped it in her hands.

She knew what it was. She'd never actually seen one in real life, but she'd read about candles in one of the library's First World books. Stems of wax, topped with a tiny fire, that people used for reading before the days of electric light.

"Candlestick."

As soon as she uttered the word aloud, it seemed to reverberate in her mind, like echoes from the past.

"Hold the candlestick, ma petite. Don't let it go. Do you understand? It's very important. Don't drop it."

And then, in a terrifying instant, Alouette was back on that cold, hard ground, side by side with her father, that enormous rock looming over their heads.

It was the same memory she'd had in the stairwell yesterday when she'd been hiding from the droids. It had been vague and blurry in her mind. But now, as her fingertips grazed the smooth sides of the candlestick, there was more somehow. As if the fog covering her past was clearing, lifting, revealing details she'd never remembered.

She could almost feel the rough dirt against her skin, the cold dampness of the ground seeping through her clothes. She could feel the pounding of her father's heart so close to her own.

He was frightened too. But why? The answer came almost immediately after her mind had posed the question.

Because we were running.
From something.
*From some*one.

She studied the candlestick in her hand. It twinkled in the light, with its slim titan stem flaring out into a six-sided base. She rotated it in her hands, studying the intricate floral patterns engraved into the metal. It was so cold to the touch and heavy in her hands. It was old, yes.

But was it also stolen?

Was that why they'd been running? Because her father had stolen this?

But what could her father want with a candlestick?

There was certainly no use for it on Laterre. After the Human Conservation Commission discovered the System Divine, they'd decided not to bring fire to the new world. It was deemed too volatile and too dangerous. Especially after half of the First World had been consumed by the deadly element in the Last Days.

Alouette clutched her hands around the candlestick and closed her eyes, letting the memory of that dark night continue to seep in. Still only bits and pieces, but the pieces were bigger. She could remember her legs aching. Her feet throbbing inside her shoes. The candlestick clutched tightly in her small hands. Her heart hadn't been pounding only because she'd been scared, but because she'd been fatigued. She'd cried out from the pain and the weariness and the terror.

And that's when her father had raised his trembling finger to his lips.

"Hush, ma petite. Hush."

They had been running. They had been *hiding.*

Alouette's eyes opened and she glanced around at the thick bedrock walls of the Refuge.

Were they still hiding?

Fear tore through Alouette, causing her body to tremble and her breath to hitch in her chest. She tossed the candlestick onto the pile of clothes and began to stuff everything back into the valise. She no longer cared if the clothes were refolded correctly. She just wanted to get out of her father's room. Away from the memories. Away from her fears. That rock felt like it was still pressing down on her, threatening to crush her. That dark, cold night still felt like it was all around her, following her.

Her father was a convict.

An *escaped* convict.

She was almost sure of that now.

So what did that make Alouette? His accomplice? His *hostage*? Tears blurred her vision as she scooped up the last armful of clothes and threw it into the valise. The candlestick, which she hadn't remembered was in the pile, toppled to the ground.

She dropped quickly to her knees and reached for the candlestick with shaking hands. It wasn't until she wrapped her fingers tightly around the stem that she spotted the crack in the metal. A tiny sliver where there once had been a seamless surface.

It was broken.

She had broken it.

"No, no, no, no, no," she whispered as she fidgeted with the candlestick, trying to push the two ends together. But somehow, she only managed to make it worse.

The crack grew wider.

And yet, as Alouette studied the fissure, trying desperately to figure out how to fix it, she realized it almost looked . . . purposeful. As though it wasn't a crack at all, but an opening of some kind.

Alouette tilted her head, the panic suddenly giving way to curiosity.

She grabbed the two ends of the candlestick and began to pull them in opposite directions, until she heard some type of mechanism inside click into place.

Then, a moment later, she let out a gasp as her entire face was suddenly bathed in a glowing green light.

- CHAPTER 27 -
CHATINE

CHATINE HAD NEVER BEEN INSIDE A CRUISEUR before. The inside was sleek and luxurious, like an extension of the Grand Palais. The walls were a seamless black plastique, slick and polished without a scratch in sight. As she took her seat, Chatine ran her hands over the soft upholstery. She'd never touched leather so soft before.

"First time in a cruiseur?" Marcellus's voice broke into her thoughts, and she turned to see that he was studying her with an amused expression.

Chatine felt her face warm. She shoved her hands in her lap and leaned back on the seat. "Are you kidding? I ride in cruiseurs all the time. This is like my thousandth time."

Marcellus clearly didn't believe her. "Right." He relaxed into his seat opposite her and announced to the vehicle, "We're ready."

A second later, the cruiseur seemed to jump five mètres in the air, leaving Chatine's stomach back down on the ground. Involuntarily, she grabbed on to the first thing she could find and gripped it tightly, trying to stifle the shriek that bubbled up in her throat.

As soon as the sensation of falling had passed, she glanced down at what she was holding and saw that it was Marcellus's knee. He met her gaze, cocking a dark eyebrow, and she quickly released her grip, leaving an obvious wrinkle in the fabric of his uniform.

She tried to lean back again and relax, but the cruiseur was already flying forward. The movement made her uneasy, and she spread her arms out across the seat to try to regain her balance.

"Your thousandth time in a cruiseur, huh?" Marcellus asked.

Chatine scoffed and turned away from him, trying to look at the passing scenery, but the vehicle had no windows. She wished she could see outside. She'd never seen the Terrain Perdu before. She'd only heard stories of the endless tundra with nothing but frozen ground for thousands and thousands of kilomètres. How long would it take them to cross it? She'd heard that cruiseurs traveled almost as fast as the voyageurs that soared around the System Divine at supervoyage speed, bringing goods and people between planets. She was *supposed* to be on one of those ships next week. But instead, she was stuck in here with a spoiled Second Estate brat.

She knew Marcellus was going to Montfer to investigate the Vangarde. That much she'd overheard when Marcellus was talking to Inspecteur Limier in the Marsh earlier. What she didn't know, however, was whether this had anything to do with what the general had told her yesterday in his office. About the Vangarde attempting to recruit Marcellus.

Chatine was not happy at the thought of returning to Montfer. She hadn't been back there since her parents were run out of town for being crooks. She could still remember the smell of the Secana Sea as her family had boarded that rickety bateau headed for Vallonay.

Unlike her parents, however, Chatine hadn't left Montfer to escape her mistakes. She'd left to escape *him*. Even though Chatine had been only eight years old at the time and hadn't really had a choice in the matter, this was what she'd told herself. She was getting away from the ghost of Henri.

And now she was going back.

Usonia better be worth it, she thought.

Chatine cleared her throat. "So, what's in Montfer?"

Marcellus averted his gaze, suddenly appearing lost in his own thoughts. For a moment, Chatine worried he wasn't going to answer her question, but then he finally mumbled, "A lead."

Chatine slumped in her seat. She was going to have to do better than that. She was going to have to dig deeper. Get him to open up. Earn his trust, just like the general had said.

But the thought made her feel sick.

Chatine was a croc. A con. A Fret rat. She could flit around like a phantom; she could lift a piece of chou bread from a stall without blinking an eye; she could rob a Second Estater while standing right in front of them. But what she was *not* and never would be was a *confidante*.

"A lead?" she repeated, trying to sound cheerful. But who was she kidding? Chatine didn't do cheerful. "Are you tracking down the Vangarde?"

Marcellus shot her a look, clearly implying she was naïve. "Yes. The Vangarde."

Chatine clenched her teeth. She was *really* bad at this. Why couldn't her job just be to follow him around without being seen? She was really good at not being seen.

She swallowed and tried again. "So, who is this lead?" She took a stab in the dark. "Some Montfer croc who's been stealing rayonettes from the Ministère and selling them to the Third Estate?"

Marcellus's head popped up and he gaped at Chatine as though she had stumbled upon some key piece of confidential information. Her hopes skyrocketed. Maybe her random guess hadn't been so random. Maybe she was actually getting somewhere.

"'Croc'?" he asked with a smirk. "Is that another one of your little phrases?"

Chatine balled her fists. "They're not *little* phrases," she fired back. "It's how we talk. It's our way of life. And if you want any hope of getting people in Montfer to talk to you, you should probably stop making fun of us."

The grin slid from Marcellus's face. "You're right. I'm sorry. Tell me what 'croc' means."

She sighed. That's not exactly what she meant. She didn't want to pass the entire cruiseur ride to Montfer defining Third Estate slang for Marcellus Bonnefaçon. "It means 'criminal.'"

"Criminal," Marcellus repeated curiously.

"Yes. So, this lead you're looking for, I'll need to know their name. So I know who to ask for when we get there."

"Why 'croc'?" Marcellus asked, ignoring her. "Where does that come from? What are the origins?"

Chatine rolled her eyes. Seriously? This was how she would be spending her day? The boy was about as interesting as a turnip. "I don't know. We don't sit around, drinking sparkles, discussing the origins of our language. It's just what they're called."

"Okay," Marcellus said, putting his hands up in a defensive gesture. "Calm down."

Chatine took a breath.

"What else?" he asked.

"What do you mean, what else?"

"What are some of the other words you use?"

"I don't know. I don't have a log on my Skin. Look, I can't help you unless you tell me who we're looking for."

"Just name a few. I want to learn more about—"

Right then, the cruiseur banked hard to the left, causing Chatine's stomach to drop again. She let out an involuntary yelp and pressed down on the seat, trying to stabilize herself.

Marcellus chuckled. "It's okay. We're just turning."

Chatine tried to play off her reaction. "I knew that."

"Really? Because you look like you're going to vomit."

Just the word made Chatine's stomach roll. She clamped her mouth shut and swallowed hard, trying to keep the sickness at bay. But she clearly wasn't fooling anyone.

Marcellus leaned forward across the small aisle between them. Chatine could smell his fresh, clean scent. It reminded her of Henri. The way the top of his head used to smell so good, so innocent, she would bury her nose in it and just breathe.

"Are you okay?" Marcellus asked, his deep hazel eyes so close to hers, she felt like she could look right through them, straight into his mind. In that brief flicker of a moment, she could almost understand why all the Third Estate girls squealed when his face appeared on their Skins. It *was* a nice face. There was no denying that.

"I'll be fine," Chatine muttered, glancing down. Her gaze landed on his hands, resting on either side of Chatine's legs. So close. *Too* close. She suddenly wanted to shove them away, push him back, but just then something snagged her attention. Marcellus's crisp white jacket sleeve had risen up his left wrist to reveal a faded bruise underneath.

What is that?

Chatine instinctively bent down to get a closer look.

"Don't look down," Marcellus said, breaking into her thoughts. "Look out the window. Trust me, it'll help."

"Out the win—?" Chatine started to ask.

"Visibility mode!" Marcellus called out, cutting off her question. The darkened plastique around them suddenly vanished, and once again, Chatine felt like she was falling. There was nothing between her and the fast-moving ground except air. She gasped as she realized that the entire cruiseur had become transparent. The walls, ceiling, and floor were crystal clear, making it seem like she was flying. Literally.

The uneasiness in her gut disappeared as she gaped at the sights around her. Stretching out beneath the cruiseur, as far as the eye could see, was a rolling, infinite landscape, dappled with large patches of ice and even larger patches of frozen, tufted grass. Strange rocks poked up from the ground, sharp and angular, stretching upward, as if trying to reach the clouds. There were no towns anywhere. No Frets, no shelters, no people. Not even a single treetop or bird in the endless white sky.

This was the Terrain Perdu.

Dead Man's Land, she'd heard people call it. Because no one had ever crossed it on foot and survived.

They were soaring right over it, the ice and rocks and frozen grass whizzing by so fast. Chatine had never once in her life used the word "breathtaking," but that seemed to be the only word that flitted through her mind now.

Breathtaking.

The vast, frozen emptiness was both terrifying and magical, all at the same time.

"It's beautiful, isn't it?" Marcellus broke into her thoughts, and it was only now that Chatine realized she was literally pressed up against the clear wall, her palms flat, her nose squished.

She pulled away and tried to shrug. "It's okay."

Marcellus tipped his head back and laughed. Chatine immediately felt her hackles rise again. "What's so funny?" she demanded.

"Has anyone ever told you, you're a horrible liar?"

No, no one had *ever* told her that before. She was starting to worry she was losing her edge. Ten minutes in a cruiseur with Officer Fancy Hair and suddenly she was turning soft.

Chatine crossed her arms over her chest, feeling her lungs flare with heat. "Did anyone ever tell you that you're a coward?"

As soon as the words were out of her mouth, she knew they had struck much harder than the casual jabbing insult she'd intended.

Marcellus's face instantly closed off, and he seemed to shrink in on himself, like he was trying to turn his entire body inside out. He slumped in his seat and stared at the passing scenery.

Chatine silently berated herself for broaching such a clearly sensitive topic. But how was she to know? Once again, she could feel how deeply she was failing at this job. She was supposed to be *bonding* with him. Not making him all sad and droopy. How on Laterre was she supposed to get any information out of him in this state?

Chatine closed her eyes and tried to think of a new tactic. A new topic. Something to break him out of this melancholy that he seemed to have fallen into. No, correction: that she had *pushed* him into.

"Mabelle."

Chatine's eyes snapped open and she glanced across the aisle at Marcellus. He was still staring at the scenery, his eyes focused on something far off in the distance. Something that, Chatine suspected, was *not* in the Terrain Perdu. Maybe not even on Laterre.

"That's who the lead is," Marcellus went on. "Her name is Mabelle Dubois. She used to be my governess. Until seven years ago, when it was revealed she was really a Vangarde spy. All this time, I'd thought Mabelle was in prison." He shook his head pensively. "All this time."

Chatine stared at Marcellus in disbelief, unsure what she should say to this, if anything. He seemed to almost be talking to himself. As though Chatine had become as transparent as the walls and floor around them.

"But it turns out she escaped. A month ago. I didn't even realize you could escape from Bastille." He laughed darkly. "Shows how much I know. Or don't know, I guess. Anyway, my father left me a message before he died. That's who I was visiting at the morgue yesterday when I . . . when you . . ." His voice trailed for a moment. "When we met. The message told me Mabelle was in Montfer and that I should go to her."

A message?

Was this what the general had been referring to when he said that the Vangarde had already made contact with Marcellus? Chatine suddenly remembered the shirt she had seen Marcellus cut off his father's dead body. The one with the Forgotten Word stitched into the fabric. But how had he been able to read it?

Marcellus went on. "I honestly don't know what I'm doing in this cruiseur right now. Or why I'm even going. To arrest her? To talk to her? To ask her why she lied to me my entire life? Making me think she loved me, when really she was just gathering intel on the Patriarche for the Vangarde terrorists? All I know is I need to see her. One more time."

Marcellus finally turned and looked at Chatine, acknowledging her presence for the first time in what felt like hours. His lips had stopped moving but his eyes were still speaking. For some reason, Chatine felt like they were saying, *Yes, I see you. I know you're there. Thank you for listening.*

And then, as the cruiseur continued to skim above the frozen ground below, all Chatine could think was:

Maybe I'm better at this than I thought.

- CHAPTER 28 -
ALOUETTE

ALOUETTE STARED UP AT THE SHAFT OF GLOWING
light, utterly mesmerized. She had never seen anything so bright, so
green, so out of place in the dark Refuge. The light fanned outward
from the candlestick, forming a small, ghostly sphere that seemed
to float in the center of the room.

It was a hologram. Alouette was certain. She'd never seen one,
but Sister Denise had told her about them. "They use light beams to
project a three-dimensional image so real, you almost feel as though
you could reach out and touch it."

Alouette now watched as the sphere began to spin. She held tight
to the candlestick, too enthralled to let go. The sphere kept turning,
becoming more defined with each rotation, until Alouette could see
that its surface was a mass of swirling clouds.

"Laterre," she whispered.

It was. It had to be. She'd seen pictures in Principale Francine's
old science books. They were images taken from deep space, when the
probes from the Human Conservation Commission had first discovered the planet all those years ago. Images that looked just like this.

The sphere began to expand further, as if Alouette were zooming in, descending toward the planet from outer space. The clouds cleared and suddenly Alouette could see the long, jagged outline of Laterre's single landmass, surrounded by ocean on all sides.

Sister Denise had been right. It was as if you could really touch the hologram. So much so that Alouette felt herself releasing the candlestick at one end and reaching out. As her fingers entered the green light, the image of the globe trembled, seeming to react to her touch.

She brushed her fingertips against the image and, even though it felt like she was brushing nothing but air, the sphere responded. It *moved.* With each drag of her finger, Laterre turned on its axis. She pushed it around and around, watching the landmass of Laterre disappear and then reappear again as the globe revolved.

Alouette withdrew her finger, letting the sphere slow to a halt. Then she poked at the giant landmass and suddenly she was zooming in again as the hologram image expanded further. She could soon make out the Terrain Perdu, the huge uninhabited area at the center of Laterre, with its barren plateaus and harsh, craggy valleys. She'd only ever seen the Terrain Perdu depicted on the maps and diagrams hand-drawn into the Chronicles. But now, on the hologram, it seemed so real. So alive. So true.

At the eastern end of the map, where the Terrain Perdu tapered away, she could see a cluster of lights. It had to be Montfer, the biggest mining town on Laterre.

Alouette swiped her finger across the hologram and the landmass swung westward, back across the vast Terrain Perdu, until she saw another, much bigger cluster of lights. This was Vallonay. The capital. Where she lived.

Under which she lived.

She prodded at the image. And, as the hologram zoomed in again, Alouette could see a vast patchwork of fermes, hothouses, and fabriques, with the outline of the Frets at the center. Three rows of old freightships forming a perfect heptagon around the Marsh. To the northeast of the Frets, standing so proud and decadent on the hill, was the half-moon shape of Ledôme.

She traced her fingers this way and that, looking closely at everything. Alouette found herself wondering what it would be like to be out there, seeing all those things in person. Touching them. Smelling them. Hearing the sounds. Going above-ground yesterday had given her a small taste. It had shown her that, even in the rusting and moldy Frets, there was so much *more* light and air than down here in the Refuge. She could only imagine how much light, how much air, how much color, how much sky there would be outside the Frets.

Then, as if the hologram were interrupting her thoughts, demanding her attention back, a red dot suddenly appeared on the map, close to Vallonay. Surprised, Alouette reached out and touched it, causing the hologram to immediately magnify. Alouette squinted at the fast-moving images. The dot was blinking just south of the city, in the dense forest that stretched onward and outward for kilomètres and kilomètres.

"Forest Verdure," she whispered, recalling the name from her lessons.

She prodded the hologram again and it whooshed in even closer. Now she could see a small lake right where Vallonay's ferme-land ended and the Forest Verdure began. And from the lake she could see a winding stream snaking into the trees and leading to a clearing. Alouette prompted the hologram to zoom in closer. The image soon became blurry, but she could just make out what looked like a group of tiny huts in the center of the clearing. Twelve small shelters that formed a perfect circle just to the north of where the red dot was blinking.

She scrolled downward, pulling the dot into the center of the map, until she could see another smaller clearing, this one with a collection of curious shadowy patterns scattered across the forest floor. The red dot pulsed and glowed furiously among these mysterious shapes, as though it were trying to tell Alouette something. Trying to point something out to her.

Alouette tried to zoom in again, but the image only got blurrier.

"What?" she whispered to the hologram. "What are these shapes?"

But just then, Alouette heard the patter of footsteps in the hallway outside her father's room. Panicked, she shoved the two ends of the candlestick back together. The green glow of the hologram, the vivid images of trees, the flashing red light—all disappeared in a heartbeat.

Gone. Vanished.

The footsteps were loud now, getting closer by the second. Alouette dropped the candlestick into the valise and snapped the lid closed. Then she shot over to the closet, hoisted herself onto the chair, and jammed the case back onto the top shelf.

Just as she was stepping down from the chair, the door to her father's room squeaked open and Alouette's gaze darted up.

It wasn't her father.

It was Sister Denise.

"Sister Laurel asked me to come find you," the sister said.

Her dark eyes scanned the room and Alouette panicked. How much had Denise seen?

The sister rubbed at her temple, near the scars where her cyborg circuitry had once been, and said in her precise monotone, "Tranquil Forme is starting now."

Alouette let out a small breath, remembering that Denise was way more interested in her gadgets than she was in the behaviors of other people.

"I'm coming," Alouette said.

Denise turned and disappeared down the hallway. Alouette picked up Katrina from where she'd dropped her earlier. She wanted so badly to take the doll with her. To hold it close to her at night like she'd done when she was a child. But if her father saw her with the doll, he would know that she'd been in his room.

So she returned Katrina to the cupboard in the nightstand, crept out of the room, and followed Sister Denise down the hallway, past the kitchen and the dining room, and into the common room. All the while, though, her mind was still back in her father's room. Bathed in the glow of that hologram. Staring at that little red dot blinking among the trees. Wondering what was hiding there.

- CHAPTER 29 -
CHATINE

"SO A BASHER IS A POLICIER DROID, A FRITZER IS A cyborg, and a cav is a dead body?"

Chatine rolled her eyes but offered Marcellus an enthusiastic "Yes! Exactly!" Or as enthusiastic as Chatine allowed herself to get. She was really getting tired of this game. And Marcellus's constant need for her to validate his efforts. He acted like being able to name Third Estate slang was the equivalent of *being* in the Third Estate. As though he were now one of them, which he certainly was not. Until that boy had a tracking device implanted in his arm, was forced to live in filth and squalor, and had to survive off stewed turnips and chou bread for a year, he would *not* know what it was like to be her. Plus, she hated the way he pronounced "basher." Like it was a fancy cream sauce dish served in the banquet hall of the Grand Palais, and not a terrifying three-mètre-high droid ready to suck the sensation right out of your limbs.

"This is great!" Marcellus said, bouncing a little on his toes as they walked. The cruiseur had dropped them at a station just outside of the Bidon, the area of Montfer where most of the Third Estate lived. "I'm learning so much. Tell me more. Like what do you call the Frets?"

"The Frets," Chatine replied flatly.

"Okay. What about Ledôme?"

"Ledôme."

"Gâteau?"

Chatine stopped walking and stared at him. "Seriously? Gâteau?"

"What?" Marcellus asked.

"You think we have a slang for gâteau? We don't even have real bread."

Marcellus bowed his head sheepishly. "Right. Sorry."

"Why don't we talk about *your* slang for a while?"

"We don't have any slang."

"Really? What about 'déchets'?"

Marcellus sucked in a breath, looking stung. "I've never used that term for a Third Estater. I swear."

"Whatever." Chatine continued walking briskly toward town.

When they arrived a few minutes later, Marcellus's reaction to the Bidon was immediate. Chatine watched him take in the collection of hovels built from scraps of metal with a mix of shock and sadness. She felt somewhat satisfied by his expression, as though she'd made her point.

"First time in Montfer?" she asked, mimicking the amused tone he'd used when responding to her reaction to the cruiseur.

He opened his mouth to say something but only a strangled stutter came out.

"Let me guess," Chatine responded for him. "You've been here but never to the Bidon slums. You spent your time touring the exploit, observing the workers, but you never followed them home to where they live. Instead *you* went back to the cushy Second Estate quartier on the *other* side of the wall."

Chatine could tell from his continued silence that she was right. And it made her even more annoyed than she had been before.

Montfer was home to the largest iron exploits on Laterre. Unfortunately, however, when the Ministère had started bringing workers out here to mine the ore and process it, they'd conveniently forgotten to bring materials to house them. So the workers were forced to make do with what they could find. Anything that came from the nearby fabriques that wasn't sent to Vallonay was collected and turned into makeshift housing.

"C'mon," she grumbled. "This way."

Marcellus followed silently behind her, and Chatine was grateful that at least his relentless questions about Third Estate jargon had ceased. He said nothing as they walked down an alleyway that led through countless metal huts. Chatine thought the Frets were pitiful, but she'd clearly forgotten just how awful the Montfer shacks were too. Their roofs, pockmarked with holes, sagged in the middle, and their ribbed and rusting walls leaned at strange angles. It was as if each shack was being sucked into the mud upon which it was haphazardly built. A river of something liquid and stinking ran through the center of the alleyway, and Chatine had to hop from side to side to avoid getting the worst of it on her boots.

But worse than the metal hovels were the people who lived inside of them. Desperate eyes watched them silently as they passed. Dirty, chapped hands extended toward them, begging for something—anything—that would keep away the chill and the hunger.

Same thing, different place, Chatine thought.

"Where are we going?" Marcellus whispered, staying close on Chatine's heels.

"The Jondrette," Chatine replied, pointing up ahead.

"What's that?"

"It's my . . ." She felt herself choke over the word. Chatine cleared her throat. "It's an inn. We can ask about Mabelle there. If she lives around here, someone at the Jondrette will know her."

"What kind of inn?"

"It was originally built to house the Ministère officials who came to Montfer to visit the exploits," Chatine explained. "So it's one of the sturdier buildings around here. That was before your friends in the Second Estate decided to construct a wall straight through the middle of Montfer and live in their cushy quartier on the other side of it, away from the riffraff."

"How do you know all of that?"

Chatine shrugged. "Everyone around here knows that."

The truth was, it was the Renards—her parents—who had recognized the empty building's potential and converted it into an inn. A place where the locals could drown their troubles—and themselves—in her father's homemade weed wine.

As they wound through the familiar pathways and passages, getting closer and closer to the building that lay at the east end of the Bidon, Chatine felt her body caving in on itself. As though her very flesh were trying to protect her from what was about to come.

Once they'd cleared the last alleyway and the rusting structure came into view, the reaction was worse than Chatine had expected. Her knees wobbled, and she felt as though she might collapse under the weight of the pain. She forced herself to keep moving, keep walking. She didn't want Marcellus to see the effect this building was having on her. But with every step she took, a new memory—a new ghost—jumped out to attack her.

Henri learning to crawl on the dirt patch out back.

Henri crying quietly in the middle of the night and six-year-old Chatine running to his crib to comfort him before their parents woke up.

Henri giggling when she kissed the small birthmark, shaped like a raindrop, on his shoulder.

Henri sitting on her lap on the metal swing that hung from the roof.

Her gaze fell upon that same roof, and suddenly she could hear him laughing. Giggling into her ear as she held him on her lap and pumped her legs, making the swing go higher and higher. There was no swing there now. Just bits of rope dangling down like abandoned nooses.

And then, all she could hear was the silence.

The silence that had hit her like a speeding cruiseur the moment she'd walked into the inn to find him gone. Her mother had sent her into town to buy vegetables, and when she'd returned, less than two hours later, she'd known in her gut that something was wrong. Something had happened.

"Where's Henri?" she'd asked her mother, running from room to room, listening for his little coos of laughter.

Her mother had been stirring a pot of stew in the kitchen. She didn't answer. Chatine searched the town, the streets, the alley behind the inn, all the while relentlessly asking, "Where is he? Where's Henri?"

Finally, a day later, her mother responded. Chatine could still remember the callous way she'd flicked her free hand, as though swatting away a gnat. "The little clochard killed him. Madeline. She dropped him on his head. We sent his body to the morgue."

That's when Chatine's whole world had imploded, like a dying star. To this day, she could still hear his soft coos and hushed sobs almost everywhere she went.

He had always been a quiet baby. Even when he'd cried, it was never loudly. It was as though he'd known, at less than a year old, that he couldn't be a burden. He had to be a good little boy so that his parents wouldn't cast him out on the street the way so many parents did when they couldn't afford to feed their children.

And yet, despite his efforts, he'd died anyway.

"Are you okay?" Marcellus broke into her thoughts, and it was only then Chatine realized she'd stopped walking. She was now just standing in front of the inn, staring at it like she was staring down an army of bashers. She touched her cheeks, and her fingertips came back wet. They felt like the exact same tears that had stung her eyes twelve years ago as she'd run to the Med Center, as she'd burst into the morgue, as she'd searched the countless gurneys for a tiny body. As she'd finally realized she was too late. It had already been disposed of. Little Henri was already minuscule slivers of ice, melting into a pit in the ground.

Chatine sniffled and wiped hastily at her cheeks. "Yes. I'm fine," she insisted. Even though she knew it was one of the biggest lies she'd ever told. She would never be fine when it came to Henri. She would never forgive that girl, Madeline. For as long as she lived.

A few weeks after Madeline had left the inn, Inspecteur Limier had shown up at their door, offering a hefty reward for the man who took her. Twenty thousand tokens. That's when Chatine had learned that he was actually an escaped convict, wanted and highly dangerous. This information had comforted Chatine. She'd felt consoled in her grief knowing that with a reward like that on his head, the white-haired man would inevitably be caught and sent back to Bastille, and Madeline would be all alone. Exactly as she deserved to be.

"So, are we going in?" Marcellus asked.

Chatine blinked rapidly, trying to dispel the phantoms from her vision.

She turned and scrutinized Marcellus, looking him up and down, taking in his crisp white shirt, pressed white pants, and the titan, Sol-shaped buttons running down the front of his jacket, marking him as an officer of the Ministère.

"What?" Marcellus asked, looking self-conscious as he patted down his shiny hair.

Chatine sighed. This was going to be a lot more work than she'd thought. "You're not going anywhere looking like that."

- CHAPTER 30 -
MARCELLUS

"IS THIS REALLY NECESSARY?" MARCELLUS LOOKED and felt ridiculous.

They were standing behind a decaying building that Théo had called an "inn." The boy had managed to scrounge up an old tarp, which he'd fashioned into a cape-like garment and tossed over Marcellus's head. He'd also rubbed mud onto Marcellus's boots, the sleeves of his coat, and the bottoms of his pant legs. Any part of his uniform that was still visible was now caked in dirt. Marcellus had half a mind to think this had nothing to do with making him "blend in," as the boy had insisted, but was more about seizing the rare opportunity to humiliate and disgrace him.

"This is an exploit town," the boy explained. "The people are harder here. Montfer is not like the Frets of Vallonay. They don't like the Second Estate here."

Marcellus scoffed. "They don't like the Second Estate in the Frets, either."

"True. But this is different. The people here, they're not afraid of fli—I mean, Ministère officers."

"It's okay. You can say 'flic' now. I know what it means." Marcellus flashed Théo a proud smile.

Théo looked like he wanted to punch Marcellus in the face.

"Anyway," the boy went on, "these people grew up inside dark tunnels and haunted exploits. You won't be able to terrorize them into talking, the way you do back in—"

"Hold on a minute. The exploits are not *haunted*."

Théo shot him a look. "Have you ever spent thirty hours straight in total darkness with only the sound of your own breathing to keep you company?"

"No."

"Then you don't know."

Marcellus schooled his expression. "Fair enough."

"Just . . ." Théo seemed to be struggling for the right directive. "Just . . . don't talk. Okay? Let me do the talking."

Marcellus opened his mouth to ask a question, but Théo cut him off. "And whatever you do, don't say 'basher.'"

Marcellus's brow crumpled. "Why not?"

"Because you say it wrong!"

"Bash-*er*," Marcellus tried. "*Bah*-shur. Ba-sher. Baaaa—"

"Stop! Just don't say anything at all. Don't do anything. Don't look at anyone. Just stand there and don't talk. To anyone."

Marcellus stood up straighter, pushing back his shoulders the way his grandfather had taught him to do since he was a child.

"No," Théo said. "Don't stand like *that*. You're poor and hungry and have lost all hope in life. Slouch!"

Marcellus tried to slouch, caving his belly in and tilting his body to the side. He felt as though he might fall over.

The boy gave him another once-over, and Marcellus could swear he saw the hint of a smile on his face. But he also knew he couldn't argue with the kid. Théo seemed to know what he was talking about. He seemed to know this town like he'd promised he did. Plus, this place—this metal-hut city—unsettled Marcellus. It was worse than anything he'd seen in the Frets. And he hadn't thought that was possible. Did his grandfather even know how bad things had gotten out here in Montfer?

"You're still too clean," Théo said, stepping back to study Marcellus's features.

Marcellus glanced down and spread out his arms, causing his tarp to rustle in the faint wind. "Huh?"

"Your face. And hair. They're not dirty enough. No one will ever believe you're Third Estate with that glossy hair and perfect skin."

Marcellus cringed, knowing what was coming next. And he was right. He watched as Théo bent down and dragged his fingers through the wet dirt. Marcellus closed his eyes as the boy streaked mud right across his forehead and cheeks.

What would his grandfather say if he could see him now? Standing there, letting a Fret rat literally cover him in dirt? He didn't even want to let his mind go there.

When he finally opened his eyes, Marcellus flinched. The boy's face was so close to his own. Closer than he had ever been. And his eyes were so . . .

Marcellus couldn't put his finger on it.

There was something about that boy's gray eyes. Something that wasn't quite right. For just a flicker of a moment, they weren't the eyes of a hardened boy from the streets of Vallonay. They were soft, tender, curious. It was almost as though . . .

What? Marcellus thought.

But again, he couldn't quite figure it out.

Théo quickly blinked and looked away, as though he'd been caught doing something he shouldn't. Marcellus felt the urge to check his pockets to make sure the boy hadn't robbed him while he'd stood there with his eyes foolishly closed. As the boy stepped back, Marcellus could swear he saw the faintest hint of pink peeking out from behind the dirt streaked on Théo's cheeks.

Was he *blushing*?

But before Marcellus could get a closer look, the boy turned and mumbled, "Okay, you're ready now. Let's go." He walked briskly toward the inn, as though he were desperate to get away from Marcellus.

A few moments later, Marcellus stood frozen in the doorway of the Jondrette.

The inn was jammed full of people, most of them standing or leaning over a long, rusted bar where two men poured dark, syrupy liquid into glasses. On a table near the bar, a woman danced in strange pointy-heeled shoes, while a child sucked on a chicken bone. Atop another table, an old man slept and drooled, despite the noise around him. Laughter, shouting, the clink of glasses, dancing feet, the whine and squeak of a stringed instrument from a distant room, and the rumble of fists as patrons demanded more drinks.

Marcellus blinked out of his trance, reminding himself that he had to blend in, just like Théo had told him. If he stood there staring like an imbécile, everyone here would know he didn't belong. But Théo didn't move either. The boy's face was blank, his mouth agape, his gaze transfixed on something in the corner of the room. But when Marcellus turned his own focus in the direction of the boy's stare, he found just an empty corner, as though the boy were looking at a ghost.

"Are you—are you okay?" Marcellus mumbled as he gently placed a hand on Théo's shoulder.

The boy startled at the touch and quickly brushed him off. "Yes. I'm fine. Give me something valuable."

Marcellus blinked, certain he'd misheard. "Excuse me?"

Théo sighed. "You really are ignorant. That's how you get information around here. No one gives anything away for free."

"Oh," Marcellus replied, feeling stupide once again as he searched around in his pockets, coming up empty-handed. "Um, I don't—"

"Your titan buttons," Théo prompted.

What? He wanted the buttons from his uniform?

The boy gave him a pointed look. Marcellus relented, reaching under his makeshift cape and pulling off one of the titan Sols from his jacket.

He dropped it into the boy's hand.

"Seriously?" Théo asked. "I thought you wanted to actually *know* where this Mabelle person is."

"I do," Marcellus replied, confused.

"Then you're going to have to do better than this."

"Fine." Marcellus reached back under his tarp and began to twist the next button on his jacket, waiting for the thread to snap. But apparently he was taking too long, because a moment later the boy huffed, shoved Marcellus's hand aside, and roughly ripped the remaining titan Sols from his uniform one by one.

Marcellus crossed his arms protectively over his chest. "Are you done?"

Théo seemed to study him for a long moment before finally taking off toward the bar. "Wait here," he called over his shoulder.

Marcellus watched the boy approach a lanky man with a ragged beard standing behind the counter. Théo whispered something inaudible to him. The man shook his head and gave Théo an unrelenting look. Théo whispered something else, but still the man's expression didn't change.

"He's refusing to talk," Théo said a moment later, returning to Marcellus. The boy's eyes raked over Marcellus's body. "What else do you have to give him?"

"Nothing. I gave you everything I have. I swear."

"What about that?" Théo asked, jutting his chin toward Marcellus's right hand. Marcellus looked down.

"No," he said, twisting the ring on his finger. "Not that."

Théo sighed. "Okay, then what?"

Dread sank into the pit of Marcellus's stomach. "I—I don't know."

Was that it? Had they come all this way for nothing? Surely there was something he could do. Somewhere else to try. Marcellus glanced up at the bearded man behind the counter. Perhaps he simply didn't know anything. Or perhaps . . .

"Tell him Marcellou wants to see Mabelle." Marcellus blurted the words out before he could stop himself.

Théo shot him a baffled look. "Marce—*what*?"

"Marce*llou*," he repeated. The nickname made him feel exposed and slightly sick, but he knew it was the only card he had left to play.

Théo shrugged and returned to the counter. Marcellus watched Théo whisper to the man, evidently repeating the nickname. Then, a moment later, the man beckoned Théo into a back room, looking over both shoulders before they disappeared behind a door on a faulty hinge.

Marcellus glanced uneasily around before finally finding a chair to sit on. When he lowered himself down, the old material squeaked and whined so loudly, every pair of eyes in the inn turned to glare at him. Marcellus flashed a smile and gave a little wave as he leaned back, trying to get more comfortable. But every move only made the chair groan louder. Finally, Marcellus decided just to stay standing. Keeping his eyes glued to the door behind the bar, he anxiously waited for Théo to return with information so they could get out of this Sol-forsaken place. But the longer Théo stayed on the other side of that door, the more Marcellus started to wonder if something had gone wrong.

Or, if something had gone very, very right.

For *Théo*.

Marcellus's cheeks heated with shame and frustration as he soon realized what had just happened.

The boy had conned him.

Again.

Théo was not coming back. He'd taken the titan buttons and made a run for it. The whole thing had been a ruse! He'd probably whispered nonsense into the man's ear, or even offered him a cut if he played along. All that friendly banter in the cruiseur and on the walk here had just been part of the con. They hadn't been *bonding*, like Marcellus had thought. Théo had been winding him up, preparing to make his play. He had no intention of helping Marcellus. He clearly just wanted to rob him.

Marcellus should have known better than to put his faith in a member of the Third Estate. Inspecteur Limier would never do that. Commandeur Vernay would certainly never have done that.

And now he was alone. A Ministère officer in an exploit town with no guide and no plan. How would he ever find Mabelle now?

"Hey! You! Boy!" Marcellus swiveled his head until he was looking into the eyes of a squat, wrinkly faced man who barely came up to his shoulder. Marcellus recognized him as the old man who was asleep on the table just a moment ago. His lips were painfully chapped, and a dark rust color stained his clothes. Marcellus could smell something sharp and bitter on his breath.

The man was waving a hand in Marcellus's face, but Marcellus wasn't sure how to respond. Théo had warned him not to speak. And despite everything that had just happened, he did agree this was good advice.

"Hey!" The man staggered slightly, the constant waving knocking him off balance. "Why don't you be a nice boy and buy an old man a drink?"

Marcellus smiled and shook his head, hoping the man would take the hint and leave. But Marcellus's dismissal only seemed to anger him.

"Whassa matter?" the man slurred loudly. "You too good for thisssplace? I can see it in yourreyes. You don' belong heeere!"

At these words, everyone in the inn seemed to turn at once, as though looking to confirm the man's accusations. Marcellus felt his throat go dry. There were too many eyes on him. And far too much distrust in those eyes. His gaze flickered to the door as he calculated just how fast he could get there without drawing even more attention to himself.

"Answer me, you worthless piece of—" The old man started to tip forward, and Marcellus put up his hands to stop the man from crashing right into him. But the drunk clearly interpreted this as an act of aggression. He jerked upright, swinging his arms violently. "Don't you push me, monsieur!"

Marcellus ducked to avoid being clocked in the face. The man stumbled from the missed punch and started to go down. His hands grappled the air, searching for something to stop his fall. They soon found the edge of Marcellus's tarp.

Suddenly, every single sound inside the noisy inn seemed to cease, and all Marcellus could hear was the ripping of fabric. The tearing of seams.

The man hit the floor with a crash, and as Marcellus glanced down, he saw white.

Dazzling white.

His Ministère uniform was exposed for the whole inn to see.

But it wasn't until six large men pushed back their chairs and started walking his way that Marcellus fully began to understand what Théo had meant about the dark, haunted people of Montfer.

And their hatred of the Second Estate.

- CHAPTER 31 -
CHATINE

WHEN CHATINE HEARD THE COMMOTION THROUGH the rickety door of the Jondrette's kitchen, she knew what she'd find on the other side before she even emerged. She would have been annoyed that the stupid pomp hadn't followed her directions and just lain low, if her heart hadn't leapt into her throat at the sight of him.

He was surrounded by six huge men. Exploit workers, Chatine could tell from the goggles hanging around their necks. The punches came at Marcellus from all angles. His fists swung wildly. Desperately. But nothing connected. There were simply too many of them to fight off, and as soon as he would turn in one direction, he'd be hit from another. His efforts were so futile, it almost looked like *he* was the drunk one of the group.

Chatine noticed a Ministère-issued rayonette on the floor, obviously kicked away the moment Marcellus had tried to use it.

One of the men landed a blow in the center of Marcellus's back, and Marcellus went down hard. Almost instantly after hitting the ground, he tucked himself into a tiny ball and covered his head with his hands. His body curled in on itself while the half-dozen men took turns kicking him in the back, ribs, and side.

Chatine had broken up her fair share of fights before. But this was different. Marcellus wasn't even *in* the fight anymore. He'd given up trying to punch back or kick back or defend himself at all. He was just huddling there, as though waiting for it to end. It was almost as though he'd been through this before. He was accustomed to being in that very position. His body knew exactly what to do.

Chatine desperately tried to figure out how to break up the attack without looking like she was coming to the rescue of a Ministère officer—an offense that would surely get her a few kicks in the ribs as well.

She pulled the seven remaining titan buttons from her pocket and stared down at them in her palm. The truth was that just one had been enough to buy the information they'd needed. And she knew that. But she also knew she wasn't going to pass up an opportunity to take that pomp for all he was worth.

She sighed and tossed the seven pieces onto the front porch of the inn. Then, she shouted the magic word that could bring any Third Estate brawl to a standstill. Sols, it could probably break up an entire revolution. "TITAN!"

The men stopped their assault and looked over at her. She pointed out the door and then pretended to lunge for the buttons. The men, as expected, were faster. They abandoned Marcellus, all diving for the shiny metal.

Chatine pivoted, dodging the men and running toward Marcellus instead. Knowing there wouldn't be much time before the titan was gone, Chatine fell to her knees next to Marcellus. There was no blood on his face and he appeared to be breathing. But he wasn't moving. He gazed, with numb and empty eyes, at his knees. "Marcellus, get up! Get up now!" Chatine yelled as she took hold of his shoulder and tried to shake him out of his stupor. "We have to leave!"

But Marcellus just curled himself tighter into his ball.

"NO!" Chatine shouted. "YOU HAVE TO GET UP NOW!"

Marcellus still wouldn't budge. Chatine glanced up, scanning the nearby tables before finding a tin of half-finished weed wine. She grabbed it and doused the side of Marcellus's face in the dark liquid. That did the trick. He startled and lifted his head.

"Marcellus," she urged. "C'mon. Those guys will be back any second. We need to get you out of here."

He appeared confused at the sight of her. "You came back?" he murmured.

"Yes. I'm here. C'mon. Get up." She maneuvered into a squat and scooted an arm under his back. "Are you ready? I'm going to help you up now."

"You came back," Marcellus murmured again, his voice dazed and dreamy.

"On the count of three, okay?"

"I didn't think you were coming back."

"One, two, three!" Chatine pushed down with her heels and heaved up. At first, Marcellus was like deadweight in her arms. But a second later, he seemed to catch on to what was happening and started to stand up. Chatine gave one final push to help him onto his feet, but the effort caused her hood to fall back, revealing the dirty brown knot of hair at the base of her neck.

She released Marcellus, grabbing for the hood and yanking it back over her head. Marcellus stumbled a bit but steadied himself on a nearby chair. She snuck a glance over at him. He was looking back at her strangely, his head cocked to the side as though he were trying to puzzle something out.

Did he see? Chatine wondered in panic.

Does he know?

Footsteps broke into Chatine's thoughts. She looked up to see the men trampling back through the front door. They froze when they saw Marcellus on his feet. Chatine reacted on impulse. Knowing they couldn't escape through the front door, she grabbed Marcellus by the hand and pulled him toward the kitchen. "Let's go!"

Marcellus stumbled behind her as she led him through the kitchen and out the back door. When they spilled out into the alleyway, she could hear the voices of the men following them. She yanked on Marcellus's hand, urging him to run faster. He seemed to finally find his legs and picked up the pace. Chatine guided him down a row of metal huts, dodging between them in hopes of losing their pursuers.

When Chatine was certain the men were no longer behind them, she dropped Marcellus's hand and slowed to catch her breath. With her hands on her knees, she sucked in lungfuls of air until she finally had enough to speak. "What on Laterre were you thinking? I told you not to do *anything* or talk to *anyone*!"

Marcellus wouldn't meet her eye as he, too, struggled to catch his breath. He glanced sheepishly at the ground. "I thought . . ." His voice dropped as he finished the sentence. "I thought you left."

For a moment, Chatine wondered if Marcellus distrusted her as much as she distrusted him. It suddenly made her respect him just the slightest bit more. "I told you I was going to find out about Mabelle, and I did."

His eyes widened. "You did?"

"Well, your little code word helped."

"Code word?"

"'Marcellou,'" she said, raising her eyebrows mockingly. "That seemed to do the trick. Apparently she's been expecting you."

"What? Where is she? What does she want?"

Chatine chuckled. "Slow down. We're meeting her in the Tourbay."

"The Tourbay? What's that?"

"The boglands. Just outside the city. This way."

She turned and continued walking. Marcellus jogged to catch up with her, his eyes alight with something Chatine couldn't quite pin-point. He fell into step beside her, and they walked in silence until they were out of the Bidon and the sad metal shacks were behind them.

As they traveled farther away from the city, the ground beneath their feet turned even softer and muddier. The mist grew thicker, swirling around them until it felt like they were walking through a wall of white clouds. Chatine admitted it was a good place for a member of the Vangarde to hide, Laterre's climate offering a natural disguise.

Within minutes, the mist was so thick that Chatine lost Marcellus in the haze. She stopped and spun in a circle, calling out for him. Then, a moment later, she heard him smacking his lips together as though he were trying to taste the mist. She rolled her eyes and moved toward the sound.

"What is this stuff?" he asked with an air of disgust.

She stepped through a pocket of fog and suddenly he was right there, standing only a few millimètres away from her. She immediately jumped back.

"It's called fog," she said impatiently.

"I know *that*," he said, flicking his tongue out to lick his lips. "I mean that stuff you poured on me in the inn. I can still taste it."

"It's weed wine."

"That's weed wine? Ugh. It's disgusting. People actually drink this?"

Chatine fought back the urge to lash out at him again with some-thing like, *Not all of us can afford to drink sparkling titan.* But instead she gritted her teeth and replied, "Yes. Some people do. I personally don't have a taste for it."

Marcellus chuckled. "Well, that's not surprising."

"Why not?"

He shrugged. "Because you're not like the rest of the Third Estate."

"Yes, I am."

"No, you're not. You're different." Then, upon seeing the sour expression on Chatine's face, he hastily added, "In a good way."

Chatine felt her cheeks start to burn. She quickly turned back toward the fog so that Marcellus couldn't see the faint smile that was spreading across her face.

"I'm not that different," she muttered. But it was quiet, barely a whisper in the thick white mist. Because the truth was, she didn't actually want Marcellus to hear.

CHAPTER 32

MARCELLUS

MARCELLUS DID *NOT* LIKE THE TOURBAY. THE boglands were wet and swampy and full of bugs. And the farther they walked into the mist, the less like an officer he felt.

What was he doing out here?

Why had he come?

And what on Laterre was he going to do when they finally found Mabelle?

This was a question he still didn't have an answer to. But he needed to find one. Quick.

His allegiance to the Ministère and his duties dictated that he should arrest her at once. She was an escaped convict. A Vangarde spy. And a possible accomplice in the murder of Marie Paresse. Yet there was something in his gut telling him he would never be able to do that. How could he possibly arrest the woman who'd raised him? Who'd loved him and cuddled him when he cried and whispered sweet lullabies into his ear when he couldn't sleep?

Marcellus gritted his teeth, reminding himself that *that* woman was an illusion. A lie. Another traitor trespassing in his life. The Mabelle from his memories didn't really exist. The real Mabelle was nothing like the one he remembered. The real Mabelle was a dangerous terrorist who *must* be captured at once and sent back to Bastille, where she belonged.

"So do you know exactly *where* we're supposed to meet her?" Marcellus asked, stepping around a patch of reeds onto what looked like a solid piece of ground. But his foot sank straight into yet another hidden puddle. This time the water came up to his knee.

That was another thing he didn't like about the Tourbay.

Marcellus's boots and half of his pants were soaked through. No matter where he stepped, the dirt seemed to disappear beneath his feet, plunging him into muddy water.

"Will you stop walking *in* the puddles?" Théo reprimanded him.

"How?" Marcellus asked helplessly. "They're everywhere."

The boy sighed. "Walk *on* the reeds. Not around them."

"Oh." Marcellus glanced at the small outcroppings of tall grass. He'd been purposefully trying to avoid them. He scooted toward the closest one and tested Théo's directions—extending his foot lightly and tapping on the ground. It held. He didn't sink. He jumped onto the dirt patch and looked up with a beaming smile, proud of his accomplishment.

But the smile dropped from his face when he saw the boy was smirking at him. "Hey," he said defensively. "I grew up in a palais, where the ground was solid."

"Oh, yeah, I feel so bad for you," the boy deadpanned.

Marcellus immediately regretted the comment. He admitted it did sound pretty obnoxious. "Sorry, this is all new to me."

"What? Walking?"

"No, *this*. Nature. Real Laterrian landscape. Exploit towns. People living in metal tents, drinking stuff that tastes like charred PermaSteel just to escape their lives for a minute. I'm just starting to realize how much they shelter us from all of that. Or maybe it's just me who's been sheltered. I don't know."

"Once again," Théo muttered, "I feel so bad for you."

"I'm not asking for sympathy," Marcellus snapped, which seemed to take them both by surprise. He quickly composed himself. "I'm saying it's not right. Officers shouldn't be kept in the dark about this stuff. We should get to know the planet we're protecting. I'm going to be commandeur of the Ministère, for Sols' sake. I should *see* all of this."

"You've seen the Frets," Théo pointed out.

"I know. But . . ."

But what? Marcellus asked himself. What excuse could he possibly have for ignoring those horrible slums for this long? For thinking it was okay that people lived like that?

Patriarche Paresse truly believed that he and the rest of the First Estate were exalted above the rest, that their money and wealth and imperial blood made them more important. And some of that privilege trickled down to Second Estaters like Marcellus. After all, it was the Second Estate who ran the Ministère, and it was the Ministère's sole purpose to manage the Regime. Which meant managing the Third Estate. Didn't that automatically make them superior? More worthy of certain privileges?

Marcellus used to believe that. He'd been fed that idea since he was a baby—usually on a titan-plated spoon. But now . . .

Well, now he just didn't know. He didn't seem to know anything anymore.

Including how to walk.

He took a step, and his foot plunged deep into another pool of water. "Sols," he swore, lifting his leg and trying to shake off the moisture.

"But what?" Théo prompted him, and Marcellus only now noticed that the boy had stopped walking and was waiting expectantly for Marcellus to finish his former sentence. "You've seen the Frets, *but* . . . ?"

Marcellus stood with his mouth hanging open, unsure how he was going to respond. And it was pretty clear from the look on the boy's face that his answer mattered. *Really* mattered.

"But . . . ," Marcellus began hesitantly. "I guess I never really *looked* that closely before."

"Shut up," the boy snapped.

Marcellus clenched his jaw. "Listen, I'm just trying to be honest and—"

Suddenly the boy's hand clapped over Marcellus's mouth, halting his words. "No, shut *up*," he whispered. "I hear something."

Marcellus froze, listening. "I don't hear anything," he tried to say, but his words were garbled through the boy's hand.

"Shhh!" Théo whipped his head around before finally focusing on one point in the distance. Marcellus followed his gaze, trying to make out something—*anything*—but the fog was too thick. All he could see was a wall of wispy gray.

Then, suddenly, the mist started to move, undulate. Like it was no longer mist, but ocean waves, and they were standing in the eye of a great storm. Through one of the swells, Marcellus could see a figure dressed in black. It was hunched over slightly, as though carrying the weight of the planet on its back. It moved slowly through the reeds, and soon Marcellus could see it was not alone. Four more figures emerged from the fog behind it.

Marcellus heard a crack and spun to see even more people surrounding them, converging from all sides. He reached for his rayonette, only to find the holster empty. Then he remembered how one of those men from the Jondrette had kicked it out of his hand. It was still lying on the floor of the inn. His heart started to hammer in his chest as he realized what a foolish decision this was. Why hadn't be brought backup? Why had he insisted on coming here alone? He looked to the boy, who appeared surprisingly calm, despite the fact that an army seemed to be materializing out of the mist.

"What's happening?" Marcellus whispered.

But it wasn't Théo who answered.

"Marcellou. I thought I'd never see you again."

CHAPTER 33

ALOUETTE

"WHEN THE SOLS ASCEND, WE GIVE THANKS," SISTER
Laurel whispered as she moved slowly out of a deep knee bend with
her arms extended in front of her and her palms facing upward.

Alouette and the other sisters followed suit, letting out long, quiet
breaths as they moved. Sister Laurel's palms almost reached the low,
uneven ceiling of the Refuge's common room before they plunged
back down and she repeated the *Sols Ascending* sequence once again.

"We give thanks for each new day," Sister Laurel continued. "We
give thanks to the System Divine that has nurtured us and cared for
us for the past five hundred and five years. And the three Sols that
rise and set in our skies."

As Alouette moved her arms and body through the first sequence,
she tried to concentrate on her breath and on keeping her thoughts
still and calm. The ten flowing sequences of the Tranquil Forme were
meant to be performed gradually, gracefully, and with the utmost
peace and focus.

But today it seemed with each move, a new image would bubble
up and erupt onto the surface of Alouette's mind.

The dingy, rusting hallways of the Frets.

Marcellus with his penetrating hazel eyes.

The message sewn into his shirt.

Those terrible droids with their haunting metal faces.

A shadowy memory of a fugitive on the run.

A number. 2.4.6.0.1.

And then, of course, the candlestick and that mysterious glowing hologram.

Alouette could still see the image in her mind: the map of Laterre, with its curious red dot flickering and pulsing in the middle of the forest.

"And now we move into *Ghostly Stars*," Sister Laurel was saying at the front of the room. "Remember to keep your steps firm but loose."

Sister Laurel took three fluid paces forward, extending her hands in an alternating pattern. The metal name tag hanging from her devotion beads winked and flashed in the room's low light. "In this sequence we give thanks to the journey of our ancestors, who traveled far from their dying First World through endless space to establish a new life on Laterre."

Alouette tried to refocus. A good sister was a sister who performed the Tranquil Forme with attention and mindfulness. She wanted to be a good sister. She really did. She tried to imagine the huge silver ships flying through the stars at hypervoyage speed, their bellies full of people, animals, prized possessions, seedlings for crops, hidden books, and most of all, hope.

But as soon as the images of the freightships formed in Alouette's mind, they quickly morphed into the dilapidated Frets they'd now become. And then Alouette was right back where she'd started.

Thinking of Marcellus. The droids. Her father. His tattoo.

The map.

What was the red dot pointing to? Where was the map leading?

And why had her father kept it hidden inside a candlestick all these years?

"Are you with us, Little Lark?" Laurel's voice punctured her thoughts.

Alouette glanced around and noticed that the other sisters were still finishing up with *Ghostly Stars* while she was already on to sequence three, *Orbit of the Divine*. Her body was moving by itself, untethered to her mind. Exactly the way Tranquil Forme was *not* supposed to be done.

She quickly repositioned herself and took a few long, loud breaths. *Focus*, she told herself. *Slow down.*

When Alouette and the sisters were done with the *Orbit of the Divine*, they moved on to sequence four: *The Darkest Night*.

"In this sequence we acknowledge the position of Laterre within the System Divine," Sister Laurel said in her quiet tone. "We honor our current season of lowest light as Laterre orbits around the back side of Sol 1 and the light from the far-off Sols 2 and 3 become invisible at night." Laurel moved one hand up and the other across, illustrating the twenty-five-year eclipse that Laterre was now experiencing, making the nights the darkest they could ever be. "Invisible, but not forgotten," Laurel reminded them as she lowered herself down into a squat. "For just because we cannot see the Sols, it doesn't mean they are not there."

As she followed Laurel out of the crouch and looped her elbow up and over in a circling arc, Alouette's gaze caught the long, raised scar on the inside of her arm.

Once again, her mind started to drift.

Back to the hologram. Back to that map. Back to Marcellus.

How his fingertips had been searching for something that wasn't there. That hadn't been there for years. Everyone who came to live in the Refuge had their Skins removed by Sister Denise. Alouette knew, like all the sisters, that if you wanted to fulfill the Sisterhood's most sacred task of protecting the library, you could not be trackable.

"Little Lark?" Sister Laurel's voice sounded like a distant echo.

Alouette blinked, just now realizing that she had come to a complete standstill. She looked up at Sister Laurel and then around at the other sisters. They were flowing through the fifth sequence—*The Gray Cloak*—but they were looking at her too. Sister Muriel's gaze, under her snow-white eyebrows, was kind but worried. Principale Francine's stare was hard and questioning, of course. And Sister Jacqui had two darts between her eyebrows, which implied she was thinking hard about something.

"Is everything okay?" Sister Laurel asked in her sweet, unassuming tone.

Alouette nodded. "I'm fine."

But as she caught herself up in the sequence, arching her arms over her head to honor the cloud coverage that kept Laterre warm enough to inhabit, she knew without a doubt that she was not fine.

Her brain was itching with questions that everyone was refusing to answer. Even Jacqui, the one sister whom Alouette could usually count on to be forthcoming, had walked right out of Alouette's lesson earlier, refusing to say anything. Sister Jacqui had just left Alouette, babbling something about knowledge and how it's acquired.

"Perhaps knowledge is in us from the very start, but it's also out there to be found."

Alouette was *trying* to acquire knowledge. She was trying to find the answers, but it seemed as though every time she tried, she just ended up with more questions.

As the group moved into the seventh sequence—*Pushing Tides*—Alouette stole another peek at Sister Jacqui. The sister flashed her a warm smile before tipping her head back and arching her arms high above her head to mimic the motion of the Secana Sea.

Alouette felt a surge of frustration rising from her belly to her throat. But she still continued through the sequence. She still swept her arms over her head; she still dropped her head back; she still stared at the ceiling of bedrock that had housed her for the past twelve years. This cave buried deep within the stone had been the only home she could remember. But now it felt like a prison. A vault full of secrets. A locked door that Alouette simply didn't have the key to.

When the sequence came to a close and she lifted her head back up, she noticed, with surprise, that Sister Jacqui was smiling at her again. But this time, there was something mysterious in her smile. Something almost enigmatic.

Was she trying to tell her something?

Alouette glanced upward again. At the low ceiling that separated her from the above-world. And suddenly, Jacqui's words echoed through her mind in a new way. With new emphasis.

"Perhaps knowledge is in us from the very start, but it's also out there to be found."

And that's when the realization hit Alouette like a collision of planets and stars.

Out there.

By the time Sister Laurel led everyone through *Sols Descending*— the final sequence of Tranquil Forme—Alouette knew what she had to do. She understood what Sister Jacqui had been trying to tell her. The answers would never be found down here. In the Refuge. Where darkness and shadows clung to everything. Where silence was everywhere.

What she needed to find was out there.

Up there.

Waiting for her in an unknown location, marked by a blinking red dot.

CHAPTER 34

CHATINE

"MARCELLOU. I THOUGHT I'D NEVER SEE YOU AGAIN."

As the woman emerged from the mist, Chatine watched Marcellus's reaction carefully. He'd said in the cruiseur that he didn't know what he would do when he saw his former governess again, and it was clear now that he still had no idea. His body was rigid and his hands were balled into fists, as though he were physically trying to hold himself back. From what? Embracing her? Seizing her? Chatine was quite certain that even Marcellus didn't know.

"What do you want?" Marcellus said in a tight voice.

Chatine could tell he was trying to sound tough, menacing even. But she could hear right through it and she suspected the woman could too. Her weathered face, etched with crisscrossing lines, broke into a kind, almost-motherly smile, and her brown eyes twinkled. As if to say, *Oh, sweet boy. Don't be like that.*

Regardless of what he did or did not intend to do, one thing was certain: The officer was scared out of his mind. Chatine had known him less than a day, but she already knew him well enough to see that. And he had every right to be. He was in the middle of the Tourbay, completely outnumbered, with no backup.

Chatine would have felt fearful too, but she knew her tattered clothes and dirty flesh protected her. She was Third Estate. It was the one time when her lowly status had actually *helped* her.

"I just wanted to see you," Mabelle said. "I've missed your sweet face. I've missed everything about you. You've grown into such a handsome man." She was close to them now. Close enough that Marcellus could reach out and strike her if he wanted. But instead, it was the woman who extended her worn and weather-beaten hand. Not in anger, but in tenderness. She reached for Marcellus's cheek, but he ducked away before she could make contact.

Any other officer or inspecteur would have already attempted to arrest Mabelle, but Marcellus was clearly torn. Perhaps it was just the fact that she was surrounded by guards—Vangarde operatives, no doubt. And Marcellus knew it would be suicide to try anything.

Or perhaps he really did care for this woman.

Despite herself, Chatine found Marcellus's reaction to the old woman somewhat endearing.

"Well, you've seen me," Marcellus said. "I guess I'll go now." He turned to leave but Mabelle caught his arm. Marcellus winced and looked down at her grip with a pained expression.

"Marcellou," the woman said again.

"Don't call me that!" Marcellus shouted, ripping his arm away from her so brusquely, one of the guards reached for an unseen weapon in his coat. Chatine readied herself to run, but after a single nod from Mabelle, the guard relaxed. "You have no right to call me that," Marcellus went on, his shaky voice seeming to gain confidence with every word. "You betrayed me. Everything you ever told me was a lie."

"Not everything," the woman replied with a warm smile. "I never lied when I told you I loved you."

Chatine watched Marcellus's face crumple, as though *those* were the words that he was most afraid to hear. And now that she'd said them, he could no longer hold on to his anger. But he seemed to try regardless. "You never loved me."

"I did," she insisted. "And your father loved you too."

Marcellus stiffened. "My father is a traitor. And a murderer."

"Your father is innocent."

Marcellus scoffed. "Of course *you* would say that."

"I say that because it's true. He never blew up that exploit. He was framed."

"Well, that's convenient," Marcellus replied with a bitterness that Chatine had yet to hear from him. It left her with a sour feeling in her gut. "A Vangarde spy insisting that a Vangarde terrorist is innocent."

Mabelle smiled, as though she expected Marcellus to respond exactly this way. "Yes, I was a spy. But that doesn't mean I didn't still care about you. I've known you since you were six months old. After your mother died when your grandfather denounced your father—"

"For being a terrorist!"

"Your father asked me to apply for the job of your governess," Mabelle went on, undeterred.

"So that you could spy on us and the Patriarche," Marcellus interjected again.

"So that I could look *after* you," Mabelle corrected. "And yes, after your father was kicked out of the Palais, we needed someone with eyes on the inside. But also, I took the job so that I could take care of you."

"And brainwash me!"

"Marcellou," the woman said tenderly, reaching out her fingers for him, but again, he was too quick. "I never brainwashed you. I tried to teach you to be kind and respectful. I tried to teach you that everyone is equal under the Sols. That no one should be imprisoned or forced to live in squalor just because they were born on the wrong side of Ledôme walls."

Marcellus crossed his arms as though he meant to argue with that, but quickly decided against it.

"My only hope was that you would grow up to think differently. Think for *yourself.* Instead of just doing whatever your grandfather told you. I tried to give you empathy. Nothing more."

As Chatine glanced between Marcellus and the old woman, she felt some of her hard edges soften. Was that why Marcellus felt so inherently different from every other officer Chatine had ever met? Was that why he seemed to look at her like she was a person and not a piece of trash to step over?

"Have I succeeded?" Mabelle asked Marcellus, tilting her head and studying him again with that affectionate gaze that felt like a punch in the stomach for Chatine. The only person who had ever looked at Chatine with that much love was Henri.

She wondered, if her baby brother were alive today, would he still look at her like that? Somehow she doubted it. He would have been thirteen this year. Old enough to be hardened by the Frets and undermined by the Regime.

Marcellus remained silent, refusing to answer the question. Chatine had a feeling he was afraid to speak, afraid that his tenuous grasp on his toughened exterior would break the moment he opened his mouth.

But Mabelle seemed to know the answer anyway. At least her smile implied that she did. "That's why I sent for you," she explained. "Because we need you."

Chatine froze, her pulse quickening. This was the moment she'd been waiting for. This was the recruitment the general had sworn was coming.

Surreptitiously, Chatine reached into the sleeve of her coat and tapped the button to start a log on her Skin. As soon as she was back in Vallonay, she would send this entire conversation to the general.

"You need me for *what*?" Marcellus spat.

The woman glanced uneasily at Chatine. It was the first time since she and her guards had arrived that she even seemed to acknowledge Chatine's existence. As though her invisibility followed her around like a shadow. But now, Mabelle was clearly sizing her up, trying to determine if she could trust her. Apparently the answer to that question was no. Chatine tugged at the cuff of her sleeve, making sure her Skin was fully covered.

"Perhaps," Mabelle began, keeping her gaze trained on Chatine while still addressing Marcellus, "we can go somewhere private to talk?"

Marcellus followed her eyeline to Chatine. "Whatever you have to say you can say in front of him."

"Him?" Mabelle repeated curiously, and Chatine wasn't quite sure if the woman was questioning her identity or her gender. She checked the position of her hood, just to be sure. It was still firmly in place.

"Yes, *him*," Marcellus repeated, irritated. "He's my guide. I trust him, and therefore if you want to say anything to me, you have to say it here."

At these words, Chatine felt a layer of warmth fall over her, staving off the chill of the icy mist.

He trusts me. Just like the general said.

"Very well," Mabelle said, her expression turning pensive for a moment. "The truth is, your father and I planned to escape Bastille together."

"And how did you escape, by the way?" Marcellus asked, the officer in him making a sudden appearance.

Mabelle just offered him a cunning smile and continued. "But your father got sick before we could execute our plan. We knew he didn't have long. So I sent you the message through his shirt."

"*You* wrote the message?" Marcellus asked. "Not my father?"

Mabelle nodded. "I thought the nickname would be your clue. Just like when you were little. Remember the clues I used to leave around the Palais for you? Leading you to a prize?"

"This is a not a prize," Marcellus muttered.

Mabelle ignored him. "I knew, given your father's relation to the general, that his body would be brought to the Vallonay Med Center for disposal, instead of the Med Center on Bastille, and that you, as his next of kin, would be called to the morgue to authorize it. Then, I just hoped you would find the message and be able to read it."

"I couldn't read it," Marcellus said, jutting out his chin like a little kid trying to make a point.

"Have you not been practicing your letters?" Mabelle asked, and in that moment, Chatine could finally see her as a governess. Telling Marcellus when it was time to go sleep, tucking him into his soft downy bed, kissing him good night.

"No," Marcellus replied sharply. "I stopped reading and writing the day I found out what a liar you were."

Chatine knew the words were meant to penetrate, but Mabelle showed no sign of the sting. "But somehow you were able to read it," she pointed out.

"I had help."

"So, you *wanted* to see me."

"I came here to arrest you."

Mabelle chuckled tenderly, like a mother laughing at her child trying to act tough. She nodded to her security detail. The guards were still standing motionless around her, like shadows in the mist. "Well, we both know *that's* not happening."

"We *will* find you. I will report this back to my grandfather, and he will send more Policier out here. Transporteurs packed full of droids. You will be rooted out and discovered."

Mabelle shook her head. "I don't think that's going to happen."

"You don't believe they can find you?"

"I don't believe you're going to tell the general about this."

Anger flashed across Marcellus's face, and Chatine wondered if he was irritated that Mabelle would think this, or that Mabelle was right. Something told Chatine it was both.

But it didn't matter. She would report it to the general anyway. This was exactly what he'd sent her here to do. This very conversation was going to get her to Usonia.

Chatine could almost feel the Sol-light on her face already.

Mabelle took another step toward Marcellus. Chatine expected him to jump back, out of her reach, but he stayed put. "We are coming back," the woman said, her voice taking on a more formal tone. "The Vangarde will rise again. We've been biding our time, building our numbers, waiting for the right moment. And it's fast approaching."

"Well," Marcellus faltered, and Chatine could hear the doubt in his voice. "We . . . will be ready for you."

Mabelle shook her head. "Not this time. There are cells rising up everywhere. In secret. This time, we will not fail."

"When does it stop?!" Marcellus shouted, his voice trembling. "How many exploits do you have to bomb before you give up? How many innocent people have to die?"

Despite Marcellus's fury, Mabelle sighed. "You still aren't getting it, are you? The Vangarde doesn't endorse acts of unnecessary violence and murder. We just want change. We want to make Laterre a better place. A more equal place. But the First and Second Estates won't allow that. They need to keep us enslaved. Because the truth is they cannot survive without the Third Estate. In our fermes, we grow the food that they eat. In our fabriques, we manufacture the goods that furnish their manoirs. In our exploits, we mine the minerals and metals they need to live. We are more powerful than they want us to know. We are the legs on which this body stands. Without us, Laterre collapses. We are trying to give the Third Estate back their power and end this corrupt system once and for all."

Chatine glanced at Marcellus to see his eyes closed, as though he was trying to summon strength from within. "Lies," he muttered to himself. "It's all lies. You're a bunch of terrorists."

"Stop parroting every little thing your grandfather ever told you!" It was the first time Mabelle had raised her voice since she'd arrived. It caused Marcellus to flinch and snap his eyes back open. "Your mind is stronger than that. *You* have the rare ability to think for yourself. If you would just shut off General Bonnefaçon in your head for one second, you could see the truth."

The woman fell silent, letting her heavy words sink into the soft ground beneath their feet.

"And once you've seen it," she went on, her voice back to its usual gentle timbre, "then you'll come to us. Then you'll join us."

Marcellus's jaw clenched. He shook his head back and forth, back and forth, as though hoping the repetitive motion would help convince him. "I will never join you."

Chatine steeled herself, fully expecting the woman to explode again. But she didn't. Instead, she smiled another knowing smile, shot a quick, distrustful glance at Chatine, and then took a step toward Marcellus. Marcellus's whole body seemed to turn to stone as she placed a hand on either shoulder and leaned in close to him.

The woman's lips moved rapidly as she whispered something into Marcellus's ear. Panicked, Chatine strained to hear what was being said. She could not miss a single word. She could not give the general any reason to go back on his promise. She took a quiet step closer to Marcellus, but it was too late. The woman was already pulling away.

Chatine wanted to scream and kick the ground. She could tell by Marcellus's numbed expression that something important had just been conveyed. Something Chatine *needed* to know if she was ever going to fulfill her end of the deal with the general and get the fric off this planet.

Suddenly the sound of music filled the air, breaking into Chatine's thoughts.

It was faint and wispy, like a song caught in a breeze. She glanced around, trying to figure out where the sound was coming from. That's when she noticed Marcellus's face. His expression had changed. He no longer looked stunned and terrified. He now looked pained and almost wistful.

Chatine cut her gaze to the old woman. Her lips were closed but the music was definitely emanating from her. It wasn't a tune Chatine recognized, but it didn't matter. She could tell from the smile on the woman's worn and lined face, as she hummed the melody to Marcellus, that this wasn't just a song.

This was a message.

CHAPTER 35

MARCELLUS

MARCELLUS'S HANDS HADN'T STOPPED SHAKING since they'd gotten back to the cruiseur. He felt cold. So very cold. And he didn't think it had anything to do with the fact that the pants of his uniform were still damp from the Tourbay.

Théo had tried to speak to him the whole walk back to the cruiseur station—asking him questions about Mabelle, his childhood, his grandfather—but Marcellus had been unable to respond. He still couldn't bring himself to speak. Finally, the boy had given up.

The landscape outside the cruiseur was dark. Sol 1 had set, and the inky black night had begun. Twelve hours of total darkness, where no light could be seen. Having been born in the season of the Darkest Night, Marcellus had never known any other sky. Apart from the fake replica that hung inside Ledôme. He couldn't even imagine what it would be like when Laterre entered the season of the Blue Dawn and the soft azure glow of Sol 3 could be seen in the night sky.

Despite the darkness outside, Marcellus's brain was alight with confusion as they glided above the frozen ground of the Terrain Perdu, back to Vallonay. Nothing about his life—his entire existence—seemed to make sense anymore. He struggled to put his thoughts and his memories in logical order, but they kept getting scrambled up in his mind.

Mabelle had insisted that his father was innocent. That he hadn't blown up the exploit back in 488. But that was impossible! Why else had they sent him to prison? Innocent people didn't go to prison.

But then Marcellus thought about Nadette, sitting in a holding cell in the Precinct, awaiting her fate for murdering the Premier Enfant. Marcellus still wasn't certain she had anything to do with it. She had loved Marie like her own child. Was it possible Marcellus had been fooled by her, too? The same way they had all been fooled by Mabelle?

And then there was the thing Mabelle had whispered to him. Just before she started humming that vaguely familiar song. Marcellus hadn't stopped singing it to himself since they'd left the Tourbay. He knew he'd heard the song before, but where? And when? And what did it have to do with what Mabelle had said to him?

"I have proof that your father is innocent. I hid it for you in my room at the Palais before I was arrested. It's been waiting until you were ready to find it."

Marcellus's thoughts were interrupted by a loud grumbling sound, which he soon realized was coming from Théo's stomach. He suddenly felt guilty for not having offered to feed the boy before. He'd been so wrapped up in his own thoughts and insecurities, he hadn't even bothered to consider that the boy might be hungry.

No, not hungry, a voice inside his head reminded him. *Starving.*

Marcellus searched the inner compartments of the cruiseur until he found two protéine bars. He handed one to Théo and began to unwrap the second.

Théo watched Marcellus carefully, as though he'd never seen a protéine bar and didn't know what to do with it. Marcellus took a small bite of his, showing the boy that it was edible.

After that, the boy did not hesitate. In the blink of an eye, he had the wrapper off and had stuffed the entire bar into his mouth, struggling to chew.

Marcellus stared, wide-eyed, as the boy swallowed it all. He glanced down at his own bar with the dainty little bite taken out of it. "Do you want this one too?"

He'd barely even formed the question before Théo lunged forward and grabbed the bar out of his hand. He wolfed that one down in a matter of seconds as well.

"I guess you were hungry," Marcellus joked.

The boy leaned back in his seat and spread his arm over the top, looking content and much more comfortable than he had on the way out here. Now the boy really *did* look like he rode in cruiseurs all the time.

"Just out of curiosity," Théo said a moment later, "why *don't* you want to join the Vangarde?"

"Because there's nothing wrong with the Regime as it is," Marcellus replied automatically. But as soon as the words were out of his mouth, Marcellus realized they were not his own.

"Stop parroting every little thing your grandfather ever told you!"

His eyes flicked to meet Théo's, and all he could see was the boy's dirty, gaunt face and his frail frame hidden beneath layers of black fabric, endless pockets, and wire stitching. Then Marcellus remembered walking through that tent city in Montfer, seeing the way the exploit workers lived. And suddenly he felt like throwing up.

"Well," he mumbled, averting his gaze. "Even if it's not perfect. Violence is not the answer."

"Mabelle said the Vangarde doesn't endorse violence."

"She's lying," Marcellus snapped, but it was too hasty. Too angry. He tried to soften his tone. "Of course the Vangarde endorses violence. Everything they do is an act of violence. They killed six hundred workers in that exploit bombing seventeen years ago."

"She also said they didn't do that," Théo reminded him.

But Marcellus didn't need to be reminded. It was all he could think about. Mabelle's whispered words were playing on an endless loop in his mind.

"I have proof that your father is innocent."

Proof? What proof? Marcellus couldn't think of anything that would exonerate his father now, seventeen years later. Plus, anything she might have hidden in her room in the Palais would have been found by now. That room had been occupied by countless Palais servants since Mabelle's arrest. Most recently, it had been Nadette's room.

"You don't believe her?" Théo asked.

Marcellus slid his gaze to him. "What?"

"You don't believe Mabelle? When she told you that your father wasn't behind the exploit bombing?"

Marcellus blew out a burdened breath. "I don't know what to believe anymore."

And it was the truth.

Suddenly everything he thought he could stand on was being shaken loose beneath his feet, like those giant tremors that used to destroy entire cities in the First World.

"So, what if you change your mind? Did Mabelle tell you how to contact her?"

"Do you *want* me to join the Vangarde?" The question shot out of Marcellus so quickly, it seemed to startle the boy.

"I don't care," he snapped, but looked slightly caught out.

"Really?" Marcellus asked. "Because it sounds like you're trying to convince me to betray my planet."

Théo looked down, rubbing at a stain on his pant leg. "Honestly, I don't give a fric what you do."

"I think you do," Marcellus said, and the intensity in his voice caused the boy to look up again. When he did, Marcellus was right there. Leaning forward, latching on to the boy's gaze. "Tell me. Tell me honestly right now. If you could change the system—if you could bring down the Regime tomorrow—would you do it?"

The boy blinked his cat-shaped gray eyes at Marcellus, and once again, Marcellus couldn't escape the feeling that the boy was trying to tell him something.

Look at me!

See me!

Understand me!

Understand what? Marcellus tried to shout back. *I'm trying to understand you.*

He collapsed into his seat with a sigh, giving up.

"It doesn't matter what I think," the boy replied quietly a moment later.

Marcellus looked at him, surprised by the answer. "It matters to me."

Théo let out a dark, humorless laugh. "Yeah, well, you're not like most of the Second Estate."

Marcellus felt his mouth go dry. He had no idea how to respond to that. Or if he even should. But then the boy seemed to startle at something and glanced down at the inside of his left arm, looking annoyed at the interruption. Marcellus watched, intrigued, as the boy tapped his Skin a few times, dismissing whatever alert had just appeared on the screen.

"Curfew warning," the boy answered his unspoken question.

Right, Marcellus thought, feeling stupide. He glanced at the clock in the cruiseur. He'd completely forgotten about the Third Estate curfew.

"Sorry," he said. "I'll make sure you don't get in trouble."

"I'll be fine," the boy shot back.

Marcellus raised his hands in the air. "Okay."

The Skin lit up again, and the boy groaned and pressed another button. As Marcellus continued to stare at the glow of the screen implanted in the boy's arm, he couldn't help but think, again, about the girl he'd met in the Frets yesterday.

Alouette.

She should have had a Skin. But instead, she had a long, rectangular scar where a Skin used to be.

"What are you staring at?" Théo grumbled as he pulled his sleeve down.

Marcellus tore his gaze away from the boy's arm. "Nothing. I was just wondering if you'd ever met anyone who *didn't* have a Skin."

He snorted. "Yeah, you."

"No, I mean, someone who's had theirs removed?"

"Only crazy Défecteurs remove their Skins. The rest of us need ours to live."

Marcellus couldn't help but laugh. "I take it you don't like Défecteurs?"

"What's to like? They're a bunch of lazy dropouts who think they're better than the rest of us because they can live outside of the Regime and survive on love, kindness, singing songs, and eating wood chips."

"I don't think they eat wood chips."

"Whatever," Théo mumbled. "They're crazy and unpredictable. I don't like crazy and unpredictable."

"Have you ever met a Défecteur?" Marcellus asked.

Théo crossed his arms over his chest. "No, and I hope I never do."

Marcellus smirked, his brain welcoming the change of topic for a minute. "Then how do you know you don't like them?"

"I don't like them on principle."

"So, you're saying they still . . . exist?"

"Of course they exist."

"But," Marcellus began uneasily, "my grandfather rounded them up years ago."

Théo scoffed. "Wow. You *do* have a lot to learn."

Marcellus cocked his head. "What?"

The boy quickly dropped his gaze to the floor. "Nothing. Never mind."

"*Where* do they exist? Where do these people live?"

The boy shook his head. "I don't know. Like I said, I've never met one."

Marcellus leaned his head back against the seat and tried to picture Alouette's face in his mind. It was getting fainter and fainter with each passing hour. He wondered if he would ever see her again. "I met this girl," he murmured. "In the Frets yesterday. I think she might be a Défecteur, but I don't know. I just can't get her out of my head."

Marcellus expected the boy to reply to this—perhaps more bitter rantings about Défecteurs—but he was strangely quiet. "Has that ever happened to you?" Marcellus asked. "Have you ever met someone that you just couldn't stop thinking about?"

"No," Théo replied flatly.

"Really? Never?"

"Never."

Marcellus sat up, suddenly struck with an idea. "Hey, maybe you know her."

"I just told you, I don't know any Défecteurs."

"But I'm pretty sure she lives in the Frets. Alouette. Does that name sound familiar?"

"No," the boy said again.

Marcellus rubbed his chin. "It's so strange. I couldn't find her in the Communiqué."

"Why would she be in the Communiqué if she's a Défecteur?"

Marcellus shrugged. "I don't know, I just thought maybe—"

"Maybe she's lying to you. Ever think of that?" There was something so cold and biting about the boy's tone that Marcellus flinched.

"You think?"

"Probably."

"Well, how do I find out? I mean, I still don't even know where to find her or if I'll ever see her again. But what if I do? What should I say to her?"

The boy stared blankly back at him. "How should I know?"

Marcellus bit his lip, frustrated. "Okay, well, will you just let me practice for a minute?"

"Excuse me?"

"On you."

"On me?" the boy repeated, still clearly not getting what Marcellus was asking.

"Yeah, you be Alouette and I'll be me."

"No. No way."

"C'mon," Marcellus pleaded. "I need help. I don't know how to talk to girls. They don't . . . they all seem so scared of me. Or they just giggle and run away. I don't know what to say to her. Just, you know, pretend to be a girl for a minute."

"Pretend to be a girl?" Théo repeated.

"Yeah, just for a minute."

The boy sighed, relenting. "Fine."

Marcellus sat up, clearing his throat. "Okay. So, I guess I'll just start."

The boy raised his eyebrows but said nothing.

Marcellus cleared his throat again. "Um, hello, Alouette. How are you?"

"Fine," Théo mumbled. "Whatever."

"I haven't seen you in a little while. Where have you been?"

"Oh, you know, around," Théo replied stiffly.

Marcellus slouched. This was not working. "No, no, you're not doing it right."

Théo stared blankly back at him.

"You need to act more like a *girl*."

"I don't know how to act like a girl."

Marcellus sighed. "Okay, so like if I grab your hand like this . . ." He reached out and took the boy's hand in his, rubbing his thumb gently over Théo's fingers. Marcellus immediately noticed the boy's cheeks turn pink beneath the layers of grime and dirt. "Yes!" he shouted, pointing at his face. "Just like that!"

The boy looked horrified and yanked his hand away. "I don't want to do this."

"But you were starting to get the hang of it."

"I said I'm done," Théo barked with such forcefulness, it plunged them back into silence for the rest of the ride to Vallonay.

When the cruiseur docked at the station inside the Frets and the doors hissed open, the boy jumped out, looking desperate to get away from Marcellus.

"Hey!" Marcellus called after him, standing in the doorway of the cruiseur.

The boy stopped and turned around, stuffing his hands into the pockets of his coat. "What?"

Marcellus searched for the right thing to say. They'd been on quite the journey together and he had no idea how to end it. He didn't feel good about simply letting the boy walk away. He pulled out his TéléCom and tapped on the screen. "Here are the tokens I owe you. For your troubles today."

Marcellus could swear he saw sadness pass over the boy's face. But he couldn't be certain in the darkness.

The boy glanced down at his Skin, which was now glowing from the transaction. "Thanks," the boy muttered, and then started to walk off again.

"Wait!" Marcellus leapt from the door of the cruiseur and jogged to catch up to Théo. "Will you do me one more favor?"

The boy rolled his eyes. "What?"

"Will you see if you can find out anything about Alouette? Ask around, maybe find out where she lives. Anything?"

"Fine," he said, and turned his back on Marcellus, once again looking anxious to get as far away from him as possible.

"I'll see you around!" Marcellus called after him, but there was no reply. The boy was already gone, swallowed whole by the night.

CHAPTER 36

ALOUETTE

IT WAS ALREADY WELL PAST HER USUAL BEDTIME when Alouette finally closed Volume 7 of the Chronicles and carried the heavy, clothbound book back to the library shelf. As she slid it between Volumes 6 and 8, making sure the spines were all aligned, she let out a deep, anxious breath. She was really doing this. This was really happening.

She was going to leave the Refuge.

She was going to leave the Frets.

She'd been working on the plan all afternoon and evening. Grateful Silence had been easy during tonight's supper. Alouette's mind had been so preoccupied with thoughts of logistics and distances and what to bring, she'd barely made a peep through the whole meal. In fact, at one point, she got so lost in her own thoughts, she'd completely forgotten about her potato stew and Principale Francine had to nudge her to hurry *up*.

That had certainly never happened before.

The plan was to leave straight after breakfast tomorrow. The timing was perfect. The sisters would be locked away in Assemblée all morning for Quiet Contemplation while Alouette was supposed to be studying in the library. She would have plenty of time to leave the Refuge and be back for lunch without anyone knowing she'd gone.

Or so she hoped.

Alouette didn't have any tokens or a Skin, so she couldn't hire a cruiseur. Which meant she'd have to walk.

After studying the maps of Vallonay and Laterre in the Chronicles and locating the winding stream that led into the Forest Verdure, Alouette had calculated that it would take a little more than two hours to walk there and back. Which meant, if she wanted to return before lunch, she'd have less than an hour to locate the clearing where she'd seen the shadowy patterns on the hologram and find where the little red dot had been blinking.

Alouette walked back to the table in the library and studied the map she'd drawn on a small piece of paper. She hadn't dared go back into her father's room to get the candlestick, for fear of being caught. Instead, she'd copied down a sketch of Vallonay and the Forest Verdure from the Chronicle maps, making sure to include any distinguishing landmarks that might help guide her. It was rough, but it would have to do.

She closed the ink pot, folded up the piece of paper, and placed it in the pocket of her tunic, trying to chase away the guilt that seemed to be following her everywhere she went. She would have to lie to the sisters. She knew this. Tomorrow evening when they asked about her day, she wouldn't be able to tell them the truth.

Just this once, she reminded herself. It was what she'd been telling herself all night.

Just this once.

Just this one thing.

This one secret.

She would leave the Refuge in the morning. She would solve the mystery of the glowing red dot. Then, when she returned, she would go back to being a good and devoted member of the Refuge who one day—hopefully, one day soon—would become a real sister.

With this last thought, Alouette tiptoed out of the library and closed the door very quietly behind her. The sisters and her father were all asleep. Everyone went to bed early in the Refuge.

Pulling a screwdriver from her pocket, Alouette crouched down so she was eye level with the handle of the library door and shimmied the small metal cover off the security panel. Principale Francine always locked the library and engaged the alarm for extra security at night. Alouette had never needed to enter the library after hours before. And she'd certainly never thought of hacking the alarm.

Not until tonight.

But her plan to leave tomorrow morning had depended upon her getting into the library, to get the information and maps she needed to find her way to the Forest Verdure. Now she just needed to reset the alarm, so no one would know what she'd done.

The two red wires that she'd pulled from their terminals slipped easily back into the ports. A small red light on the panel flashed twice, indicating the security system was engaged.

After snapping the cover back into place and sliding her screwdriver back into her pocket, Alouette crept down the corridor to her bedroom, where she quietly twisted the handle, slipped through the door, and closed it silently behind her.

She nearly let out a shriek when she turned around to find Principale Francine sitting on her bed, waiting for her.

"Good evening, Alouette," the sister said evenly.

Alouette's heart kicked in her chest and her cheeks grew instantly hot. Why was the director of the Refuge in her room?

"Everything all right?" Principale Francine peered up at Alouette over her half-moon glasses.

"Yes, yes," Alouette blurted out, while hurriedly searching Francine's face for signs of suspicion. But the sister just looked back at her with a steadfast, unreadable gaze. "I . . . I couldn't sleep," Alouette babbled on. "So I went to the kitchen for some water." She glanced down at her empty hands and quickly added, "Which I drank."

It was already happening.

She was already lying.

And she was dreadful at it.

Principale Francine looked at Alouette for a few long, interminable seconds, and Alouette's heart knocked even faster behind her ribs. The sister could see right through her. Alouette had no doubt about that.

"I was hoping to have a word with you." The sister motioned to a spot on the bed next to her. "Will you sit?"

Alouette swallowed hard.

"Of course," she said, and sat down.

But as soon as she did, Principale Francine was on her feet. Alouette watched, terrified, as the sister began to pace the small room with her hands clasped, viselike, behind her back. Even though it was late, the sister's steel-gray hair was still scraped back into an impeccable, unforgiving bun.

Does she know?

Of course she knew. She knew *everything*. She was Principale Francine! She knew about the Frets. The boy with his bleeding head. The snooping around in her father's room. She knew about the old valise. The candlestick. Alouette hacking the lock and sneaking into the library to draw the map. She knew it all, didn't she?

And now she'd come here to punish Alouette.

What would the sentencing be?

The last time Alouette had ever been punished by Francine was when she was six years old, two years after she and her father had come to live in the Refuge. Alouette had been playing with her father's small cooking pot, banging it on the door of the Assemblée room. The sisters were deep in prayer, but Alouette was so excited to test out an old First World code that Sister Denise had taught her, she couldn't help herself.

H-E-L-L-O, she'd rapped on the door, using a series of different taps for each letter. The wooden door sounded like a deep, booming drum under the pot. She was just playing, having fun. Except Principale Francine hadn't seen it that way. She'd given Alouette double chores for a whole day and extra handwriting assignments for a week.

And that was just for banging a pot.

She couldn't even imagine what might be in store for her now.

"Alouette," Principale Francine said. "The sisters and I convened earlier today"—she stopped pacing and stared down at Alouette—"to talk about *you*."

Alouette's stomach dropped. This was it, wasn't it? All the sisters knew, and now this was the end. The end of all her plans. She was never going to be able to leave the Refuge tomorrow, was she? They would keep a constant watch on her, making sure she didn't escape or snoop or hack ever again.

She'd never get to the Frets or the forest.

"You have been working very hard, Alouette. Very hard indeed . . ."

She'd never find out the secret of the candlestick and the blinking red dot.

"You have been diligent with your lessons and industrious with your chores. You dust and tend to the books in the library with care and attention. . . ."

She'd never find out the truth about her father.

"Your Tranquil Forme is shaky at times, but you work hard to perfect your sequences. You are a devoted daughter and an asset to our community. . . ."

Wait. What?

Finally, Alouette tuned in to what Principale Francine was saying.

Instead of stern words and a list of punishments, Francine was *praising* her. Alouette wasn't sure she'd ever been praised by the Principale.

"You are making us all very proud."

Alouette's jaw almost dropped. "I am?"

Principale Francine cocked an eyebrow like she did in her lessons when Alouette wasn't grasping a concept. "Of course you are, Little Lark."

"Oh, I—I—" Alouette stuttered. "Thank you."

She didn't know what else to say. She was too stunned.

Then the sister reached into the pocket of her tunic and pulled out a long string of metallic beads.

"Your devotion beads," Alouette said.

Why was Principale Francine showing Alouette her devotion beads? She'd seen them a million times before.

"No, these are *your* devotion beads."

Alouette looked from the beads to Francine. *"What?"* Her voice was shaky.

"They're yours," the sister repeated.

"B-but . . . how? And why?"

Principale Francine gave a quick, efficient nod. "Because you are one of us now. Well, you will be soon, when you take your final vows, which as you know, takes some time to prepare for. But I wanted you to have these now."

Alouette felt numb with shock as the sister leaned down and ceremoniously strung the beads around her neck. The weight of the necklace was heavy and significant. Heavier than Alouette had imagined it would be. It was as though she could feel the responsibility that these beads represented.

Alouette's hands shook as she reached up and took hold of the metal tag hanging from the center of the necklace. It looked the same as the one that hung from all of the sisters' devotion beads. But as

Alouette flipped it over, she could see that instead of saying "Jacqui" or "Francine" or "Muriel," her tag read:

LITTLE LARK.

The breath hitched in Alouette's chest as she ran her fingers over the engraved letters. She had to make sure this was real. That these beads were real. That this wasn't just the same dream she'd had for years. Ever since she and her father had arrived at the Refuge and Alouette had learned about the ways and the sacred tasks of the Sisterhood, she'd fantasized about this moment.

And now it was actually happening.

Alouette expected to feel a joyful burst of pride. She'd succeeded. She was a sister. She'd become an official member of the Sisterhood. She should feel elated. Proud. Accomplished. She should be commending herself on all her hard work over the past twelve years.

But Alouette couldn't bring herself to think about the past twelve years. All she could think about was the past twelve hours. How she'd broken the rules. Betrayed the sisters. *And* her father. Left the Refuge without telling a single soul.

And how, tomorrow, she planned to do it all over again.

Clearly oblivious to the storm of emotions brewing inside her, Principale Francine gave another quick nod and a rare hint of a smile. "Welcome, Sister Alouette."

Alouette pulled her face into a smile too and managed to utter an enthusiastic "Thank you."

But in that moment, she felt less like a real sister than ever.

- CHAPTER 37 -
CHATINE

AS SOON AS THE SHADOWS OF THE FRETS ENVEL-
oped her, Chatine yanked back her hood and fell to her knees, trying desperately to suck in air. That entire cruiseur ride home, she'd
felt like she couldn't breathe. The walls of that blasted vehicle had
been closing in on her, a millimètre every second, until she felt like
she was being squeezed to death.

She unzipped the front of her coat and let the cold air rush in. For
once in her life, she was too warm and the biting wind of Laterre's
night was unusually refreshing.

She should never have agreed to play that stupide game of his.
Everything had been going great until then. She'd succeeded. She'd
gotten the exact intel that the general had asked for.

"Pretend to be a girl," she whispered, mocking Marcellus in a disdainful tone. "You be Alouette." She spat on the ground. "I would
rather *die* than be that wide-eyed Défecteur bimbo."

Chatine wasn't sure why, but there was something about that
girl that she didn't trust. Even though she'd only seen her for a
few seconds in the hallway of Fret 7 as she was running away, she

could feel it in her gut. And Chatine's gut was rarely ever wrong.

When the cold air had finally calmed her down, Chatine stood and zipped up her coat. As soon as she pulled the hood back over her head, she started to feel like herself again. Not the blushing, bumbling idiot whom she'd barely recognized back in that cruiseur.

She pushed back her left sleeve, tapped her Skin, and accessed the log she'd captured in the Tourbay. She pushed play and listened carefully, waiting for the conversation between Marcellus and Mabelle to begin. But all she could hear in her audio chip was static. She glanced down at the screen of her Skin, which showed nothing more than a dizzying scramble of colored pixels.

Sols. They must have blocked the signal somehow. To make sure neither of us could log it.

Chatine groaned and dismissed the useless file.

She'd just have to remember everything that was said.

She tapped at the screen to send an AirLink request to General Bonnefaçon. She didn't expect him to actually connect. It was already late at night and Chatine was planning to just send a message to relay her good news, but after a few seconds, his face appeared on the screen.

"Good evening, Renard," the general said in that same pretentious accent. Why did the Second Estate have to talk like that? All clipped and haughty.

"Good evening." Chatine tried to emulate the inflection, but she just came off sounding like an idiot.

"I hope that you being outside after curfew means you have been busy acquiring information for me."

Chatine straightened her spine, as though her confident posture would translate across the AirLink. "It does, actually."

The general's lips twitched into a smile. "Excellent, do tell."

Chatine swallowed and prepared herself to tell the general everything that had happened in the Tourbay—every word that was said, every twinkle in Mabelle's eyes, every falter in Marcellus's speech—but it was suddenly as though her voice were caught in her throat. As she thought about Marcellus's tormented expression in the cruiseur on the ride back to Vallonay, she felt a strange wave of sickness pass over her. It was a sensation she'd never remembered experiencing before. She cleared her throat and swallowed again, trying to dispel the acid feeling in her stomach. But it wouldn't go away. For some reason, the idea of reporting Marcellus's actions to the general was making her physically ill.

No, she commanded herself. *Now is not the time to go soft. Not when you're this close.*

"Yes?" the general prompted.

He's nothing but an arrogant Second Estate pomp. He means nothing to you. And you certainly don't mean anything to him.

Chatine opened her mouth, which was bone dry. "I—we—"

The general sighed. "I'm a very busy man, Renard. Do you have information for me or not?"

Chatine glanced up at the dark sky, thinking about Usonia. Sollight. Freedom.

Then she forced herself to think back to the cruiseur. To that suffocating space. To Marcellus leaning close to her, grabbing her hand.

"You be Alouette . . . pretend to be a girl."

"He was summoned to Montfer." The words spilled out of her like water out of a busted pipe. "He got a message from his former governess, asking him to meet her there."

The general's eyes narrowed with realization. "Mabelle Dubois."

"Yes. We went to Montfer and met her in the Tourbay. Those are the bog—"

"I know what the Tourbay is," the general interjected.

"Oh, sorry. Anyway, she was surrounded by bodyguards. Vangarde operatives, I assume. I counted eight. Which means there might have been a cell nearby."

Chatine shivered as she said the words, the weight of her actions finally starting to sink in.

What are you doing? Have you lost your mind?

She was ratting out a Vangarde cell. This was the very thing she *didn't* want to get involved in. Regime politics. Revolutions. Wars.

You're doing what you have to do, she reminded herself. But for the first time in as long as she could remember, her usual excuse didn't comfort her.

"And Mabelle tried to recruit him?" the general confirmed, pulling Chatine's thoughts back to her Skin.

She glanced uneasily around. The Frets were quiet. Deserted. It was well past curfew. "Yes, but he turned her down. Obviously. He's very loyal to the Regime."

Something inscrutable flickered across the general's face. "What else?"

Chatine thought back to the misty boglands. To the tune that Mabelle had hummed to Marcellus. She was almost certain the song was some kind of code. Something only Marcellus would know. "I don't think the Vangarde is finished with Marce—with Officer Bonnefaçon. I believe they will make contact again. Soon."

"Is that all?"

"I'm sorry," Chatine rushed to say. "I tried to log the conversation, but they'd jammed the signal somehow. The file on my Skin was nothing but static."

"Hmm," the general said cryptically, and Chatine was starting to feel uneasy.

She waited for him to speak again, to tell her she had done her job well. Her task was complete. Her voyageur to Usonia would be prepped immediately. But he remained so silent and still that, for a moment, she wondered if the AirLink connection had been lost.

"So," she prompted. "My reward?"

"Your reward?" the general echoed, as though the words were unfamiliar to him.

"You promised me passage to Usonia if I tailed Marcellus when the Vangarde made contact and reported back to you."

The general stared at her through the screen, pensive and foreboding. "That's not exactly what I said."

Chatine felt panic rise up inside her. She tried to keep her voice calm and steady, but it was a losing battle. "Yes, you did. You said if I delivered the information you needed, then you would—"

"Ah," the general said, "you see, that's where we have a differing of opinion."

"A differing of opinion?" Chatine's hands balled into fists. "About what?"

"About what information I ultimately need."

Chatine's pulse pounded in her ears. She didn't dare speak, for fear that she would unleash every Third Estate curse word under the Sols.

The general's expression softened momentarily, as though he were actually apologetic for what he was about to say. "The truth is, our intelligence on the Vangarde and their activity is still embarrassingly limited. They're recruiting and plotting and gaining momentum, and we have no idea where they are. Every day that their whereabouts remain a secret is another day lost in this battle. We need to find their primary base of operations so we can wipe them out completely."

"How is that my problem?" Chatine asked through gritted teeth. "I told you everything that happened in Montfer. I fulfilled *my* end of the bargain."

"Yes, you've proven to be quite resourceful today. Marcellus trusts you and apparently the Vangarde trusts you as well."

"Actually, they don't. They jammed my Skin signal, remember?"

"They allowed you to get close to them."

"That doesn't mean I can find their base."

The general sighed. "Well, I hope, for the sake of your future, that's not true."

Fire raged inside of Chatine. "You can't do this!" she shouted. "We had a deal. You can't just change the deal. I want my passage to Usonia."

"And you will get it," the general replied calmly. "As soon as you identify the location of the Vangarde's secret base."

"How on Laterre am I supposed to do that? I have no idea where they're hiding! They could be anywhere! They could be in the Terrain Perdu for all I know!"

But the general did not appear to be concerned. "You're not thinking rationally, Renard."

"What?"

"As you just said, the Vangarde is not finished with my grandson. They will attempt to make contact again soon. Which means, right now, he is your best lead to finding the base."

Chatine wanted to scream. She wanted to march up to Ledôme right now, drag General Bonnefaçon out of his stupid leather chair, and wring his thick neck. But she knew that was impossible. She'd never even get *inside* Ledôme on her own, let alone inside the Palais, let *alone* be able to drag the general anywhere.

Why was she always coming so close only to fail? Only to have it all ripped out from under her? First the Capitaine and now the general.

"Keep me posted on your progress," the general said as his arm extended toward the screen, ready to disconnect the AirLink.

"Wait!" Chatine called out, but it was too late. The general's face vanished from her Skin, and Chatine stood in the middle of the darkened streets of Vallonay, completely alone.

She couldn't believe this was happening. A classic bait and switch. She knew the move well. The general had conned her. As easily and as swiftly as she'd conned countless people.

What was she going to do now? How was *she*, of all people, supposed to find the location of a secret revolutionary base?

Chatine sighed and reached into the pocket of her coat, feeling around for what she had stolen tonight in the cruiseur. She pulled out Marcellus's titan ring. The one that *used* to be on his left hand. The idiot had been so distracted mooning over Alouette and acting out his little role play, he hadn't even noticed Chatine swipe it from his finger when she'd pulled her hand away from his.

"Stupide pomp," she muttered as she turned the sparkly object over in her palm, trying to make out the detail in the faded, sporadic light of the few working streetlamps.

As she walked deeper into the Frets, making her way home to Fret 7, Chatine slipped the ring onto her finger. Even though Marcellus had worn it on his pinky, it was loose around her thumb. And, as much as she depised herself for thinking it, she liked the look of the ring on her finger. She liked the way it made her skin tingle. Like she was carrying a small part of him around with her.

But still, she would not keep it. Tomorrow morning, she would take it straight to the Capitaine to see how much she could get for it.

It was definitely worth something. Probably not enough to close the gap between what she had and the exorbitant price the Capitaine was now demanding for passage to Usonia, but every little bit helped. Especially now that she was practically starting over.

She had very little hope of ever finding the Vangarde's secret base for the general. She didn't even know where to start.

With Marcellus, the clear, rational voice inside her head finally spoke. *Just like the general said. You start with Marcellus. He's your best chance.*

Chatine pulled her coat tighter around her and continued walking home. Maybe she would feel better after a night's sleep. Maybe everything would look different in the morning. Everything would make sense.

But as she neared the entrance to Fret 7, Chatine could swear she heard footsteps behind her. She spun around only to find the pathway empty and dark. Then, a moment later, something heavy and scratchy was thrown over her head.

Chatine clawed at the fabric, fighting for breath. But something—or someone—was holding it tight around her neck. She tried to run. She tried to scream. But before she could get a single sound out, she felt a hard thud on the back of her head and the planet spun out from under her.

- PART 4 -
THE BLADE

The written word evaporated, like dew on a blade of grass. One day it was there, and then it was gone. Forgotten. Laterrians no longer needed symbols inked and scratched on a page. They had images glowing on their wrists and words chiming in their ears.

There was no place for books. For history.

No place to learn from the mistakes of the past.

From *The Chronicles of the Sisterhood*,
Volume 2, Chapter 18

CHAPTER 38

CHATINE

THE VANGARDE BASE.

That was Chatine's first thought as rough hands set her down in a chair and bound her wrists behind her back.

She'd found it. Or, rather, *they* had found *her.* The Vangarde had probably been watching her since she and Marcellus had left Montfer. Possibly even before that. Maybe they'd been watching her for her entire life. She didn't know what these people were capable of. She didn't know what kind of surveillance they had on this planet. For all she knew, they were more powerful and pervasive than even the Ministère.

They'd heard her speaking to the general. They knew she was a spy. And now she would pay.

Chatine might have been scared if she weren't so distracted trying to figure out how to activate the disabled tracker on her Skin so she could transmit her location back to the general and claim her reward.

Someone yanked the sac from her head, and Chatine's vision started to clear.

She blinked her eyes, taking in her surroundings, trying to memorize them.

All around her was thick gray PermaSteel. The ceiling was only a mètre or two above her head, and the walls were held together with giant gray rivets. The room seemed to press in on all sides. Dirty puddles, edged with salty tide marks, dotted the floor. An old life vest lay in one of these puddles like a bloated carcass, lit up by a gloomy shaft of light. She turned as far as her restraints would allow to see where the light was coming from, and she glimpsed, in the far corner of her eye, a small round window encircled by riveted PermaSteel.

And that's when whatever courage she still had vanished.

This was *not* the Vangarde base.

This place she knew.

This was a place she swore she'd never set foot in again. A place she'd grown up avoiding at all costs.

This was the Grotte, a retired cargo bateau that used to carry people and goods over the Secana Sea from one side of Laterre to the other. But now, as it sat idle in Vallonay's sprawling and ugly docklands, it served as the main headquarters for the Délabré. The Scum of Laterre is what her father's merciless gang of lowlifes should really have been called.

Chatine wasn't frightened of the majority of her fellow crocs. For the most part, her kind kept to a code. There was a mutual respect among cons. But the Délabré were not just crocs or cons. They didn't just run scams. They were pure filth. Inside and out. They caused pain just to see it on people's faces. They maimed and cut and crippled just for the fun of it. They were the kind of people who enjoyed watching others suffer. It was for this reason that Chatine avoided the docklands at all costs. She never wanted to end up in the very situation she was now in.

She could hear footsteps behind her. She tried to turn to see who was coming, but her restraints held her firm. It didn't matter, though. She could smell his breath even before he arrived.

"Well, well, well," said the voice of Monsieur Renard. "If it isn't my little progeny, *Théo*." The emphasis he put on her fake name was immediately understood:

I hold all the power. One word from me and everyone will know your secret.

Chatine remained silent, trying to keep her face blank. The last thing you wanted to do in the face of the Délabré was show fear. It was their main source of sustenance.

Her father leaned in close. Chatine held her breath. The foulness permeating from him was suffocating. "Little Théo, running around the planet with officers of the Ministère. Very interesting. Isn't that very interesting?"

Two others stepped out from opposite sides of the chair, flanking Chatine. Claque and Hercule. She sucked in a breath when she saw them. Although barely taller than Chatine, Claque was lean and tough with a cunning half smile. He moved like an insect, all angles and purpose, and was known for collecting toes. Hercule, on the other hand, was so gigantic he had to crouch under the bateau's low ceiling. His biceps were as big as Chatine's head, his torso looked like it was taken off a droid, and his huge brow hung heavy and low over his eyes like he was some sort of monster. The gang used him to instill fear in people, but Chatine knew his size was all he had going for him. His brain was filled with fog.

It was Claque who you had to be afraid of. In addition to chopping off toes, he was known for running one of the most profitable blood bordels in the Planque. He lured girls in with food and money, then sucked the nutrients from their blood to sell to the upper estates. Most of them were never seen or heard from again.

"Théo's been busy, we hear," Claque said. "Riding around the whole fric-ing planet in cruiseurs. Getting cozy with officers."

Chatine swallowed. So that's what this was about. They'd seen her with Marcellus.

"Sounds like a pretty nice con," her father said, nodding to Claque. "Doesn't it?"

"A *very* nice con," Claque agreed.

"I'm just sad that we were left out," her father said, his lips tugging down theatrically. "I don't like being sad."

"And I don't like people who break the rules," Claque said, sneering.

Dread trickled all the way down to the soles of Chatine's feet as her brain scrambled for her next move. If she told them the truth—that she wasn't running a con, she'd turned snitch for the general—the consequences would be disastrous.

On the other hand, if she let them go on thinking she was scamming Marcellus for largs, she'd be expected to fork over a percentage. That was the rule that Claque was referring to. Anyone running a large-scale con in the Frets had to share the wealth with the Délabré or say good-bye to a toe or two. But she didn't have a percentage to give them. All she had was Marcellus's stupide ring. She couldn't exactly split that ten ways.

She rubbed her bound hands together, feeling for the metal around her thumb. But her skin was bare.

"Looking for this?" Monsieur Renard pulled the titan band out of his pocket and gave it a flick. It spun gracefully in the air before landing in his outstretched hand. He studied it. "Looks valuable. Definitely titan."

Chatine closed her eyes for a moment, summoning strength. Her father was a different person around the Délabré, especially around Claque. Yes, he was always insufferable, but it was as though they brought out the cruelty in him. When he was inside these walls, he wasn't her father anymore. They didn't share blood, or a shady past in Montfer, or a couchette. He was the formidable leader of a feared gang. Nothing more.

And it terrified Chatine.

"You've been holding out on us," Claque said. "And we're not happy about it."

"I swear that's all I have." Chatine spoke for the first time, surprised by the lack of tremble in her voice.

Her father made a *tsk* sound with his teeth and shook his head. "Oh, my *son*. I'm so very disappointed in you."

"Look, it's early. I'll get more. I promise."

"That's not what I mean," Renard replied. "I mean, I'm disappointed that you would *lie* to your own father."

"I'm not lying."

Renard shared an inscrutable look with Claque. Claque turned to Hercule, who had yet to say anything in this entire conversation. Although that was typical. As soon as he opened his mouth, the illusion of threat usually went right out the window. So he'd been trained to keep his lips shut tight.

Hercule nodded and walked past Chatine, out of her field of vision. She desperately wanted to spin the chair around so she could see what he was doing. She knew it was never smart to turn your back on a Délabré. She could hear a rustling sound behind her. Her mind raced to identify it. Then, a second later, Hercule appeared again, and Chatine's heart sank with a thud when she saw what he was carrying.

It was her sac of stolen trinkets.

How had her father found it? Had Azelle ratted her out? Had Monsieur Renard gone on one of his snooping missions through the couchette and found it under the floor grate in her room?

Hercule dropped the bag to the ground, and as Chatine heard the clanking sound it made as it hit the steel floor, all of her former composure and control instantly vanished. "Give it back!" she yelled. "Give it back, you lowlife croc!" She fought against her restraints, wriggling and twisting until the chair nearly tipped over. But it made no difference. The ropes were too tight. There was no way she was getting out of here like this.

"Calm," Claque said in that eerie whisper of his. "Calm. We *will* give it back. As soon as *you* give us our cut of the Bonnefaçon job."

Chatine did manage to calm herself. But not because Claque told her to. Because she was suddenly struck with an idea.

It was risky, but she didn't have much of a choice at this point.

She *had* to get her collection back. That was years of hard work. Eight *thousand* largs' worth.

"Like I said," Chatine began, fighting to keep her voice steady. "It's still early. But I promise it's going to be big."

Claque crossed his arms over his chest, looking skeptical. "How big?"

Chatine scoffed. "The boy is the grandson of the general. He lives *in* the Grand Palais. And I swear as soon as I get what I'm after, you'll have your cut. And it will be big, okay?"

That seemed to satisfy the man, and the doubt slid from his face, replaced by a greedy smile. "I like big."

Chatine tried to match the expression. "Who doesn't?"

"How long are we talking here?" Renard asked.

Chatine's mind raced. She had to get off this planet before these Délabré goons came after her for their cut. Finding the Vangarde base was a long shot, but it was her only chance now. She had to try. She just needed more time.

"Two weeks," she announced. "Max."

And in the meantime, she thought bitterly, *I'll find a way to steal my trinkets back.*

Claque exchanged a look with her father and then turned back to her. "You have three days."

"Three days?!" she fired back. "That's impossible. You don't understand. This con is complex. I'm talking multiple layers of deception. I'm talking—"

"Three days," Claque repeated as his gaze fell on her feet. "Or we start taking our *cut* in other ways."

Chatine felt her blood turn to ice as she thought of all those hobbled people in the Frets, their disobedience to the Délabré visible to everyone they passed.

"Fine," she said, even though she knew there was no way she could get the information the general was after in three days. Marcellus was still her only lead on finding the base, but she didn't know when, or even *if*, the Vangarde would contact him again. It was a lost cause.

Monsieur Renard held up Marcellus's ring. "We'll take *this* as your down payment." He slid the band onto his finger, and Chatine felt a wave of revulsion at seeing the officer's shiny ring on her father's grimy hand.

She struggled against her restraints again. "Can I go now?"

Hercule started to walk toward Chatine, but her father stopped him with a hand. Instead, Renard pulled a knife from his back pocket. He slowly stalked toward the chair, disappearing behind her. She felt a jerk as his knife cut through the ropes around her stomach, releasing her from the chair. He moved on to her bound hands. She could feel the cold steel of the blade resting against her wrists. Then, in one swift motion, the ropes were gone and the blade nicked her palm.

She yelped in pain and pulled her hands to her, seeing dark red blood ooze out of the small cut. "What the—" she started to ask, but was silenced by her father's heavy breath on her ear.

"Just remember," he whispered low enough that neither of the others could hear, "I know exactly how much that blood is worth."

- CHAPTER 39 -
MARCELLUS

THE ENTIRE WAY BACK TO LEDÔME, MARCELLUS HAD managed to keep his mind off Mabelle and the strange encounter he'd had with her in Montfer. But the moment he walked into the Palais, it was as though all those thoughts he'd been successfully holding back flooded in, finally breaking through the dam he'd built around them in his mind.

Suddenly, everywhere he looked, Mabelle was there. Objects and locations around the Palais that had been safe for years—that Marcellus had worked so hard to *make* safe—became minefields again.

She was tapping her fingernail against the screen of her Skin, reminding him it was time to go to bed. She was bounding up the imperial staircase, chasing him while his five-year-old self ran and shrieked with glee. She was scooping him off the ground, lifting up the bottom of his shirt so she could blow bubbles on his bare stomach while he laughed so hard it hurt.

Had that all been a lie?

An eleven-year deception?

Had it all been an act so she could gather intel on the Regime?

Thankfully the Palais was quiet as Marcellus climbed the imperial staircase and headed into the south wing that he shared with his grandfather. It was late. The moon hung low in the TéléSky outside the vast Palais windows. Everyone had retired. He was grateful for the calm.

The last few days had been such a whirlwind with the assassination of the Premier Enfant, the cancellation of the Ascension, the riots breaking out in the Frets, his father's death, Mabelle summoning him to Montfer, telling him that the Vangarde's numbers were rising every day.

It's happening, isn't it? Marcellus thought as he walked the long corridor to his rooms. *Everything my grandfather and the Patriarche have feared for years is coming to pass. The Vangarde is resurfacing. A new rebellion is beginning.*

The thought made him shiver. Marcellus had listened to people in the Ministère talk about the failed Rebellion of 488 for his entire life. He'd heard so many horror stories about the death toll—on both sides: the innocent lives lost, the gruesome scene of mangled, torn-apart bodies lining the streets. He used to have nightmares about that rebellion. He'd been less than a year old when it had happened, and it still haunted his dreams.

Now just the thought of it starting all over again—of Marcellus having to witness it, *fight* it—made him sick to his stomach.

But, of course, he would fight. He would stand up for the Regime. He would protect his planet as he'd been raised and trained to do. He didn't care how many people the Vangarde were able to recruit, the Ministère was still stronger. The Ministère would always be stronger. They would find these terrorists. They would root them out before they had a chance to do any more harm.

"The Vangarde doesn't endorse acts of unnecessary violence and murder."

Marcellus felt his hands clench at his sides as he walked the long corridor to his rooms.

Lies, he reminded himself. That's what Mabelle did. She lied. She had done it his whole life.

"I have proof that your father is innocent. I hid it for you in my room at the Palais before I was arrested. . . ."

Marcellus shook his head, trying to rattle the memory loose. He'd spent too many years of his life believing what that woman had to say; he was not going to start again now.

And yet, as Marcellus continued down the hallway, he found himself walking straight past his door, clear out of the south wing, all the way back down to the servants' wing. His breath was labored, his muscles were tight and coiled, as though they were already preparing themselves for the rebellion.

He halted in front of the door of Nadette's room.

The room that once belonged to his own governess too.

The doorway had been blockaded with orange lasers, forbidding anyone from entering while the Ministère finished collecting evidence relating to Marie's murder. But Marcellus was able to poke his head into the room and glance around. It had been scrubbed clean by Ministère forensics specialists. The linens had been stripped from the mattress. The drawers had all been opened and emptied. Even the carpet had been ripped up from the floor, revealing cold, sterile concrete underneath. The only thing still left in the room was the framed artwork, but even that had been taken down and set to lean against the bed so that the walls could be checked for secret compartments.

Marcellus had to laugh. The Ministère had done his job for him. If *anything* had been hiding in this room, they would have found it by now. He would have gotten an alert on his TéléCom.

Which only confirmed exactly what Marcellus had suspected.

Mabelle was still lying.

Marcellus released a breath and turned to leave, suddenly becoming aware of a presence standing behind him. He jumped at the sight of his grandfather's piercing eyes, staring at him from the dim light of the hallway.

Marcellus clutched a hand to his chest. "Grand-père," he said. "You scared me."

His grandfather stepped into a small shaft of light, illuminating his face.

"Is everything all right?" Marcellus asked, blanching at his grandfather's stony expression. Had the Vangarde already attacked? Had the rebellion started? Was someone else dead?

"I heard you went to Montfer today," the general said, ignoring Marcellus's question.

For a moment, a bolt of panic shot through Marcellus. *How does he know?* What *does he know?* But then he remembered that he'd told Inspecteur Limier about it, and Limier had wanted him to take Sergent Chacal with him. Was that what this was about? That he'd left without backup?

Marcellus stood up straighter. "Yes. I went to follow up on a Vangarde lead. I'm sorry for leaving Chacal behind. The lead was hot and I couldn't wait."

"A lead?" the general said with an edge of curiosity that made Marcellus's gut twist with guilt. He rarely ever lied to his grandfather, and now he knew why. He was miserable at it.

"Yes, sir."

"Find anything?"

Marcellus's heart thudded loudly in his chest. He knew this was his moment to come clean. He'd failed to tell his grandfather about the shirt, about the message, about Mabelle's summoning; and now he had a second chance to right the situation. To tell him everything that he now knew about Mabelle. His grandfather could have a fleet of Policier patroleurs dispatched in the next hour. They'd find her. They'd put her back on Bastille where she belonged.

He could still hear Mabelle's voice in his mind.

"I don't believe you're going to tell the general about this."

This was his chance to prove himself. To prove he had what it took to replace the irreplaceable Commandeur Vernay. To prove his loyalty to the Regime and the Bonnefaçon name. This was his chance to be the man his father could never be.

"My only hope was that you would grow up to think differently. Think for yourself."

I am thinking for myself! Marcellus silently shouted back at the memory.

His head was starting to pound like it might actually explode. And his grandfather was still watching him, waiting for a response, waiting for the truth.

When Marcellus finally spoke, he didn't feel like he was even in his own body. He could hear his own voice, but it was as though he were no longer standing in this hallway.

"No, I found nothing," Marcellus heard himself say. "It was a dead end."

Something inscrutable flashed over the general's face, and Marcellus felt his throat go dry. After a long moment, his grandfather finally said, "That's a shame."

Marcellus felt his whole body relax. But he was still anxious to get away. "Yes, it is. Well, I'd better get to bed."

He pushed past the general and started down the hallway, feeling his grandfather's eyes on his back the whole time.

"Of course. Big day tomorrow."

Marcellus froze and slowly turned around. "What?"

"Have you not checked your AirLink messages?"

Panic returned to Marcellus's gut as he realized he hadn't yet turned his TéléCom back on. "Not yet. I've been . . . busy."

"Yes, you have," the general said, and before Marcellus could figure out what on Laterre he meant by that, he added, "Nadette is being executed in the Marsh tomorrow morning."

"WHAT?" Marcellus spat before he could stop himself. Upon seeing the look of confusion on his grandfather's face, he attempted to flatten his expression. "I mean, why isn't she being sent to Bastille like all the others we've rounded up?"

"The others didn't kill the Premier Enfant." The general took a step toward Marcellus. His frame seemed to fill the entire width of the hallway. "The Patriarche is demanding retribution."

Marcellus fought the urge to argue that the Patriarche didn't have a reputation for making rational decisions. Especially in times of duress. The last time he'd demanded something, the general had lost his best commandeur.

But Marcellus knew this was not the time to bring up Vernay. His grandfather would surely only shut him down again.

"Do you disagree with the choice of punishment?" General Bonnefaçon asked.

"N-n-no," Marcellus stammered, berating himself for such a foolish reaction. "We've just never had a public execution before. In the entire history of Laterre."

Something that resembled irritation passed over the general's face. Marcellus knew he was treading on unstable ground. "We've also never had a direct attack against the First Estate before. Do you suggest we treat the *murderer* of the Paresse heir the same way we treat a petty thief?"

"No," Marcellus managed to utter, casting his gaze to the floor.

"We must make an example of her."

Marcellus nodded. He could hear in his grandfather's voice that he was rapidly nearing a precipice. If he crossed over, there would be no turning back. His only option was to defuse. "Yes, sir."

"New crimes call for new forms of punishment."

"New *forms* of punishment?"

"We've commissioned a device for the occasion. The government of Reichenstat has been using it for years. But of course, we've improved upon it. Made it more efficient. I've heard stories of people on that backward planet being hacked to pieces before they died. It's inhumane, really. Nadette's death will be fast and relatively painless."

Device?

Efficient?

Relatively *painless?*

Marcellus instinctively felt bile rise up in his throat. With some effort, he managed to swallow it back down. He knew he might regret what he was about to ask, but he had to ask it anyway. If he didn't, he might wonder for the rest of his life.

"But, sir. What if she's innocent?"

It was a question that seemed to echo deep within him, through all eighteen years of his life. It was a doubt that had been planted as a seed years ago, abandoned, neglected, forgotten. But now, after the events of the past two days, it had slowly begun to grow. Break ground. Blossom.

His grandfather took another step toward him, his eyes narrowing. Marcellus fought the urge to turn and run down this hallway, climb into his bed, and hide under the covers until Mabelle came to comfort him. The same way he used to do when he was a child and his grandfather would scold him.

But he was no longer a child now.

"Marcellus," his grandfather's voice was clear yet full of warning. "If you're going to be commandeur one day, you cannot let your emotions and ties to the past skew your judgments of the present. Nadette is as guilty as your father. And she, too, must pay the price for her treason."

CHAPTER 40

CHATINE

BEEP. BEEP. BEEP.

Chatine rolled over in her bed and swatted at the surface of her Skin, trying to stop the intrusive noise. She had no doubt it was a reminder to go to the Med Center for her monthly Vitamin D injection. But she was way too tired for Ministère reminders.

Chatine had barely slept at all last night. Her conversation with the Délabré had been replaying in her mind.

Three days. She had three days to get off this planet. Or figure out a way to steal more stuff from Officer Bonnefaçon to pay off Claque and her father. Otherwise she'd wind up hobbled, selling her blood *and* her soul in the bordels so that the First and Second Estates could have their precious face creams and youth injections.

Beep. Beep. Beep.

Chatine dragged her eyes open. The familiar emblem of the Ministère—two crossed rayonettes guarding the planet of Laterre—flashed on her Skin, informing her of an incoming Universal Alert. She glanced to the other side of the bed, but it was empty. Azelle had obviously already left for work.

Chatine sank back against her pillow as the face of General Bonnefaçon filled the screen on her arm. She nearly shrieked aloud at the sight of it.

Feeling stupide, she took a deep breath, reminding herself that this message was going out to *all* of Laterre. Not just her. But between her cowardly reaction to the sight of the general and her behavior in the cruiseur yesterday, Chatine did *not* like the person she was turning into.

"Bonjour, fellow Laterrians," the general began. "I bring you promising news this morning. We have apprehended the person responsible for the murder of Marie Paresse, the Premier Enfant of Laterre. Her name is Nadette Epernay. She was the child's former governess, and we have no doubt that she was affiliated with the terrorist organization known as the Vangarde."

Chatine stared wide-eyed at the screen. The Vangarde were responsible for killing the Premier Enfant? No wonder the general was so desperate to find their base.

"Mademoiselle Epernay must pay for her brutality against the Regime," the general continued. "She must pay for this murder. Which is why, this morning, as a punishment for her crimes, she will be executed in the Vallonay public marketplace."

Executed?

Chatine felt a shiver run down her spine.

In all her life, she had never heard of a convict being executed. Convicts were too valuable. They were needed to mine zyttrium on Bastille. According to Azelle, the supply in the TéléSkin fabrique was dwindling by the day. If anything, they needed *more* prisoners.

"Once this punishment has been carried out," the general went on, "life on Laterre will continue as normal. Barring any other interruptions, the Ascension will soon be rescheduled. Thank you for your attention this morning. Vive Laterre."

As the Ministère emblem filled the screen once more, Chatine let out a heavy sigh. Her plan this morning was to tail Marcellus, in hopes that he would lead her to more information about the Vangarde. But she knew this development was going to make that task much more difficult.

Thirty minutes later, the Marsh was in a state of anarchy. It was so crammed full of people, waiting to watch some poor girl meet her grisly end, they were practically on top of one another.

Chatine sat in the center of the rainy marketplace, watching the crowd from one of her favorite surveillance spots—on top of the head of Patriarche Thibault Paresse. Not his real head, of course, but a half-mètre version of it that stood atop a giant bronze body. Thibault Paresse had been the very first Patriarche of the Regime and the founder of Laterre. His statue had been erected in the Marsh years ago, long before Chatine was born, as a reminder to the Third Estate of how this "great man" had shepherded their ancestors away from the collapse of the First World.

Now the statue sat crooked in the middle of the marketplace, like it might topple over at any second. The bronze had worn off in several places, leaving Thibault with what looked like a very unfortunate skin condition.

All of the stall owners seemed to be taking full advantage of the execution today. Chatine could hear vendors calling out prices for carrots, potatoes, and chou bread that were nearly double the normal price. Fresh barrelfuls of seaweed had been carted in for the occasion. Cheap sustenance for the poor. It was rough going down, but it could keep you from starving to death. And Chatine could smell the unmistakable scent of roast chicken wafting from the direction of Madame Dufour's stall. The old croc always roasted a chicken when the Marsh was crowded. It was how she seduced customers to her stall.

As Chatine scanned the sea of people milling around below,

waiting for something to happen, her gaze zeroed in on a girl standing at the south entrance of the marketplace, wearing a long gray robe-like garment with billowing sleeves.

Chatine's stomach lurched.

It was the girl. The girl Marcellus had been all moony-eyed over in the cruiseur yesterday. The one he'd made Chatine play in that stupide game of his.

Alouette.

Chatine narrowed her eyes, studying the girl. She remembered Marcellus's desperate questions about her, pleading for Chatine to find out more about her.

There was one thing for certain—that girl did *not* live in the Frets. Her pristine gray shoes were enough to tell Chatine that. Nothing stayed that clean in the Frets.

She *had* to be a Défecteur.

But Chatine had always assumed Défecteurs were dirty too. Didn't they live in the woods, in mud huts? That girl didn't look like she'd ever even *seen* mud before.

She was completely out of her element. And it was starting to attract attention.

Chatine noticed Old Man Gonesse sizing her up from a few mètres away, clearly getting ready to swoop in and make his play for whatever she was carrying in her pockets. Chatine turned away, perfectly content to just ignore the whole thing. Let the stupide girl get picked apart by Marsh vultures. What did it matter to her?

But then, a moment later, Chatine spotted that unmistakable silver raincoat, immaculate wavy hair, and clean face. Marcellus. He was making his way through the crowd, heading right toward the girl. Chatine's mind whirled. If the officer located Alouette, Chatine probably wouldn't see him for the rest of the day. He'd whisk her off somewhere, with an obnoxious smile on his face, and attempt to get all those desperate questions of his answered.

In short, the girl would only distract him.

And Chatine didn't have time for distractions. She needed Marcellus to stay on task. *Her* task.

How was he going to lead her to the Vangarde base if he was off being lovesick with some brainless Défecteur?

And on top of all that, Chatine simply didn't trust the girl. Every time she laid eyes on her, something clanged in Chatine's chest. Like a warning bell. The girl was bad news.

Which meant that Chatine had no choice but to intervene.

- CHAPTER 41 -
ALOUETTE

ALOUETTE HAD NEVER SEEN SO MANY PEOPLE ALL AT once. Hundreds, maybe thousands, of bodies filled the giant space in front of her, all of them scurrying, shoving, talking in hurried voices. Some even shouted amid the mishmash of stalls.

It didn't take long for Alouette to figure out she was in the Marsh, the large open-air marketplace in the center of the Frets. Although, she had no idea *how* she'd gotten here. Her plan had been to leave from the back of Fret 7 and avoid the marketplace altogether, but somehow she must have gotten turned around.

Alouette wondered if the Marsh was always so raucous, so frenetic. So fraught. Like soup on her father's stove, the crowd seemed to be simmering and waiting, itching to boil over.

She'd been here for only a few minutes and already she felt overwhelmed. Alouette couldn't believe her eyes, or her ears. Even her nose was having a hard time taking in the heady smell of sewage, trash, and rotting vegetables.

Alouette gripped her fist tighter around her hand-drawn map, trying to summon strength from it. This small piece of paper was supposed to lead her straight to the Forest Verdure. Straight to her father's secret past. Straight to the answers to all her burning questions. She hadn't dared keep it in her pocket. She was too afraid it would fall out and get lost.

Besides, the deep pockets on her tunic were full of other important items: A flashlight that she'd swiped from Sister Denise's workbench. A small bottle of fresh water, because she knew from the Chronicles that the drinking water up here wasn't always safe. And in her right pocket, she'd managed to also stow her favorite screwdriver. She wasn't even sure what she might need it for, but she felt more prepared having the tool with her.

Alouette unfolded the map and peered down at it, trying to figure out how she'd gotten so turned around. It appeared that if she could just find her way to Fret 15, she would be back on track. She could walk straight south to the lake that bordered the Forest Verdure. From there, all she had to do was follow the stream that would take her to the clearing where she'd seen the blinking red dot on the hologram.

"Okay," she murmured under her breath. "You can do this. Find Fret 15."

She had only a few hours until Assemblée was over, which wasn't long. If she was going to get out to the forest and back before the sisters came out of Quiet Contemplation, she needed to get moving. Alouette touched the front of her tunic, feeling her devotion beads lying cold against her chest, and finally took a tentative step out from the cover of the darkened hallway and into the Marsh.

And that's when she felt it. The tiniest drop of moisture on her nose. As light as a feather. Alouette stopped again and looked up. The roof of the old freightship that used to cover the market had rusted and crumbled away, revealing big patches of sky.

The *real* sky!

Her mouth tweaked into a smile.

For as long as she could remember, she'd only seen bedrock above her head. But now, here it was. The gray Laterrian sky. It seemed so much higher, so much more vast, than she'd ever pictured in her mind.

As she marveled at the thick clouds, she felt another two drops, this time on her forehead and cheek.

And she just couldn't help it.

She opened her mouth to catch a raindrop on her tongue, as she'd always imagined doing when she was a kid. It tasted salty and almost sharp.

"Bonjour, ma chérie, you got some chou bread for me?" Alouette jumped as a rough hand grabbed her wrist. She whirled around to see a large man with drooping eyes staring at her with a crooked, snarling smile. "I haven't eaten in days."

Alouette fumbled for words. "Oh my Sols! I didn't bring any food with me. I'm so sorry. I should have brought something."

How could she not have thought about all the starving people up here? She'd been so preoccupied with her plan to get out to the forest, she'd completely forgotten to bring any food with her.

"Come on, lovely," said the man as his hand tightened around Alouette's wrist. "You got that clean skin and pretty curls. You must be pocketing something good."

His face was too close to hers, and Alouette could see something dark and sinister in his eyes. She tried to pull away, but his long black fingernails dug into her flesh through her tunic.

"Give Old Gonesse something to eat, yeah?" The man's breath smelled of sour milk and old onions.

Alouette's pulse began to race. She gave her arm another tug, but the old man held tight.

"I really am sorry, but I don't have—"

The next words evaporated off her tongue, because suddenly, all around her, the world seemed to halt. Everyone stopped what they were doing and stared down at the glowing rectangles implanted in their arms. Even the old man with the crooked smile let go of Alouette's wrist and was now gazing down at his Skin.

Then, in eerie unison, every single gaze lifted and focused on something in the distance.

Something Alouette couldn't see.

Or understand.

"It's starting," the old man hissed before disappearing into the crowd.

Then, in a flash, the marketplace exploded with noise and movement and energy. It was as if a stopper had been released, and suddenly people flowed and gushed around her, shoving from every direction. *In* every direction.

As Alouette tried desperately to fight her way out, her feet tripped and staggered until she felt herself falling. Fear bloomed in her chest. A cry for help rose up in her throat. Her feet were nearly off the ground when she felt someone grab her sleeve and yank her out of the swarm.

It was a boy.

"This way," he shouted.

He tugged again on Alouette's sleeve, compelling her forward. She continued to stumble slightly as he pulled her past stalls and through tightly packed walkways, but he held fast to her tunic until they'd reached a quiet spot in the middle of a nest of booths selling old kitchenware.

"What's going on?" Alouette asked, struggling to catch her breath.

But the boy didn't answer. He seemed distracted, anxiously glancing over Alouette's shoulder as though searching for someone.

Even with his big black hood and ratty clothes, Alouette could tell the boy was small and skinny. Underfed, most likely. But there was also something familiar about him. Oddly familiar.

"What's happening?" Alouette tried again.

The boy blinked and focused on her, his expression incredulous. "The execution."

Alouette's eyes widened. "The *what?*"

The boy said nothing; he only looked out over the sea of heads. Alouette followed his gaze and spotted a platform in the center of the marketplace. The area was surrounded by a team of droids, their metal skulls and gleaming eyes looming over everyone in the Marsh. Alouette's blood froze at the very sight of them. But the restless crowd seemed to be moving right toward them, and now Alouette could see why. Up on the platform, three droids slowly began rolling out some type of machine. It was a huge, terrifying device that looked to be made entirely of PermaSteel. Two rectangular columns stretched four or five mètres into the air, joined near the bottom by a flat rectangle jutting out to one side. The whole apparatus looked almost like a bed, with posts way too tall for its frame.

Alouette shivered as she stared at the device. This thing—this curious, unfathomable contraption—was going to execute someone? *Kill* someone? It didn't seem possible. She'd read of such things happening on the First World. But never here.

The porridge she'd eaten for breakfast rose up in Alouette's stomach as her mind raced through everything she'd learned about Laterre. "But the Ministère doesn't execute people," she said quietly to the boy.

"Exactly. That's why everyone's all riled up." The boy rolled his eyes.

"Who are they executing?" Alouette asked.

The boy shot her a look of disbelief. "Have you been living under a rock?"

"A rock? Well, not exactly, but—"

"Haven't you been getting the alerts?" The boy glanced at her sleeve, but then seemed to remember something and sneered. "Oh, right, your *kind* doesn't get alerts."

"My kind?"

The boy shook his head. "It's the governess. Nadette Epernay. She murdered the Premier Enfant. At least that's what they're telling us."

"The Premier Enfant is dead?!"

The boy pushed back his hood a little farther and stared up at Alouette. "Are you telling me you really didn't know?"

But Alouette didn't get a chance to answer because at that moment, a fresh surge of people barreled toward them, and she and the boy were flung apart. Alouette stood on her tiptoes and searched desperately for a sign of him.

Just as she spotted the boy's hood, she was suddenly knocked backward when a woman slammed into her. Alouette stumbled, trying to find her footing. But by the time she regained her balance, the boy's black hood was gone.

She opened her mouth to call to him, but no sound came out. She didn't know his name. And even if she did, there was no way her voice would carry in all this commotion. Everywhere she turned, people were shouting.

"Look, look. Here she is!"

"That's her! The monster!"

"She's not a monster. She's just a baby."

Alouette spun in a frantic circle until her gaze landed on a young woman standing on the platform, shivering in a flimsy blue shirt and pants. Two droids gripped her with huge metal fists, squeezing her arms so tight, the color drained from the woman's skin. The terror and rain that splashed across her face made her look ghostly and disfigured.

This was the murderer of the Premier Enfant?

A girl who couldn't have been much older than Alouette?

Alouette had barely had time to take in the news that the child had been killed, and now this woman, this *girl*, was going to be executed for the crime? Alouette's stomach clenched and her legs felt wobbly beneath her.

"Get on with it! Just kill her!" someone in the crowd shouted.

"Yeah, give us our Ascension back!"

There was some laughter followed by more angry shouts.

"Arrête! She's innocent."

"Yes, look at her! There's no way she did it!"

"Of course, she did it! Kill her!"

More outcries and peals of laughter swirled around and buffeted Alouette. The noise, the commotion, the shouting, the girl's wide, petrified eyes. It was all too much.

Alouette suddenly wished she were back in her warm bed, inside the Refuge's tight, safe walls. She wished her father were there to take her into his strong arms, shield her from this terrible place, and tell her it was going to be okay. She wished she'd never come out here.

She squeezed her hand tightly around the map. As though it had the power to stop all of this.

"Shut up!" someone shouted right next to Alouette, startling her. "She's saying something."

More calls for quiet echoed around Alouette, and she looked back toward the platform. The two droids pushed the girl facedown onto the flat steel bed of the device. But she was resisting, and with her head thrust upward, she was shouting.

"I didn't do it! I swear I'm innocent! Please. Please! Help me!"

The droids thrust her down harder, forcing her head onto the block as four clamps suddenly protruded from the PermaSteel surface. They rose up like metallic creatures, encircling her wrists and ankles before squeezing shut. The governess let out a terrified shriek.

"I loved her!" she shouted, the sound muffled by tears and her face being pressed into the metal slab. "I . . . I loved that little girl like she was my own."

Alouette leaned forward, trying to hear what the young woman was saying.

"We . . . we played. Every morning, we played. I was the Fairy

Queen and she was the Princess." The governess was sobbing now, stuttering and fumbling over her words. "We lived in a . . . a magic castle. There was a dragon. It was Marie's dragon. Poor little Marie. We looked after it. We fed it magic turnip juice and . . ."

Alouette swallowed a lump in her throat as she remembered her own games from when she was little. Her own magic castles and imaginary dragons.

Suddenly, a somberness seemed to descend on the Marsh, shifting the energy in the crowd. There were no more shouts, only mutterings and whispers.

"I don't think she did it."

"She looks just like my daughter."

"The poor thing."

"Oh my Sols, please save her. Spare her!"

Alouette could hear the girl's shuddering sobs punctuated by sparse, halting words: "Innocent." "Please." "Dragon."

Then, a strange, high-pitched buzzing noise permeated the air, growing louder and louder. The crowd fell nearly silent, and Alouette watched in horror as the top of the contraption flickered, like it was waking up from a long slumber. A blinding flash and a thin beam of light ignited between the two PermaSteel columns. The beam was bright blue and vibrating. Restless.

The crowd sucked in a collective breath.

"It looks like a blade," Alouette heard someone whisper. It sounded like a child.

The beam—the blade—started to glide slowly downward between the columns, sizzling and flashing as it moved, sending small blue sparks into the thick, wet air.

Alouette's gaze flitted back to the young girl lying beneath it. Her face was now hidden by her cascading auburn hair, but her slim neck was exposed.

And it lay right in the path of the beam.

Suddenly, everything became horribly and terrifyingly clear to Alouette.

"No! No!" The words rushed from her mouth. "No! No! No!"

The beam kept lowering, making its fatal descent between the twin columns. The girl's limbs went rigid, as if she could sense what was coming next.

Alouette's stomach rolled and heaved, and her legs began to shake. "No!" she cried again, but this time the word was lost in a shudder.

The beam hovered just centimètres above the girl's unblemished neck. There wasn't so much as a breath in the entire crowd. Alouette tried to steel herself, wondering if she might faint. She heard a soft sizzle and then suddenly someone grabbed her from behind, clamping a hand over her eyes.

"Don't watch," a deep voice whispered close to her ear.

She knew the voice.

There was only one person it could be.

He'd saved her.

Saved her from the awful sight.

Saved her from witnessing the horror of the Ministère's heartless sentence.

But he couldn't save her from the girl's screams.

Or the smell of burning flesh.

- CHAPTER 42 -
MARCELLUS

MARCELLUS WISHED HE'D LOOKED AWAY TOO.

He wished he could stop staring.

But, as he shielded the girl's eyes, he couldn't seem to pull his own eyes away from what was happening on the platform. They were transfixed by the horror. The blue beam didn't drop fast. It moved slowly, painstakingly, with tiny blinding sparks whirling and disappearing into the air like miniature fireworks. When the laser finally reached Nadette's neck, there wasn't a sound in the Marsh. It seemed like even the droids held their nonexistent breath.

There was no blood. The burning-hot laser cauterized her flesh too quickly for blood to spill. But the smell was enough to turn even the strongest stomachs. Marcellus felt himself gag and cough. He was barely able to keep himself from being sick. The sight of the young girl's head thumping into a metal can beneath the device, Marcellus knew, would never be erased from his memory.

Not ever.

Marcellus's breathing was coming in heavy, sharp gasps. He tried to remind himself of little Marie and the painful way she'd died too.

But that just made him feel worse. Marie's little face. Nadette's kind smile. The way they used to call out to each other through the long corridors of the Palais as they played. The same way he had done with Mabelle.

The memories cycled in his mind, blurring into one another. Nadette and Marie. Mabelle and Marcellus. Two Palais governesses accused of being Vangarde. Two convicted.

One now dead.

A low, pained groan shook Marcellus from his thoughts. He turned toward the girl next to him. The girl who called herself Alouette.

He had found her again.

He'd doubted he ever would.

And yet, as he'd been patrolling the crowds, surveying for signs of hostility, there she'd been. Staring up at Nadette, her face aghast, desperately shouting something he couldn't hear. As soon as he'd laid eyes on her, Marcellus had leapt into action. He knew he had to protect her from what was about to happen. He had to shield her from the horror. The girl had seemed so innocent to him in the Fret hallway. She'd panicked at the sight of a few droids. He couldn't imagine what she might do if she'd seen *this*.

But now she was standing there, gaping at the platform, where the droids were dragging away what was left of Nadette's body. Marcellus hadn't even noticed he'd dropped his hand from her eyes.

"Are you okay?" Marcellus asked. He raised a hand to comfort her but soon realized he didn't know where to put it. On her shoulder? On her arm? Over her eyes again?

He let it fall back to his side.

The girl was mumbling something incoherent. Marcellus wondered if it was even coherent to her. It sounded like babble. Her eyes were glassy, and her breaths were rapid and shallow.

Was she going into shock?

She was still staring at the platform. The body was gone. All that was left was that gruesome machine. A Reichenstat invention, his grandfather had said. Made more efficient by Ministère cyborg scientists. All Marcellus could see now was a horrible contraption he wanted loaded onto the next voyageur and launched into deep space.

"Officer Bonnefaçon?" Inspecteur Limier's clipped voice reverberated through Marcellus's audio patch, pulling his attention away from the girl and the contraption. "Are you there?"

Marcellus stepped away from the girl, out of her earshot, before reaching into his pocket and unfolding his TéléCom. "I'm here."

"The crowd is getting restless. We need to be prepared for another riot. I've already ordered more droids to be sent from the Precinct."

Marcellus stood up a little straighter, glancing anxiously around. The crowd did seem to be growing more agitated. They were still shouting at the platform, pushing and shoving at one another to get a closer look at the deathly contraption.

"What do you want me to do?" Marcellus asked the inspecteur.

"Get out of there."

Marcellus blinked, surprised. "What?"

"Leave the Marsh. Now."

"No," Marcellus immediately replied. "I can't. I need to stay and protect the Regime. I need to do my job."

"And we saw how well that turned out on Ascension day."

Anger flashed inside Marcellus. He was about to respond when suddenly Limier was shoved backward by a mob of people. His face momentarily vanished from the screen. When he returned a few seconds later, he was shouting, trying to be heard above the noise. "The future commandeur of our Ministère can't risk his life in a Third Estate riot. You're the general's grandson. You're a target. If anything happens to you, the general will never forgive me. Get out, Bonnefaçon. That's an order!"

"Inspecteur," Marcellus argued, but the connection was already cut.

With a frustrated sigh, Marcellus pocketed his TéléCom and walked back over to Alouette. She was still staring fixedly at the platform. Even as the crowd continued to push in from all sides, she didn't move. She seemed frozen to the spot.

"Hey." Marcellus maneuvered in front of her, blocking her view, forcing her to look at him. She did. And for a moment, Marcellus was speechless. He'd forgotten just how striking these eyes were. So vast and dark with a sparkle and a depth he'd never seen before. Certainly not anywhere on Laterre.

"Are you okay?" he asked again, the urgency in his tone rising.

Alouette seemed to snap awake from her trance. "Yes," she said. But then, a second later, she shook her head violently and yelled, "*No!* No, I'm not okay. Why did they do that?" She jabbed a finger toward the platform and the terrible machine. Her big eyes gleamed with heat and fury. "She was just a girl. How could they do that?"

"She murdered Mar—" Marcellus started to say the girl's name, but it hitched in his throat. "The Premier Enfant."

"But they can't. It's a mistake." Alouette's voice grew more impassioned. "Death punished with more death? That never worked on the First World. I thought the Regime knew that. I thought that's why they left it behind."

She was rambling now, and Marcellus found himself wondering again who this girl was.

Who talked like that?

"We should learn from history, not repeat it." She stared at the now-empty platform, where, only a few moments ago, Nadette had been alive. "It's not right."

As the crowd's shouts escalated, so did Marcellus's anxiety. This was no time to stand around discussing the morality of Nadette's execution. Limier was right. Another riot felt imminent.

Marcellus raised his hand and wrapped it around Alouette's closed fist. Her skin was cold and clammy, and she startled at his touch.

"Can I take you home?" Marcellus asked. She shook her head. "I think I should take you home. Where do you live?"

Alouette shook her head again. "No, I have to go," she said, and yanked her fist from him.

But as she did, something fluttered out from her hand. Marcellus swooped down to catch it and found himself holding a small, crumpled, cream-colored object, almost like a piece of paper. The kind they used to use in the First World.

Marcellus turned over the object and unfolded it.

It *was* paper.

And on it, someone had drawn a map. A map leading to a place Marcellus knew well. A place he visited whenever he needed to escape. The one place where he could always feel safe and alone.

Marcellus stared, dumbfounded, at the crude drawings of trees. The circular formation of small huts. The lake. The stream. There was no doubt in his mind. Marcellus was looking at a map of the old Défecteur camp in the forest.

But that camp had been deserted long ago. If this girl *was* a Défecteur, as he'd assumed, why would she want to go there?

The girl snatched the paper from his hand. "I have to go," she said again.

Stunned, Marcellus looked up at her. "Is that where you're going?"

A look of trepidation passed over her face, but she didn't respond.

"I know where that is," Marcellus said.

Her eyes flashed wide. "You *do*? You know—"

But the rest of her words were drowned out. The crescendo of shouts rose into one raucous, pulsing cry. Marcellus couldn't make out exactly what they were saying—something about "the blade"—but he could feel the energy in the air shift. Then he could feel the pressure at his back. The mob started to rush the platform, shoving into Marcellus and Alouette. A few people managed to climb onto the platform and began to attack the deadly contraption, shouting, "Down with the Ministère!"

Marcellus spun in a slow circle, assessing the threat. The newly ordered droids were already being dispatched into the fray.

He thought briefly of Inspecteur Limier's directives. *"You're a target. . . . Get out, Bonnefaçon. That's an order!"* But he felt like his mind was being torn in half. Part of him wanted to disobey Limier. Stay and defend the Regime. Be the commandeur he wanted so badly to be. But the other part knew Limier was right. He was a target. Which meant anyone near him would be in danger too.

His gaze landed back on Alouette, then on the map still resting in her hand.

"Come on," he said. "I'll take you away from here. Right now. I'll take you where you want to go."

He held out his hand. The girl looked at his palm and then up at his face. She studied him for a few long seconds.

"It's okay," he said softly. "You can trust me."

Marcellus felt the crowd push in harder around them.

The girl stared down at his outstretched hand for another long moment. Then she took a deep breath and slipped her hand into his.

- CHAPTER 43 -
CHATINE

CHATINE WASN'T SURE HOW IT HAD HAPPENED. ONE minute the entire crowd seemed to be calling for the girl's head, and the next they were calling for justice for the dead governess. No, not just calling. Shouting. Screaming. And then they were fighting.

Sometimes Chatine swore her entire estate was delusional. They looked to an impossible lottery to save them from their miserable lot in life. They ate up every false word the Ministère fed them about honest work and honest chances. And now they were scrapping like stray dogs over a found chicken bone, creating weapons out of everything and anything they could find, attacking officers and Policier deputies and even droids.

Who attacks a droid?

Idiots, Chatine thought as she watched a man leap onto a droid's back and the droid toss and turn trying to get him off.

Chatine sank to her knees and began to crawl through the fray. Her mother had actually taught her this trick years ago, crawling around on the grimy floor of the Marsh. It was a surprisingly efficient way to move through a crowd, as well as an excellent angle from which to reach into people's pockets.

But Chatine wasn't concerned with pinching random trinkets and measly scraps of bread right now. She was looking for Marcellus. After losing Alouette, she'd finally spotted him again roaming the crowds in the center of the Marsh. Right before the awful contraption had sliced off that girl's head like it was nothing more than a piece of meat on the Patriarche's carving board. The stench was still trapped in Chatine's nostrils. She'd smelled seared flesh before—this was the Frets after all, medical procedures were often performed on the fly—but there was something about this particular stench. This particular flesh. It made Chatine's stomach roll.

In the end, she'd looked away.

She had plenty of disturbing memories to populate her nightmares. She didn't need any more.

But then the stupid boy—Marcellus—had vanished like smoke.

Chatine glanced up just in time to see three bashers barreling toward her, obviously in pursuit of someone. She tucked her knees into her chest and rolled adeptly to her left, landing safely under a stall. By the pungent, sour smell, she guessed it sold cabbages. And not fresh ones.

Chatine peered out just in time to see the droids apprehend the person they were looking for: a woman now dangling from one of their grasps. She swung her arms and kicked wildly.

Still fighting, Chatine mused with disbelief.

Did the woman even know what she was fighting for? Or were they all just following the horde? Feeding off the frenetic energy that Chatine could feel vibrating in her bones?

If what Mabelle had said about the Vangarde being nonviolent was true, then their plan was not working.

"This is ridiculous," Chatine muttered aloud.

"Shhh!" came a voice from behind, startling her. She spun around to see a boy hiding in the shadows under the stall. She hadn't even noticed him when she'd first rolled under here, which made her anxious. Chatine noticed *everything*.

The boy was skinny, his clothes no more than a bunch of rags. But something perched on his head glinted. Two discs of plastique, circled in PermaSteel. It was a pair of goggles, like the kind Chatine remembered the exploit miners wearing in Montfer. Except these were so big on the kid, they covered most of his head. He looked like an oversized insect.

The boy scowled at Chatine. "They'll find us," he whispered, holding a hand to his lips.

"Sorry," Chatine whispered back.

She vaguely recognized the boy. She'd seen him hanging around the Frets before, but she didn't know his name. "Oublies" was what his kind were called around here. Homeless and parentless. Abandoned or orphaned.

Forgotten.

Basically, just another Fret rat like her.

"You can't stay here," the boy told her. "This stall and the inside of the Thibault statue are all part of my turf."

She fought back a smile.

Definitely like her.

"You can go *inside* the Thibault statue?" Chatine asked, wondering why she had never thought of that before.

The boy flashed a wicked grin. "Yes! It's totally fantastique in there. The perfect place to hide from bashers." His grin turned to a scowl. "But don't get any ideas. Like I said, *my* turf." He pointed to the ground Chatine was sitting on and then at Chatine. "And *you're* trespassing."

"I'll be gone in a second." She peered out of the stall, scanning the crowd for Marcellus.

"Rent is ten largs a minute." He held out his arm and pulled up his sleeve to reveal his Skin, waiting for payment.

Chatine tucked her head back inside. "I'm not paying you."

"Then get out," he said.

Chatine sighed. "I'm just looking for someone. As soon as I find him, I'll leave, okay?"

"What does he look like?"

"Stupide hair, stupide shiny raincoat, smiles like a sot."

"Officer Bonnefaçon? Oh, yeah, I saw him."

Chatine perked up. "You did. Where? When? Which way did he go?"

The boy crossed his arms over his chest. "That kind of information will cost you."

Chatine groaned. "How much?"

"Twelve largs."

"Three."

"Seven."

Chatine rolled her eyes and tapped her Skin against his, transferring the tokens. "Fine. Now tell me, what do you know?"

The boy glanced at his Skin, confirming the validity of the transaction. Then he looked up. "What do I know about what?"

"The officer."

"What officer?"

Chatine gritted her teeth. "Officer Bonnefaçon. You said you saw him."

The boy leaned back on his haunches. "I didn't see anything."

If Chatine hadn't been so impressed by the boy's ability to con her, she would have slapped him right now. And if she hadn't been preparing to leave this planet, she might even have asked to team up with him. "You're pretty despicable, you know that?"

He smiled. "Thank you."

"You should work for the Ministère."

The boy shook his head. "No can do. I've already got an employer."

"And who's that?"

He peered around the stall suspiciously and then leaned forward, gesturing for Chatine to do the same.

"Can you keep a secret?" he asked.

"Yes."

"I'm a spy," he whispered. "For the Vangarde."

Chatine clamped a hand over his mouth. "Don't joke about that."

"I'm not joking." The boy's muffled voice tickled against her palm. She pulled it away.

"If they hear you even utter that word, they'll bring you in. It doesn't matter how young you are."

"I'm not young," the boy snapped back, sitting up straighter, as though to try to make himself look taller.

"Right. I didn't mean young. I meant—"

"The Vangarde trusts me. I'm their eyes and ears in the Frets."

"Please stop saying that word."

"Are you afraid of them?" the boy asked, tilting his head.

"I'm not afraid of anything," Chatine fired back, even though she knew it wasn't true. She was afraid of plenty. She rubbed the small cut on her palm that was just starting to scab over, remembering the threat her father had made to her last night.

"They're nice," the boy said. "And they pay well."

Chatine shook her head. So this was what the Oublies did for fun? They played Vangarde spy? "Just be careful, okay? If you get caught doing anything—"

"Please," he interrupted her. "You're talking to Roche. Roche doesn't get caught."

"Roche." Chatine repeated the name, remarking at how well it fit him. "I like that."

"Gave it to myself," he said proudly. "After my parents were shipped off to Bastille."

Chatine lowered her head. "I'm sorry to hear that."

"Don't be. They were heroes. Spies just like me. They got captured in the line of duty."

She doubted that was true. But she smiled anyway. Because she, too, could remember a time when she used to make up stories about her parents. Anything to turn them into better people than they were. "They sound great."

"But that won't happen to me," Roche assured her.

"I'm sure it won't."

"Because I've got something my parents didn't have."

"What's that?" Chatine asked, enjoying the charade. It was a nice distraction.

But before Roche could answer, Chatine heard a voice outside of the stall. She froze.

"Shhh," she commanded Roche, pointing upward. Roche fell silent and listened.

"Can I take you home?" the voice said.

Chatine would recognize it anywhere, now.

"I think I should take you home. Where do you live?"

It was *his* voice.

Officer Bonnefaçon's.

"Is that where you're going? I know where that is."

His tone was soft and sweet. Chatine felt her pulse start to slow. Like his voice alone was enough to calm her. Suddenly, all the other sounds in the Marsh—the rumbling of droids, the shouts of the angry mob, the soundtrack of her *life*—faded into the background, and all she could hear was his voice.

"Come on," she heard him say. "I'll take you away from here. Right now. I'll take you where you want to go. . . . It's okay. You can trust me."

Chatine closed her eyes, allowing herself a moment to just imagine. Just pretend.

That he was looking at her right now.

That he was saying those words *to* her.

That he *would* take her away from here. Far, far away. To another planet. Maybe even to a whole other system. One that had a friendly sky and Sols that actually gave a damn about what happened to you. She took a breath and waited for him to say more. She wanted so badly to cling to this moment. To trust him. To forget everything that was happening outside this stall and just listen to him speak.

But he didn't.

The deafening sounds of the uprising came rushing back to her, crashing into her until she felt like every Third Estater with a weapon was suddenly charging *her*.

She blinked her eyes open and listened again. But the officer's voice had vanished, sucked up into the melee. And then she remembered her real motivation for finding Marcellus: Right now he was her only hope of getting off this planet.

"What was that about?" Roche was staring at her with a baffled expression.

"Nothing," she muttered. "Stay here."

"Of course I'm going to stay here. This is *my* turf, remember?"

Chatine peered out through the small gap between the stalls.

"And you still owe me rent," Roche reminded her. "It's been four and a half minutes. At ten largs a minute that's . . ." He paused, attempting to do the calculations in his head.

Chatine glanced desperately around the Marsh, just managing to spot the top of the officer's head disappearing into the swarm, his glossy silver raincoat getting swallowed up by a sea of shredded rags. And bobbing up and down behind him was a halo of springy black curls.

Chatine's pulse immediately spiked again.

Fric!

"Ten plus ten plus . . . ," Roche said, counting quietly on his fingers. "That'll be two hundred largs."

Chatine crawled out of the stall. "It's forty-five largs! And you can use the seven you conned from me as a down payment."

She jumped to her feet and chased after Marcellus and Alouette, weaving through bodies made of flesh and steel, ducking rayonette pulses that shimmered through the air searching for targets. But the crowd was too thick. By the time she squeezed out of the Frets, she knew she was too late. He was helping the girl onto the back of his moto. He was strapping a helmet onto her head. He was climbing onto the seat. He was pulling her arms around the waist of his silver coat, telling her to hold on.

And then he was revving the bike into gear, gripping the handlebars, and steering them away from the Frets.

"I'll take you away from here."

As she watched them disappear over the horizon, Chatine suddenly felt like *she* was the one on that platform, lying under that blade. But it wasn't her head the beam was aimed at.

With a growl, she kicked at the dirt and turned back to the Frets, clutching a hand to her chest, right over her heart, as though making sure there wasn't a giant, bleeding wound there.

- CHAPTER 44 -
ALOUETTE

LOW BRANCHES SLAPPED AND CRACKED AT ALOUETTE'S visor as the hovering vehicle weaved in and out of the trees.

Moto, she thought to herself, recalling the entry in the Chronicles about transportation. *A one- to two-person doorless vehicle—similar to a First World motorbike—that travels at speeds up to 200 kilomètres per hour.*

Her fingers and arms ached from holding so tightly to Marcellus, but she didn't dare loosen her grip around his sleek raincoat. The moto was moving too fast, skimming through the trees with the ease of a deer bounding and dancing through the forests of the First World. That is, before all the First World forests were cut down or burned up by the dirty air.

But these trees were so alive and vibrant. Brilliant green with thick tangles of even greener undergrowth that stretched out like a vast rug beneath them. It all felt like a dream, except her dreams were never like this. So colorful and vivid and *fast*. It was like someone had sped up the world and thrown pails of paint on everything.

Marcellus barely spoke to her during the ride. Just a few words, here and there, asking if she was okay. His voice was clearly being broadcast through some special technology in their helmets. But to Alouette, it seemed like he was speaking right inside her head.

Alouette could barely form a reply, though. She was still in shock. She couldn't believe what she'd just done. She'd left the Marsh with a stranger.

But she couldn't think about that now. She had to focus on what she'd come for: answers about her father and the truth about her past.

The glowing red dot on the hologram.

That was the only reason she'd said yes to the boy. Because she had to know. She had to find out what was hiding here in the Forest Verdure.

After weaving along the bank of the stream that snaked through the trees, Marcellus entered a clearing and slowed the moto to a halt. Alouette glanced around, recognizing the circle of small shelters. It was just like the clearing she'd sketched on her map.

How does he know about this place? Alouette wondered as she stepped off the bike and felt the spongy forest floor beneath her thin soles.

She pulled off her helmet and stared at her surroundings. Everything was magical. The small shelters were crudely made from mud and branches, but they were beautiful with their low-slung doors and thick mossy roofs. The huts were snugly encircled by tall trees, shooting straight up into the dappled gray and white clouds above.

"This is it, isn't it?" Marcellus asked, studying her. "The place on your map?"

"Yes," she said. "It is."

"Did you . . ." Marcellus swallowed. "Did your family live here?"

Alouette almost laughed at the question but caught herself just in time. He was serious, wasn't he? He really did think she might have once lived out here.

Why on Laterre would he . . . ?

But then it hit her. What if he was right? What if she and her father *had* lived here before they had come to the Refuge? What if this was where they'd been hiding?

"How do *you* know this place?" she asked guardedly.

Marcellus seemed saddened by the question. "I come out here to . . ." He paused. "I don't know, to get away from everything. It's peaceful. And quiet."

"Does everyone know about this place?"

Marcellus shook his head. "No. No one comes out here anymore. Ever since the Ministère found it and—" He stopped talking and looked to the ground, as though he were worried about saying the wrong thing. "Anyway, no one comes out here now but me."

Alouette's mind scrambled to put pieces together. The Ministère found this place, and then what? They kicked everyone out? They sent them to Bastille? Everyone except her and her father? Perhaps that was when they'd run away and escaped to the Refuge.

But where was her mother during all of this? Was she already dead?

"So, you don't recognize it then?" Marcellus was looking at her again, waiting for an answer.

Alouette shivered and rubbed her arms, trying to warm them in the cold, damp air. She wasn't sure how to answer that. She was wary about saying too much to this stranger. She still knew so little about him.

"Maybe," she said, avoiding his gaze. But she could still feel his eyes on her, studying her. The way he looked at her—like she was a secret to be uncovered—unsettled her. But there was something else, too. When his eyes were on her, a strange tingling started at the nape of Alouette's neck and traveled down her spine.

She couldn't explain it.

She wanted it to go away.

But then again, she wanted it to stay, too.

She prayed he wouldn't ask any more questions. Her mind was

too crammed full of her own questions. And the truth was, she was desperate to get away from him. Not because she didn't enjoy being with him—she did. More than she should. But she needed to explore this place on her own.

The hologram had shown her a smaller, nearby clearing: the one with a strange scattering of dark shapes on the ground. The red dot was positioned right over it. She knew it was significant somehow, but she didn't know why.

She shivered again.

"Are you cold?" he asked.

"I'm fine." But her teeth chattered.

"I'll get some wood and make a fire."

"You can do that?" Alouette's eyebrows shot up. "Build a fire, I mean?"

Marcellus looked surprised. "Can't you?"

She shook her head. "No."

Another strange look flashed over his face before he finally turned and headed toward the trees. "Wait here. I'll be right back."

Alouette watched him go, and as soon as he was out of sight, she pulled the map from her pocket. She peered down at her own sketch, trying to make out which direction she should go. She scanned her surroundings, looking at the trees and the sky above. Back on the First World, people would guide their way using the Sol and the stars. But Laterre's clouds, as always, hung like a blanket over the forest. According to Sister Jacqui, the Sols hadn't been visible on Laterre in over nine years.

The sky held no answers.

She would simply have to circle the camp until she found the clearing. She hitched up her tunic so it wouldn't snag on the uneven ground and headed into the trees in the opposite direction of Marcellus.

But it was difficult to walk in the forest. The undergrowth was thick and tangled, and when her canvas shoes did find the ground, they sank into the dark soil, which was matted with dead leaves and rotting vines. She moved slowly through the damp vegetation. Minutes passed, branches creaked, and fat raindrops dripped from the trees above. Yet still she found nothing. No clearing. None of the strange shadowy shapes she'd seen on the hologram. Only more trees and more twisting undergrowth.

"Where is it?" she murmured to herself.

Alouette looked at her map again and tried to study it as she walked. But her foot snagged on the uneven ground and she tumbled, thrusting out her hand to break her fall. Something sharp scraped against her palm.

"Ow!" she cried.

Wincing with pain, Alouette looked down to see a pile of large rounded stones scattered around her, hidden beneath the knee-high grass and shrubs.

Are these . . . ?

She urgently pushed the grass aside until she could see that the stones were arranged in the shape of a crescent moon.

She scrabbled a few mètres to her left, her fingers scraping at the damp ground until she came across another collection of stones, this time placed in the form of . . .

"A star!" Alouette cried aloud as she leapt to her feet and stared down.

Just as she expected, from this angle the stones disappeared, hidden beneath the undergrowth. But not completely. The grass and weeds weren't able to grow on *top* of the stones, which meant, every few mètres, there was a shadowy gap in the forest floor.

An outline left by the stones beneath.

A shape.

She sucked in an elated breath.

This is it!

This was the smaller clearing she'd seen on the hologram map.

But a moment later, her hopes fell again as she realized she still had no idea what she was looking for. The place felt no more familiar than the camp. She spun around and around, and then weaved in and out of the stone formations, searching for clues. Any clues.

But nothing jumped out at her. What was this place? What were these stones? Their arrangement was definitely purposeful, but she had no idea what it could mean. And, most important, why were they marked on her father's map with a blinking red dot?

Alouette didn't really know what she'd expected to find here. But she had expected to find *something*. Something clear and obvious. An answer to all her questions. But now all she had were these stones, clusters and clusters of them, buried in the grass, surrounded by trees. Endless trees under an endless gray, unfathomable sky.

"Amazing, right?"

The voice made her jump.

It was Marcellus. He was standing on the edge of the clearing, his arms full of sticks. He began walking toward her. "It took me forever to figure out what these stones meant. I assumed it must be some sort of ritual or something. You know, for the Défec—" He cleared his throat. "The people who lived here." He cocked his head and looked straight at her.

She leaned forward, waiting for him to continue. "And?" she prompted. "Did you figure it out?"

He frowned, like he was expecting a different reaction. "Yes, it's a graveyard. At least that's my best guess. They buried their dead here. Like they used to do in the First World."

Alouette blinked. This was *not* what she'd expected him to say.

"Buried their dead."

Marcellus's words rang in her ears as she spun in another slow circle, peering down at the curious shadows and stones in the grass.

A graveyard?

Suddenly, Alouette's heart violently skipped behind her ribs.

Maman?

Is she buried here?

Alouette closed her eyes and tried to conjure up something. Anything. A face. A burial. Tears. People crying. Digging. A hole in the ground. But nothing appeared. Before the Refuge, there was only darkness.

Darkness, and now that one hazy memory.

"Hush, ma petite. Hush."

Alouette shuddered.

"You're freezing," Marcellus said tenderly. "Come back to the camp. I'll show you my fire-building skills."

He picked out a small stick from his bundle and waved it playfully, grinning.

For a moment, Alouette saw him as a little boy, eager and adventurous. It made her smile too.

She followed behind him as he walked out of the clearing, back toward the camp.

"Did you find what you were looking for?" Marcellus asked, and, even though his voice was light and conversational, Alouette could hear the desperation in his words. He wanted to know more about her. He wanted answers. Answers she couldn't give. Not even to herself.

She glanced back at the clearing. The mysterious stones had already disappeared among the tall grass and wild shrubs, like memories lost and overgrown with time.

"I did," Alouette said. She turned back, praying that Marcellus couldn't tell what a terrible liar she was.

CHAPTER 45

MARCELLUS

THE GIRL WAS LYING.

That, Marcellus could be sure of. It was written all over her face. She was hiding something. She'd always been hiding something. But what? That was the big mystery.

What had she come out here to find?

Why was she acting like she didn't even recognize this place? When he'd told her about the graves, she'd looked astonished. Like the ritual of burying the dead was completely foreign to her. An unfathomable thing.

They arrived back at the camp, and Marcellus dropped the sticks he'd found into the fire pit. He then sat down and started to arrange the wood. Alouette sat beside him, watching him carefully. She had a studious way about her. Like someone who always drank in the world with her big eyes. He liked that about her. As he struck the match and lit the flame, he couldn't help stealing glances at her. The fire clearly delighted her. Almost as much as it had delighted him the first time he'd made one.

And then she spoke. Quiet and contemplative, almost as though speaking to herself. "Prometheus."

"Prometheus?" Marcellus repeated, the word sounding clumsy and foreign in his mouth. "What's that?"

She stared at the flames. "He stole fire from the gods and gave it to the humans. Although, some say he was stealing it back. The human race already had fire, and Zeus had just hidden it as a punishment."

Marcellus turned and stared at Alouette. It was as though she were speaking another language. Zeus? Gods? Stealing fire? He wondered if this was one of those nonsense Défecteur fables his grandfather had told him about.

"A punishment for what?" Marcellus asked, suddenly finding himself desperate to know.

She smiled at him and his chest squeezed. "Oh, it's a long story. I was just thinking how you're kind of like Prometheus."

Marcellus wondered if that was a compliment or not. "How so?"

"Man had fire back on the First World. Then we came here, and the fire was taken away because it was thought to be too dangerous and destructive. And now you've brought it back."

Marcellus hesitated, unsure how to continue. "But I didn't—I mean, I just found this place. The fire was here."

Has she never seen fire before?

Marcellus thought all the Défecteurs used fire in their camps. But maybe not. Maybe she was from one of the other camps across Laterre that had been shut down over the years. Or maybe the rumors were true. Maybe some Défecteur tribes really had managed to evade his grandfather's roundups.

"Why don't you have a Skin?" he asked, trying to sound as casual as possible. He knew he had to be careful. He didn't want to sound like he was interrogating her, for fear of scaring her away. If she really was a Défecteur, then he, an officer of the Ministère, would be considered her enemy. Yet, for some reason, she didn't seem to be afraid of him.

Alouette looked up suddenly, like he'd woken her from a dream.

Marcellus noticed how the flames of the fire reflected and danced in her eyes. It made him momentarily forget what he had just asked her. But it didn't matter. It was clear she wasn't going to answer him anyway. Her gaze quickly returned to the fire.

He tried to reel the conversation back in. "I'm sorry. I'm just curious about you. You're so . . ."

She turned toward him again and their gazes latched like a pair of magnets, making Marcellus's face flush with heat. She seemed so intrigued by what he was about to say. And Marcellus suddenly felt as if his entire future with this girl hinged on his next word.

"So, what?" she asked.

A thousand responses fluttered through his mind, each seeming more ridiculous and inappropriate than the last.

Strange.

Beautiful.

Entrancing.

"Mysterious," he finally said.

"Mysterious." She echoed the word back to him, like she was saying it for the first time, trying it out. Then she laughed. "I've never thought of myself as mysterious before."

"Oh, but you are."

She bit her lip, which made her look both thoughtful and vulnerable at the same time. "What makes me mysterious?"

"Well, let's see." He began counting on his fingers, keeping his voice light and playful. "You can read the Forgotten Word. You don't have a Skin. You acted like you've never seen a droid before. You wanted me to take you out into the Forest Verdure but then acted like you've never been here. And you seem to appear and disappear into thin air." He watched her carefully for a reaction, wondering if he'd let himself go too far. But all he could read on her face was amusement. "Maybe," he went on, with a sudden stroke of inspiration, "you're a ghost."

She laughed, and in that moment, with that perfect sound bouncing between them, Marcellus felt as though he could fly.

"Maybe I am a ghost," she admitted with a small smile.

He felt himself smiling too, something he definitely didn't do enough these days. "A ghost who lives in the Frets?"

"Maybe."

"You use that word a lot," he pointed out.

She shrugged. "It's a good word."

"It's a *mysterious* word." He pointed to another finger, adding this to his growing list.

"Maybe," she repeated with an even bigger grin.

Marcellus laughed and shook his head. He looked back into the fire and watched the flames lick and curl around one another. There was something so tender and intriguing, gentle yet strong, about this girl. It both fascinated him and maddened him. The longer he sat with her, the more he felt as though he were being pulled into her. But at the same time, she was still a blank slate to him. A paradox in a strange gray tunic with eyes that seemed full of both wisdom and innocence at the same time.

And then, just as quickly as the laughter had come, the sadness followed. Marcellus squeezed his hands together, as if he were wringing out the loneliness that was welling, suddenly and unexpectedly, inside his chest. "I've just never met anyone like you."

When Alouette looked over at him, the smile had vanished from her face too. Now her eyes were wide with concern. It was as though she'd sensed the sadness in his voice and felt the inexplicable shift in the air around him. Were his emotions that obvious?

Maybe to her, they were.

Alouette took a breath and sat up straighter. "It's because of my father. He doesn't like me going up—" She seemed to cut herself off. "He doesn't like me going outside. He forbids it. So I guess I am sort of like a ghost."

Marcellus startled at the honesty in her voice. She was answering his questions. She was letting him in. "Never?"

Alouette shook her head, and her eyes darted back to the fire. "Never."

His brow furrowed. "Why?"

"He's . . ." She seemed to struggle for the right word. "Protective. And . . ."

"Strict," Marcellus finished for her.

Alouette looked surprised. "Yes. How did you—"

"My grandfather is the same way."

"Strict?" Alouette confirmed.

Marcellus nodded. "It's only because he wants so badly for me to succeed. I mean, I do too. But it's hard. He's very . . . private. He never talks about anything."

Alouette chuckled. "Neither does my father."

"I feel sorry for him sometimes. He's been through so much. Especially this year. He lost a very dear friend in the fourth month. Actually, she might have been more than a friend, but I'll never know because there's no way he would ever tell me that."

Alouette tilted her head, watching him with that studious expression of hers. Like she was trying to memorize every word he said. "Do you ever try to ask him about it?"

Marcellus scoffed. "I've tried. But he shuts down whenever I mention her name. It's hard for him to talk about that kind of stuff. He's lost a lot of people in his life. My father—his son. My mother. And now her."

"It sounds like you've lost a lot of people too. I'm sorry."

Marcellus swallowed. "Thanks."

"How did she die? Your grandfather's friend."

Marcellus stared down at his hands, kneading them mercilessly. It felt good to have someone to finally talk to about Commandeur Vernay—about all of this—yet he still felt oddly guilty. Like he was betraying his grandfather's trust. "The Patriarche sent her on a dangerous mission, which my grandfather thought was a bad idea from the start. She never made it back." Marcellus flinched a little at this understatement. The commandeur had been captured and executed by firing squad along with her entire unit, when they were caught trying to assassinate the Albion queen.

"Wait, who is your grandfather?"

Marcellus's gaze shot up. It took him a few seconds to decipher the alarm in her dark brown eyes.

She doesn't know.

All his life, he'd assumed everyone knew who he was. The First Estate. The Second Estate. Even the Third Estate. Sometimes it felt like the whole of Laterre had their eyes trained on him, waiting to see how he would turn out. Would he become like his grandfather, a great leader? Or would he become like his father, a traitor?

But this girl. Somehow *she* didn't know.

And that made her more intriguing than ever.

Suddenly, Marcellus understood why she was here with him. Why she had agreed to come with him. Why she didn't seem afraid of him. If she found out he was related to the man responsible for rounding up Défecteurs on Laterre, he'd surely never see her again.

"Uh . . . um," he stammered, trying desperately to undo the panic on her face. "He's . . . no one important."

Her eyes narrowed, as though trying to decide whether or not to believe him. He quickly maneuvered the conversation back to where it had begun. "Anyway, yeah, he can be a little hard to live with sometimes. But he raised me." He paused. "Actually, he didn't. I mean, technically he's my guardian, but he's a very busy man. I was raised by a governess." His voice fell. "Her name was Mabelle."

"Mabelle," Alouette repeated. "From the message on the shirt?"

Marcellus felt his fists clench at the memory of seeing Mabelle in the boglands. "Yes."

"Did you go to her in Montfer?" she asked. "Like the message said?"

"I . . . ," he began, flustered. He still wasn't sure what to make of that trip. It had all been so confusing. Mabelle's words whispered in his ear. The song she hummed to him. The look of betrayal on Théo's face when Marcellus had told him that the Regime was fine the way it was. "I did," he finished, "but it turned out to be nothing."

One of Alouette's eyebrows rose, and she studied him for a few moments, as though she could see right through him. Read his thoughts. Just like the ghost she claimed to be. When she spoke again, he was certain she would call him on the lie, but instead she said, "Your governess. Isn't that what that woman was today? The one who was executed? A governess?"

Marcellus felt a stab in his chest at the memory. He'd miraculously been able to chase it away for the past hour, but now it came roaring back to him like a dying flame come back to life.

"Yes. Nadette. She was the Premier Enfant's governess."

"I just don't understand why they killed her," Alouette went on. The heat was beginning to build in her eyes again. The fury he'd seen back in the Marsh. "They've never executed anyone before."

"They had to make an example of her. They can't punish the murderer of the Paresse heir the same way they'd punish a petty thief. New crimes call for new forms of punishment." The words charged out of him so quickly, he didn't realize they were his grandfather's words, not his own, until it was too late. He felt sick to his stomach at the realization. He sounded like a programmed droid.

"Stop parroting every little thing your grandfather ever told you!"

The memory of Mabelle's words made him shudder.

"But killing her is murder too, isn't it?" Alouette countered, her voice hoarse but firm. "It's no different from what she did. Or what they claim she did."

"You don't believe she did it?" The question shot out of Marcellus like a pulse from a rayonette, desperately seeking a target.

His urgency seemed to startle Alouette. "I don't know. Do *you* think she did?"

And there it was. The question he hadn't been able to answer. At least not to himself. And definitely not to his grandfather. But to her? To this strange, mysterious ghost-girl who talked like she was from another time? Another planet? Who didn't know who he was?

He somehow felt like he could say it to her.

"No." The word was barely a whisper, as quiet as a thought. "I don't."

Their eyes locked for another long moment. And then it was as though she'd ripped open a door. The words began to whoosh out of him, like air that had been trapped in a dark, solitary cell on Bastille.

"I don't know what to think anymore. About anything. They took Mabelle away when I was eleven. They told me she was a traitor. And she *was*. She admits it! But before that, she was . . . I don't know, she was like a mother to me. She really seemed to care about me."

"Maybe she did," Alouette said tenderly.

"Maybe." Marcellus caught Alouette's eye as he said the word, and they shared a smile. "We used to play all sorts of games. Like hide-and-seek in the gardens. One time, she hid in the fountain. Right in the middle!" Marcellus couldn't help smiling at the memory. "My grandfather was so angry when we trooped home, both of us soaking wet."

Alouette smiled back at him. "She sounds fun."

"She was. She taught me the Forgotten Word, too."

Her eyebrow shot up again. "You know the Forgotten Word? Why couldn't you read the message in the shirt then?"

Marcellus sheepishly dropped his eyes back to the glowing fire. "After she was taken away, I guess I just sort of . . . forgot it all."

"I'm sure you remember *some* of it."

Marcellus shook his head somberly. "No. It just looks like gibberish to me now."

"That's nonsense. I bet you can still read it if you try." Alouette glanced around, as though searching for something. She tipped her head down to the collar of her tunic. "Here!" she said, pulling out a long string of metallic beads hanging from her neck. Fastened to the end was a shiny silver tag. "Read this."

She beckoned him closer, and Marcellus scooted a centimètre to his left so that he could lean in and see the letters engraved into the metal.

"What is this?" he asked, gesturing to the beads.

Alouette's face closed down again, as though he'd said the wrong thing. Why was he always saying the wrong thing?

"It's . . . ," she began. "They're . . ." But she shook her head, like she was having an internal argument with herself. "Just read it."

He peered at the engraving again. The letters looked vaguely familiar, but he couldn't make sense of them. Their meaning was clouded by time.

"I can't."

"Yes, you can." She scooted closer to him. So close Marcellus could feel her breath on his skin, warm and sweet like a hint of the honeysuckle he sometimes smelled in the gardens in the early evening. "Just try."

He looked back down at the tag. He could tell there were two words. He remembered that much. But the letters just hung together, a blur and a jumble of tiny lines.

"The first word is tougher," Alouette said. "Maybe try the second."

He stared hard, really hard, squinting at the letters. Why was he so stupide? Why couldn't he just remember?

"Just sound it out," Alouette encouraged him. "One letter at a time."

He could hear Mabelle saying the same thing to him.

"Sound it out, Marcellou. You can do it."

And then, like fog evaporating in front of him, the first letter began to take shape in his mind. His tongue instinctively pressed against the roof of his mouth, forming a sound.

"L . . . ," he said aloud, surprising himself nearly as much as Alouette.

"Yes!" she exclaimed, getting just as excited as Mabelle used to. "That's it! Keep going."

He stared harder. The fog was still heavy. He tried to hold Mabelle's face in his mind. Not the worn, weathered face he'd seen yesterday in Montfer, but the young, jubilant face of his governess all those years ago. The one who danced with him in fountains and hid with him under tents made of sateen sheets. As she slowly came back to him, so did the letters.

"A . . . R . . ." He looked over at Alouette and she grinned, nodding.

"Yes. You're almost there."

"L . . . AR . . . LAR." He strung the sounds together. When he reached the last letter, he paused. It was a straight line with two smaller lines jutting out from it at opposite angles. As he stared at it, a strange clucking noise suddenly sprang from his tongue, as if it had been hiding there, just waiting for him to find it all these years later.

"L . . . A . . . R . . . K!" he shouted, grinning wildly. "It spells 'lark'!"

"Yes, that's what it says!"

Then they were grinning at each other, looking into each other's eyes.

"What does it mean?" he asked.

"It's my nickname. Little Lark. See, there's the word 'little.'" She pointed at the first word on her tag. "That's what they—" She stopped, seemingly catching herself again. "That's what my father calls me."

He smoothed over the tag with his thumb. "I like it. It's a bird, right? The lark. A bird from the First World?"

She nodded. "A bird that sings early in the morning. Apparently, when I was little, I would sing every morning, as soon as I woke up."

Their eyes met again, and Marcellus realized the loneliness that had clenched in his chest earlier was gone. It had been replaced with a fluttering. Like a million tiny wings. He felt the sudden urge to pull her toward him, wrap his arms around her, press his lips to hers. . . .

But then she spoke again, and it was like ice-cold water splashing over his head.

"Marcellou. That's *your* nickname, right? I remember it from the message."

Marcellus let the silver tag slip from his hands. "Yes," he murmured.

She didn't move away. She stayed close, her head cocked to one side. She was studying him again. Those observant eyes penetrating his. "Is that what your grandfather calls you?"

Marcellus scoffed at the question. "Are you kidding? General Bonnefaçon is way too busy and important for silly nicknames."

It was out of his mouth before he even realized what he'd said.

The reaction was immediate. It was as though she'd been bitten. Alouette jerked back from him so fast, Marcellus flinched. "What did you just say?"

He tried to cover. "I—I said my grandfather is too busy and important for nicknames."

But she was too shrewd. Too clever. She'd heard what he'd said. "But you called him something. Something else." Her voice was shaky, guarded. "Your grandfather is General Bonnefaçon?"

"Yes, but don't worry, I—"

It was too late, though. Marcellus could see it in her eyes. The light flickering off. The sparkle extinguishing. Her face closed down again. It was as if every layer he'd worked so hard to peel away over the past hour had flipped back into place.

"So you're Marcellus *Bonnefaçon*?" she confirmed.

He swallowed, suddenly wishing he could take back what he'd said. Anything to bring back the sparkle that had been there just a moment ago.

But it was gone.

Like the dying embers of the fire.

Alouette shivered fiercely.

"You're still freezing. Here, take this." Marcellus leapt up and began to unbutton his raincoat. But before he could even get the garment off his shoulders, Alouette was on her feet, backing hurriedly away from him.

"I need to go. My father. He'll be looking for me." Her voice was rushed and breathless. She would no longer meet his eye. "Can you take me back to the Marsh now?"

Resigned, he buttoned up his coat again. "Yes," he said. "Of course."

And, as they walked back to his moto, Marcellus knew. He felt it in his gut, like a kick.

He'd lost her again.

CHAPTER 46

ALOUETTE

MARCELLUS BONNEFAÇON.

As the moto swerved through the trees and the wind battered against her helmet, all Alouette could hear was his name looping and cycling in her mind.

Marcellus Bonnefaçon.

How could it be true? The boy she'd tended to in the hallway. The boy with the deep laugh and the kind smile who'd built a fire and sat beside her just a short while ago. The boy whom she was now holding on to as they raced back through the forest.

He was the grandson of General Bonnefaçon.

Alouette knew all about the general from the Chronicles and her lessons. She knew he was the leader of the Ministère and the head advisor to current Patriarche Lyon, as well as his late father, Patriarche Claude. The general was one of the most powerful men on the planet. And here Alouette was, the daughter of a convict—an *escaped* convict!—riding on the back of a moto with his grandson.

But Marcellus wasn't just the general's grandson.

When he'd offered Alouette his raincoat, she'd seen the shiny epaulets of his uniform. The crisp white jacket. The row of sparkling titan buttons. She knew exactly what they were.

And more important, what they *meant*.

Officer Bonnefaçon.

It's why he'd been in the Frets the other day. And in the Marsh today for the execution. He wasn't *just* a member of the Second Estate. He was an officer of the Ministère!

She'd been a sister for barely a full day, and she'd already messed up. She'd put the Refuge and the library in danger. If the Ministère was somehow able to find the Refuge now and destroy all the books the sisters had worked so hard to protect for nearly 150 years, it would be all her fault.

As they swerved and rumbled through trees, Alouette tried to remember what she'd told Marcellus back at the fire. How much had she revealed? She hadn't said anything about the Refuge or the First World books that were hidden there. She was sure of that. Which meant she hadn't broken the vow of secrecy. But still, had she told him enough for the Ministère to track them down?

It was as though Alouette had forgotten everything the sisters had ever taught her. "Be an observer," Sister Jacqui always said. "Be present and awake to your world."

But Alouette hadn't been present or awake. And she certainly hadn't been observant. She'd let the warm fire and the deep hazel eyes of Marcellus lull her straight to sleep.

"Imbécile," she muttered aloud.

"What was that?" Marcellus's voice reverberated through her headset.

Startled, Alouette looked up and realized they were out of the trees. The forest was now behind them, and they were passing by the sprawling fermes on the outskirts of Vallonay.

"Nothing," she replied.

The moto sped onward until the Frets rose up in front of them and Marcellus finally pulled the vehicle to a stop at the edge of the Marsh. Alouette immediately scrabbled off the bike.

"Thanks for the ride," she muttered, avoiding Marcellus's gaze. "I should get going now." She yanked at the strap on her helmet, but she couldn't manage to unfasten it. Her fingers were shaking too much.

"Wait," Marcellus said, hurrying over to her. "Let me help you."

With ease, he unlatched the strap and slipped the helmet from her head. But his fingers caught in her hair, and he let out an awkward chuckle. For a moment, their gazes locked and Alouette could feel a shiver work its way down her spine.

He's the general's grandson, she reminded herself. *Officer Bonnefaçon.*

Her cheeks started to burn with anger. But she wasn't sure whom she was angry with. Herself for not having realized it sooner? Or him for not telling her?

"I have to go," she said hastily, breaking the strange current streaming between them.

She started to back away.

"No, wait, I—"

"Why didn't you tell me?" she blurted out.

Marcellus looked startled. "What?"

"You could have told me who your grandfather is. Or were you purposefully keeping it a secret?"

"No," Marcellus rushed to say. "I wasn't keeping it a secret. I thought you knew." His voice grew quiet as he stared down at the ground. "I thought everyone knew."

Alouette shrank back, feeling more stupid than ever.

"Look," Marcellus said, stepping toward her again. "I'm not going to tell him, if that's what you're worried about. I'm not going to—"

But his words were cut short by a chorus of shouts, followed by a deep rumbling sound.

They both turned toward the marketplace. A swarm of people were charging straight toward them, shouting, with their fists in the air. Some were throwing rocks, others were grabbing vegetables and loaves of chou bread that had tumbled from the upturned stalls. Behind the crowd, Alouette spotted a pack of droids, like giant flashing, shimmering insects, trampling anything in their path.

She froze at the sight.

Marcellus grabbed her by the hand and pulled her out of the way. The mob streamed past them, the droids clanking in pursuit.

"It isn't safe here," Marcellus said, his expression anxious. "I should really escort you home."

Alouette's stomach flipped.

No! No way! He most certainly could not escort her home. She'd already done enough damage today. She wasn't about to lead him straight to the Refuge's door.

"I'm fine," she snapped. "I can get home on my own."

It was a lie. She wasn't sure if she *could* get home on her own. She had no idea how far she was from Fret 7 and the mechanical room. Or which direction to go to get there. She was completely turned around. She scanned the Marsh, searching for something—anything—familiar, but it all looked like another world to her. Another planet, even.

She could just make out the head of Thibault Paresse in the distance, towering over the chaos like a bronzed Sol. She remembered the execution taking place on a platform right near there. Perhaps if she headed toward it . . .

Marcellus tugged on her sleeve again. "At least let me see you again. Tomorrow? Will you meet me somewhere? Anywhere? Please."

His fingers released her sleeve and slid down her arm until he was holding her hand. No, not just holding. *Squeezing.* Alouette felt her knees buckle just a little. She looked down, unable to bring herself to meet his eyes again, for fear of what she might say. What she might agree to.

This boy seemed to cast a spell over her.

A dangerous spell.

"I don't think so," she said hastily.

She could never see Marcellus Bonnefaçon again.

Not tomorrow.

Not any day.

But still Marcellus didn't release her hand. "*Please.* I'm sorry I didn't tell you about my grandfather. Let me make it up to you. We could go anywhere you want. I could take you back to the Forest Verdure. Or to Ledôme. Have you ever seen Ledôme? I could show it to you! We could—"

But Marcellus never finished the sentence, because suddenly a hand clamped down hard on his shoulder.

A big hand.

A very *familiar* hand.

Alouette's eyes widened and her heart leapt into her throat.

Then came the voice, equally familiar, and more terrifying than it had ever sounded to her.

"Let go of my daughter."

- CHAPTER 47 -
CHATINE

CONDITIONS IN THE MARSH HAD NOT IMPROVED. IN fact, they'd only gotten worse.

Chatine watched from a high beam overlooking the marketplace as five men clobbered a droid and actually brought it to the ground. She witnessed a group of rioters tear apart the new execution contraption—which people were already starting to call "the Blade"—like they were fighting over the carcass of a rabbit. She saw a Policier sergent fall at the hands of broken pipes. He was nearly beaten to death before a pack of bashers arrived to scatter the protesters and load the sergent into a med cruiseur.

Chatine had thought this whole spectacle would be entertaining to watch. After all, she had no stake in this fight. But as the shouts of anger and cries of pain grew louder, Chatine actually found herself feeling a little unsettled.

Her heart began to pound. She suddenly felt too exposed. Too vulnerable. The rioting, the violence—she'd never seen the Third Estaste this riled up before. Nor the droids so eager to inflict punishment. But she couldn't leave. She had to keep a lookout for Marcellus.

He was still her best chance at finding the Vangarde base. The stupide pomp had to come back eventually, right? And Chatine would be there waiting for him when he did.

Directly below her, a droid dragged a writhing, ranting woman through the aisles of the marketplace. She was putting up an impressive fight. She even managed to break free from the basher's grasp for a moment. But the second she tried to run, a paralyzeur pulse was buried deep into her calf and she collapsed to the ground with a snarl.

It was only then that Chatine recognized her.

It was Madame Dufour.

Chatine had always had bad blood with the old woman. But now, as she watched the droid march back toward her and scoop her up by the back of the neck, she almost felt sorry for her.

Until she remembered the scent that had wafted from Dufour's stall earlier today.

Chatine had never moved so fast in her life. Within a minute, she had reached the catwalk directly over Madame Dufour's stall. She peered over the edge. And there it was.

Tucked behind the stall on a plate hidden from view from anyone on the ground, the chicken was roasted to a perfect crispy brown. Her stomach growled. She was *so* hungry.

With her mouth already watering, she swung down from the catwalk and landed in a crouch inside the abandoned stall. She reached for the leg, but before she could wrap her hand around the bone, the plate was suddenly yanked out from under her.

"Hey!" she roared. She was fully prepared to fight anyone— including the Patriarche himself—for that chicken. That is, until she looked up and saw who was standing over her.

"Are you sure you should be here right now?" Her father sneered as he ripped a leg from the chicken and tore a piece of juicy flesh from the bone with his teeth. "Shouldn't you be out working this Bonnefaçon con you've cooked up?" He licked his grease-stained lips. "This is delicious."

"Give it back," she snarled.

Her father arched an eyebrow, clearly not about to do anything of the kind. He took another bite and rapped his fingers against the edge of the metal plate, making a harsh clanking sound. Chatine's gaze darted toward Marcellus's ring, shoved up around her father's weathered knuckle.

"I don't need to remind you of what's at stake here, do I?" Monsieur Renard asked.

Chatine glared, her cheeks flaming, as her father continued to knock the ring rhythmically against the plate.

Tap. Tap. Tap.

"No," she said through gritted teeth.

Her father stuffed the entire chicken leg into his mouth, raking his teeth against the bone. When he pulled it out again, all the meat was gone. Only the fatty tendons remained. He smacked his lips together. "Good. Because remember, *Chatine*, a child who doesn't bring in enough largs as a boy, must pull her weight as a girl."

The cut on the inside of her palm throbbed, as though her father were pressing his knife into her skin a second time.

He would, wouldn't he?

She was his own daughter, but she knew that wouldn't stop him. He'd send her off to the blood bordels in a heartbeat. There was no point in fighting.

There never had been.

"Why is it always me?" she fired back. "Why don't you ever threaten to send Azelle to the bordels? She's only two years older than me. Her blood is still worth something."

Monsieur Renard dropped the clean chicken bone onto the plate and reached for a wing. "Azelle brings in plenty from her fabrique job. And it's always smart to have someone *inside* the system. She serves her purpose."

Then, with the plate of chicken still in his hands, her father scooted out of the stall and sauntered right back into the fray, as if he were taking a moonlit stroll through one of the Palais gardens. As if the riots didn't faze him at all.

Chatine let out a growl of frustration and kicked at an empty turnip crate. She was furious at her father for threatening her. She was furious at Marcellus for running off with the Défecteur girl. But most of all she was furious at herself for letting it all happen.

By the time she made it back to her lookout point near the center of the Marsh, more droids had arrived and the situation was finally starting to come under control. People were being thrown into Policier transporteurs by the dozens. Some of them were stoic, calling out, "Honest work for a *dis*honest chance!" and some of them cried, begging for mercy and apologizing for their actions. Regardless, they all ended up heading to the same place: the Prisoner Transport Center to await passage to Bastille.

Chatine checked the time on her Skin. Marcellus and Alouette had been gone for over an hour. As she watched Inspecteur Limier wrestle a Third Estate lowlife into the transporteur, Chatine once again cursed herself for letting Marcellus get away. She'd been so focused on the girl—keeping her away from him—she hadn't been doing her actual job. And she'd lost him because of it.

But then, just as Limier managed to slam the door behind the thrashing croc, she heard a new kind of commotion ring out in the marketplace below her. It wasn't the usual whir of droid sirens or the bellowing of a mad woman with a makeshift weapon. It was Marcellus's voice shouting, "Let go of her!"

A low growl followed the sound, and then someone yelled, "Stay away from my daughter."

Chatine scanned the stalls, searching for the source of the voice. She saw nothing at first. But then she spotted a gigantic figure trampling past the nearby statue of Patriarche Thibault, dragging a girl behind him. Officer Bonnefaçon was chasing after both of them.

Chatine couldn't see the figure's face. It was concealed by a dark hood hanging low across his brow. But she was certain it had to be a man. A very *large* man. And the girl he was dragging had wide, bewildered eyes and infuriatingly clean clothes.

It was most definitely *that* girl again.

Alouette.

"Please, Papa." She was crying. "I'm sorry. I'm so sorry."

"I am an officer of the Ministère!" Marcellus shouted at the man, sounding more intimidating than Chatine had ever heard him. "I command you to release her at once, or I can and will arrest you."

She snorted. *So* now *he stands up for something?* Where was all this gumption back in the Tourbay? Of course, then he didn't have a sparkly eyed bimbo to fight for. He only had pathetic little Théo.

Chatine felt a stab of something sharp and hostile in her chest. She pushed it away and focused back on the hooded man, who was now almost directly underneath her. He was still dragging Alouette behind him.

Marcellus pulled out his rayonette and aimed it at the man with shaking hands. "Stop! Or I'll paralyze you!"

But the hooded figure turned around and knocked the weapon right out of Marcellus's grip, with what looked like nothing more than a flick of his fingers.

Marcellus stared at his weapon on the ground before deciding on another tactic. With a roar, he ran after Alouette's father and jumped onto his back. The man was so large and strong that Marcellus looked just like that rioter who'd tried to attack the massive Policier droid earlier. Alouette's father thrashed and beat at Marcellus over his shoulder. But Marcellus had seemingly found some untapped strength that impressed Chatine. He held on tight, strangling the man.

Alouette screamed. "NO! Please! Stop! You're hurting him."

But Chatine wasn't sure whom she was screaming at. Whose side was she on? Her father's or Marcellus's?

Perhaps even *she* didn't know the answer to that.

The hooded man gave one final heave, bending forward and launching Marcellus over his head. Chatine watched wide-eyed as the officer flew through the air.

In that moment, it was as though the entire marketplace froze. The riots came to a halt. The droids seemed to power down. Every pair of eyes in the vicinity turned to see Marcellus crash into a vegetable stall, sending grungy carrots and withered cabbages flying.

Panic shot through Chatine as she stared down at his body slumped on the muddy ground.

Unmoving.

Then, a moment later, the stall let out a loud creak, buckling to the left as its rusting corrugated roof crashed into the base of the old Patriarche statue. The rickety statue swayed ominously, like the men whom Chatine used to see drinking too much weed wine at the Jondrette. With wide, unblinking eyes, Chatine watched as the giant Thibault Paresse wobbled and let out a deafening screech.

"Watch out," a nearby stall owner yelled. "It's falling!"

Someone screamed, and Chatine couldn't be 100 percent sure it wasn't her. Her gaze flicked from the tumbling statue to the person who still lay on the ground, directly in its path.

Marcellus.

"No!" Chatine shouted, and this time, it really was her.

- CHAPTER 48 -
CHATINE

CHATINE LEAPT DOWN FROM THE BEAM, LANDING
hard in a crouch. She felt something in her left ankle twist awkwardly, but she didn't stop. She dove toward Marcellus, shoving
him out of the way.

Crash!

Trash swirled, mud splattered, and people screamed as the huge
bronze figure of the founding Patriarche hit the ground, right where
Marcellus had been just a second ago, and cracked in half at the
waist.

"Marcellus?" His name scratched in Chatine's throat as she
slumped down next to him, her heart hammering at her ribs. He still
wasn't moving.

"Come on, *get up*, you stupid pomp," she whispered.

His eyelids shot open, and before he could even focus on Chatine's
face in front of him, he scrambled to his feet, practically shoving
Chatine out of the way as he glanced around the marketplace.

Something cold and bitter squeezed in Chatine's chest.

He was still looking for *her*, wasn't he?

Still trying to save *her*.

Chatine turned away in disgust and pushed herself to her feet, immediately feeling the pain shoot through her left ankle. *Fantastique*, she thought as she started to hobble away. She couldn't watch this anymore. The boy was a fool. Alouette's father clearly wanted her to have nothing to do with Marcellus, and yet here he was, chasing after her like a sot.

"Oh my Sols!" someone shouted, and Chatine turned back to see a woman pointing at the fallen, cracked statue. "There's someone under there!"

Chatine's eyes traveled the length of the giant Patriarche, from his enormous head lying facedown in the mud to his broken left foot on top of the wreckage of the collapsed stall.

And that's when Chatine saw it.

Pinned under the massive bronze boot was an arm. A child's arm. Chatine tried desperately to make out whom it belonged to, but there was too much rubble. Too much debris covering the rest of the body.

Chatine stood frozen to the spot, staring helplessly at that arm. Those unmoving, untwitching little fingers as lifeless as the plastique doll arm that lay under the grate next to her bed.

Before she could even react, a figure emerged from the crowd, running toward the statue. His raincoat was no longer spotless silver. It was stained with mud.

"Quick!" Marcellus called out to the small crowd that had started to gather. "Help me!"

The officer waded through the debris, flinging trash and wreckage to the side as he dug his way to the bottom half of the broken statue. Chatine watched in a semi-trance as Marcellus pushed aside a broken plank from the old stall, revealing the face of the young boy pinned beneath the Patriarche's foot.

Chatine's stomach rolled again.

It was Roche.

The boy she had met less than two hours earlier hiding underneath the cabbage stall. He wasn't moving.

"We need to get this off him!" Marcellus yelled.

Chatine flinched, coming out of her trance. She ran toward the base of the statue, ignoring the stabbing pain in her ankle. Marcellus locked eyes on her and silent understanding flowed between them.

They slid their hands under opposite sides of the Patriarche's ankles.

"One, two, three," Marcellus counted out.

Chatine heaved upward with all her strength. She could feel the blood rushing to her face, and her fingers went numb. Across from her, Marcellus gritted his teeth, and the tendons in his neck popped out from the effort.

The statue didn't move a single centimètre.

Two more men joined them, one of them gripping the statue's left knee, the other slipping a hand through the gap formed between Thibault's torso and lower half. Together, they all lifted like they were trying to pull an entire planet from orbit.

The statue shifted, but only slightly.

Roche let out a soft whimper as the enormous structured settled back down onto his arm. Chatine shuddered out a breath. He was still alive.

"We're going to get you out!" she told him. "Don't worry!"

They needed more help.

Chatine stepped away from the statue and scanned the crowd. She spotted Inspecteur Limier a few mètres away. Why the fric wasn't he helping? Or at least sending in some of his metal-headed bashers?

"Inspecteur!" she called out.

But it was as though Limier weren't even in the same marketplace. He was barely on the same planet. Something in the distance had caught his attention. His circuitry flashed more wildly than Chatine had ever seen before. She followed his gaze through the crowd. It wasn't difficult. She could have easily drawn a line straight from Limier's flickering face to the hooded figure.

Alouette's father had stopped and turned, maybe to see what had silenced the crowd again. But he was not looking at the commotion around the fallen statue. He was looking straight back at Inspecteur Limier.

Chatine's gaze flicked back and forth between the two men. She could almost see the electrical charge in the air. Like lightning caught between two conductors. Limier's eyes were narrowed, his lip curled into a snarl. The hooded man's eyes were wide with alarm.

"It's not moving. We need more help!"

It was Marcellus's panicked voice that finally made Alouette's father pull his eyes away from Limier and look over at the collapsed statue. At the young boy pinned beneath the bottom half. At the men grunting with effort but getting nowhere.

His eyes narrowed in concern. He glanced again at the inspecteur, indecision playing across his face.

And then it was as though something snapped inside Alouette's father. He released his daughter and stalked back through the Marsh, pushing people and debris aside until he reached the foot of the statue. With his large hand, he gestured for Marcellus and the other men to move aside. He bent his legs—as thick as PermaSteel beams—until he could maneuver his hands underneath the statue. With a deep, guttural growl, he pressed upward from his feet, using all the power of his legs, back, and arms. Sweat immediately beaded on his forehead. His face twisted grotesquely from the effort. But slowly, the old Patriarche's legs began to lift. A sliver of a gap opened up.

Alouette's father dug his heels into the mud and grunted again as he continued to hoist up the bottom half of the statue. Finally, when the gap was large enough, Marcellus and the two other men rushed forward to pull Roche to safety. He was deathly pale and clutching his crushed arm, but otherwise he looked unscathed.

Chatine's mouth fell open as a gasp of disbelief escaped. She couldn't believe what she was seeing. Four of them had attempted to lift that statue. Four of them had failed.

But this one man—this *giant*, droid-like man—had done it.

Once Roche was clear, Alouette's father released his grip. The bronze statue collapsed to the ground with a loud *crash*, and the hood covering the man's head fell back against the nape of his neck, revealing a head of hair so white it was almost blinding.

Chatine felt a jolt of recognition.

She'd seen that hair before.

She knew that man.

He rushed to pull the hood back up and then quickly glanced around to search for something in the crowd. Chatine had only one guess whom he was looking for.

The man's gaze landed, again, on Inspecteur Limier, who was now pushing his way through the throngs of people, the cyborg wiring on his face still blinking so rapidly, it looked as though something had short-circuited.

The man grabbed his daughter by the hand and began to pull her away again. Limier attempted to follow, but the crowd was too thick. Soon, his attention was pulled to Roche, who was being tended to by Marcellus. Chatine watched Marcellus yell urgently into his TéléCom, demanding that a médecin come to the Marsh immediately.

Chatine felt the urge to stay with Roche. To make sure he was okay. But there was a stronger urge thrumming through her at that moment. An urge that went way back. A desperation to confirm the realization that was already starting to take shape in her mind.

She tugged at her hood, pulling it farther over her face, and took a few paces backward, melting herself into the crowd like smoke. Then she did what she was best at: She started to follow her mark. She pursued Alouette and her father through the Marsh, keeping a safe distance as she weaved around crowds and stalls, until she watched them disappear into Fret 7.

Inside the first hallway, Chatine lost sight of them. But when she stopped and listened, she heard two faint voices. Chatine followed the sound, creeping around corners and hugging the walls to remain unseen. When she finally caught up to the hooded man and his daughter, they were disappearing into the old mechanical room on the ground floor.

Trying her best to ignore the sharp pain in her ankle, Chatine sidled up to the door and glanced around the corner. Strangely, Alouette and her father had vanished.

Then Chatine heard the *clank* of metal. The sound reminded her of the noise the grates made when she hid her sac of trinkets under the floor of her couchette. She crept up to a large rusted machine and peered around it.

And that's when she saw Alouette slowly lowering herself into a narrow opening in the floor. She watched in awe as the girl's head disappeared underground.

Chatine almost laughed at the irony of the situation. Défecteurs living right under the Frets. She had to hand it to those dropouts. They were certainly crafty.

But Chatine wasn't concerned with *where* they were going. As she watched the large man start to climb down into the hole after his daughter, his hood slipped back from his head again, and Chatine was able to see his whole face.

In a flash, all her suspicions were confirmed.

The white hair.

The huge shoulders.

The giant hands.

Chatine closed her eyes and let herself drift back to that night.

The night the white-haired man came to their inn in Montfer.

She could still see him standing in the doorway, ducking to

avoid hitting his head on the low entryway. She could see the beautiful hand-painted doll in his hand. She could see Madeline's smug little face as the man told her she was his daughter and took her away.

Chatine's eyes fluttered open and her heart hammered in her chest.

It was the same daughter she had just watched disappear underneath Fret 7.

The same girl who had killed Chatine's little brother.

She had been living right under her nose this entire time.

- PART 5 -

LITTLE LARK

*Of all the twelve planets in the System Divine, Laterre was the
coldest, wettest, and darkest. The rain fell, the clouds never cleared,
and the Third Estate were hungry. Hungry and wet and cold.
Some cheated and conned. Others sold blood from their veins. But
most gathered points and dreamed of living out the rest of their days
under blue skies and gleaming Sols.*

And the rest of their nights under stars.

Stars in an artificial sky.

From *The Chronicles of the Sisterhood,*
Volume 7, Chapter 15

- CHAPTER 49 -
ALOUETTE

THE SILENCE IN THE REFUGE HAD NEVER BEEN SO deafening.

Alouette sat in the small kitchen, her hands shaking in her lap. Her father sat across from her. He was staring down at his own hands, his face as flat and hard and unreadable as the bedrock behind him. His cropped hair glowed like ice under the kitchen's single lamp, which hung just above his head.

Since they'd returned from the Marsh ten minutes ago, he'd said only seven words: "Sit down, Alouette. I need to think."

And so, while the sisters were still locked behind their Assemblée doors, they sat. Just the two of them. The quiet punctuated every now and again only by an echoing drip from the nearby sink.

Alouette had tried to speak, but her father had raised his finger and shushed her with a fierceness she'd never seen before. At least never directed at her—not until today. She wasn't sure if her hands were shaking now because of his silencing . . . or because of his silence.

She was used to her father being quiet. He'd always been a man of few words. But this? This was different.

Alouette was frozen to her seat, terrified. Terrified he might start to speak, even yell. Terrified he might *never* speak and they would spend the rest of the day like this, twin stars trapped in a soundless orbit.

As they sat, memories of the day kept popping up and bubbling over in Alouette's mind.

The crowds in the marketplace. The awful execution. The Forest Verdure with its giant trees and strange graves. Marcellus's eyes. His green-brown eyes, so full of kindness and sadness. And secrets . . .

He was no longer just Marcellus Bonnefaçon. She could never think of him that way again. From now on, he would always be *Officer* Bonnefaçon. The grandson of the general.

And then Alouette thought about the Marsh.

Being pulled away, yanked by her father through the crowds.

The little boy, stuck.

And her father . . .

"How did you lift that statue?"

The question darted out of Alouette before she could think to stop it. It wasn't even one of the questions she'd really wanted to ask.

After a few very long moments, her father looked up. This time, though, he didn't raise his finger or hush her. This time, his eyes bored straight into hers. Deep and dark and glimmering. They seemed to hold a million questions. A million frustrations. Or, even worse, a million disappointments.

Whatever it was, his look made Alouette's stomach roll with nerves and her heart ache with grief. For a moment, all she wanted to do was slink down off her chair, fall to the ground, and curl into a ball on the cool kitchen floor.

"The boy was hurt," her father finally said before his gaze slipped back down to his hands.

Alouette knew better than to point out that her father hadn't answered her question. He'd only said *why* he'd lifted the statue, not *how*.

There'd never been any doubt in Alouette's mind that her father was strong. But now, after what she'd seen in the Marsh, it was clear that her father's strength was something different. Her father had succeeded in lifting that huge bronze statue all alone, where three men and that scrawny boy in the black hood had failed.

Where had her father gained strength like that?

Unconsciously answering her own question, Alouette shifted her gaze from her father's white hair down to his right bicep. It was covered with his shirt sleeve, but she could just about make out the contours of those five dimpled bumps.

2.4.6.0.1.

His prisoner tattoo.

That's where such strength had come from, she realized. Or worse, perhaps it was his incredible strength that had put him on Bastille in the first place.

Her father looked up again, but this time his eyes were bleary and dazed. It was like he was waking from a dream, only to be confused by the reality he'd woken into.

"Papa?" Alouette whispered.

He blinked, then straightened his back and wide shoulders. "We'll have to leave very soon. Maybe tomorrow."

Alouette stared over at him, stunned.

"I'll have to secure us passage," he went on. It was suddenly as though Alouette wasn't even in the room with him. Her father had slipped into some kind of trance. "He knows where I am now. It's the only way."

Alouette had no idea what her father was talking about.

"Passage?" she whispered, scared to interrupt him.

"Reichenstat would be far enough away," he muttered, standing up and pacing the small kitchen. "I probably should have just taken you there to begin with."

Alouette's eyebrows flew up. "Reichenstat?"

Why was he talking about a planet worlds away from Laterre?

"I should have enough funds to get us there and some left over to start a new life." Her father paused, running his hands over his coarse white hair. "Hopefully enough."

It was like the row of lights in Sister Laurel's plant propagation room turning on, one after another. Everything suddenly emerged into light and Alouette now understood what her father was rambling about.

"We're going to Reichenstat?!"

The words burst out of her so loudly that her father immediately raised his finger and shushed her again.

Alouette lowered her voice to a frantic whisper.

"But, Papa, we can't go to Reichenstat. Laterre is our home. This is where we live. Here, with the sisters. In the Refuge." She waved her arms around at the kitchen. "You're their cook. And I'm a sister now. Look!" She reached into the front of her tunic and pulled out the string of devotion beads that Principale Francine had given her just last night. The sight of them—the thought of losing everything she'd worked for—made her chest tighten and her breath snag in her throat.

Hugo stared at the beads as though he couldn't make out what they were. Then his head snapped up. Alouette saw determination in his eyes and heard resolution in his voice as he said, "It's not safe for us here anymore, Little Lark. We need to leave as soon as possible."

Alouette's hands began to shake harder. "Papa, is this about me leaving the Refuge today? I promise, I really promise, I will never do that again. I know that was a stupid thing to do. It was unsafe. But I won't ever do it again. I promise."

But her father simply shook his head and said nothing.

"Please, Papa, listen to me. We can't go to Reichenstat. It's so far away. Where would we live? We don't know anyone there. How would you find work? The Chronicles say it's cold on Reichenstat.

Very cold. Snow and ice covers most of the lands." Her voice cracked. "We don't have the right clothes."

"Alouette," her father said after sighing heavily. "We have no choice. It's too dangerous here for us now. It's time to leave. I suggest you start packing."

Panic seized Alouette as she watched her father turn toward the door of the kitchen. For a moment, all she could do was silently open and close her mouth. But just as her father was about to duck under the doorway, her voice finally came to her.

"No!"

Her father stopped and looked back.

"No," she said again. The sound harder. Her voice firmer. "I'm not going. I don't want to go to Reichenstat. I can't go."

His forehead furrowed. "This is not up for debate, Little Lark."

Alouette pushed herself up from her seat and hurried toward her father. "Yes, it is. You can't keep making decisions for me. You can't keep hiding things from me and expecting me to just go along with it. This is my home. This is *our* home. It's where we belong. I'm not leaving." The words came out in a breathless, desperate rush.

Her father let out a weary sigh and cast his gaze to the floor. "We can't stay."

"We can. I promise, we can, Papa." But she could tell her pleas were doing nothing.

"This is about that boy, isn't it?" her father snapped, his voice deep and stern.

"No," Alouette shot back. And it was the truth. She didn't want to see Officer Bonnefaçon ever again. She couldn't see him ever again. But suddenly, now, when she thought about flying off to Reichenstat—about being so far away from him—for some reason she felt sick and dizzy.

"You don't know what you want," her father said, a note of sadness mixed in with the anger. "You are a child; you don't know what is best for you. I do and so I am taking you to Reichenstat for your safety."

"I am not a child!" Tears pricked at Alouette's eyes, and she angrily swatted them away. "Not anymore."

"Well, you are still too young to make decisions for yourself," Hugo said with an air of finality before he started again toward the door.

Frustration and despair suddenly erupted inside Alouette. "I may be young, but at least I am not a criminal!"

Her father stopped in his tracks, frozen for a few beats. Then he turned and gave her a long, silent stare.

Heat bloomed in Alouette's cheeks and her stomach flipped. But she couldn't stop now that she'd started. Nor could she stop the tears that were streaming down her face. "I know you were on Bastille. You're a convict. A thief, perhaps. Maybe even a murderer! I don't know because you never tell me anything. You leave me to guess and assume and think the worst." She was sobbing now. Hysterical. But she managed to point at his arm. "I know all about your past, Prisoner 24601."

Her father just continued to stare at her. The lines on his face looked deeper than ever, and his eyes were flat and hard.

Finally, he cleared his throat and said, "Pack your things, Alouette. We leave tomorrow."

- CHAPTER 50 -
MARCELLUS

THE NEXT MORNING, MARCELLUS AND HIS GRAND-
father walked in silence. Two peacocks skittered out of their way
as they moved along the wide avenue, lined with tall cypress trees,
toward the gates of the Ministère headquarters. The early morning
Sols shone just above the horizon line in the TéléSky.

The weather in Ledôme was always programmed to be comfortable: warm but not hot, dry but not too much. Yet, this morning,
Marcellus's skin pricked and sweltered under his stiff uniform. He
was tired, too. He'd lain awake most of the night with thoughts of
Alouette cycling through his mind.

Her father seemed like a dangerous man. The way he'd pulled that
statue off the child by himself. Who had that kind of strength? And
was it that strength that kept his daughter locked away and afraid to
leave? Alouette's face had looked so terrified and ashamed when her
father had found her. He shuddered at the thought of what might
have happened when they'd arrived back home.

Wherever that was.

Marcellus squeezed his hands into fists as he walked. He couldn't believe he'd let them get away. After Alouette's father had pulled the statue off the boy, Marcellus had been so preoccupied with calling for help and getting the injured boy to the Med Center, he hadn't even noticed them slip into the crowd. The next time he'd looked up, the two of them were gone. Both vanished like ghosts.

"General Bonnefaçon."

Inspecteur Limier's voice punctured Marcellus's thoughts. He'd appeared suddenly behind them on the path, without a single audible footstep.

"You're late," Marcellus's grandfather stated without breaking his stride or turning his head. They were currently passing under the massive marble arch that marked the entrance to the Ministère grounds. Its towering roof and sculptured sides gleamed in the artificial Sollight. The inspecteur maneuvered his way between Marcellus and the general, and Marcellus found himself having to fall a few paces behind.

"An important matter detained me," said the inspecteur.

"And what is that?" the general asked.

"LeGrand is still alive," Limier announced.

Marcellus noticed his grandfather's shoulders stiffen and his neck muscles twitch.

"Not this again, Inspecteur," General Bonnefaçon said.

"But I saw him, sir," Limier persisted. "This time, I'm certain."

The desperation in the inspecteur's tone was so unfamiliar, so strange for someone usually so impassive and composed. "He was in the Marsh yesterday. The old statue of Patriarche Thibault collapsed on top of a child. He lifted it into the air as though it were made of feathers. I would recognize that incredible strength anywhere. It was Jean LeGrand. I have no doubt."

Marcellus nearly tripped over his own feet. Limier was clearly talking about Alouette's father. But how did he know him?

"I'm sure you were mistaken," the general said.

Mistaken? Marcellus had never known a cyborg to make a mistake.

Cyborgs were built for precision and accuracy. Médecins, inspecteurs, scientists, all of them. The only reason they were surgically enhanced was to *avoid* mistakes.

"Sir, the man lifted a seven-mètre-tall bronze statue by himself," Limier said, that same urgency in his voice. It was as though someone had removed his circuitry in the middle of the night, turning him into a regular man, with regular emotions.

"There's only one man on Laterre with that kind of strength," Limier went on, "and that's Jean LeGrand. He's an escaped convict, and he needs to be brought to justice."

An escaped convict?

Marcellus's grandfather ground to a halt, causing Marcellus to nearly crash into him. The general turned toward his most trusted inspecteur, and Marcellus could see the frustration and disappointment in his eyes.

"I shouldn't have to remind you, Inspecteur, that this obsession has already cost you years of your life. Don't let it distract you from the bigger problems we now face on this planet. You are Laterre's most senior inspecteur. You command the Policier of the planet's largest city and capital. I cannot lose you to this pointless infatuation again. LeGrand has been dead for twenty-five years. And he's *still* dead. Stop chasing ghosts."

Ghosts.

Marcellus felt a chill run down his spine as a million puzzle pieces seemed to suddenly clatter into place. Alouette's fear. Her father's strength. Her skittishness. His fury.

The secrecy.

So much secrecy.

Her father wouldn't allow her to leave home. When she'd found out that Marcellus was the grandson of General Bonnefaçon, she'd completely freaked out.

Marcellus had thought it was just because she was a Défecteur.

But now he realized it was more than that. The Défecteurs were known for harboring fugitives, claiming they didn't agree with the Ministère's laws. It was one of the reasons his grandfather had initiated the roundup efforts to begin with.

And now Marcellus was more than certain that there were still tribes of Défecteurs out there. Living among them. Hiding people like Alouette and her father.

An uneasy silence had fallen between the three men. They continued to walk the avenue toward the headquarters of the Ministère. Marcellus could see the building in the distance, its two identical black towers jutting majestically toward the TéléSky. Behind its arched doorways and lavishly carved windows, there lay a maze of hallways, offices, and state-of-the-art tech labs.

It was a building Marcellus both respected and feared. It represented everything that had ever made him feel safe on this planet, but at the same time, it represented a future he was unsure he was ready for. A future that had been thrust upon him the moment the Patriarche decided to ignore his grandfather's sage counsel and send Commandeur Vernay to the planet Albion to die.

But there was still so much Marcellus had to learn. So much strength he had to find before he would ever be anything like his grandfather's closest confidante.

And yet, there were still so many ways in which he knew he'd *never* be like Commandeur Vernay. He knew Vernay would have disobeyed Inspecteur Limier's orders in the Marsh yesterday. She would have pulled rank and stayed to help control the riots. She wouldn't have run off into the forest with a Défecteur. But most important, Commandeur Vernay would have turned Alouette in the moment she saw the scar where her Skin should have been.

But Marcellus also knew, without a shadow of a doubt, that he could never turn Alouette in. Not then, and not now. Not even after he'd learned she was living with a wanted criminal.

That's how weak he really was.

That's how ill-equipped he was to do this job. To work in that building. To one day be not only commandeur, but general of the Ministère. To follow in his grandfather's footsteps.

He would always, *always* be one step behind him.

Just as he was right now.

"The Third Estate is getting out of hand." The general's voice broke through the silence. He clearly wanted to get to what he considered to be the most important business of the day. "Yesterday's riots were embarrassing to the Regime. And even though we managed to restore order to the Marsh, the execution has stirred up unruly factions in the Third Estate, and now the turmoil has moved into the fabriques. We need to work quickly."

Limier nodded. "Affirmative, General." It was as though his previous concerns were nothing but distant memories—discarded bytes of data dispatched to the back corners of his enhanced brain. Marcellus wished it were that easy for *him* to forget. "Do you believe the Vangarde is behind this?"

"I do," the general replied. "And they're gaining momentum because of all the destruction and chaos."

"Do you really think this is what the Vangarde wants?"

The question slipped out so involuntarily, Marcellus didn't even realize he'd said it aloud until his grandfather and Limier stopped in their tracks. Eerily and silently in sync, they both turned their heads to face him.

"This seems like *exactly* what they would want," his grandfather said in a warning tone.

Heat rose to Marcellus's neck. "I mean, it's just . . ." He cleared his throat, trying to gain control of his wavering voice. "I'm just wondering what their plan is. The Vangarde. Are they making demands? It all seems kind of disorganized, doesn't it? What are they expecting will come out of these riots and commotion? Surely they would have a better plan?"

As soon as the words were out of his mouth, he regretted them.

The general arched his left eyebrow. "They're *terrorists*. They want anarchy, bloodshed, and mayhem so they can swoop in and overthrow our Regime." He glared at Marcellus. "Our beautiful Regime."

Marcellus swallowed hard and nodded. "I see. So, how do you plan to deal with it? The riots, I mean?"

His grandfather halted in front of the sleek plastique doors of the Ministère headquarters and turned back to his grandson. "They had a saying on the First World: The best way to stop a fire that's blazing out of control"—he shared a look with Limier that made Marcellus's stomach turn—"is with more fire."

- CHAPTER 51 -
CHATINE

CAREFUL NOT TO WAKE ÁZELLE SLEEPING NEXT TO
her, Chatine got out of bed and tested out her ankle. It was still
slightly swollen and tender from trying to save the stupide pomp
officer in the Marsh yesterday, but thankfully she was able to put
weight on it. She pulled on her black pants and coat, and with a
sigh, twisted her pale-brown hair into a knot. She was getting really
tired of hiding it. She should cut it all off and be done with it. She
still had a few weeks left before it would be long enough to sell to
Madame Seezau for the full two hundred largs, but she prayed she
wouldn't be here that long.

"You're up early."

Chatine turned to see Azelle stretching her arms above her head,
the left side of her face creased from the pillow.

"I have something I need to do this morning," Chatine muttered
as she tucked her hair under her hood and slid her feet into her boots.

Azelle giggled.

"What?" Chatine shot her sister a look.

"You're always so cryptic," Azelle said.

Chatine scoffed. "Yeah, well . . ." But she had no idea how to finish the sentence, so she just let it hang. Plus, she had to be cryptic. She knew Azelle would never approve of what she was about to do.

Last night, after Azelle had gone to sleep, Chatine had retrieved the plastique doll arm from beneath the grate in the floor. It was the one thing her father's gang hadn't stolen from her. Then she'd lain in bed and thought about the day the white-haired man had appeared at the inn to take Madeline away. She thought about the doll he'd brought for her and how he'd called her "ma petite." But mostly, Chatine thought about what had happened two weeks later, when Inspecteur Limier had knocked on the door of their inn, searching for an escaped prisoner named Jean LeGrand. Searching for *them*.

Offering a reward so high, it had made Chatine's head spin.

"Twenty thousand tokens for any information leading to the apprehension of LeGrand and the girl."

"Are you going out?" Azelle asked, breaking into Chatine's thoughts.

Chatine bent down and picked up the tiny plastique arm, which now lay on the floor next to her bed. It must have slipped from her hand when she fell asleep. "Yes, but—"

"I'll walk with you!" Azelle was suddenly up and pulling on her work uniform. "I'm going to go into the fabrique early today. Now that the Ascension is going to be rescheduled, I need to store up as many points as I can get." Chatine watched her sister do a little skip as she went to slide her feet into her shoes.

"No," Chatine said automatically, slipping the doll arm into the pocket of her coat. The last thing she needed right now was Azelle prattling on the entire way through the Frets, distracting her from what she had to do. "I can't wait."

Before Azelle could argue, or even finish putting on her shoes, Chatine ducked out of the bedroom.

The minute she was through the door, she heard the soft rumble of her father's snores. Chatine glanced up to see him slumped forward in a chair, his arms folded on the table with his head resting on top of them.

If it weren't for the snores, Chatine would have thought he might be dead.

If only she could be so lucky.

The situation was all too familiar. The empty carafe of weed wine on the table. Her parents' bedroom door shut tight. He'd come home from the docks drunk and belligerent again, after hanging out inside the Grotte with the Délabré. Her mother had evidently locked the door on him, leaving him to drink until he passed out.

Chatine knew this might be her only opportunity.

She crept closer to the table and, with the precision and delicacy of a médecin, wrapped her fingers around his left wrist. She gently tugged until her father's hand was free, causing his head to clunk down hard on the table. He stopped snoring.

Chatine cringed and withdrew, waiting for him to wake up. But her father barely even stirred.

She rolled her eyes. The man was completely out. Ten bashers could barrel through here, and her father probably still wouldn't wake up.

She roughly grabbed his hand and yanked Marcellus's ring off his little finger. She had to pull hard to dislodge it from between the folds of her father's thick skin, but eventually it came loose and Chatine slipped it into her pocket. She released Monsieur Renard's hand and let it fall with a *thump* back down on the table.

The snoring resumed.

Pathetic, Chatine thought as she strolled out the front door of the couchette and slammed it shut behind her. When it swung open again a moment later, Chatine readied herself to run. But it was just her sister.

"Hi!" Azelle said breathlessly as she stepped into the hallway, combing a hand through her hair. "I'm ready. Now we can walk together."

Chatine sighed and started down the hallway of Fret 7. "Fine. But you have to walk fast."

As expected, Azelle started talking the moment they left the couchette. She launched into a long-winded story about a girl at her fabrique who blew all her tokens on a new dress that was now hanging useless in her closet because the girl had no place to wear it.

Chatine was actually grateful when the familiar chime of a Universal Alert blasted into her audio chip and the emblem of the Ministère appeared on the inside of her arm. It was the only thing capable of quieting Azelle.

"Another one?" Azelle said inquisitively as she turned her gaze to her Skin. "Do you think they're announcing the date of the rescheduled Ascension?"

Chatine shrugged. "Your guess is as good as mine."

But as soon as the general started speaking, Chatine knew that the news was not good. There was a graveness in his voice that sent a shiver down Chatine's spine. "Hello again, fellow Laterrians. We at the Ministère are greatly disappointed in the unruly behavior of the Third Estate following yesterday's execution, not to mention profoundly saddened. The Patriarche prides himself on taking good care of his people and maintaining a just and harmonious planet. This rioting and ransacking demonstrate to us that you are ungrateful for the Regime's generosity and support. We have provided you with jobs so that you can feed and clothe your families. Yet some of you are choosing mayhem over honest work and orderliness. We have provided you with a strong and dedicated Policier force, led by devoted and loyal inspecteurs, to keep the peace on our beautiful planet, yet some of you have chosen to attack the very people who have committed their lives to protecting you."

The general glanced away and shook his head, as though physically unable to continue.

Chatine scoffed. What a farce. Did he honestly believe he was fooling *anyone* with this charade?

She glanced over at Azelle, who was staring wide-eyed and desperate at her Skin.

Apparently, he did.

The general cleared his throat and continued. "I'm afraid your actions have left us little choice. Those who turn against their Regime—against their Patriarche—must be separated from those who are loyal. They cannot continue to receive our love and support if they choose to fight against us." He paused and narrowed his eyes. "Therefore, *anyone* caught rioting or looting will be arrested and sent immediately to Bastille. Anyone who colludes, conspires, or abets rioters—including those who fail to report disruptive activity—will have *all* their Ascension points voided, among other severe punishments. We at the Ministère firmly believe in honest work for an honest chance, therefore dishonest work must result in an immediate loss of that chance."

Chatine inhaled a sharp breath. This was not good. Not good at all. She, personally, couldn't care less about these threats. But she knew her estate. And she knew this announcement would have the opposite effect the general was intending. This would *not* encourage people to calm down and go back to work. It would only make the people angrier. They didn't like these kinds of threats. Especially when it involved their Ascension points.

The sound of muffled sobs pulled Chatine out of her thoughts. She glanced down at her Skin to see that the general's face was gone. The screen was asking if she wanted to replay the announcement. She swiped it off and turned toward Azelle.

Her sister had stopped walking and was staring into her darkened Skin, crying quietly.

Chatine's first instinct was to keep going and leave her behind. Let brainwashed Azelle have her little meltdown. Let her lament the shattered state of her beloved planet. But just as Chatine was preparing to mumble some excuse and duck down the next hallway, Azelle let out a sad little whimper that pulled Chatine to a halt.

She sighed and sidled up to her sister, resting a hesitant hand on her shoulder.

"Azelle," she said, trying to infuse her voice with sympathy. But it came out flat and clumsy. "It's going to be okay. The general wasn't talking about you."

Azelle sucked in a shaky breath. "How do you know?"

"For one, you're not out there rioting or looting, are you?" Chatine almost laughed at the thought.

Azelle sniffled and finally looked up from her Skin. Her cheeks were puffy and her eyes bloodshot. "No, but my whole fabrique is causing trouble. Yesterday, after that horrible execution, a group of workers got really rowdy. They were shouting bad things about the Patriarche. And then they started breaking things—"

"That wasn't you—" Chatine tried to interrupt.

But Azelle shook her head. "You heard what the general said. If you don't report what you see, your Ascension points will be deleted! I saw what those guys were doing. I saw them smash one of the machines, and I didn't do anything to stop it. That means I've colluded!" Azelle hiccupped, and her voice raised an octave. "I worked so hard for my points. And I'm so close to winning, Chatine. I can feel it."

Chatine fought the urge to roll her eyes at her sister's delusion. How could she possibly, after all of this, still be thinking about the Ascension?

"The Ascension is the only reason I have to get up in the morning. It's the only reason I have to live. If I lose all my points, what will I have left?" Azelle buried her face in her hands and broke into sobs.

Chatine wished she could think of more to say to her—something to make her sister feel better. Perhaps even bring her a little hope. But she'd lived on this planet for eighteen years. She knew such words didn't exist.

As she stared at her sister, crying helplessly into her hands, a dull ache started to pulse in Chatine's chest. For the first time in her life, she was starting to realize that she and Azelle were not that different after all. In fact, they were eerily similar.

They both just wanted out of this life.

And they were both delusional enough to believe it could be done.

Chatine laid a gentle hand on her sister's arm. "You should probably get going, right? You don't want to be late to work."

Azelle seemed to break from a trance. Her head snapped up, and she rubbed her damp cheeks with the heels of her hands.

In that instant, staring into her sister's tearstained eyes, Chatine could almost see herself. See what she would have looked like as an obedient member of the Third Estate. As a rule follower. As a girl.

The two sisters had always shared similar features—the same clear gray eyes, the same dainty nose, the same high cheekbones—but it wasn't until right this very moment that Chatine had been able to see the resemblance.

"You're right." Azelle sniffed. "I should go. Thanks, Chatine."

And before Chatine could react, her sister threw her arms around her waist and squeezed. Chatine stiffened at the embrace, unsure what to do. Azelle was too close. This whole situation brought back too many dark, painful memories.

The sweet scent of Henri's hair. The feel of his tiny body in her arms. His blanket gathering dirt and dust in a corner.

"Okay," Chatine said, patting her sister on the back. "Good. So, um. Have a nice day."

Azelle finally pulled away but didn't leave. For a moment, she just stared at Chatine with a sympathetic expression on her face that made Chatine squirm inside. It was as though her sister could see right through her. Right into the dark depths of her.

Then Azelle reached out and brushed away a strand of hair that had evidently fallen out of Chatine's bun. She tucked it back under Chatine's hood and smiled. "I like that you're cryptic," she whispered before turning and vanishing down the hallway.

As Chatine watched her sister disappear, she thought about all the walls that were swiftly closing in around her: The general's warning to the Third Estate. The Délabré gang waiting for a cut of a con that didn't exist. Her failure to locate the hidden Vangarde base.

She pressed her hand against the small lump in her pocket—the arm of Madeline's doll.

A piece of something that once was whole.

A reminder of the kind of life that could never be hers. Or Azelle's. At least not here.

Once again, Chatine found herself thinking about the day Inspecteur Limier had appeared at the inn in Montfer, asking about a runaway convict.

She took a deep breath and continued out of Fret 7, reminding herself that this was her only option. Then, before she could second-guess herself, she turned in the direction of the Policier Precinct, praying that someone there was still willing to pay for information about the whereabouts of Jean LeGrand.

CHAPTER 52

ALOUETTE

REICHENSTAT.

Her father was taking her to Reichenstat. She'd barely seen Laterre, and now her father was shipping them off to another planet entirely.

It was almost lunchtime and Alouette still hadn't left her room. She'd missed supper last night, and now she'd missed breakfast, too. But she didn't care. She wasn't hungry.

She didn't want to leave the only home she'd ever known.

Alouette had cried deep into the night until she'd finally fallen asleep, curled in a huddled ball under her blanket. When she'd awoken this morning, her pillow was still damp from tears, and her chest throbbed with an ache so sad and deep, it seemed it might crack her ribs wide open.

She'd been so foolish. She should never have snuck out of the Refuge and disappeared into the Forest Verdure with Marcellus.

She'd known there would be consequences for what she'd done.

But not this.

Never *this*.

Alouette rubbed at her swollen eyes and checked the time on the small clock beside her bed. Her father had said they were leaving today, but she hadn't heard from him all morning.

"Reichenstat." She whispered the word aloud.

It felt as alien and foreign as the planet itself.

Suddenly, all the anger and frustration she'd felt last night came rushing back to her.

She'd only just been made a sister, a real sister, and now they had to leave. She touched her devotion beads, still around her neck, and thought of all the years she'd been working so hard with her studies, with her chores, with her Tranquil Forme. All for nothing.

But there was something else, too. Some other ache deep inside her chest.

"This is about that boy, isn't it?"

Her father's words came back to her, and Alouette's cheeks unexpectedly warmed. A realization was blooming within her that she was having a hard time accepting. Maybe her father was right. Maybe part of this *was* about the boy. At least, in some way.

Alouette shut her eyes tight. She could still feel his touch on her palm from when he'd held her hand in the Marsh. The urgency in his fingers when he'd begged her to meet him again.

"Tomorrow? Will you meet me somewhere? Anywhere?"

Alouette's eyes sprang open and she let out a laugh, which sounded more like a sob. There was no chance of that now, was there? Even if Marcellus weren't the general's grandson and therefore a threat to her entire way of life, it wasn't like she could meet him. She would soon be on board a voyageur heading to a planet worlds away. Laterre would soon be a tiny speck, a distant glow, in the vast sky. A place she would probably never see again.

How could her father do this to them? To her? To the sisters? Had he even thought of them? What if she really had put the Refuge and the library in danger? She couldn't just leave the sisters to clean up *her* messes.

With this last thought, Alouette rolled over and screamed, long and hard, into her pillow.

"Alouette?"

She startled at the sound of her name and looked up. Sister Muriel was standing in the doorway of Alouette's room. Her neat curls glowed white, and her wrinkles seemed even deeper now—etched with concern. Her devotion beads clacked slowly through her aged fingers.

"Are you all right, Little Lark?"

Alouette pushed herself up to sitting and rubbed at her face. "Yes, yes, fine," she said, but her voice was shaky.

"Are you sick?"

Alouette shook her head. She was worried her voice might crack if she spoke again. Muriel was always so kind, so sweet and caring. Alouette could feel tears pricking at her eyes at the thought of never seeing her again. Never seeing *any* of the sisters again.

"We were wondering if you might both be ill."

Alouette furrowed her brow. "Both?"

Muriel stepped into the room. "Your father said you weren't at supper last night because you felt unwell. And when there was no breakfast prepared this morning, we assumed he might be sick too." Muriel was threading her beads even faster now. "But then we found the door to his room was open and he wasn't inside. Jacqui looked in the library and Sister Laurel's propagation room. Even in the laundry. But he's nowhere to be seen."

"He didn't prepare breakfast?" Alouette blurted out.

She could barely keep up with what Muriel was saying. Her mind was still stuck on the first point. Her father *always* made breakfast. He always made every meal. Even on those days, those very few days, that her father felt ill, he still went to the kitchen and prepared meals for the sisters and Alouette before returning to his bed.

Muriel shook her head. "We don't know where he is. We were hoping you might know."

Suddenly, something cold and hard clutched at Alouette's stomach. It clutched so fiercely that she shot up from her bed. As soon as she was on her feet, she started to run. She scooted around Muriel and out the door.

"Little Lark?"

But Muriel's worried shout was just a faint echo behind Alouette, who was now sprinting full tilt down the hallway.

When she arrived at her father's room seconds later, it was just as Muriel had described. The door was ajar, but there was no one inside. With her heart thudding behind her ribs, she pushed the door wide and switched on the light.

Hugo Taureau's bed was made, the sheets and blankets stretched and tucked with fierce precision under the mattress. His room was always sparse, but now it felt even more bare for some reason. Maybe she was imagining it, but it felt like there was a cold chill in the air too.

The chill of emptiness.

Alouette's gaze ran anxiously over the room again before she hurried over to the closet and pulled back the curtain.

"What?" Her word came out as a gasp.

The shelves were empty. Everything was gone. His shirts and pants, his aprons, his underwear and shoes. All of it.

Gone.

Where were all his things? Maybe he'd already packed for Reichenstat. But why wasn't he here? Why hadn't he been in to see her this morning, to make sure she was packing too?

Then Alouette spotted something. The shelves weren't completely empty after all. Up on the highest shelf, she could see her father's old valise peeking out. Something shifted inside her. She felt a flare of hope. Alouette grabbed the nearby chair, stepped up, and pulled the case down.

But as soon as the valise was in her hands, she knew that it was too light.

She carried it over to the bed, popped the latches, and lifted the lid.

All the old clothes she'd found earlier were gone. The candlestick, too.

Only two things remained.

Glinting and flickering under the room's dim light, the beautifully engraved titan box that Alouette was certain had once belonged to her mother sat in the bottom of the case, and right beside it lay Katrina. Her childhood doll. Her father had left them both for her.

"Little Lark? Is everything okay?"

It was Muriel's voice again, but Alouette didn't turn around. She kept staring into the valise at the small box. At the soft yellow fabric of Katrina's dress. At the two things in the world that truly belonged to *her*.

And that was when the crushing realization finally hit.

"He's gone."

- CHAPTER 53 -
MARCELLUS

"NO RESULTS FOUND," THE TÉLÉCOM ANNOUNCED.

Marcellus sighed and lowered the screen, staring out into the bustling studio of the Ministère headquarters in Ledôme, where his grandfather had just finished broadcasting his Universal Alert to the Third Estate.

For the past twenty minutes, Marcellus had been searching the Communiqué for anything he could find on Alouette LeGrand. But the girl was still a ghost. The only result he'd managed to produce was the one for Jean LeGrand, confirming what his grandfather had told Inspecteur Limier earlier this morning:

Escaped from Bastille in 478 ALD.

Deceased in 480 ALD. No surviving relatives.

Except he wasn't deceased. Marcellus had seen him just as clearly as Limier had sworn to see him. The image in the Communiqué had been taken before his hair had turned white and his skin had wrinkled around the eyes, but everything else matched perfectly with the man in Marcellus's memory.

But why was there no mention of a daughter?

Staring out into the crowded studio, Marcellus spotted his grand-father surrounded by admirers, people queuing up to offer their words of gratitude and congratulations on such a compelling and effective speech.

Marcellus cringed. Was he the only one who thought that this kind of threatening approach wasn't going to work? That it would only make things worse? Nadette's execution had riled up the Third Estate more than Marcellus had ever seen. The people were angry and starving. They were attacking droids, for Sols' sake. They didn't need more threats; they needed someone to pacify them. Throw them a lifeline. They needed someone to show them that the Ministère and the Patriarche were on their side.

Apparently he *was* the only one who thought like that, because after the alert had ended, the entire room had broken into applause. Inspecteurs, sergents, officers, even the aides had cheered. They all seemed to think that General Bonnefaçon's tactic was the right one. But they hadn't been in Montfer. They hadn't seen the metal shacks of the Bidon. They hadn't looked into Théo's eyes when Marcellus had sworn that the Regime wasn't flawed.

"My only hope was that you would grow up to think differently. . . . I tried to give you empathy."

And none of them had been raised by a Vangarde spy for a governess.

"AirLink request pending from Sergent Chacal." The voice of his TéléCom pulled Marcellus back to the room. He blinked and tapped on his screen to accept the request.

"We got one." The startling words came before Marcellus could even offer a formal greeting.

Sergent Chacal's angular face filled the whole of the screen, as though he were purposefully leaning in to the microcam to get his point across.

There was no leaning necessary. His words spoke volumes.

"You got one?" Marcellus echoed in disbelief. "As in one of *them*?"
There was only one "one" these days.

"Affirmative, Officer," Chacal said. "He's Vangarde, all right. He's
been running messages for them in the Frets. We need you to get
down here right now to interrogate him."

"Me?" Marcellus asked, confused. "Why can't you do it?"

Interrogation was definitely more of Chacal's specialty than his.
The sergent could force all kinds of secrets from the lowliest of lowlifes. If his cruel glare and fierce voice didn't work, then the metal
baton that he kept strapped to his belt would always do the trick.

"Because he says he knows you," the sergent replied.

Marcellus blinked into the TéléCom. He could see his own
reflection blinking back at him from the corner of the screen. His
thoughts immediately flitted to Mabelle. Had she sent someone for
him? Someone to try to recruit him again?

"And no one else has been able to crack this one," Chacal went on.
"So we figure, why not give the future commandeur a try?"

Marcellus knew this was meant to be a jab. It was no secret that
most people in the Policier disapproved of how fast Marcellus had
moved up the ranks. Everyone knew it was due to the fact that he was
the grandson of the general. But, like all the jabs they threw at him,
he chose to ignore this one too.

"Where is he?" Marcellus asked.

"He's being held down here at the Precinct."

Marcellus nodded dazedly and mumbled something into his
TéléCom that vaguely sounded like, "I'll be right there."

The giant, windowless building of the Precinct was bustling with
activity. Noisy, furious people being herded into holding cells and
interrogation rooms, sergents shouting out instructions, trying to
maintain some semblance of order. As soon as Marcellus walked in,
the frenetic energy of the place slapped him across the face, and he

nearly turned around and walked back out. It was almost as though he could feel the walls shaking.

"Took you long enough." Sergent Chacal was suddenly beside Marcellus. He was the only one in this whole building who actually looked *happy* to be here. His small, compact body was almost twitching with excitement. Which was to be expected. Sergent Chacal was completely in his element. He loved nothing more than rounding up troublemakers.

"Where is he?" Marcellus asked, glancing around nervously.

"We've got him in interrogation room two. Real piece of work, that one. Have barely been able to get a word out of him all day."

"How do you know he's Vangarde, then?"

The Ministère had been rounding people up for two days, but everyone had denied any association with the Vangarde.

"He copped to it," Chacal said.

Marcellus balked. "He *did*?"

"Yup. Admitted to the whole thing. He was in the Med Center yesterday, being treated for a broken arm, and he was bragging to anyone who would listen about being a Vangarde messenger. But when we brought him in here today and asked him about where the messages were going and what they said, he clammed up."

Marcellus felt his chest tighten. As he followed Chacal down the hallway to interrogation room 2, he pictured every possible kind of person behind that door. A man-beast as frighteningly huge as Alouette's father. A formidable guard like the ones who had flanked Mabelle back in the Tourbay.

Chacal clapped him on the back when they reached the door, and with an unhelpful smirk said, "Good luck." Then he turned and left Marcellus alone in the hallway, presumably to go and watch this charade from the monitoring room with the rest of his deputies. Marcellus could already envision them sitting around laughing, taking bets about how long he would last in there.

With a deep breath, Marcellus reached out and turned the handle. He pushed the door open wide, his gaze immediately landing on the person occupying the steel chair in the center of the room.

A very *small* person.

Marcellus bit his lip to keep from laughing. Was this a joke? Had the guys down here at the Precinct decided to pull a prank on him?

It was a child.

A *boy*.

As skinny as one of the Patriarche's titan toothpicks.

Marcellus curiously took in his large gray eyes and the pair of goggles on his forehead. He recognized him. He *did* know him. This was the same boy whom Marcellus had tried to save in the Marsh yesterday.

Tried, but failed.

In the end, it had been Alouette's father—this mysteriously *un*-deceased Jean LeGrand—who had saved him with his incredible strength.

Marcellus was grateful to see that the boy was relatively unharmed. His left arm was bandaged, but in his right hand, he held a half-eaten carrot, which he drummed against the surface of the table.

Annoyed at what was clearly a Precinct prank, Marcellus turned to leave, prepared to march out that door and tell Chacal enough was enough. He was tired of being the joke around here.

But then a voice stopped him.

"Old Chacal thinks I'm Vangarde, doesn't he?"

Marcellus spun around and stared at the boy. He couldn't have been much older than twelve, but his voice sounded more mature.

"That's what he told you, right? That I'm a Vangarde." The boy stopped drumming his carrot and pushed his goggles farther up his forehead. He flashed Marcellus a wide grin.

"Yes," Marcellus said. "That's what he said."

"I'm not."

"Well, I know that. And I'm going to get this sorted out right away and get you released." He turned back toward the door.

"Unless, I *am*."

Marcellus stopped in his tracks again. Was the boy *in* on the prank? Had Chacal and the others offered to give him a loaf of chou bread if he played along?

"Then you'd be in a whole lot of trouble for releasing me, wouldn't you?" The boy let out a roar of laughter much deeper and gruffer than one would ever expect from such a scrawny body.

"Is this a joke?" Marcellus asked outright.

"No," the boy replied while nodding his head.

Marcellus sighed. This was pointless. But he knew if he gave up now, he'd never hear the end of it from Chacal. Or worse, Chacal would get on his TéléCom to Limier and report back that Marcellus was being soft on a criminal with suspected ties to the Vangarde. And Limier would *definitely* tell his grandfather.

Marcellus needed to play along and keep up this charade until he could figure out how to get the boy released.

"So," Marcellus said, lowering himself into the chair across from the boy, "you've been working with the Vangarde?"

The boy stared hard at Marcellus. His gaze was so intense, Marcellus felt the urge to look away. As though *he* were the criminal under investigation. Not the other way around.

"Like I'd tell you, if I was," the boy finally said.

"Why wouldn't you tell me? You can trust me. We go way back to the Marsh, remember?" Marcellus leaned forward and offered the boy a kind smile.

"Because you'd send me off to Bastille with the rest of them," the boy said, pointing up toward the moon. "Although I guess you're going to send me there anyway. That's how it goes, right? Doesn't really matter what happens in here. Once you're marked, you're marked."

Even though Marcellus couldn't have agreed more with the boy's shrewd observation, he didn't respond. Instead, he pointed to the boy's arm. The boy rolled his eyes but didn't hesitate to offer up his Skin for Marcellus to scan. Marcellus aimed his TéléCom at the small implanted screen in the boy's arm. The TéléCom elicited a soft beep before reciting the statistics of the boy's profile into Marcellus's audio patch.

"Roche. Last name unknown. Homeless. No known parents."

"Homeless?" Marcellus repeated with concern.

"Well, I *wasn't*," the boy said, "until you came and knocked my house down."

Marcellus blinked at him, confused.

"Thibault Paresse. Giant bronze man in the Marsh. Founder of Laterre. Any of this sound familiar?"

"You live in a statue?"

"Live*d*," the boy corrected. "Past tense."

"And your name's Roche?" Marcellus asked, lowering the TéléCom.

Roche gave a comical salute. "Aye, aye. How very perceptive of you, Officer."

"And you're an orphan?"

"I'm not an orphan," Roche shot back. "I'm a free agent."

He took a big bite out of his carrot and chewed noisily.

Marcellus almost laughed but managed to contain it. "So, Free Agent Roche. Can you tell me why Sergent Chacal brought you in here?"

"Aren't you supposed to be figuring that out for yourself, Monsieur Officer? That's why they gave you the uniform and nice polished boots, isn't it?"

Marcellus ignored him and asked, "What do you know about the Vangarde?"

The boy took a few more raucous chews on his carrot. "They killed the Premier Enfant, didn't they? They're up to no good."

Bitterness rose in Marcellus's throat at the reminder of poor little Marie. He quickly swallowed it down.

"Chacal says you were bragging about delivering messages for them."

The boy laughed, as though this was the most ridiculous thing he'd ever heard. "I was on painkillers. I also bragged that I was the Patriarche's uncle. Did he tell you that part? Probably not. Those drugs you got there in the Med Center are whacked. You should just give *those* to your suspects and you'll be able to ship them *all* to the moon."

Marcellus smiled. He admired the boy's gumption. He was smart. The way so many of the Fret rats were. He clicked on his TéléCom, bringing up a live AirLink feed of the monitoring room. He was hoping to get a look at Chacal's expression so he could figure out how much longer he would have to keep up this farce.

The room was filled with deputies, but Chacal wasn't there.

Had the wretch just up and left? He clicked on the view of the Precinct's foyer and that's when he saw them.

Both of them.

Chacal had his strong, rough hand wrapped around the arm of a frail, wispy boy in an oversized black coat and scuffed-up boots. Marcellus's heart leapt into his throat.

Théo.

What was he doing here? What had he gotten himself into now? It was as though trouble followed that boy.

Chacal was dragging Théo through the foyer, presumably to another interrogation room. As Marcellus watched, something hot and primal growled in the pit of his stomach. He felt a deep-seated urge to protect the boy. From everything. And especially from deputies like Chacal. He clicked his screen to activate the sound.

"I swear, I'm not pranking you, Chacal!" Théo was saying. "I've seen him with my own eyes. His name is Jean LeGrand and there's a reward on his head."

"It's 'Sergent' to you, déchet," Chacal spat back. "Now get in there." He kicked open the door to an interrogation room and wrestled Théo inside.

"Everything okay, Officer?" Roche asked, pulling Marcellus's attention away from his TéléCom. Marcellus glanced up to see an amused look on Roche's face. And suddenly an idea came to him. A perfect solution.

Marcellus leapt to his feet. "Wait here," he told Roche.

As he pocketed his TéléCom and raced toward the door, Marcellus was reminded of what the Patriarche liked to say when he was out hunting in the Palais gardens and was able to line up the perfect shot, bringing two helpless pigeons plummeting to the ground.

And that, mon ami, is how you shoot two birds with one bullet.

- CHAPTER 54 -
CHATINE

STUPIDE! CHATINE REPRIMANDED HERSELF AS SHE collapsed onto the chair in the dingy interrogation room. *Stupide! Stupide! Stupide!*

Why on Laterre had she decided to waste her time chasing after a twelve-year-old reward that was probably no longer valid? She should have been focusing on her task for the general. She should have been tracking down Marcellus and doing everything in her power to find the Vangarde base. This was what she got for trying to be crafty. For thinking she could find another way out.

Chacal shut the door behind him, looking delighted to be alone with her. Thankfully, he didn't know she was a girl. Otherwise, she was *sure* this meeting would go differently. She didn't trust most of the Policier, but she trusted Chacal least of them all. Even less than Limier. At least Limier was a cyborg. His integrity was programmed in.

Chacal had none.

"So," he said, pacing in front of her. "What's the littlest Renard doing at a Policier Precinct?"

Chatine sighed and crossed her arms over her chest. "I told you. I came for the reward on Jean LeGrand, the escaped convict. It's supposed to be twenty thousand largs."

Chacal nearly choked. "Twenty thousand? For a convict? Now I know you're pranking me."

"Look it up. You'll see."

Chacal cocked an eyebrow, clearly trying to decide whether or not he believed her. Finally, he pulled out his TéléCom and ran the search.

"Just as suspected," he said, returning the device to the pocket of his uniform. "A lie."

Chatine sat up straighter. "What? No, it's not."

"LeGrand died twenty-five years ago. There is no record of an official Policier reward for his capture."

"B-b-but," Chatine sputtered, feeling more desperate and confused by the second. "That can't be right. It came from Inspecteur Limier himself. He came to Montfer looking for him and that idiot daughter of his twelve years ago. I was there. I heard it with my own ears. He offered—"

The door to the interrogation room opened, cutting Chatine off from her ramblings.

"That'll be enough." She recognized the voice, but not the tone. Her gaze swiveled to see Marcellus standing in the doorway.

Chacal flicked his gaze at him and scoffed. "Don't worry, *Officer.* I've got this under control."

Chatine fully expected Marcellus to back down, bow out of the room with a mumbled apology. But he stood rigid in the doorway, looking more severe than Chatine had ever seen him.

"I said, that's enough," Marcellus repeated. "I'll take this from here."

Chacal groaned like this was all a huge inconvenience to him. He turned and looked up at Marcellus. "Go back to interrogation room two. This is nothing you need to concern yourself with. Just another lying déchet trying to—"

"Don't call him that!" Marcellus fired back, startling both Chatine and Chacal. Sols, even the officer himself looked a little surprised by his own outburst.

Chacal studied Marcellus as though trying to figure out whether to take him seriously.

Chatine watched the face-off between the two men with fascination. The way Marcellus was holding himself, with his shoulders pushed back and his chin jutted out slightly, made Chatine's stomach do a small backflip. She did *not* like the sensation one bit.

"I will continue this investigation," Marcellus said, standing his ground. "And you, Chacal, are free to go."

The sergent continued to glare at Marcellus, and Chatine wondered who would back down first. She would have placed largs on Marcellus. Big largs.

She would have lost.

The sergent's cheek quivered as though he were chewing on the inside of it. And then finally, with a grunt, he tore his eyes away from Marcellus and stalked out of the room.

"Vive Laterre," Marcellus called after him.

"Vive Laterre," Chacal muttered in response, slamming the door behind him, and then he was gone.

And Chatine was alone with Marcellus.

Of course, it wasn't the first time they'd been alone together. It wasn't even the second time. But it was the first time Chatine was aware of this thrumming sensation inside of her. Like her heart had grown to the size of a Sol and was pulsing wildly in her chest.

Marcellus began to pace the room. Chatine watched him with a mix of curiosity and annoyance.

What is he doing here?

Had he come just to save her from Chacal?

The thought made the thrumming grow stronger.

Marcellus stopped and turned toward her. He was fidgeting, as though whatever he was about to say was weighing on his nerves. His right thumb and forefinger found his left hand and rubbed absently at his pinky. Then he flinched and glanced down at it, shaking his head. "I keep forgetting it's not there," he murmured, as though speaking to himself.

Chatine instantly knew he was talking about the ring. The one that was currently sitting at the bottom of her coat pocket.

"My ring," Marcellus went on. "It went missing a few days ago. I feel sort of lost without it." He looked up and caught her eye.

Does he know?

Does he suspect me?

She reached into her pocket and rubbed her fingertip against the cool metal. "I'm sorry," she offered. "Was it very . . . um . . . valuable?"

Marcellus dropped his gaze to the floor and laughed. "No. It was worthless, actually. Made of fool's titan. It just had sentimental value. It belonged to my mother."

Chatine threaded her finger through the ring in her pocket. This was the perfect opportunity to get on the officer's good side. She could say she found it on the floor of the cruiseur. She could swear she hadn't known it was his until now.

Marcellus steeled himself, as though coming to a decision about whatever he'd been debating in his head. He pulled out his TéléCom and began tapping the surface. Chatine craned her neck to see the screen. In a small window, she saw herself, sitting in this very room. She glanced around to look for the microcams, but they were invisible. Hidden in the walls. When she looked back at Marcellus's TéléCom, however, the window had gone dark.

He'd disabled the security feed.

Why had he done that?

Then, suddenly, Marcellus was beside her. Closing the distance between them in two long strides. He crouched down next to her chair, his head just coming up to her shoulder. She could smell his hair. It smelled like the scent of fresh fabric wafting out of the vents of the garment fabrique.

How annoying.

Chatine tried to breathe through her mouth.

"Théo," Marcellus's voice was a rushed whisper, as though he were afraid of the walls listening. "I need your help."

Marcellus placed a hand on her arm, and Chatine tensed.

She tugged on the ring still looped around her finger, drawing it slowly to the edge of her pocket. She wondered what he'd do when she gave it back. Would he thank her? Smile that gleaming smile at her? *Hug* her?

Chatine suddenly felt breathless at the thought.

"I heard you mention Jean LeGrand," Marcellus went on. "What do you know about him? What about his daughter, Alouette? Did you find out anything else about her?"

Chatine let the ring slide off her finger. It plummeted to the dark corner of her pocket. She glanced down at his hand, still clutching her arm like she was his lifeline. And suddenly she became angry.

Very, very angry.

She didn't want to be his stupid lifeline.

She didn't want to be anyone's lifeline but her own. She didn't want to be the one Marcellus Bonnefaçon came to for help with his love life. She wanted to be the one he came to for . . .

Well, it didn't really matter what Chatine wanted.

It would never happen. Nothing she ever wanted would *ever* happen. And how could it? He didn't even know she was a girl! He still looked into her eyes and saw Théo. The wily Fret rat. His errand *boy*.

She launched out of her chair, moving to the other side of the room, as far away from him as possible. "Yes, I did, actually."

Marcellus appeared confused by her sudden movement, yet

annoyingly still hopeful. "You did? What? What did you find out?"

"Her name is not Alouette. It's Madeline."

Marcellus stood back up, his expression inscrutable. "Madeline," he repeated the name in a daze, and Chatine despised the way it sounded on his lips. Like a song.

"Yes. Just as I suspected, she's been lying to you this whole time. She's a liar."

And a murderer, Chatine added in her mind. She waited for her words to trigger a reaction. A flash of disgust on the officer's face. She'd settle for even a flicker of irritation. But she saw none of that.

Marcellus immediately tapped on his TéléCom and started speaking into the screen. "Search Madeline LeGrand."

Chatine watched his expression fall with disappointment as he stared at the flickering screen.

And that's when she knew. That's when she finally understood.

Marcellus was fascinated by that girl, liar or not. He might even be falling in love with her.

"Will that be all, Officer?" Chatine snapped.

Marcellus glanced up from his TéléCom and blinked at Chatine, as though he couldn't remember who she was or why she was there. "What? Oh, no. Wait. What were you saying to Chacal about a reward?"

Chatine sighed. She really didn't want to be here any longer. But she had a feeling Marcellus wasn't going to let her go until she told him everything she knew about the girl. "Madeline used to live with my family in Montfer. Until one day her father—Jean LeGrand— came and took her away. A few days later Inspecteur Limier showed up looking for him. He offered twenty thousand largs for information leading to his capture."

Marcellus's forehead crumpled, as though these details didn't add up.

"Twenty thousand?" he repeated. "For a criminal? That's way too high. That doesn't make any sense."

"Yup. That's what Chacal said. You two really cracked this case wide open." She walked over to the door. "So, can I go now?"

Marcellus hurried to the door and put his hand on it. "Wait. I have another favor to ask you."

Chatine groaned. She *really* regretted coming here. "What?"

Marcellus ran a hand through his thick, wavy hair. His previous confidence had vanished, and he was back to looking completely unsure of himself. "I need you to interrogate a suspect for me."

- CHAPTER 55 -
MARCELLUS

THERE WAS SOMETHING ABOUT THÉO THAT WASN'T adding up for Marcellus. The boy was hiding something. Every time Marcellus looked into his fierce gray eyes, he could see something buried underneath. A secret. A concealed layer.

The problem was that Marcellus had no idea what that layer contained.

He supposed everyone who lived in the Frets had secrets. Dark secrets that kept them alive. But he didn't have time right now to go searching for this boy's secrets. He had too many other people's secrets he was trying to deal with.

Alouette had lied to him.

About her name. About living with an escaped convict.

What else? Marcellus wondered. *What else is she hiding from me?*

"Why would you need *me* to interrogate a suspect for you?" Théo asked, his question pulling Marcellus back into the room.

Marcellus tapped at his TéléCom, bringing up the security feed for the Precinct. "We can't get him to talk," he explained to Théo, trying to reclaim that confidence he'd walked into this room with. "I thought maybe you'd have more luck."

He placed the TéléCom down on the table in front of Théo so he could see the screen.

Théo bent forward and Marcellus watched his dirty face pale.

"His name is Roche," Marcellus began. "He's allegedly been—"

"He's innocent!" Théo shouted, startling Marcellus. "Don't believe anything he says. He's just a kid. He's playing around. Trying to feel important. Please. You have to let him go."

Marcellus felt his heart warm at the protective quality of Théo's voice. "So, you know him?"

Desperation flashed in the boy's eyes. "Yes. I know him from the Frets. Believe me, whatever he's told you, he's lying."

Marcellus nodded and held Théo's gaze for a long, reassuring beat. "I believe you."

Théo seemed to visibly relax, his shoulders falling away from his ears.

"Unfortunately," Marcellus went on, "Chacal doesn't. The kid was bragging about delivering messages for the Vangarde, and Chacal thinks he was telling the truth. Of course, the boy now claims he was lying, but that's not enough to release him. If he admits to *you* that he was lying—in confidence when he thinks we're not listening—I might be able to get him released."

Théo looked confused. "So, what exactly do you want me to do?"

"Go into the interrogation room and pretend that you're another suspect. Tell him that we brought you in for questioning. Try to get him to talk truthfully." Marcellus thrust the TéléCom into Théo's hands. "Take this. Tell him you stole it off me. It'll earn you credibility."

The boy stared back at Marcellus, looking impressed.

Sols, Marcellus was impressed himself. Maybe hanging out with this Fret rat had rubbed off on him. Maybe he *would* make a decent commandeur one day.

He pointed to the TéléCom. "Click this in front of him and tell him you're disabling the microcams. The window will go dark, but I'll still be able to see you from the monitoring room. I'll connect to your audio chip, so I'll be able to hear everything you hear, and I'll be able to guide you through the whole thing."

Théo hesitantly took the TéléCom, glancing at Marcellus as though suspecting that this might be a trap.

Marcellus nodded. "It's okay. I trust you."

For a brief moment, Marcellus swore he saw a tiny smile break onto the boy's face, but it was gone so fast, he couldn't be sure.

Without a word, Théo folded up the TéléCom and slid it into the pocket of his coat. Marcellus opened the door and led Théo into the hallway. He stopped in front of interrogation room 2.

"Are you ready?" he said with a wink.

Théo nodded but there was something in his eyes. An uncertainty that made Marcellus feel sort of queasy.

"The sooner you can earn his trust and get him to admit this was all a game, the faster I can release him."

Théo nodded again, and Marcellus sucked in a breath.

Here it goes.

He unlocked the door and ripped it open. "You can't lie to the Ministère and get away with it!" he bellowed, doing his best Chacal imitation. He grabbed Théo by the shoulders and gave him a shove, careful to push just hard enough to make it look real, but not hard enough to do any harm. Théo stumbled into the room, turning back to hiss at Marcellus.

"Get in there and cool off!" Marcellus spat. "I'll be back to try again."

Marcellus slammed the door and hurried down the hall to the monitoring room. Chacal was already there, along with a few of the other deputies.

"Nice tactic," Chacal said. "Get the déchets to do your work for you." He flashed Marcellus a goading grin, as if waiting to see if Marcellus would react the same way he did in the interrogation room.

Marcellus glared back at him. "Just give me your TéléCom, Sergent."

Chacal reached into his pocket and reluctantly handed over the device. "What's wrong with your TéléCom?"

Right then, as if answering the sergent's question, Théo's voice rang out through the monitoring room's speakers. "Look what I copped off the pomp."

All eyes turned toward the giant monitor where Théo was pulling Marcellus's TéléCom out of his pocket and brandishing it toward Roche.

Chacal turned back to Marcellus with wide eyes. "Are you crazy? You let him have your TéléCom?"

Marcellus waved him off with one hand while the other expertly tapped buttons on Chacal's screen, connecting to Théo's audio chip. "Can you hear me?" he spoke clearly into the device. "Touch your nose if you can."

On the screen, the boy rubbed at his nose.

"How did you do that?" Roche asked Théo, looking impressed.

Théo snorted. "Easy. I swiped it from his pocket when he was dragging me in here. You put up enough of a fight with one hand, they don't notice what you're doing with the other."

Marcellus could feel Chacal seething beside him. "This better work, Bonnefaçon."

Marcellus ignored him again, addressing Théo instead. "Now pretend to cut the feed."

Théo pulled the second chair closer to Roche and sat down. He flashed him a cunning smile. "Watch this." He tapped at the screen and Roche's eyes went wide. "Now we're alone," Théo said, looking pleased with himself. He leaned back in the chair and put his feet on the table like he was going to take a nap.

"What did they bring you in for?" Roche asked a moment later, still gaping at Théo as though he hung Bastille in the sky.

Théo shrugged. "Same as you. Blah, blah, blah. Vangarde. Blah, blah, blah. Suspected enemy of the Regime. Only difference is, I'm not joking around. I told you not to joke around about this stuff. I told you it was serious."

Roche studied Théo for a long time, then flicked his gaze to the blackened TéléCom on the table between them. Marcellus felt himself leaning in to the screen.

C'mon, he silently pleaded. *Just admit this is a huge joke so we can all get out of here.*

Roche folded his arms across his chest. "I'm not joking around."

Théo scoffed. "Yes, you are. That's what you Oublies do, you make up games in the Frets to keep yourself busy and—"

"It's not a game!" Roche whispered, and Marcellus felt a shiver at the urgency in the boy's tone. "There's a real rebellion brewing."

Théo gritted his teeth. "I *know*. Which is why you need to stop messing around."

"I'm not messing around. Like I told you before, the Vangarde trusts me. They pay me to run messages for them in the Frets."

Marcellus glanced at Chacal out of the corner of his eye. The wretch was chuckling to himself. He was *enjoying* this.

Théo rolled his eyes. "No, they don't."

"They do!" Roche insisted. "I swear."

"And how long has this been going on?" Théo asked in a high-pitched voice.

Chacal snorted. "Sols, when is that boy going to become a man already?"

"Shut up," Marcellus snapped, keeping his gaze trained on the monitor.

"A whole year," Roche said proudly.

"Prove it," Théo challenged. "Tell me one of the messages."

Marcellus nodded. This was good. The boy was much better at this than he was.

Roche scratched his nose, his confidence ebbing ever so slightly. "I can't."

"Because, wait, let me guess. They're top secret, right?" Théo was clearly mocking him.

"No," Roche replied. "Well, I mean, yeah, they are. But I can't tell you what any of them said because they're all written in the Forgotten Word."

Marcellus felt ice in his veins.

WHAT? he thought at the exact same moment that Théo blurted out, "What?!"

Roche looked pleased by the reaction. "That's right. The Vangarde uses the Forgotten Word to pass messages to one another."

Marcellus's mind started to spin.

He's joking.

He has to be joking.

This is all part of the game.

But there was something niggling at Marcellus. A small itch at the back of his mind. A shiver of premonition that ran through him.

It makes sense.

What the kid was saying actually made sense. What *if* the Vangarde was using the Forgotten Word as their secret language? It would be the perfect code. No one could read it or write it anymore. Marcellus had met only two people in his life who could.

Mabelle.

And . . .

A lump formed in his throat. Marcellus coughed, reached for a mug of water on the nearby table, and guzzled it down. He suddenly felt a craving for some of that disgusting dark brown weed wine that Théo had thrown in his face at the Jondrette. It would certainly dull the throbbing that was starting in his head.

Alouette.

She knew the Forgotten Word. She didn't have a Skin. She wasn't in the Communiqué. She was secretive. And skittish. And lived in hiding.

Right, Marcellus assured himself. *Because she's a Défecteur and the daughter of a criminal.*

But then another voice screeched into his mind. A very different type of voice. The voice of doubt.

What if she *wasn't* a Défecteur, like he'd thought? What if she was something else? Something far more dangerous . . .

He immediately shoved the thought away. It was ridiculous. It was ludicrous. The kid in the interrogation room was *joking*! He wore industrial exploit goggles on his head, for Sols' sake! He was playing around. Marcellus was spiraling all because of some stupid prank from a twelve-year-old Fret rat.

And yet . . .

The thought wouldn't go away. It lingered. It hovered. It was a dark, gray cloud soaked with rain, threatening to break open and destroy everything.

Everything.

"Well, isn't that convenient," Théo was saying to Roche on the screen; the signature sarcasm that Marcellus had come to know so well was back in his tone. "The secret spy messages you've been hired to deliver are written in a language you can't even read."

"They are," Roche insisted.

"Then where are these Forgotten Word messages? Do you have any with you?"

Roche shook his head. "Nope. I ate the last one before they took me to the Med Center, so those flics couldn't get their hands on it."

"You ate it," Théo confirmed doubtfully.

"Yup. Stuffed it right down my throat. It tasted better than chou bread."

"How do I know you're not—"

"Ask him if he remembers any of the words!" Marcellus barked into Théo's ear, causing him—and everyone in the monitoring room with Marcellus—to jump.

"What are you doing?" Chacal asked, stepping up beside Marcellus. But once again, Marcellus ignored him. He approached the wall and placed his palms flat against the screen. He pressed and pressed as though he could reach right through it and manipulate the entire conversation with his hands. Change the outcome of whatever came next.

Théo tilted his head, questioning Marcellus's directive.

Marcellus repeated it. Slower this time. Clearer. But with the same sense of urgency. "Ask him if he can remember any of the words from the messages. If he's been delivering them for as long as he says, he has to remember *something*. Turn on the TéléCom, ask him to sketch what he remembers."

Annoyance flashed over Théo's face. He clearly didn't like where Marcellus was going with this, but Marcellus didn't care. He had to know. He had to put his suspicion to rest. This nonsense had gone on long enough.

Théo pulled the TéléCom toward him and swiped on the screen. "Fine," he said to Roche. "If you've really been running secret Forgotten Word messages for the Vangarde for a whole year, you have to remember something they've written." He pushed the TéléCom across the table with one finger. "Write something."

Roche balked, leaning away from the TéléCom as though it might bite him.

"You can't, can you?" Théo taunted.

Roche bit his bottom lip, looking torn.

"Because, admit it, you made this *all* up. There are no messages. You were never hired by the Vangarde. You've never even spoken to a member of the Vangarde, am I right?

Even though he could tell Théo was trying to sound like his usual tough, cavalier self, Marcellus could hear the desperation in his voice. Théo wanted—no, *needed*—Roche to cave. He needed him to confess that he'd been lying all this time. That it was all a sham.

And, ironically, Marcellus needed the exact same thing.

Their desperation was perfectly aligned.

Roche glanced down at the TéléCom, his stoic expression starting to crumble, his shoulders starting to slouch. Marcellus could see, in the monitor, the pulse of the boy's throat as he swallowed. As his body admitted the defeat before his voice could.

Marcellus felt himself sag so deeply in relief, he feared he might drop right to the ground. He closed his eyes. He tried to gain control of his racing heart.

It's over.

It was nothing.

Just a game.

"Actually," Roche said, "there is one word they've been using a lot lately."

Marcellus's head snapped up, and on the monitor, he saw Roche hesitantly reach out and pull the TéléCom toward him.

"Oh yeah?" Théo asked doubtfully. "What's that?"

Roche's face twisted in concentration, and for a moment it looked as though he really was trying to reach into the back corners of his mind and wrench something loose. He poised his fingertip over the screen of the TéléCom. His tongue slipped out the side of his mouth as he seemed to fall into a deep, focused trance.

Then, slowly, he started to trace something onto the screen.

Marcellus hurriedly tapped the monitor in front of him to mirror the TéléCom Roche was using. He blinked in disbelief at the long vertical black line that was appearing in front of him. The monitoring room was silent. Everyone—even Chacal—looked as though the fate of the planet rested on this twelve-year-old kid's scribbles.

Roche finished his line and immediately started another. This one was horizontal, branching out, at a right angle, from the bottom of the first line.

L.

Marcellus recognized it immediately.

"That's it?" Théo mocked. "That's all you remember? You drew a corner."

"Wait," Roche told him without looking up. "There's more."

Théo sighed, growing impatient with what he clearly thought was a farce.

Marcellus watched with a bone-dry throat as the boy—an orphan who claimed to be a Vangarde spy—shakily sketched out three more letters on the TéléCom.

Marcellus stared at the enormous screen in front of him, feeling like the entire planet of Laterre had just tilted on its axis. And maybe it had. Maybe this was the end for all of them. Maybe the Last Days had finally come to this world as well.

Because Marcellus wasn't sure how he was going to survive after this moment.

How *any* of them were going to survive.

Images and voices and colors swirled in his mind, like mist caught in a brewing storm. Mabelle. Walking out of the fog. Humming that haunting tune.

Little Marie Paresse. Convulsing. Vomiting. Her face turning blue.

Alouette. Sitting next to him at the fireside. Smiling that dazzling smile. Disappearing into the crowd like a phantom.

General Bonnefaçon. Standing in that darkened hallway of the Grand Palais. Uttering his menacing warning. *"You cannot let your emotions and ties to the past skew your judgments of the present."*

But that's exactly what he'd done, wasn't it? He'd let his emotions skew his judgment.

Marcellus was sure of it now.

Chacal clapped him on the back, startling Marcellus out of his reverie. "Any idea what that gibberish says?"

Marcellus felt his head fall into a dazed nod. "Yes," he said, still staring unblinkingly at the wall.

At the letters that had just appeared in front of him as though written by an unseen hand. By a *ghost*.

"It says 'Lark.'"

- CHAPTER 56 -
ALOUETTE

ALOUETTE'S FEET POUNDED SO HARD ON THE FLOOR tiles, the whole Refuge seemed to shake. Her breath was rough and jagged in her throat, and her heart beat like a hammer inside her chest. In one hand, she gripped Katrina, her doll, and in the other, the titan box.

"Jacqui!" she cried, bursting into the bedroom that Sister Jacqui shared with Sister Denise.

Sister Jacqui, who was alone in the room, dropped a bag she'd been holding and spun around. "Little Lark?"

"You said . . . you said . . . ," Alouette began, but she couldn't find the words. She couldn't find the breath.

Sister Jacqui rushed forward and took Alouette by the elbow, guiding her into the room. "Shhh. Come here. Sit down." Jacqui gestured toward the bed, littered with books. Jacqui and Denise were the only two sisters who shared a room in the Refuge, and everywhere—every shelf, table, chair, and surface, including their bed—was always covered in Jacqui's books or Denise's disassembled gadgets.

Alouette lowered herself down between two of the books. Jacqui sat next to her. But a moment later, Alouette sprang back up. She couldn't sit. Her body felt too wound, too taught.

She started to pace.

"You said that knowledge is within us, but that it's also out there to be found." Alouette's voice was fast and shaky. "You said that, and so I did. I went out there. I had to. I had to find out." She couldn't stop the words now. It was like someone had jammed on the kitchen faucet and the water was flowing, hot and fierce and gushing. "I had to find out if it was true. About Papa. I just wanted to know. And now—" A sob caught in her throat. She swallowed it down. "I've messed up everything. Now he's gone. He's gone to Reichenstat. He said we would both go. But he left without me. He's taken all his things. His clothes. Everything . . ."—she held out her shaking hands, which still held the doll and the box—"except these."

Sister Jacqui looked at Alouette for a moment and then at the objects clutched in her fists.

"Take a deep breath," Jacqui coaxed, reaching out to rest a calming hand on top of Alouette's.

Alouette did as she was told, although her breath still came out ragged and trembling.

"And another," Jacqui said, nodding and breathing with Alouette. "Now, let's start from the beginning."

With the air in her lungs and the sister's hand on hers, Alouette's legs finally loosened. She sat back down next to Jacqui.

Part of her knew that if she told Sister Jacqui everything, if she really did start at the beginning, then it would also be the end. The end of Jacqui's unwavering trust in her. The end of being sworn in as a sister. Maybe even the end of her welcome here in the Refuge.

But then another part of her knew she couldn't hold it in any longer. Everything inside of her, all the secrets she'd been keeping, all the lies she'd been telling, were like seedlings in Sister Laurel's propagation room. Now that they'd sprouted from the soil, there was no stopping them growing up into the light.

She had to tell Jacqui the truth. It might be the only way to keep them all safe.

"It started when the boy got hurt," she began, her voice still shaky and hurried. "I was trying to fix the old security monitor, and that's when I saw him. He was injured and bleeding. I couldn't just stand there and watch. I knew what to do to help him. I knew I needed to apply pressure and clean his wound and . . ." She took a deep breath. "And so I went outside. I left. Without telling anyone."

Alouette stopped and glanced at Jacqui from the corner of her eye. Her cheeks burned with guilt. She steeled herself for the shock. The look of betrayal. The harsh words. But Jacqui simply nodded her head, indicating for Alouette to go on.

Alouette took another deep breath and kept talking. She told Jacqui about leaving the Refuge and finding Marcellus and cleaning up his bleeding head with the old shirt. She told the sister about the terrifying droids and the convict with the bumps on his arm.

"They were just like Papa's," she said.

"It's okay," Jacqui said, rubbing Alouette's back like she used to do when Alouette was little and she couldn't sleep.

Alouette swallowed and continued her story. She was careful not to leave anything out. She told Jacqui about finding the candlestick and the hologram map in her father's room, hacking the library's security alarm so she could get to the Chronicles after everyone had gone to sleep, and then sneaking out again when the sisters were in Assemblée the next day. She choked down a sob as she relayed the part about the horrible execution, but she smiled a little as she told the sister about the ride on Marcellus's moto and the mysterious camp in the forest with its fire pit and little circle of huts.

All the while, Jacqui never reacted. She just nodded and listened. As though Alouette were simply telling her a story about scrubbing the Refuge floors.

"And then . . . ," Alouette said, bracing herself for the worst of it. "And then, I found out who Marcellus really was. I was so stupide not to have read the signs before. I put everyone in danger. He's . . . he's . . ." She swallowed. "He's the general's grandson. And an officer of the Ministère."

Jacqui glanced down at her lap, and Alouette couldn't tell if she was angry or surprised or something else.

"I'm sorry," Alouette rushed to continue. "I'm so, so sorry! I feel horrible. Because it turned out to be nothing. I put the Refuge in danger. I put the *library* in danger. For nothing. The flashing dot just marked some old grave site. I think maybe it's where my mother is buried."

Jacqui made a clucking noise with her tongue, pulling Alouette out of her spiral of panic. The sister appeared to be struggling with what she was going to say next.

"What?" Alouette asked curiously. "What is it? Tell me."

"Little Lark, your mother is not buried. Her dust was scattered in Montfer, where she died. Your father told me."

Suddenly, it felt like everything was vanishing in front of Alouette.

First her father.

And now her mother, too.

Pieces were beginning to fall out of place. The story she'd crafted in her mind about the camp and the graves and the candlestick wasn't making sense anymore. If her mother wasn't buried in that clearing, then why did her father have a hologram map leading there?

Would she ever find out?

Would her father's secrets be buried forever?

Would she even see her father again?

"Oh my Sols, Jacqui, I was so horrible to him! He came to get me from the Frets. He dragged me back here, and I said the most terrible things. I called him a criminal." She gasped for breath, and hot tears sprang to her eyes. "That's why he left, isn't it? Because of me. Because I hurt him. I pushed him away, and now he's gone! He's . . ."

The sobs took over. They heaved up through every muscle and fiber of Alouette like waves. She couldn't control them. She couldn't stop them. Until she looked up and saw the person standing in the doorway. And suddenly, they stopped on their own.

Sister Denise was dressed in a long gray jacket with a stiff, high collar, just like the ones Jacqui and Laurel always wore when they went on supply runs.

How long had she been there? How much had she heard?

"Are you ready, Jacqui?" Denise asked in her familiar and composed monotone. "It's time."

"Okay," Jacqui replied, squeezing Alouette's hand before releasing it.

Alouette's gaze spun back to Jacqui, and for the first time since she'd entered the room, she noticed that Jacqui, too, was wearing her above-world coat. Alouette peered down at the floor and realized the bag Jacqui had dropped when she'd first come in was the same bag the sister always took up to the Frets.

"Are you going on a supply run?" Alouette asked, confused.

It wasn't the right day for a supply run. And why was Denise going too? She never went up to the Frets. It was always Sister Jacqui and Sister Laurel.

"Not today," Jacqui said as she pushed herself up from the bed and began buttoning her coat.

"So where are you going?" Alouette asked.

A look flitted between the two sisters before Jacqui finally said, "There's something Denise and I have to do. You will understand soon."

Panic surged through Alouette. They couldn't leave too. Alouette couldn't stand to see another empty room in the Refuge today.

"Are you going to find my father?" As soon as the thought crashed into Alouette's mind, the ache in her chest began to ease. "That's it, isn't it? You're going to find him?"

But Sister Jacqui shook her head. "We aren't going to find Hugo.

Your father has his own path. You will see him again, though, I am sure of it."

The sister crossed the room and retrieved a large book from one of her shelves. She flipped through the pages and pulled out a loose leaf of paper. Then she crossed back over to Alouette and held it out.

"I never agreed with the decision to keep this from you. But it's what he wanted."

Alouette let the doll and the titan box drop into her lap as she reached for the yellowed paper. It took her a moment to figure out what it was, but finally she recognized the familiar, loopy handwriting of Sister Bethany, the first sister to compose and compile the Chronicles. Then Alouette's eyes fell on the words: "Bastille," "convicts," "metallic tattoos."

"The missing page?" Alouette whispered, utterly stunned. "From the Chronicles? You had it all along?"

She shot an accusing look at Sister Jacqui.

"He was ashamed, Alouette," Jacqui explained. "And he wanted to protect you. That's all he ever wanted."

Then Sister Jacqui leaned over, picked up her supply sac from the floor, and pulled it onto her shoulder.

Alouette momentarily forgot the page in her hand as her fear and confusion came charging back. "I don't understand," she cried out. "Where are you going? Does this have anything to do with what I did? Or Marcellus Bonnefaçon?"

Jacqui smiled. "Not exactly. And I wouldn't worry too much about Marcellus Bonnefaçon. He's no danger to us."

Alouette's brow furrowed. "What? How do you know? And what do you have to go do?"

Sister Jacqui sighed. "That, I'm afraid, I'm not allowed to tell you." She shared another inscrutable look with Sister Denise. "Remember everything we've taught you. And remember"—she reached forward and tapped the beads hanging from Alouette's neck—"you're one of us now and you're strong, Little Lark."

Then, before Alouette could reply, Jacqui turned and followed Sister Denise out the door.

For a few moments, Alouette was left stunned, openmouthed, gawking at the empty doorway. Then, suddenly, something shifted inside her. A feeling that something was escaping her. Everything was slipping through her fingers.

"Wait!" she shouted, scrambling to her feet.

Alouette charged after the two sisters. But by the time she was halfway down the hallway, she could hear the Refuge's PermaSteel door clanging shut.

They were gone.

Just like her father.

Alouette looked around the empty hallway, at the low ceilings and the thick, rugged walls. The ache in her chest had returned full force.

Somehow everything had changed, and yet, at the same time, nothing had changed at all.

She was right back at the beginning.

Back in the darkness where she'd always been.

Meanwhile, her father was probably already aboard a voyageur bound for Reichenstat, speeding across the System Divine, moving farther and farther away from her with each passing second.

Alouette glanced down at the page in her hands and ran her fingertips across the ripped edge. She remembered learning about voyageurs from Volume 11 of the Chronicles. How they were used to transport goods and people to the other planets in the System Divine. She remembered studying drawings of their long bodies, massive thrusters, and Y-shaped wings. Their powerful engines allowed them to travel from one planet to the next, when in supervoyage mode, or even as far as distant galaxies, when in hypervoyage mode.

But passages were so expensive, it was only the First and Second Estates who could ever afford to take those trips.

"I should have enough funds to get us there. . . ."

When her father had said this to her yesterday, Alouette had thought he was just rambling, possibly not in his right mind. But now she was wondering if what he'd said was true.

But how did he have the funds?

Alouette suddenly felt incredibly stupid. She closed her eyes, letting the shame of the moment wash over her.

Of course.

Her father was a criminal.

An escaped prisoner.

The funds were undoubtedly *stolen*.

But Alouette had searched his entire room the other day, and she hadn't found anything that looked like it might be stolen except the . . .

The yellowed page dropped from Alouette's hand and fluttered to the ground as she felt the world shift ever so slightly.

The candlestick.

The hologram map.

It wasn't leading to anyone's grave. It was leading to her father's hiding place. He'd buried something out there in the woods. Something he didn't want found by anyone but him. Which meant he couldn't secure passage on a ship to Reichenstat until he'd uncovered it.

Alouette's heart was suddenly alight with hope and the promise of redemption.

She knew how long it took to get to that clearing. She'd ridden there on the back of Marcellus's moto, but her father would most likely be on foot.

Alouette might still have time.

Time to stop him. Time to apologize for all the things she'd said to him. But most of all, time to tell her father that she would travel to the farthest planet of the System Divine if it meant she could still be with him.

- CHAPTER 57 -
CHATINE

LARK?

Chatine sat in interrogation room 2 across from Roche, who had just finished scribbling nonsense on Officer Bonnefaçon's TéléCom and was now pushing it toward her with an I-told-you-so expression on his face.

And it *was* nonsense, wasn't it?

No one still wrote or read the Forgotten Word. It had become a lost language. A cryptic code of their ancestors. A useless device.

When Roche had first started dragging his fingertip across the surface of the screen, Chatine had been absolutely, 100 percent sure it would be utter gibberish that came out. He was just playing around. Refusing to give up the farce.

But now she wasn't so sure.

She'd heard Marcellus's voice through her audio chip after Roche had finished. She'd heard the tremor in his tone.

"It says 'Lark.'"

What on Laterre did "Lark" mean?

She glared at Roche. "Where did you learn this word?"

Roche shrugged. "I told you. It's been in the messages. A *lot*."

Chatine was losing her patience. This kind of talk was surely going to get him sent to the moon. She was supposed to be directing suspicion *away* from him, but from the evident shift she'd heard in the officer's voice, it was clear that her questions—and Roche's *stupide* answers—had been doing just the opposite.

She leaned in close to Roche and locked eyes with him, trying to convey the direness of the situation in a single glance. "Look," she whispered hoarsely, even though she knew everyone could hear. Marcellus Bonnefaçon and probably half of the Policier force were watching her right now. She suddenly wished she had the capacity to disable that TéléCom for real. "You need to stop lying to me. You need to stop right now. This is serious. We could both get—"

Just then the door to the interrogation room was flung open and a figure in white rushed inside. The person was moving so swiftly and with such ferocity, Chatine could barely register his face.

That is, until he slowed down.

Until he grabbed Roche by the collar and ripped him out of his seat.

"Where did you learn that word? Where have you been delivering messages? Where are the Vangarde hiding?"

If Chatine hadn't been staring straight at him, she would never have believed that this angry beast of a man—this white gust of wind—was Marcellus. He shook Roche, causing the kid's oversized goggles to pop off his head and clatter to the floor.

"Where are they?!"

"Stop!" Chatine begged, pulling on his arm. "He's just a kid. He doesn't know anything."

Marcellus blinked and focused on her. For just a shiver of a moment, Chatine could swear that he saw her. *Really* saw her. His gaze seemed to cloud over. His expression softened. His brow furrowed like he was piecing it all together. As clearly as if she had let down her hood, scrubbed her face clean, and revealed herself to him.

Then the moment was over, and Marcellus turned back to Roche.

He set him back down on the ground. "Sorry," he muttered.

But Chatine barely had time to register the apology, because just then Roche charged at her. The top of his head smashed into her stomach, and she staggered back, hitting the wall. The impact knocked the wind out of her.

"You mouchard!" he screamed. "You lying, cheating, sniveling snitch!"

Roche backed up and started to come at her again, but this time Marcellus hooked his elbow around Roche's chest and held him back. The kid fought. He squirmed. He kicked. He yelled. "You betrayed me! You betrayed your entire estate!"

Suddenly, another uniformed figure burst through the door. It was Chacal. Chatine watched in horror as the sergent didn't even bother trying to help Marcellus restrain Roche. He just pulled out the long metal baton from his belt and aimed it at the boy's right knee.

Roche yelped and went down hard. But that did nothing to stop the tirade pouring from his lips. "You are a good-for-nothing, lowlife traitor. I can't believe you work with *them*. I can't believe you would sell me out to these flics!"

Chatine felt the insults in every bone of her body. The pain in her stomach from the impact of Roche's head was nothing compared to the agony she was feeling now. This boy—this one of her own—was right. She was a lowlife, sniveling traitor. She *was* a mouchard.

And not just in here. Not just in this room with him. For the past week she'd been doing something she swore she'd never do. She'd been spying for the Ministère. For the *general* no less.

All so she could fulfill her own selfish desires.

All so she could leave them behind.

Chatine was born into the Third Estate of the Regime. The bottom. The underbelly of the planet. The scum of Laterre. And yet, she'd never felt lower than she did right now.

She'd never cared about any of them. She'd never been loyal to her own kind. But there was something about Roche—something about his eyes and his dirt-stained face and his clever talk—that triggered a sensation deep within Chatine. A feeling she hadn't felt in years.

Empathy.

Chacal wrapped a hand around Roche's scrawny arm and began to drag him from the room. Chatine knew exactly where they were taking him.

There was only one place you got dragged to in this building.

Roche was going to a holding cell to await transport to Bastille.

"No!" Chatine exploded, pushing herself off the wall and diving toward Chacal. "Arrête!" Her hands were balled into fists. Her teeth were bared. She felt as though she could have easily torn that flic apart.

If she had been able to get to him.

Marcellus stepped in front of her, blocking her path. She feigned left, then spun right, but the officer was ready for her. As though he was anticipating her movements.

"You can't take him!" Chatine screamed at Chacal over Marcellus's shoulder. "He's just a kid! He doesn't know what he's talking about. He's making it all up."

She tried to ram Marcellus with her shoulder, fighting to get to Roche, but Marcellus grabbed her by the arms, holding her back, his nails digging into her skin through her coat.

"Bonnefaçon," Chacal said as he dragged Roche out the door. "Control your déchet friend."

Chatine felt Marcellus's body tense at the word, but he held his ground. His grip didn't loosen.

She thrashed. She punched. She flailed.

But she was too weak. She might have had the brains and the Fret smarts, but she didn't have the strength. She didn't have enough food to have the strength. She was no match for the strapping, well-*fed* Bonnefaçon protégé.

The door to the interrogation room closed with Chatine on one side and Roche on the other. And she had a sickening feeling it would be like that forever. She would never see him again. He would be shipped off to Bastille, and it was all her fault.

"You can stop this!" Chatine felt her knees go weak. "You have to stop this. Don't let them take him to Bastille."

Marcellus's gaze drifted toward the door. He seemed to be lost in a mix of pity and confusion. He released Chatine and collapsed into one of the nearby chairs, running his fingers through his dark hair.

Chatine dropped to her knees. If she couldn't stop them with her fists, maybe she could stop them with her words. "Please." She no longer cared that her voice sounded high and whiny. She just needed to undo what she'd done. She needed to take it all back. Even if that meant she was discovered for who she really was. "He's not what you think! You're making a mistake!"

"Am I?" Marcellus roared, launching out of his chair so quickly, it flew out from under him and crashed into the wall. Marcellus looked shocked by his own strength. Chatine scrambled up, suddenly afraid of getting kicked like a dog at his feet.

But then, a moment later, Marcellus's face crumpled. "I'm sorry," he whispered. The old, soft, gutless Marcellus that Chatine had grown accustomed to was back. "I'm sorry. I don't know what to do anymore. I don't know what to think. I can't just release him after he's admitted to working with the Vangarde. Sols, I'm losing it. I'm losing my grip on everything!"

Fire rose up inside of Chatine again. How dare he pretend to be tormented? How dare he stand there, deliberating Roche's fate like he deliberated what flavor tarte to have for breakfast? He knew nothing of suffering. None of the Second Estate did.

Marcellus ran his fingers through his hair again. It was already all mussed up from the last time, but now it looked like he'd washed it and let it dry in a windstorm. His loose curls, finally broken free, twisted every which way.

"Do you believe him?" he asked a moment later. "Do you believe he's working for them?"

"No," she said automatically.

Because it didn't matter what she did or did not believe. She couldn't let Roche go down for this. She couldn't be responsible for sending him to Bastille.

"No?" Marcellus repeated vacantly.

"He's making it up. He's trying to feel important in all this chaos. He can't possibly be involved."

"Then how did he know that word?"

Marcellus's question sank like a stone inside Chatine's chest. The graveness in his voice confirmed all her suspicions.

The word had significance.

"Lark?" she asked, and she swore she saw Marcellus flinch.

His hand fell from his hair and he looked at her. "Yes. Does that mean something to you?"

Chatine released a breath, grateful that, for once, she didn't have to think about the answer. She didn't have to contemplate its implications, carefully align it in her head with all the lies she'd already told that day.

She could just tell the truth. "No." She crossed her arms over her chest. "What does it mean to you?"

Marcellus continued to look at her, his gaze intensifying with every passing second, until Chatine could swear that he was about to answer her. That he, too, was going to tell the truth.

But she would never know.

Because a second later, Marcellus's TéléCom lit up on the table, pulling their attention toward it. Chatine could see Inspecteur Limier on the screen, his circuits flashing the way she'd only seen them do in the face of grave danger.

Marcellus reached for the TéléCom. "Go ahead, Inspecteur," he said.

Then, Chatine watched as Marcellus's expression went from confusion to horror in a heartbeat.

CHAPTER 58

MARCELLUS

"WHAT DOES IT MEAN TO YOU?" THÉO ASKED
Marcellus, his arms crossed over his chest like a challenge.

A war waged inside of Marcellus. It was a battle bigger than the
failed Rebellion of 488, bigger than even the Usonian War of Independence, which broke the planet free from Albion's reign.

Because it wasn't just a war over territories and governments and
control.

It was a war over his mind.

A war over his heart.

A war over a single word.

"Lark."

What does it mean to you? That was the ultimate question Marcellus
was faced with. And he had a feeling that however he chose to answer,
it just might decide the rest of his life. He turned toward Théo. The
boy's piercing stone-gray eyes were waiting for him, waiting for a reply.

But Marcellus never got the chance to give one.

Because a second later, his TéléCom lit up on the table and
Inspecteur Limier's sharp, clipped voice rushed into his ear.

"Officer Bonnefaçon. We have a very serious situation in the Fabrique District."

Marcellus's stomach lurched as he reached for the device and accepted the connection. He'd never heard the inspecteur's voice sound so grave.

"Go ahead, Inspecteur."

The inspecteur's cold, orange eye stared at Marcellus through the screen as he spoke. "There's been an incident in the TéléSkin fabrique. Someone has set off an explosif."

"Wh-what?!" Marcellus sputtered. "Are the workers okay?"

The inspecteur's facial circuitry flickered once as the data was accessed. "The device was rudimentary, and the damage was contained to the processing department."

Marcellus cringed. *I knew that Universal Alert would only make things worse.*

"The Communiqué shows twelve lives lost," Limier went on. "I'm AirLinking you the profiles now. The families are being notified presently over their TéléSkins."

Marcellus tried to blink his surroundings back into focus. The words were too foreign. They belonged in another time. On another planet. Delivered to another officer.

It's happening again.

Suddenly all he could see was the face of his dead father in the morgue.

The man responsible for the last explosion on Laterre. Seventeen years ago.

That explosion had put an end to a revolution.

This one, he feared, had the power to start one.

"Officer Bonnefaçon?" Inspecteur Limier's voice pulled Marcellus back to the room. "Officer?"

"Yes. I'm here."

"We are preparing an immediate cleanup effort," Limier stated evenly. "It's now more important than ever that life continue as normal on Laterre. That people go to work so that our Regime can go on functioning."

Continue as normal? Marcellus thought, sickened. Twelve people were dead. Wiped out from existence like burned-out stars. Just like that.

What about their families? All the people getting heartless, automated alerts on their Skins right now? How would *they* just continue as normal?

But still, Marcellus heard himself saying, "Yes, of course, Inspecteur."

"Your grandfather would like you to return to the Ministère headquarters right away. He will be holding a briefing shortly."

Marcellus nodded. "I will be there."

The connection blinked out, and Marcellus dropped the TéléCom into his lap. The razor-thin device suddenly felt as heavy as a stone.

"What is happening?" he whispered aloud.

He got no reply. It was only then he realized he was alone in the room. The door was ajar. And the boy—Théo—was gone.

Marcellus gaped at the empty space, trying to figure out when, during the conversation, the boy had slipped out.

"Lucas Fontaine. Third Estate. Fret 12."

Marcellus's gaze was pulled back to the TéléCom lying on his lap. The profiles Inspecteur Limier had sent were now scrolling on his screen.

Faces of the dead.

"Anouk Duchêne. Third Estate. Fret 20." Marcellus reached for the device to silence it. He couldn't handle this right now. He needed to think.

"Azelle Renard. Third Estate. Fret 7."

Renard?

Marcellus's hand froze. He stared down at the image on the

screen. A pretty girl with cat-shaped eyes, high cheekbones, and a slender face. The resemblance to Théo was incredible. It was almost as though Marcellus were looking at a female version of the boy he'd come to know over the past few days.

He glanced back at the empty space where Théo had stood only moments ago, and suddenly a knot the size of a planet formed in his chest.

"The families are being notified presently over their TéléSkins."

"Sols!" Marcellus swore, leaping out of his seat. As he raced down the hallway of the Precinct, toward the exit, he gripped the TéléCom tightly in his hand, bellowing into the screen. "Locate Théo Renard!"

Outside the Precinct, it was raining. Hard. As though the Laterre sky were weeping for everything it had lost this week.

"No location found," the TéléCom announced. "Tracker disabled."

Marcellus wiped the fat raindrops from his eyes and stared down at the screen.

Disabled? The Third Estate can disable their trackers?

He let out a sigh as he jumped on his moto and started the engine. There was still so much he had to learn about this planet.

Starting with how to find someone who clearly didn't want to be found.

- C H A P T E R 59 -
CHATINE

ALONE.

Chatine was alone again. She sat on the roof of the textile fabrique, staring down at the pile of rubble below, the rain falling thick and heavy on her hood and dripping into her eyes. Most of the neighboring building was still intact, but the section in front of Chatine was a tangle of shattered mortar and twisted metal. A few spirals of lingering smoke tried to rise from the debris, only to be snuffed out by the wet air.

The alert she'd received from the Ministère when she was in the Precinct was still playing in an endless loop on her Skin. Chatine had yet to find the energy to turn it off. She could hear the message only in bits and pieces now.

"Please accept our condolences . . . Her body is being transferred to the Vallonay Med Center . . . grateful for her loyalty to the Regime . . . May she rest with the Sols."

Staring down at the place her sister once worked, Chatine felt like the only person left on this entire planet. She was used to it, though. She had always been on her own. It was the one constant in her life she could count on. She was born alone. She'd practically raised herself alone. She'd spent the first five years of her life *alone*.

But then Henri had come and for that brief, blissful year, she hadn't been alone anymore. She'd finally had a friend. A companion.

Then he died and Chatine was alone again.

Of course, she'd always had Azelle. But they'd never been close. As small children, they'd squabbled constantly. As they grew older, however, Azelle had tried to reach out to Chatine. Tried to become her friend. But after Henri died, Chatine had decided friends were overrated. Plus, Azelle was so different from the rest of their family. It was almost as if she didn't have a drop of Renard blood in her veins.

But somehow—by some curious joke of the Sols—Chatine and Azelle had been born into the same family. They had shared a bed and scraps of food. But they'd never shared secrets. Chatine had never told her sister of her plan to escape to Usonia. Because she knew, if she did, Azelle would only laugh at her and tell her how foolish she was being. The same way Chatine had laughed at Azelle's foolish plan to win the Ascension.

Maybe Chatine *should* have told her.

Maybe she wouldn't have laughed.

Maybe she would have pleaded for Chatine to take her, too.

And maybe Chatine would have said yes.

She wanted to think, now, that she would have said yes.

That they could have found a life on Usonia together.

But it didn't matter anymore. Because Azelle was gone. And her sister's hope of ever finding a better life—won or earned or otherwise—was gone too.

And now Chatine felt more alone than ever.

The crushing absence of her sister hit harder than she ever imagined it would. And she couldn't shake the feeling that it was somehow her fault. That everything was *her* fault. The Délabré finding her stash. Roche getting arrested. And now this.

But that was ridiculous. She knew that. She hadn't done this. She hadn't set that explosif. It had probably been some stupide worker, trying to make a point by blowing up the building where the Skins were made. Destroying the machines that manufactured the chains for the Third Estate.

Regardless of who did it, it was done.

An entire section of the fabrique was gone.

The only evidence that it had ever been there in the first place were these smoking remains. This massive, cavernous chasm in the side of the building. And the matching chasm that had opened up inside of Chatine, threatening to consume her whole.

As she stared into them both, Chatine found herself wondering if maybe Azelle had had the right idea this whole time. Maybe they *were* all better off just following the rules, going to work every day, checking in and out on their Skins, praying to the Sols to win an impossible lottery year after year.

Being dutiful servants of the Regime.

Because look what the alternative had gotten them.

Another pile of ashes.

Chatine knew what this meant. Something big was coming. A storm was brewing. A storm the likes of which even the rain-soaked people of Laterre hadn't yet seen.

And Chatine did *not* want to be around to see it.

"Hey."

Chatine jumped and turned to see the last person she ever expected to see on the roof of a fabrique. But there he was. His crisp white uniform was stained from the ash and dust mingling with the moist air. He sat down next to her on the edge of the building and peered over the precipice, into the charred wreckage below. He sucked in a breath and leaned back.

"Do you always like to be up so high?"

"Yes. Always." Chatine felt herself stiffen beside him, slipping back into her regular disguise. But with him, it wasn't just the disguise of Théo, the wily *boy* of the Frets. It was more than that. Whenever she was around Marcellus, she felt as though she had to be another level of another person. The best version of her fake self. She had to be the craftiest. The smartest. The quickest. The snarkiest.

She had to be *memorable.*

That's what it was, she now realized. All this time, she'd been desperate for him to remember her. She didn't just want to fade into the back of his mind when his training was over and he returned to his easy life in Ledôme. She wanted to be the Fret rat he could never forget.

"You're a hard person to track down, you know that?" He flashed her a cryptic smile that Chatine couldn't quite interpret.

"Been looking for me long, Officer?" she asked in the most teasing voice she could muster.

But it felt forced.

And stupid.

And desperate.

And she was tired of being memorable.

Now she just wanted to go back to hiding.

"Yes, actually," Marcellus replied in all seriousness. "After you ran out of the Precinct, I looked everywhere for you."

Chatine felt her heart do a double beat behind her ribs. She scorned it.

"Well, here I am!" She opened her arms wide, as though gesturing not to this building, not to this run-down Fabrique District, but to all of Laterre. To all of the System Divine. To this whole Sol-forsaken universe.

Then, before she could even fathom what she was doing, Chatine was on her feet. She was standing at the very edge of the building, at the edge of the world, gazing down into the dark abyss. She opened her mouth, and as loud as her lungs would allow, she shouted, "Here

I am! I'm right here! Do you see me? Because I've been here this whole time! This whole fric-ing time."

So much for going back into hiding.

Marcellus leapt to his feet. "What are you doing?"

"I'm screaming!" she screamed back.

He grabbed her by the sleeve of the coat and pulled her away from the edge. "Well, can you at least scream a little farther back? You're making me nervous."

Chatine turned toward him, opened her mouth, and let out the wildest, most maniacal laugh she'd ever heard coming from her own lips. "Am I making you nervous, monsieur? Do you not want me to die? Do you not want me to fall over the edge of this building and plunge to my death? Wouldn't that make life easier for you? One less Third Estate scum to deal with? One less body to freeze to death in the Frets? One less mouth to *not* feed?"

In that moment, Marcellus looked genuinely frightened of her. "W-w-what?" he stammered. "Of course not! What are you even talking about?"

"Would you miss me, monsieur?" Chatine went on. She had lost her mind. She knew that. But she no longer cared. "Would you be sad if I died?"

"Yes," Marcellus said. His face was full of torment. She was making him uneasy. She was glad of it. "Of course I would be sad."

"Why?" Chatine insisted. "Why would you be sad? Why would you even care? You don't seem to care about anyone else who dies around here. Another Third Estate body in the morgue. Another pile of frozen dust to scoop up. What's it to you? You don't care. None of you do!"

Marcellus's lips pressed into a firm, angry line. "We care," he said, but then a second later amended his statement. "*I* care."

"Why? Why do you care what happens to me?"

Marcellus looked saddened by the question. As though he felt like this wasn't a question he should have to answer. But Chatine didn't agree. It was not only a question he *had* to answer, but a question she *needed* him to answer.

"Why?" she asked again.

"Because . . . ," he began uncertainly. "Because you're my friend, Théo."

Chatine let out another laugh. This one, however, was dark. Spiritless.

Miserable.

"Théo," she repeated with an air of disgust. "Théo." Then her voice grew quiet. Pensive. "That's my name. That will always be my name to you. It's not the kind of name you sing. It's not the kind of name you fight for. Or stand up to white-haired giants for. It's the kind of name you say with spite and pity. *Théo.*"

Marcellus shook his head. He was not following her. He could not comprehend the nonsense she seemed to be spewing.

And yet, Chatine thought, *he's still here.*

He hadn't left. He hadn't walked away.

He's still here.

"What are you talking about?" Marcellus finally asked.

But Chatine didn't respond. Because there were no words that could make any of this clear. Forgotten or otherwise.

There was only the truth.

There was only her.

She reached up, and with her freezing, numb hands, Chatine began to rub at her cheeks, her forehead, her chin. Her skin pulled. Her flesh screamed. But she didn't stop until it was all gone. Until she'd scraped away every layer of grime and filth. Years of conceal-ment. A lifetime of hiding in the dirt.

Marcellus watched her with silent curiosity. His eyes wide. His jaw slack.

At what moment did he see it? she wondered. At what moment did he realize her ultimate con?

Was it in the arch of her cheekbones?

The feminine point of her nose?

The slender slope of her jaw?

Or was he still in the dark?

Not for long, though.

Chatine took a deep breath and slowly lifted her hands to her hood. As she peeled it back, she saw Marcellus's face shift. She saw the comprehension begin to dawn like a cloud drifting away from a Sol. But it wasn't until she unwound the knot at the base of her neck and shook out her long hair that the light finally broke through.

Chatine self-consciously touched the ends of her hair, which now fell almost to the middle of her back.

And she waited.

For what, she wasn't sure.

A question?

A laugh?

An arrest?

But Marcellus just stood there, staring at her. Speechless, yet not silent. A small guttural sound escaped the back of his throat.

"*Chatine*," she said quietly. "That's my name."

Then, she took one step forward and pressed her cold lips against his.

PART 6

THE VANGARDE

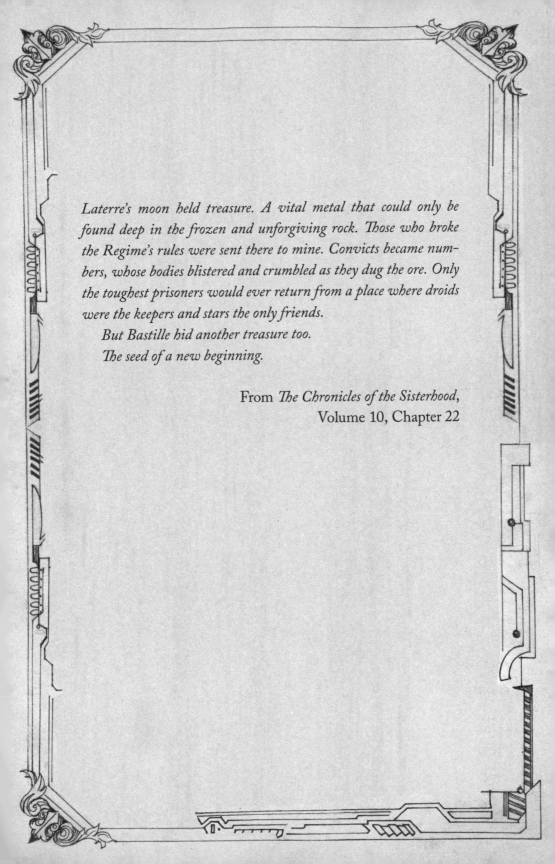

Laterre's moon held treasure. A vital metal that could only be found deep in the frozen and unforgiving rock. Those who broke the Regime's rules were sent there to mine. Convicts became numbers, whose bodies blistered and crumbled as they dug the ore. Only the toughest prisoners would ever return from a place where droids were the keepers and stars the only friends.

But Bastille hid another treasure too.

The seed of a new beginning.

From *The Chronicles of the Sisterhood*,
Volume 10, Chapter 22

- CHAPTER 60 -
MARCELLUS

MARCELLUS BARELY HAD TIME TO REGISTER WHAT
had happened before the boy was kissing him. No, not the boy. The
girl. She was a girl. She'd been a girl this whole time.

This whole time!

Marcellus couldn't wrap his mind around this. His memory skid-
ded back through every conversation, every look, every movement.
What had he overlooked? How hadn't he seen it?

The profile on the Communiqué said the boy's name was Théo.

But now Théo was Chatine, and Chatine was kissing him.

Deeply, intensely, endlessly.

His lips . . . *Her* lips were so cold on Marcellus's own, but her body was
so warm. It arched against him. Almost involuntarily, his arms slipped
around her narrow back, pulling her closer. His fingers weaved through
her hair, which was now loose and wet and tangled down her back.

It was wrong.

This kiss.

It was all wrong.

Yet Marcellus couldn't pull away. There was something crackling

between them. It couldn't be stopped. Her kiss was hungry, demanding, needy. Everything else seemed to fall away. Vanish. The smoke
from the destroyed fabrique. The rain falling everywhere. And all the
deception, too. All the lies. Even the word "lark" had flown away.

Until there was nothing but Chatine's rain-soaked lips on his.

Marcellus stepped into her, pressing himself against her. Kissing
her back with the same fervor and desperation. And in that instant,
Marcellus felt infinite. For the first time in his life, he felt unstop-
pable. Invincible, even.

"Good evening." A voice caused Marcellus to jump back as though
Chatine had bitten him. It was a familiar voice. An unsettling voice.
The one voice on Laterre that could bring Marcellus crashing back
to solid ground.

"Grand-père?" He glanced around wildly, expecting to see his
grandfather's pristine white uniform looming over him.

But the roof of the fabrique was empty. They were still alone.

"I have not heard from you in some time."

There it was again. His grandfather's voice. But where was it coming from? Marcellus's shaky hands reached into his pocket, searching
for his TéléCom.

"I do not appreciate being kept waiting."

Marcellus finally managed to unfurl his TéléCom but frowned
when he saw the screen was empty. His grandfather was not speaking
to him.

Then who on Laterre . . .

Marcellus glanced up to see the boy—the *girl*—punching frantically at the inside of her arm.

At her Skin.

It seemed Marcellus's audio patch was still synced with the chip
in Chatine's ear from when he'd connected to it at the Precinct. He
could still hear everything she could hear.

"I'll expect a full report from you by tomorrow morning, otherwise—"

Marcellus just managed to catch a glimpse of the general's face before the message was abruptly cut off.

"Why is my grandfather AirLinking you?" Marcellus asked, still unable to make sense of it.

Chatine shook her head and waved her hand. "It was nothing. Just one of those silly Universal Alerts we're all forced to listen to. Just forget it."

She took a step toward him and wrapped her hands around his neck, pulling his mouth back toward hers. But Marcellus jerked away. "Wait. That doesn't make sense."

A Universal Alert?

But his grandfather had been sitting in his office during that message. And General Bonnefaçon didn't send Universal Alerts from his personal study. Marcellus grabbed Chatine's wrists, disentangling her grasp from around his neck. She tried to yank her left hand free, but Marcellus held tight, maneuvering it around so he could see the screen implanted in her flesh.

She fought. She struggled. But once again, he was stronger.

He pressed play.

". . . otherwise I'll be forced to call off our deal. We're running out of time. Marcellus is still our best lead to the Vangarde base, but if you can't finish the job, then I'll find someone else who can."

There was a finite beep, marking the end of the message, followed by silence.

Deafening, all-consuming silence.

Everything inside Marcellus went rigid. He could do nothing but stare openmouthed at the girl.

"You're working for him?" Marcellus finally broke the silence. His voice deep and slow, dark and quiet. "For my grandfather?"

The girl actually had the nerve to scoff at this. And *laugh*. Like it was all a joke. Like his life, his loyalty, his shattered trust were just one big joke. "No. Of course not. I would never work for that pomp."

"You're lying!" Marcellus spat, releasing Chatine's wrist and stepping away from her. He could feel his pulse thumping in his neck. "You're spying for him. On *me!*"

She didn't say anything. She kept her eyes pointed downward. At her Skin. Rubbing the darkened screen where General Bonnefaçon's face had just been.

"Look at me!" snapped Marcellus, although his voice cracked over the words.

Finally, her gaze crept upward. So slowly, it was painful.

As Marcellus looked into her gray eyes—glimmering like rainwater—he could see it now. They were so delicate. So feminine. He wasn't sure how he'd missed it before. His fists tightened until his fingernails cut into his palms.

"Is that what this was all about?" he asked, his voice thick with disdain. "The disguise? The kiss? Everything?"

"No!" she cried out, her eyes suddenly full of desperation. "No, it wasn't like that. I swear."

But Marcellus ignored her cries. In fact, they only made him angrier. "All this time I thought you were helping me, but you were just hoping I would lead you and my grandfather to the Vangarde?"

"I'm sorry," Chatine tried. "I can explain."

"Save your explanations. I know how this works. I'm not stupid. You're poor. You're hungry. You're freezing. You'll do anything for a larg, isn't that right? Isn't that how your *kind* operates?"

He felt dirty thinking it. He felt even dirtier saying it. But it was true. She'd just proven it was true. All this time Marcellus had thought that this boy—*girl*—was different. But she wasn't. She was just a lying, cheating con artist like the rest of them.

"Please." Chatine grabbed his hand and squeezed it. "Listen to me. It's not what you think. I mean, it was at first, but it's not anymore. I swear it's—"

"Why should I believe you? Why should I believe anything you say . . . *ever*? Roche was right. You *are* a traitor."

Marcellus roughly yanked his hand from hers. He was finished. He didn't want pitiful "pleases" and excuses. He just wanted to get away from her. Away from this rooftop. This girl, with her pathetic, cat-shaped gray eyes. Away from her lies.

He turned and started walking across the craggy rooftop.

"Marcellus, wait!" she called out.

He spun around, anger flashing in his eyes. "That's Officer Bonnefaçon to you," he spat. "You would be wise to remember your place, déchet."

CHAPTER 61

CHATINE

SOMEWHERE BEYOND THE DENSE CLOUDS, THE SOLS were setting and night was descending over the streets of Vallonay.

The Darkest Night.

Until this very moment, Chatine had never quite understood the name of the current season of Laterre's orbit. She'd always known darkness, that much was certain. Her entire life, thus far, had been one of near-constant darkness. But this was a different kind of dark. This was a darkness that seeped into her skin, that eroded her bones, that blackened her heart.

Rain came down in droves. It was crooked. It was sideways. It was everywhere. It splattered up from the ground, attacking her from below.

As Chatine continued walking back toward the Frets, she pulled her flimsy coat tighter around her and readjusted her hood. Her hair was back in its usual knot and her face was streaked with mud again. She reached into her pocket, sliding her fingers over the curve of Marcellus's ring.

She could still hear his words tumbling around in her mind. He thought she was the scum of Laterre. He'd called her a liar. He'd called her a déchet.

He was right.

She *was* garbage. She was worthless. While Azelle—sweet, innocent Azelle—had tried to live an honest life, Chatine lied and cheated her way through everything.

The memory of Marcellus's eyes as he'd watched the general's message play on her Skin was enough to punish her for a lifetime.

The fric with him.

Chatine had expected the Frets to be in an uproar. But everything was eerily quiet and deserted. It was as though the news of the bombed fabrique had shocked everyone into a stunned silence. And now they were just lying in wait. Waiting to see what the Ministère would do. What the planet would do.

But Chatine had no time for waiting. She was done waiting.

The fric with Laterre.

She had to leave. She had to get as far away from this planet as possible. Usonia, Reichenstat, Kaishi, Novaya. She'd even live on Albion with the mad queen if she had to. She no longer cared where she went, just as long as it wasn't here.

But she was out of options.

The deal with the general was obviously off. There was no way she would ever find the Vangarde base now.

And all of her stolen trinkets were still in the hands of the Délabré, who had given her until tomorrow to dole out their share of a make-believe con. If she didn't produce the largs, she would lose even more than she'd already lost.

Which meant there was only one way to get the amount she needed.

When she arrived at the mechanical room in Fret 7, she paused before the doorway, summoning the strength to do what she knew she had to do. Then she pulled back her sleeve and tapped to waken her Skin. Chatine took a deep breath and stared at the metal grate that covered the vent in the floor. It looked so innocent and unassuming. One would never know that it had been concealing a convict.

A convict that someone was willing to pay twenty thousand largs to find.

She tapped her Skin. When it prompted her to specify a recipient, she spoke slowly. "Inspecteur Limier."

Then she waited for the AirLink to be accepted.

This was it. Her only shot. Her last-ditch effort.

There might be no record of the reward for Jean LeGrand in the Ministère Communiqué, but Chatine didn't care. She now understood that this was not a Ministère matter. This was clearly a *personal* matter. She'd seen the way the inspecteur and the white-haired man had looked at each other in the Marsh yesterday. There was something significant there. An ancient rivalry. One that spanned years, if not decades.

Inspecteur Limier's face suddenly appeared on her Skin, startling Chatine even though she'd been the one to initiate the connection. She could tell from his surroundings that he was riding in some type of vehicle. Possibly a transporteur.

"Renard," the inspecteur said. Was it only *her* name that he pronounced with that mix of irritation and amusement? As though she was not only a nuisance to him but also a joke?

"Inspecteur," she replied. She fought the urge to imitate his same tone. "I'm contacting you about a very urgent matter."

The circuitry in the inspecteur's face flashed once. "Yes?"

Chatine took a breath, keeping her voice light and airy. "Twelve years ago, you came to Montfer, offering a reward for information leading to the whereabouts of a criminal named Jean LeGrand."

Limier cocked an interested eyebrow, prompting her to continue.

"I'd like to claim that reward."

There was silence. Limier's face was very still. If it weren't for the flickering lights on his cheek, Chatine might have thought the AirLink had dropped. But then, a second later, the inspecteur started to laugh. It wasn't a mirthful, human laugh. It was a bleak, robotic laugh that sent a chill down Chatine's spine.

"What?" she asked uneasily. "What's so funny?"

"You," the inspecteur said through his mechanical chuckles. "All of you. You duplicitous Renards are all the same. Corrupt. Dishonorable. So willing to turn on anyone. Even one another."

Chatine's forehead crumpled. What was he talking about?

Limier's laughter came to an abrupt halt. "I'm sorry, Théo," he said, his voice once again emotionless and dry. "But I'm afraid you're too late."

Chatine felt her knees wobble. She grabbed on to a nearby pipe to keep from collapsing. "What?" she managed to utter. "No, that can't be. I just saw him yesterday."

How could she be too late?

"As did a lot of people," Limier pointed out. "As did I."

Chatine glanced around at the empty Fret hallway. Had the Policier already raided this place?

"So, you know where he is?" Chatine asked, her voice trembling. She refused to give up. She refused to accept the fact that her last hope—her last chance of escape—had led to yet another dead end.

"Yes," the inspecteur said. "I've just received an AirLink, not a few minutes ago, from someone claiming the same reward. In fact, they already have LeGrand in custody. They sent me proof. I'm heading there right now to resolve this matter once and for all."

Chatine felt the blood drain from her face. She released the pipe she'd been clinging to for support and stood up straighter. "Who?" she asked through gritted teeth. "Who has him in custody?"

But she didn't have to wait for an answer. She already knew.

Inspecteur Limier let out another gloomy cackle, and now Chatine understood the reason behind his amusement. "Your parents."

- CHAPTER 62 -
MARCELLUS

THE MARBLE FLOORS SHOOK BENEATH MARCELLUS'S feet as he charged down the hallway of the Grand Palais's south wing. Every muscle, every tendon and sinew, every nerve ending inside of him was on fire. He'd never known anger like this. It rushed through him, again and again, like an endless looping wave.

Everyone had deceived him.

Everyone had lied to him.

Alouette.

Théo—or Chatine or whatever her name was.

Even his own grandfather.

All along, that Fret rat had been spying for the general. Trying to lure Marcellus in so he would lead her to the Vangarde base and she would get a big, fat reward from his grandfather. And like a true imbécile, Marcellus had been sucked right in. Taking her along to Montfer, treating her like a friend, helping her, feeding her, telling her things he'd never told anyone before.

Kissing her.

He wiped his mouth with the back of his hand, the anger burning inside him so fiercely now, it felt as if it were going to consume every molecule of air in his lungs. Every last cell in his body.

As he strode onward down the corridor, the crystals in the chandeliers clinked, the paintings vibrated on the walls, and the china vases wobbled on their ornate side tables.

But he kept moving, as straight and unswerving as a paralyzeur pulse. With a single target in mind.

"You hired her to spy on me?"

The words tore out of Marcellus as he burst through the heavy double doors of his grandfather's study.

The general looked up from the TéléCom on his desk. For a moment, he appeared startled. But then, with the swiftness and precision of a seasoned Ministère officer, he pulled his expression into something more neutral.

More unreadable.

"Take a seat, Marcellus."

But Marcellus ignored him. He rushed forward, planted both hands on the surface of the huge desk, and glared at the general. "You sent her to spy on me!" His voice was thick and trembling, yet filled with all that anger. "You hired her to use me."

"You need to calm down," the general said, keeping a steady gaze on Marcellus. He lifted his chin and his lip curled, ever so slightly. "This is not the behavior of a Ministère officer."

Marcellus banged a palm onto the desk, making the TéléCom jump. "But you clearly don't *think* of me as an officer, do you? You never have. You've never trusted me. Was I ever in line for commandeur? Or was that just a decoy? Because you knew, in your heart, that I could never replace your precious Vernay."

The flinch happened so fast, Marcellus almost missed it. The general pushed himself up from his seat, so he was eye level with his grandson. "Marcellus, you need to use your brain. You are not stupide. Although, I must say, you're acting that way right now."

Marcellus leaned in closer to his grandfather, refusing to look away. "I've been on trial my entire life. Ever since the day I was born, you've been waiting for me to screw up. To become a traitor. To let you down. Do you know how that feels? To have someone watching you like that? Waiting like that?" The words were tumbling out of him now, hot and furious and violent. "To have someone—your *own* grandfather—never fully believing in you?"

The general raised a hand. "Quiet, Marcellus." His voice was so low, it almost sounded like a growl. "Like I said, you're not using your brain. If you were, you'd realize you are a target."

The general moved around the side of the desk, until he was standing right beside Marcellus.

Marcellus started to tremble. But he clenched his fists and forced himself to face his grandfather.

"A target for the Vangarde," the general clarified in the same low monotone. "They want you, Marcellus. With your notoriety as my grandson and the blood of one of their former operatives in your veins, you could be a very useful pawn in their game." He leaned in so close, his face was centimètres away from Marcellus's. "I was trying to protect you."

Marcellus could feel his cheeks burning, his hands shaking. "I don't need protecting. And I don't need to be a pawn in one of *your* games either. I don't need some Fret rat—some *girl*—chasing me around, luring me into her plans. *Your* plans. Pretending to be my friend." Much to his annoyance, his voice cracked on the last word.

The general eyed Marcellus for a long moment before throwing his head back and letting out a cruel, jarring laugh. "Oh, Marcellus. You fell for her, didn't you?"

"*I did not*," Marcellus bellowed, but his cheeks were burning.

Was there anything his grandfather didn't know about him?

Was there ever a single moment he hadn't been watching him?

Waiting for him to make a wrong turn?

"Trust me, you don't want one of *those* girls, Marcellus," his grandfather said, his expression returning to neutral. "Fret girls are nothing but trouble." He raised an eyebrow, as if considering something. "I suppose, with some soap and a hot shower, she could be quite pretty. Pretty *enough* . . ." His grandfather paused. "For a déchet."

"Stop!" Fury exploded through Marcellus, and before he could think about what he was doing, he lunged at his grandfather. *"Arrête!"*

But the general was too quick, too strong. He caught Marcellus's fist in his own.

"Dear boy," he said, gripping Marcellus's hand and squeezing it. Hard. "You are so weak. Just like your father." His mouth twisted into a sneer. "Your good-for-nothing, traitor father."

Marcellus tried to yank his hand away, but the general's grasp was too tight. "I am *not* my father!" he bellowed, hot and fierce, into his grandfather's face.

He yanked his hand again, but this time the general released it, causing Marcellus to stumble backward.

"I am not my father," Marcellus said again as he attempted to right himself.

"No?" the general asked, cocking his head. "It seems like you're very much like him. Weak and pathetic and fraternizing beneath your estate."

Marcellus reared up again. "If my father was weak, if he was a traitor and a coward, then whose fault was that? *Whose?*" Never in all his life had he ever spoken like this to his grandfather. It was terrifying and invigorating at the same time. And now that he'd started, he couldn't be stopped. "It was your fault, wasn't it? You were his father. You raised him. You failed, General Bonnefaçon. You're the failure. You're the weak one. You couldn't even stand up to the Patriarche when he sent Commandeur Vernay to Albion. And now she's dead. Because of *you.*"

And then it came.

Sudden, like a crack of lightning to his stomach.

His grandfather punched him, and Marcellus went down. Straight to the floor.

"You are a stupide boy!" He kicked Marcellus hard in the stomach. Again and again.

"See!" the general roared. "Look at you! You are pathetic. You can't even fight back. You never can!"

The pain was searing. The blows kept coming. Worse than ever. His grandfather had never beaten him like *this* before. Marcellus couldn't breathe. He couldn't think. All he could do was bury his head into his hands and curl up his legs to try to protect his stomach.

"Come on!" his grandfather yelled again. "For once in your life, show me, Marcellus. Show me you're not weak. Show me you're not just like your father!"

But Marcellus couldn't. He couldn't fight this man. He never could. The general was too strong, and Marcellus was too fearful. He wasn't a fighter. He would never be a fighter. He would never be the officer his grandfather wanted him to be.

Hot tears pooled in his eyes.

His grandfather was right.

He was weak.

He was a fool.

He was nothing.

It was almost a relief when the kick came to the back of his head and everything went black.

CHAPTER 63

CHATINE

FRIC! CHATINE PACED THE LENGTH OF THE MECHAN-
ical room in Fret 7, cursing everything and everyone on this
Sol-forsaken planet.

Why hadn't she contacted Limier the moment she saw Jean
LeGrand disappear under that floor grate yesterday?

Because she was stupide, that's why.

Because she'd foolishly decided to go to the Precinct first. And
now her parents had Jean LeGrand, and they were going to claim the
entire reward for themselves. Twenty thousand largs!

Chatine racked her brain, trying to figure out where they had
taken him. Where was Limier heading when she'd contacted him?
From the view of the rushing scenery through the window, it didn't
appear to be inside Vallonay city limits.

Which made sense. Her parents would never have led Inspecteur
Limier to the old Grotte at the docklands. That was sacred Délabré
ground. Plus, she wouldn't be surprised if they were doing this all
on their own. If her father had chosen to not even involve Claque or

Hercule, or any of his other despicable friends. That was the first rule in being a Délabré: Never trust a Délabré.

Fric! Fric! Fric! Chatine continued to pace.

Her father must have seen the white-haired man in the Marsh yesterday. He must have recognized him as Jean LeGrand and undoubtedly remembered the reward that had been offered. How could he not?

It was just as Inspecteur Limier had said. The Renards were all the same.

Well, *now* they were.

Chatine stopped pacing, as the crushing ache was suddenly back in her chest, threatening to squeeze her to death. Azelle had been the only honest one among them. She had been the only one who *wouldn't* have called in for that reward. Because she would have been too busy dutifully assembling new Skins. She probably wouldn't have even recognized the white-haired man who'd come to take Madeline away.

But Chatine would never forget him.

Just like she would never forget *her.*

That worthless, wide-eyed clochard who had killed Chatine's brother. Who had captured Marcellus's heart. Who was probably with him right this very second, comforting him, stroking his hair, telling him to forget Chatine and her lies and the feel of her lips against his.

The girl who was beautiful and clean and . . .

Emerging from the gap in the floor right this second!

The grate scraped against the metal floor as the girl climbed through the narrow opening. Chatine dodged behind a rusty old contraption, concealing herself from view.

Madeline—or Alouette or whatever the fric her name was— carefully replaced the metal grate, stood up, and set off toward the hallway. As Chatine watched her go, she marveled at how different the girl looked. And it wasn't just the new gray coat with its double buttons, enviably thick fabric, and upright collar. Nor was it the knee-high boots, which had replaced those ridiculous slippers she was always running around in. No, there was something in the girl's gait. In the way she marched out of the room.

This girl was confident. She was focused. She was determined.

It instantly made Chatine suspicious.

She peered around the corner of the mechanical room doorway and watched as the girl strode purposefully in the direction of the Fret exit.

Chatine chewed on her lower lip. She had no idea where her parents were hiding LeGrand.

But this girl clearly had a destination in mind.

Chatine slipped out of the mechanical room and back into the shadows of the Frets. Right back where she belonged.

As she weaved alongside Frets 6 and 5, it soon became obvious where the girl was heading. And Chatine really didn't want to go back in there.

Chatine hung back, unseen, as Alouette approached the giant and ominous black cube of the Vallonay Policier Precinct. Alouette slowed to a halt in front of the moto-docking station and stared up at the looming structure, as though trying to decide whether or not to go inside.

This is where she's going? To the Policier?

Then Chatine noticed the girl pull something out of one of the pockets on her coat. It was yellowish-white, the color of an old eggshell. Alouette unfolded it the way you would a TéléCom, but it was certainly not a TéléCom. It almost looked like *paper.*

Chatine slithered out of the shadows but stayed close to the wall as she took a few steps toward Alouette. She squinted to try to make out what was on the page. It didn't appear to be the Forgotten Word. Instead, there was some sort of picture. It was crude, as if it was hand-drawn. She could see something sleek and long with a gently curved underside.

Wait, Chatine thought. *Is that a . . . ?*

Chatine received the answer to her barely formed question a moment later when Alouette walked straight up to one of the hovering motos charging at the docking station, opened her coat, and pulled a strange-looking tool from an even stranger-looking belt that was cinched around her waist.

Chatine watched in disbelief as the girl inserted the tool into a gap between the moto's engine and its display console. Then, with a swift flick of her wrist, she popped the shiny silver cover right off.

What on Laterre does she think she's doing?

Alouette pulled a small flashlight off her belt and held it between her teeth, aiming the beam at the bike's interior. After consulting her paper again, she reached inside and pulled free two wires. Next, her hand went to a pouch on the other side of her belt. She pulled out a pair of clippers, which she used to trim the ends of the wires. Replacing the tool, she then removed something thin and metallic from the same pouch. Chatine thought it resembled the strips of circuitry implanted in Limier's face. She watched as Alouette threaded the wires through the wafer-thin filament.

Suddenly there was a hiss and a small shower of sparks.

Chatine stifled a gasp.

But Alouette looked completely unfazed.

She simply slipped the wires back into the body of the moto, popped the cover back on, consulted her paper one more time, and then hit a small switch near the handle. The narrow strip of lights lining the bottom of the moto blinked to life, and suddenly the vehicle was airborne, lifting farther off the ground as the engine idled quietly.

Chatine couldn't believe what she'd just witnessed.

That girl had hacked a Ministère moto!

Chatine had never seen anything like that in her life. She didn't even know that was possible. And she thought she knew *every* possible con, cheat, swindle, and hack there was.

Despite the fact that Chatine hated this girl with every bone in her body, she couldn't help but feel impressed. Seriously impressed.

Alouette returned her tools to the belt and her paper to her pocket, straddled the bike, and engaged the throttle. The vehicle responded instantly to her touch, juddering as though eager to get going.

Alouette glanced over both of her shoulders into the darkness, and then, with a twist of her wrist and a kick of her foot, she was off, rushing past Chatine in a blur of lights and wind.

Chatine stared blankly at the girl's vanishing form, still trying to make sense of everything that had just happened. Then, five seconds later, she realized her only lead on the reward had just whooshed past her, and she was still standing there like an idiot.

She leapt into action and ran toward the last remaining moto hovering at the docking station. She tried to remember everything the girl had done, but with no tools and absolutely no knowledge of the inner workings of a moto, she was helpless.

Chatine had no other choice. She had to do it her way.

She rolled up the sleeve of her coat and tapped at her Skin. When the screen prompted her to speak, she pulled her face into a grimace and recited her message, alerting the sergent on duty that someone had just stolen a Ministère moto and taken off, out of the Frets.

Then she slipped underneath the hovering moto and waited.

Less than a minute later, Chatine heard the front doors of the Precinct whoosh open and the sound of footsteps approaching.

It had to be silent.

It had to be fast.

It had to be debilitating.

She readied herself, steadying her breathing and coiling her muscles. The footsteps grew louder, and then the two giant black boots appeared on either side of the moto. The vehicle sank a millimètre as Sergent Chacal settled into its seat.

Do it now!

She snaked her arm up from under the idling moto and took hold of the metal baton that was fastened to the sergent's belt. With the grace of a cat, she gently slid the baton from the holster.

Almost there, she told herself. *Just a few more centimètres.*

The weapon eased out little by little but then snagged on something. Chatine felt her arm halt.

A blast of warm air rushed across Chatine's face as the sergent started the engine, adjusting the throttle. Chatine gritted her teeth and gave the baton a strong tug. It lurched free from the holster, but the force of her pull knocked it out of her hand, and it fell to the ground with a *clank* that seemed to ring out across the entire planet.

"What on Laterre?" Chacal said, leaning over the left side of the bike.

Chatine snatched the baton and rolled right, vanishing under the shadow of the moto.

But Chacal must have seen something, because suddenly he was off the seat. He was bending down. He was crouching to peer under the vehicle.

He was in the perfect position.

Chatine stood up. "Good evening, Sergent," she said pleasantly.

Chacal's head whipped up but Chatine had the baton ready. As it made contact with his face, Chatine heard a satisfying *crunch*. She wasn't sure if it was the sergent's nose, cheek, chin, or all of the above, but it didn't much matter. Blood splattered Chatine's face and hair, and Chacal went down hard, letting out a very unmanly, high-pitched yelp as he hit the ground.

"That's for Roche," she said, dropping the baton next to his head.

Then she straddled the bike, revved the engine, and sped off after Alouette.

- CHAPTER 64 -
MARCELLUS

MARCELLUS FELT NOTHING AT FIRST, EXCEPT THE cold floor beneath him.

"Look at you! You are pathetic. You can't even fight back."

Marcellus's eyes fluttered open. He stared at the burnished, decorative ceiling of his grandfather's office for a few moments before his gaze slipped over to the nearby windows. From where he lay, Marcellus could see the TéléSky that hung over the Palais gardens. It was inky and deep blue, a suggestion of the night to come. Sols 1 and 2 had already set, but Sol 3 was still dangling low on the horizon.

"Show me, Marcellus. Show me you're not weak. Show me you're not just like your father!"

Marcellus winced, his head pounding and his ribs aching. He wondered if he'd ever be able to get up from this cold, hard floor.

He wondered if there was any point.

Nobody would care if he did or didn't, would they? No one would care if he never got up again. There was no one left to care. His grandfather had beaten him senseless and no doubt left for more important Ministère matters. Chatine was a backstabber and a spy.

And Alouette? The kind girl who'd tended to his bleeding head? The intriguing girl he'd opened up to? The girl with those huge dark eyes that made him believe he could trust her? *She* was a member of the Vangarde, a rebel, and a terrorist. Like Mabelle. Like his father.

His cold, dead terrorist father.

As he watched the last Sol finally slip away and the TéléSky glow deep indigo in its wake, Marcellus thought of his father stretched out on that table in the morgue. He remembered how weathered and trampled and beaten his father's body had been from all those years on Bastille. Then he wondered how long he himself would have lasted there, if he'd ever been in his father's place.

"I am not *my father!"*

Marcellus's own words came back to him now, and he suddenly realized just how true they were. Marcellus *wasn't* like his father, because there was no way he would have survived on that cold and icy moon for all those years.

"No," he murmured, his voice soft and raspy.

Julien Bonnefaçon had been no coward. He hadn't been weak. He'd been strong. So much stronger than Marcellus could ever be.

Probably stronger than even the general himself.

Marcellus almost smiled at the thought.

The pale-blue glow of Sol 3 had dimmed, and now stars were emerging in the TéléSky. One after the other, they popped out of the darkness, appearing exactly where they would be in the real sky, if the clouds on Laterre would ever part long enough for them to be seen. Soon there would be thousands of them.

Like lights alive in the dark night sky.

Suddenly, as Marcellus gazed through the window, he found himself humming.

Just like the stars, the song seemed to come from nowhere—popping out of the dark corners of his mind. Yet the tune felt deeply familiar. The notes, the pace of the melody felt so old and so new at the same time.

As he hummed, the rhythm and notes grew stronger, more fully formed in his brain. And then the words came.

"*Bright stars . . . ,*" he sang between hums. *"Always shining."*

The words were coming to him in fragments. Disjointed lyrics that, like the tune, were so familiar to him, it was as though he were finding an old friend. Finding something he'd lost but had never in his heart truly forgotten.

The song seemed to give him new strength, and he was able to sit up. His head still ached, but his body somehow felt less fragile. Less brittle and sore.

"Lights alive in the dark night sky."

Outside, the stars in the TéléSky multiplied, each of them shining and twinkling so brightly. Maybe the kick in the head had done something to his brain, but it seemed like the stars were responding to him. Hearing his melody. And singing back.

Soon the entire song had pieced itself together inside him.

> *"Bright stars most high.*
> *Lights alive in the dark night sky.*
> *Always shining,*
> *Forever shining,*
> *Living truth in twinkling eyes."*

Marcellus sang the tune over and over. Each time his voice was stronger. Each time its familiarity grew and bloomed in his chest.

Until finally, he knew it. Like he'd never *not* known it.

He knew exactly where he'd learned it.

And, more important, the last place he'd heard it.

Then he was on his feet. He was moving. Running. It was as though every ache and pain, every bruised rib and tender patch of skin, had suddenly healed itself. He swept out of his grandfather's office, down the hallway, and through their private salon and dining rooms. He took the stairs down two at a time, then three at a time. He was almost flying.

He kept running. Soon he was leaving the opulent corridors of the First Estate wings and entering the dingy hallways of the servants' quarters. He threaded between waitstaff and gossiping serving maids.

He didn't stop until he reached the room.

Her room.

The door was open. The orange security lasers were gone, but other than that, the room was just as it had been the last time Marcellus was here a few days ago. The empty drawers, the stripped bed, the bare floor with the ripped-up carpet still rolled to one side. The paintings were still there too, just as he'd hoped, leaning on the floor, stacked against a bare wall.

He rushed into the room and started flicking his way through the heavy frames.

"No . . . no . . . no . . . ," he murmured as he pushed a few of the pictures aside.

Then he found it.

The one he'd come for.

He pulled it out from the stack and propped it up against the empty bed. He knelt down before it and gazed into the canvas. It was just as he remembered from when he was little. The rich blue of the sky. The earthy green of the trees and hills. The paint so thick it was like frosting on a gâteau. And of course, the swirling yellows of the stars, dotted and burning in the sky.

Mabelle used to sing the song to him, close to his ear, as they both stared at this painting. He would always come to her room when he couldn't sleep. Or when his grandfather had yelled at him. Or worse. Mabelle would snap on the little light by her narrow bed and he would climb in beside her. She would wrap his little body in her arms, she'd press her lips to his wrist, which was usually still tender from the general's rough grip, and they'd both gaze up at the painting. She would sing, and he would hum.

He could still hear her voice now. The way it would rise in the middle and then drop to a soft, mournful low note on the last line.

"Living truth in twinkling eyes."

It was this song that Mabelle had hummed to him back in the boglands of Montfer. He was certain of it. He just wasn't sure *why*.

Marcellus reached out and touched the canvas. The paint felt rough and surprisingly hard under his fingers. He traced the green hills and then the gangly trees, pointing up like arrows into the sky. Then his forefinger moved across each star, until it landed on the biggest and fieriest one of all.

The paint was thickest here, on this glowing star. But, as he looked closer, Marcellus noticed it was chipped.

Like it had once been disturbed.

"I have proof that your father is innocent. I hid it for you in my room at the Palais before I was arrested. It's been waiting until you were ready to find it."

Marcellus paused and glanced back toward the door. The hallway outside the room was empty. He looked back at the painting, sucked in a breath, and finally scratched at the glowing yellow star with his nail.

The paint cracked and crumbled off easily.

Buried in the chalky, yellow dust was a shiny object. Marcellus flicked at it with his finger, and a tiny, metallic microcam fell into his palm.

CHAPTER 65

ALOUETTE

SOMEONE WAS FOLLOWING HER.

Alouette was sure of it.

She had never been more terrified in her life. It was getting darker by the second, and the trees of the Forest Verdure whipped by so fast, they were like a continuous green blur in the moto's high-intensity headlight. Her knuckles had cramped from gripping the handles, and her face was constantly being scraped by small branches and snapping leaves.

And now there was someone behind her.

She could see a headlight flickering in the fog in the corner of her vision. Another moto, to be sure. Whoever it was seemed to be keeping perfect pace with Alouette. Every time she'd tried to lose them, by banking to the left or cutting through a narrow gap between the trees, they were right there. Right behind her. Turning the same turns, cutting through the same trees.

Relentless and persistent.

Someone must have seen Alouette take the moto from the Precinct and given chase. A sergent? An inspecteur, perhaps? A droid?

Could droids even ride motos? She had no idea. Whoever it was—
whatever it was—she couldn't shake them.

"Lean into the curves," Alouette murmured to herself through
gritted teeth. Another tree loomed large in the mist in front of her,
and she unsteadily steered the moto around it. "Trust the vehicle."

In the pages she'd copied quickly from the Chronicles earlier,
she'd found blueprints of the moto's mechanics and circuitry. As well
as notes on how to drive one. But reading about riding a moto was
a lot different from actually riding a moto. Alouette had discovered
that very quickly. As she'd wobbled away from the Policier Precinct
and careened toward the forest, she had honestly feared for her life.

Marcellus had made it look so easy yesterday, when he'd dipped
and weaved through the trees. But it wasn't easy. Not at all. Driv-
ing this moto was like trying to drive a hovering, untamed beast. A
hundred-kilogramme beast that could buck and flail at any moment.

And being chased by the Policier on top of that definitely didn't
help.

"Papa," she whispered into the cool night air.

She had to think of him. He was the only thing keeping her going.

Alouette had to find him.

She'd managed to locate the lake just outside the Forest Verdure,
and now she was following the winding stream that led to the abandoned camp where Marcellus had taken her and where she swore her
father must have buried something valuable.

Please, Sols, she silently begged. *Please let him still be there.*

The headlight of the other moto flashed in her vision again, as
though reminding Alouette that it was still there. Still following.

And then Alouette was struck with a horrifying realization.

If her father *was* still at the camp, then she was leading whoever
was behind her straight to him. She was leading the Policier directly
to an escaped convict.

Alouette instinctively twisted the throttle as far as it would go.

She had to drive faster. She had to shake whoever was following her. The moto bucked upward and launched to its new speed. Her body jolted back.

"Lean in." She recited the words from the Chronicles aloud, bending forward until her chest was almost touching the handlebars.

After she'd finally regained her balance, Alouette braved a glance over her shoulder.

"No!" she shouted.

The light was still there. Except now it seemed even closer, beaming even brighter through the trees and fog.

Alouette could see she was getting close to the camp. She had to think of another plan.

Suddenly, Sister Jacqui's voice echoed in her mind.

"Be present and awake to your world, Little Lark."

The words caused her to blink and take in her surroundings with new eyes. As though the words were actually waking her from a deep sleep. As though she were seeing the trees, the blanket of fog, and the beam of her own headlight in front of her for the very first time.

"Be present and awake to your world."

And then the idea came.

Alouette jammed on the brakes and leaned hard to the right to yank the moto into a deep, fast swerve. The vehicle drifted and spun under her before finally coming to a stop. She was now facing the opposite direction.

Facing her pursuer.

She snapped off her headlight and waited in the darkness, listening to the sounds of the forest, listening to the sounds of this world. The fog was thick all around her. She was encapsulated in it.

But more important, she was hidden by it.

Then she heard the sound she'd been waiting for. The low purr of the other moto's engine and the swift snapping of branches and leaves as it blazed through the trees, speeding toward her.

Not yet, she told herself. *Just a few seconds more.*

The sound of the engine grew louder, and Alouette poised her finger on the dashboard.

Wait for it. . . .

The other moto crashed through the mist.

Now!

Alouette flicked on her headlight, illuminating the wall of fog around her in a dazzling, blinding glow. A haze of scattered light.

The rider tried to regain control, but they were momentarily blinded by the glowing fog. The moto careened straight into a tree, sending them flying off the bike and tumbling to the ground. They rolled three times before finally coming to a halt, facedown in the undergrowth.

Alouette jumped off her moto and slowly approached the wreckage. The other vehicle lay twisted and hissing at the base of the tree, completely destroyed. She sucked in a breath. She'd only wanted to momentarily blind the person following her. Slow them down so she could throw them off her trail. She hadn't meant to *hurt* them.

"Oh Sols," she whispered. "Please don't be dead."

Her heart thudded behind her ribs as she took a hesitant step toward the unmoving body. It was small. Too small for a Policier sergent or inspecteur. And she could now see that the rider was not wearing a white uniform, but rather was dressed all in black.

Had she killed a *child*?

With shaky hands, Alouette reached toward the rider's shoulder. She wanted to flip them over so she could see their face, assess their injuries. If they were still alive, perhaps she could . . .

The body let out a low groan and Alouette leapt back.

She watched in relief as the stranger slowly, painstakingly pushed themselves to their knees and stood up. When they finally turned around, Alouette's eyes widened. It was the boy from the Marsh. The one she'd lost in the crowd.

Why was *he* following her?

The boy still looked dazed from the fall. He stood with his hands resting on his knees as though fighting to stay conscious. There was something different about him. His hood wasn't covering his head. And Alouette could just make out a tangled knot of ash-brown hair at the base of his neck.

Alouette could hear his labored breathing, and her surprise morphed back into guilt. She opened her mouth to apologize, but suddenly the boy stood up and locked eyes on Alouette. There was something so fierce, so venomous, in his stare, Alouette was stunned into silence.

No one had ever looked at Alouette like that before.

So much animosity radiated off the boy, Alouette felt like she was being punched in the stomach. But she couldn't look away. The darkness in the boy's gaze seemed to hold her captive.

And yet, the longer she stared back at him, the more familiar he became. It was that same sensation she'd had in the Marsh. The sensation that she knew him. That they'd met before.

The boy swallowed, looking like he was about to say something—*trying* to say something—but nothing came out. It didn't matter, though. His stare spoke louder and with more hatred than any words could have.

Suddenly, out of nowhere, a name whispered through Alouette's mind. Like a rustle of wind through the trees. It was a strange name. A vaguely familiar name.

Chatine.

Then she heard something else.

The sound of footsteps. The crackle of twigs. Someone else was nearby.

She finally tore her gaze from the boy and looked in the direction of the noise. Through the swirl of mist and trees, Alouette spotted a faint glow of light in the distance.

Her father's light?

It had to be. She must be closer to the clearing than she'd thought. Which meant she wasn't too late. He was still there!

She glanced back one last time at the boy before darting into the trees. She moved through the darkness, toward the glow. Branches snagged at her coat and vines twisted up from the ground to trip her, but she didn't stop. As she got closer to the source of light, she could hear more noises. The sounds of scuffling, scraping, and thudding.

"Papa!" she called out, finally stumbling into the clearing.

But the sight in front of her wasn't at all what she expected. Hugo Taureau was sitting on the ground, slumped against the base of a tree, his hands bound behind his back, a filthy cloth stuffed into his mouth.

"Papa!" Alouette shouted again as she ran toward him. But she managed only a few paces, because suddenly, out of the corner of her eye, she saw a strange ripple in the damp air, like the invisible molecules around her were quivering. Then something harsh and fiery and hot exploded in Alouette's left leg.

She let out a scream before crumpling to the ground.

CHAPTER 66

MARCELLUS

"ONE NEARBY DEVICE FOUND," THE TÉLÉCOM informed Marcellus. "Microcam. Unknown model. Unknown origin. Attempting to connect. Please wait."

Marcellus shuddered out a breath and began pacing. He was back in his bedroom in the south wing, his door bolted shut, the drapes drawn. The entire walk back from the servants' quarters, Marcellus had felt as though the microcam in his pocket were as heavy as a stone. This had been way worse than walking around the Palais with his father's prison shirt tucked into his uniform. With every butler, maid, and advisor that he passed, he became increasingly certain that they would take one look at him and just *know*.

Know that he was smuggling Vangarde property. Know that he was betraying his grandfather and his Regime with every step that he took. With every second that he didn't smash the device under the heel of his shoe.

He *had* considered throwing it away. For a flicker of a moment, he'd entertained the idea. But then he'd touched his bruised cheek

and ribs and stomach, and he'd once again felt the sting of his grandfather's words.

"You are so weak. Just like your father."

And the moment had passed very quickly.

Marcellus stopped pacing and peeked tentatively over at the
microcam sitting on his bed, next to the TéléCom. He felt like a
child peering out from behind a chaise during a game of hide-and-
seek, waiting to see if his seeker had found him.

Except in this scenario, if he was found, he'd be incarcerated.

He'd be banished.

He'd be disowned.

Just like his father.

His heart banged violently in his chest.

"Attempting to connect," the TéléCom repeated. "Please wait."

Marcellus wondered if the TéléCom would even be able to connect
to this strange device. He'd instantly recognized it as a surveillance
microcam, but it was definitely not a Ministère-issued unit. This one
was crudely made, as though it had been crafted in a small, outdated
workshop, cut off from the state-of-the-art, cyborg-run tech labs that
lined the third floor of the Ministère headquarters.

Marcellus wrung his hands together. What if the TéléCom
couldn't connect?

Or even more terrifying, what if it *could*?

Marcellus honestly couldn't decide which outcome he would prefer.
If the TéléCom failed to connect, then he would never have to watch
whatever was on this microcam. He could just go on living his life
like the past week had never even happened. Like he'd never removed
the shirt from his father's back. Never ventured out to Montfer. Never
seen his old governess again. Never befriended a traitorous Third
Estate Fret-rat girl posing as a boy. Never looked into the endless dark
brown eyes of a Vangarde operative posing as a Défecteur.

But Marcellus knew, even before the TéléCom displayed its final verdict, that he didn't want that. Despite how harrowing and heart-breaking and painful this last week had been, he didn't want to pretend that none of it had happened.

He didn't want to go back to being that cowardly, ignorant, spoiled Second Estate *pomp* he'd once been.

He'd seen too much now. He'd come too far.

The TéléCom beeped.

"Connection successful."

Marcellus sucked in a breath and tentatively walked back to his bed. He scooped up the device and stared at the screen. The TéléCom was now displaying the microcam's contents.

There was only one item.

A lump immediately formed in Marcellus's throat as he recognized the date attached to the footage. It was two days before an explosif went off deep inside the copper exploit, killing six hundred workers.

Four days before his father was sent to Bastille.

Two weeks before the people stopped fighting, Citizen Rousseau was arrested, and the Rebellion of 488 finally came to an end.

This was it. Marcellus could feel it in his bones.

This was the "proof" Mabelle had been talking about.

With shaking hands and a pounding heart, he hovered his fingertip a millimètre above the screen, took a breath, and clicked play.

A moment later, his grandfather's face filled the entire screen, as though he were looking directly *into* the microcam. Looking straight at Marcellus.

"Sols!" Marcellus shrieked, and dropped the TéléCom onto the bed.

What on Laterre . . .

Marcellus blinked down at the device. His grandfather's face still peered up at him from the screen.

"AirLink request pending from General Bonnefaçon," the TéléCom announced.

Marcellus breathed out a sigh of relief. His grandfather had sent him an AirLink request right as Marcellus had pushed play on the footage.

Feeling stupide for reacting like a child afraid of his own shadow, Marcellus picked up the TéléCom and poised his finger to accept the request. It was an instinctual movement. A reflex.

When the general requests an AirLink, you accept.

That's it.

There's no other way to be.

For Marcellus, there *had* been no other way to be for as long as he could remember.

But now, curiously, he hesitated.

"AirLink request pending from General Bonnefaçon," the TéléCom repeated.

But all Marcellus could hear in his mind was his grandfather bellowing, *Connect, you worthless coward! Connect!*

Marcellus glanced up and caught sight of his own reflection in his titan-framed mirror. His hair was wild and unruly, and he could already see the bruise starting to form on the side of his neck, beneath the edge of his collar. Always in a place that could be hidden. Never anywhere visible. Otherwise all of Laterre would know General Bonnefaçon's dirty little secret.

Marcellus felt the familiar urge to fix his hair, adjust his clothing. To make himself more presentable. Like a Ministère officer should be.

But instead, he simply reached out and hastily tapped the screen.

"Request declined," the TéléCom announced, reminding Marcellus of what he had just done.

Marcellus winced, waiting for the guilt.

Yet, all he felt was relief.

Like he'd stripped off a layer of heavy, sopping-wet clothes.

In fact, he was so shocked by the unexpected sensation, he didn't even notice that the footage from Mabelle's microcam had started to play until he saw his grandfather's face again. This time it wasn't close up on the screen, but far away and obscured by shadows. He was sitting at his desk in his study. The one right down the hall from Marcellus's rooms.

How had Mabelle managed to hide a microcam inside General Bonnefaçon's office without him noticing?

"My apologies," the general was saying, "but this feels rash and impulsive. I'm certain we can come up with another solution if we—"

"This is the only solution," another voice replied. It was stern and unyielding.

Marcellus couldn't see who else was in the room. The person speaking must have been out of the microcam's range.

"You've let this rebellion get *way* out of control," the voice continued. "That Citizen Rousseau woman is ruining everything my ancestors worked so hard to achieve. It's time to end this."

"Monsieur Patriarche," his grandfather said in a placating tone. "I strongly advise against this approach."

Monsieur Patriarche?

This must be the former Patriarche—Claude. He died two years ago, in 503, fifteen years after this footage was captured. Marcellus remembered attending the funeral when he was sixteen. That's when Lyon—the current Patriarche—inherited the Regime.

"I thank you for your counsel, as always," Claude replied. "But my mind is made up. I don't have time for this anarchy. I have enough on my plate right now dealing with that incompetent son of mine. The whole business with that Villette girl is a disaster."

Marcellus snorted. Even Lyon's own father knew he was a joke.

"I told you I would handle that," the general said, and Marcellus could hear his grandfather's composure starting to slip.

"It doesn't seem like you have been handling *anything* lately, General. Which is why I'm taking control of the situation."

The general paused, clearly collecting his thoughts. When he spoke again, his voice was hushed, almost pained. "Have you considered the number of casualties this tactic will incur? Six hundred workers are scheduled to be in the copper exploit at any given time."

"Good," the Patriarche replied coldly. "That should be enough for the rest of them to see what kind of monsters these people are. I want rescue teams on call, ready to try to get people out. The Vangarde will look like terrorists and we'll look like the heroes. Citizen Rousseau won't stand a chance after this."

Marcellus grabbed hold of his bed to keep the room from spinning.

"Yes, Monsieur Patriarche," the general replied, but he sounded far from convinced. "Although we must be extremely careful. This can never be traced back to the Ministère or the whole plan will backfire."

"You're absolutely right," Patriarche Claude replied. Marcellus heard a shuffling of something, and then a moment later, the man was on the screen. His back was to the microcam, but Marcellus recognized his short, stocky frame. "We will need to pin this on someone. A suspect who can't be doubted."

When the general spoke next, his voice sounded haunted and hollow. "You already have someone in mind."

"I do," the Patriarche said firmly, and for a long time, the two men just stared at each other, exchanging silent words and accusations. The general rested his elbows on his desk and leaned forward, his face falling into a shaft of light, so that Marcellus could now see his features. Even though he was seventeen years younger, he looked exactly the same. Stoned-faced and hardened. Yet, in that instant, Marcellus saw something else in his grandfather's eyes. Something very, very foreign.

Fear.

The Patriarche was the first to break the silence. "Ever since your son betrayed his planet to join the Vangarde, your own loyalty to the

Regime has been called under question. I hear whispers about it all over Ledôme. I can't have a general whose loyalty is doubted."

"Monsieur Patriarche," the general replied, sounding appalled, "surely, there's someone else who—"

"There is no one else. Julien must take the fall so that your reputation remains untarnished and the Regime remains steadfast."

The general swallowed visibly, and Marcellus could almost read the defeat in his eyes. "Yes, Monsieur Patriarche. I will take care of it."

Marcellus jammed his finger at the TéléCom, ending the playback. His breath was coming out in ragged gasps. His knees were buckling. It felt like the floor beneath his feet was cracking wide open, and any minute he would fall straight through to the fiery core of Laterre.

His father had gone to prison for that bombing.

He'd lived seventeen years on a cold, dark moon for that bombing.

He'd literally frozen to *death* for that bombing.

And it was a lie. It had all been a lie.

The Patriarche was the one who'd ordered the bombing.

His father had joined the Vangarde, but the Vangarde had never been behind that senseless act of murder. They were never the violent, lowlife terrorists Marcellus had been taught to believe.

The Ministère was. The Patriarche was. The Regime was.

His grandfather had sacrificed his own son to save his reputation. To save face with the Patriarche. He was the true terrorist. The true murderer. The true coward.

And Marcellus had been blindly following in his footsteps the whole time.

CHAPTER 67

ALOUETTE

ALOUETTE COULD SEE HER LEG STRETCHED OUT IN front of her. Yet there was nothing. No feeling. No sensation. It was as if it weren't even a part of her body anymore. It was someone else's leg lying on the wet forest floor.

She could feel her heart, though. It was pounding inside her chest. She fought against the metal wound around her wrists, binding her to the base of the tree. But the wire was tied too tight, and all she managed to do was dig the cable deeper into her skin. She glanced over at her father, bound to the same tree beside her, with the dirty cloth still stuffed into his mouth. Alouette couldn't understand how he hadn't managed to break free. He appeared to be tied up with the same type of wire. Clearly he was stronger than a thin piece of metal?

A single lamp stood in the tall grass in the middle of the clearing, illuminating a few of the strange gravestones. An open sac lay next to it, the contents spilled out. Alouette could see her father's clothes strewn in a haphazard pile and his titan candlestick lying on the ground.

"Would you look at that," a voice said, and Alouette glanced up into the eyes of a woman clutching a rayonette in her hands. "We asked the Sols for one fugitive, we got two!"

She was standing next to the man who had tied Alouette to the tree. He was small—a third the size of her own father—but there was something quick and menacing in the way he moved.

"Yes, ma chérie," the man replied with a wolfish grin. "The Sols are shining on us after all."

Where the man was all narrowness and angles, the woman beside him was all girth and gigantic curves. And every time Alouette looked at them, something strange and unsettling stirred deep inside her.

An ache.

A fear.

A familiar terror.

As if her father could hear her worried thoughts, Alouette felt his hand brush against her own, reassuring her. Telling her, in his silent, subtle way, that all would be fine.

But there was something about this couple. There was a wickedness in their eyes that made it impossible for Alouette to feel reassured.

"We lost our dear Azelle today, our precious daughter," the man said, pulling his lips into what Alouette assumed was supposed to look like a frown. "She was such a hard little worker, that one. A true asset to the family. Kept up a nice stream of largs coming in when times got tough." His menacing grin returned as his greedy eyes settled on Alouette. "But then, ta-da, just like that, our luck changes. And now, we're going to be rich!"

Rich?

Was that what this was about? Did these people know what her father had buried here?

"Oh my, how you've grown," the woman was saying. It took a moment for Alouette to realize she was speaking to her. She waddled up to Alouette and hooked a finger under Alouette's chin. "Our little Madeline. It's so lovely to see you again."

At this, Hugo immediately shouted something angry and incomprehensible into his gag. But Alouette couldn't understand why her father was so upset when the woman had clearly mistaken Alouette for someone else.

"You don't remember me, do you?" the woman asked, withdrawing her hand so quickly, her fingernail scraped against Alouette's skin.

When Alouette didn't respond, the woman kicked her dead leg. *"Do you?"*

Hugo's face twisted and pulled, as though he were trying to fight against his restraints but couldn't. Instead, he shouted again into the dirty cloth.

"Calm down, old man"—the woman waved the rayonette—"or I'll give you another blast in the neck. That'll settle you back down."

Alouette struggled to hold in the gasp that rose to her lips. The woman had shot her father in the neck? No wonder he'd been unable to get away. Nearly his whole body must be paralyzed right now.

"Besides, she can't feel a thing," the woman went on, turning back to Alouette. "Can you, *Madeline*?"

Alouette stared up at the woman, completely dazed.

Why did she keep calling her Madeline?

Alouette could tell the woman was waiting for her to respond, but she had no idea what to say.

"I don't believe this!" the woman exploded, her eyes suddenly wild and full of rage. "You lived with us for nearly four years! I raised you from a squealing baby. You ate our food and slept under our roof. Then you just disappeared into thin air, without so much as a thank-you! And now you don't even remember us? The kind Renards who took you in when your mother couldn't even afford to buy you chou bread?"

"Well, what did you expect?" the man snapped. "She was always an ungrateful little clochard."

Alouette's mind was whirling. What was this woman talking about? She *had* to be mistaken. There was no way Alouette could have lived with these terrifying people. These *Renards*. Surely, she would have remembered them.

The woman snorted. "And stupide."

The man—Monsieur Renard—smirked at Alouette. "Stupide, to be sure. You never did do anything right. We used to send you out to the Tourbay to collect reeds for the wine. It would take you hours to come home."

Madame Renard cackled. "She probably forgot where she was supposed to go."

Alouette flinched. That strange fear inside of her throbbed. It was as though there was a memory there, trying to break free. Trying to take shape. She could feel her fingers curling into fists behind the tree.

Remembering the cold handle.

The blisters.

The weight of a pail filled with reeds covered in sticky, dark mud.

"And then this one," Monsieur Renard said, crashing through the tenuous threads of her memory. His beady gray eyes flitted from Alouette to her father. "He showed up, with his fancy clothes and snooty airs, and took our little mademoiselle away before we could train her to actually be of some use."

Monsieur Renard gave Alouette's father a nasty kick to his thigh.

"Don't!" Alouette cried out, speaking for the first time since she'd arrived in the clearing. "Please, don't."

"How sweet," Madame Renard cooed. "She really loves him, doesn't she?" She winked at Alouette. "Well, don't you worry, Madeline. We love old Jean LeGrand too. We love him a *lot*."

Alouette's head started to pound. Who was Jean LeGrand? Why were these people calling both of them by different names?

Everything was wrong here.

It had to be.

And yet, there was a part of her—that part that still ached deeply inside of her—that wondered if any of it could be true.

"That's right," Monsieur Renard said, puffing up his scrawny chest. "That hefty reward on his head is going to solve *all* of our problems."

"Reward?" Alouette blurted without thinking.

The woman snickered and nudged her husband with her elbow. "Did you hear that, chéri? She doesn't know about the reward." Then she glanced back at Alouette. "Still the little bimbo, aren't you? You don't know a thing."

The words hit Alouette like another paralyzing pulse from the rayonette. Because the woman was right. Alouette really didn't know anything, did she? She'd thought herself so clever these last few days, with all her snooping and creeping around and stealing of motos. When really, she was just as stupid and ignorant as always.

"Turns out our good friend LeGrand here is worth a pretty larg," Monsieur Renard said to Alouette. "Not long after he took you away, Inspecteur Limier came around asking for him, offering a big fat reward to anyone who could help find him. Lucky for us, the reward is still good and that fritzer flic is on his way here right now to pay us twenty thousand tokens for this rotten croc." The man tilted his head back and shouted into the sky, "We're going to be rich as Patriarches!"

He grabbed his wife's hands and started to dance with her. The two spun in a circle, cackling and singing at the top of their lungs, "Twenty thousand largs! Twenty thousand largs!"

After they'd danced themselves breathless and finally come to a halt, the woman's gaze landed back on Alouette and her face fell into a theatrical scowl. "I will say, though," she said with a forlorn sigh. "We could really have used that money back then. Those were hard times. No food. Too many debts. We lost our inn. We were so poor, we even had to sell one of our babies. My poor little Henri." She let out a long, dramatic sniff that was clearly supposed to be a sob. "My one and only son—"

A loud cracking noise suddenly reverberated from somewhere in the woods, interrupting Madame Renard. She clutched the rayonette with both hands and swung it toward the trees behind her. "What was that?"

Monsieur Renard laughed. "Now, now, love. Don't get your culottes in a bunch. It was just a falling branch."

But Alouette could no longer focus on anything that was going on around her. It all seemed to be happening in a fog. All she could think about was what Madame Renard had told her. That she had lived with them. That her father had a twenty-thousand-token reward on his head. That a Policier inspecteur was on his way here right now to take him back to Bastille.

It was all too much.

She turned to her father, her eyes begging for him to tell her that it was all a lie. That these wicked people were making it up. But her father wouldn't even look at her.

"Is it true, Papa?" she demanded. "Tell me! Is it true?"

"Hear that?" Monsieur Renard nudged his wife. "She calls him Papa. Like he was her real father." The man crouched down low in front of Alouette, staring deep into her eyes, until Alouette no longer felt the numbness only in her leg. She felt it everywhere.

"But you know it's not true, don't you, my pretty?" The man sneered. "He's as much your father as I am. I doubt you'll ever know who your real father is. Blood whores, like your maman, tend to get around. They'll do anything for an extra larg."

Hugo tried to fight against his restraints again, but the paralyzeur in his veins was still too strong. His neck muscles bulged from the effort and his face contorted. But apparently it was still enough to frighten Monsieur Renard, because he scuttled away from Hugo like a rat.

"That's not true!" Alouette shouted, even though she knew she had absolutely no authority in the matter.

Madame Renard threw her head back and guffawed. "Of course it's true! Why do you think she dumped you with us in the first place? Because there was no father to dump you with!" She flicked the rayonette toward Hugo. "This one bought you from us like a sac of potatoes at a market stall. He's definitely not your *Papa*."

Alouette turned back to Hugo. This time her voice was soft, tentative, pleading.

"Papa?" she whispered.

Hugo slowly lifted his gaze to meet hers. The gag was still in his mouth. But it didn't matter. He didn't need to speak. His eyes said everything.

It was all true.

- CHAPTER 68 -
CHATINE

CHATINE WAS NOT USED TO HIDING IN TREES. SHE was used to hiding in the skeletons of broken-down, mold-ridden former freightships. She much preferred the Frets, though. That maze of leaky pipes and exposed beams made sense to her. This tree on the edge of what could only be an abandoned Défecteur camp was jagged and scratchy and far too noisy.

Below her, her croc parents had Jean LeGrand and his daughter tied to the base of a tree and were now dancing like idiots, celebrating their incoming reward. Chatine knew she had to think and act fast, before Inspecteur Limier arrived. She guessed, from their Air-Link conversation earlier, that he was traveling by transporteur. Those hulking vehicles could never make it through these dense trees. Which meant he would be forced to traverse the Forest Verdure on foot.

She glanced around the clearing for something she could use as a weapon, cursing herself for not taking Sergent Chacal's baton with her after she'd smashed in his pomp face. Through the tall grass, Chatine spotted a peculiar collection of stones, arranged in some kind of pattern. They were big enough to knock someone out, but not big enough to do permanent damage. She could stash her parents' unconscious bodies in the woods and be ready to claim the reward when Limier arrived.

She shimmied toward the trunk of the tree and tested her weight on the next-lowest branch, gingerly pressing her foot down to make sure it would hold her.

"I will say, though," her mother was saying below her. "We could really have used that money back then. Those were hard times. No food. Too many debts. We lost our inn. We were so poor, we even had to sell one of our babies. My poor little Henri. My one and only son—"

The branch snapped. Chatine plummeted. She desperately reached out for something to grab on to. Her hands just barely caught the end of another branch, and she managed to haul herself onto it. The commotion had surely given her away, but Chatine could no longer bring herself to care. Her body, her mind, everything had gone numb. Like a droid had emptied an entire round of paralyzeurs straight into her veins.

The forest seemed to go dark. Empty. Silent. Until all she could feel, taste, hear, see, and smell were her mother's words.

"*. . . we even had to sell one of our babies. My poor little Henri.*"

No. That couldn't be true. Sell Henri? Her mother was lying. She was just playing one of her mind games, toying with Alouette and her father to try to evoke sympathy.

Henri is dead, Chatine affirmed silently in her mind. *His little body was sent to the morgue. My mother told me . . .*

But then her heart started to thunder as she remembered.

I never saw the body.

I went to the morgue. I searched the cavs, but it wasn't there. I always assumed they'd already disposed of it.

Her gaze shifted down to her Skin as she thought of the alert she'd received tonight about Azelle.

"Please accept our condolences . . . Her body is being transferred to the Vallonay Med Center . . . May she rest with the Sols."

Had Chatine ever seen an alert for Henri? On her own Skin or on her parents'?

The answer slowly turned the numbness in her veins into a red-hot rage.

It was true. Her mother had *sold* her little brother. Sold him like he was a sac of turnips or a jug of weed wine. Sold him like he was nothing. Like he wasn't Chatine's sky and stars. Like he wasn't the only good thing in her life.

She'd told Chatine the baby was dead.

She'd blamed Madeline!

She'd said the girl had dropped Henri on his head.

Chatine had lived with that horrible image in her mind for the past twelve years. It had haunted her in every waking moment and in every tormented dream.

And it had been a lie.

But even more incomprehensible was that Chatine had believed it. She should have known better than to believe anything her parents had to say. They were crocs, the very worst kind. They lied to everyone. Even to each other. *Especially* to each other.

But this lie was different. It had changed Chatine. Every single day it had turned her a little darker. A little angrier. For the past twelve years, it had slowly been forming her into the person she now was:

The girl in the black hood who hid in the ceilings of Frets. Who watched and listened to the world beneath her. Who dreamed impossible dreams of escape. Who was always, constantly, bitterly, eternally . . .

Alone.

And who was now watching her entire life vanish into the mist like it had never existed in the first place. Like it had been built upon nothing more than unstable air.

Chatine stared down at the girl who sat on the cold, wet ground, her hands bound behind her back, her face a canvas of fear and disbelief.

She hadn't killed Chatine's little brother.

She was innocent.

She was just as much a victim of the Renards as Chatine was. As little baby Henri was.

Then a thought struck Chatine so hard, she lost her balance and nearly fell out of the tree again.

Is he still alive?

Suddenly, a loud clanging alarm sounded through the forest, and Chatine was blinded by a beam of light so bright, it seemed to illuminate the entire wood. A few seconds later, five hulking, towering droids stomped out of the trees and into the clearing, their sirens whirling and the orange beams from their eyes sweeping the ground.

"Halt!" one of the droids bellowed. "By the order of the Patriarche, you are commanded to halt. Abandon any weapons you have in your possession. Anyone who makes any sudden movements will be immobilized."

Chatine froze. She wasn't yet sure whether she'd been detected, but if she hadn't, she wanted to keep it that way.

Far below, her parents froze too. Her mother dropped her rayonette. Her father shot his hands into the air. It was the first time she'd ever seen her father so willingly obey a basher. But Chatine knew he was not freezing for them. He was freezing for *him*.

A man emerged from the trees a moment later, the circuits on his face flashing and flickering as he surveyed the scene.

"Inspecteur Limier!" her father sang out, sounding, for once in his life, overjoyed to come face-to-face with the enemy of every croc in the Frets. "So lovely to see you on this fine evening. How are you doing, mon ami? Feeling good? Feeling fit? Cyborg circuits functioning in fine form, I see."

The inspecteur did not look amused by her father's playful banter. Then again, the inspecteur *never* looked amused. He flicked his gaze toward the white-haired man, still bound and gagged next to Alouette. Chatine noticed the look of fear that flashed on the fugitive's face. His worst nightmare come true.

"That's right," Monsieur Renard said, his hands still high in the air. "We got him. One Jean LeGrand served fresh to you on a titan platter." Her father beamed at the inspecteur, like he was expecting a compliment and a pat on the back. "We'll take the twenty thousand in tokens or titan blocs. It's all up to you, of course."

The inspecteur nodded curtly and made his way toward the two bound prisoners. He looked LeGrand up and down, as though checking to make sure he was real, before turning his sights on Alouette.

He clucked his tongue. "If it isn't little Madeline. Alive and well. I thought you were dead. Pity. It would have made all of this so much tidier."

LeGrand yelled something inaudible beneath his gag and attempted to kick Limier in the shins, but the large man's legs were weakened by the paralyzeur still pumping in his veins, and the inspecteur easily stepped back, out of range. "What's that, LeGrand?" he taunted. "I can't quite make out what you're saying." He reached forward and pulled the gag down.

"Leave her alone, Limier!" LeGrand bellowed. "She does not concern you! This is between us. Let her go. You can have me. But let her go."

"Why don't you let *me* decide what does and does not concern me," Limier said, his voice eerily steady.

"Limier," LeGrand growled. "I'm warning you."

But Limier turned away from the white-haired man. "Be patient, LeGrand. I'll deal with you in a minute. First I have some Délabré scum to take care of."

He flicked one hand toward Chatine's parents. "Arrest both of them."

The droids sprang into action, turning toward the two scraggly crocs, who still had their hands in the air.

One droid managed to get hold of Madame Renard, who kicked and squirmed and tried to slap the basher in the face, but Monsieur Renard was faster. Before Limier had even finished his command, he was already sprinting through the trees. A droid took off after him, and a moment later, Chatine heard a familiar warbling sound, followed by a sickening *thump* as the rayonette pulse found its target.

"What the fric is this?" Madame Renard spat, still struggling in vain with her droid. "You can't do this! What about our reward?"

Limier let out a mirthless chuckle. "Reward? You honestly think I would *ever* give money to a Renard?"

Chatine immediately felt the sharp sting of betrayal. Not on behalf of her parents—Limier could do whatever he wanted with those liars—but on behalf of herself. She, too, had put her hopes on that reward. And she had no doubt that if she had been able to successfully play out her plan, she too would have seen it ripped right out from under her. She wasn't sure why this should surprise her. She'd never trusted Limier. But the twenty thousand largs had blinded her. Just as they had clearly blinded her parents.

Chatine heard a strange noise—a scuffling of some sort—and her gaze was pulled back to Alouette and LeGrand, still tied to the tree. Except Alouette was writhing now, kicking and fighting against her restraints as though she'd gone mad.

"Hush, Little Lark," LeGrand said soothingly. "Hush."

Chatine froze.

What did he just say?

She was almost certain she had misheard him from this distance.

But then the girl bucked again and LeGrand repeated it. This time, louder. "Little Lark. Please look at me."

And that's when Chatine knew she had not been mistaken.

She had not misunderstood.

She knew what she'd heard.

And suddenly, every bit of anger in her blood melted away and all she could feel was hope.

A surge of deep-rooted, untapped, unexpected, unforeseen hope.

Little Lark.

Jean LeGrand had just called Alouette "Little *Lark*."

Her ears were ringing at the sound of that word. There was no way it was a coincidence. Chatine had seen the reaction on Marcellus's face after he'd read that word. After Roche had scribbled it onto his TéléCom.

"Lark."

That word had meant something to him. That word had gotten Roche sent to a holding cell to await passage to Bastille.

But it wasn't a word, was it?

It was a name.

It was a person.

It was *her*.

She could remember Marcellus shaking Roche, demanding to know, "Where are they?"

Chatine had known he was talking about the Vangarde, but at the time, she couldn't fathom how Marcellus had made the connection. Now she could.

That girl down there, whispering desperate, tearful pleas to Jean LeGrand, she wasn't a Défecteur. She was one of *them*.

She was a member of the Vangarde.

That gap in the floor of the mechanical room wasn't a Défecteur hideout as Chatine had originally thought. It was something else. Something the Ministère had been searching for for the past seventeen years.

Something worth a one-way ticket to Usonia.

While the two droids continued to wrestle with her parents, Chatine carefully climbed back down the tree and landed softly on the wet ground. She moved quickly, darting across the undergrowth and leaping over the small rocks that blocked her path. When she was far enough away—out of earshot of even the droids—she pulled back her sleeve. She tapped the screen in her arm to initiate an AirLink and pronounced the name painstakingly slow, so the Skin wouldn't—*couldn't*—miss a single syllable.

"General Bonnefaçon."

- CHAPTER 69 -
ALOUETTE

ALOUETTE WISHED THE RENARDS HAD GAGGED HER, too. It would have made it easier to keep the scream locked inside. She felt it bubbling, burning, ready to burst out of her.

Her father was not her father.

He'd paid for her.

Bought her like a loaf of bread from these people.

These *Renards*, whose faces tickled the frayed edges of her memory as they were carried off by droids.

And this creature—this uniformed cyborg—knew her father. He knew *her*. He'd called her the same name those people had called her: Madeline.

It was all too much. Everything was too much. She couldn't take it anymore. She kicked and squirmed and fought against her restraints. She felt the rough bark of the tree scraping at her wrists, but she didn't care. She needed to get out. She couldn't be here any longer with this stranger who claimed to be her father. Who'd lied to her for almost her entire life. About everything. Even her *name*.

"Hush, Little Lark. Hush," Hugo whispered to her.

But those words—those same words that had once calmed her—now only made her angrier, more restless. More determined to flee.

"Little Lark," Hugo spoke again. "Please look at me."

"No," she spat. "I never want to look at you again!"

"Alouette," her father said. All the regret and tenderness in his voice was gone. "You need to listen to me. This man—Inspecteur Limier—he's very dangerous. I need you to—"

"I've waited a long time for this, LeGrand." The chilling words broke though the cold air. Alouette looked up.

Into the gloom.

Into the dark forest.

Into the eerie, terrifying orange eye of the cyborg who was now stalking toward them with the purpose and fastidiousness of a para-lyzeur pulse. The long grass parted like oceans as he stalked forward, and his oblivious black boots kicked and pummeled at the grave-stones under his feet. It was only now that Alouette realized they were alone with him. The droids had all vanished into the trees.

"Too long," the inspecteur said.

Alouette felt Hugo stiffen beside her. "Look, you can have me, but let Alouette go. She has nothing to do with this. This is between you and me."

Alouette watched, alarmed, as the lights flashed on the inspec-teur's forehead and cheek. "So that's what you're calling her now, is it? Alouette?" The inspecteur leaned in close to her, his orange eye whirring and clicking. "What's the matter? You didn't like the name your déchet mother gave you?"

"Leave her alone," Hugo growled.

The inspecteur's lip quirked into an unsettling smile as he stood up straighter and pulled his rayonette from its holster, brushing his thumb tauntingly against the lever on the side. When he spoke again, his voice was impassive, almost businesslike. "I won't be releasing you or her. You are a criminal and she is the daughter of a worthless blood whore. The Regime has no use for either of you."

"Limier," Hugo implored. "How many times must I tell you? I'm a changed man. I've learned to be decent. Moral. Good. I'm no longer the—"

"You will never change, LeGrand," the inspecteur shot back, his grip around the rayonette tightening. "Never. Criminals don't change. You are as permanent, fixed, and unchangeable as this." Limier bent down and, with the tip of his weapon, tapped five times against Hugo's upper arm. "2460 . . . *1*." He spat the last number.

"Fine," Hugo said. "Then send me back to Bastille. Just let her go."

"What good would it do to send you back there? You'll only escape again. I've chased you across Laterre. Hunted you down for far too long. You've evaded me one too many times, LeGrand." Limier clicked his neck to the side, and Alouette could swear she heard metal parts grinding. "I'm done chasing you. This is where the hunt ends."

Alouette blinked up at the inspecteur, and suddenly it was as though a blanket of fog was slowly lifting from that memory lurking in the back of her mind.

She and her father huddled on the cold, wet ground.

An enormous rock pressing down on them.

The sound of footsteps.

"Hush, ma petite. Hush."

They had been running. They had been hiding.

From *him*.

Inspecteur Limier's thumb came to rest on top of the lever on the side of his rayonette. Then, with the flick of his finger, he pushed it until it could go no farther. Until the weapon was armed to its fullest capacity.

"Your next flight will not be to the moon, LeGrand, but to the Sols."

Alouette felt like she'd been shot by another paralyzing rayonette pulse. But this one wasn't aimed for her leg, it was aimed for every vital organ in her body. She could feel them all freezing up at once, shutting down. Her heart slowing. Her lungs gasping. Her brain clouding over.

This cyborg—this half man, half machine—wasn't going to send her father back to prison. He was going to kill him. She was going to have to watch him die right next to her.

And suddenly, in a blink of an eye, the world became crisp and clear again.

Hugo Taureau—or Jean LeGrand, or whatever his name was— might not have been Alouette's real father, but he was the only father she'd ever known. And just like he'd said to Limier, he *was* decent, moral, and good. He'd loved Alouette. That much he'd never lied about. That much she could be sure of.

That, and the fact that she could *not* let him die.

Alouette pushed against her restraints again, but it was no use. They were too tight. She needed something to cut through them. She needed some type of tool or—

Alouette's head snapped up, and for the first time since she'd learned the truth from the Renards, she looked at Hugo. She turned and stared *hard* and purposefully into his eyes.

Listen to me, she said silently.

His eyebrows rose subtly in response and Alouette nudged her chin toward her coat. Hugo's gaze darted down, but his expression remained clouded. He wasn't getting it. He didn't understand. She glanced up to see Limier glaring down at them, the armed weapon glistening in his hand. She needed more time.

That much, at least, Hugo *did* seem to understand.

"Limier," Hugo began. "I thought you were a man of justice. Of *reason*. So think about this reasonably. I stole a loaf of chou bread. That was my only crime. How is that punishable by death?"

Alouette could hear the subtlest twinge of mocking in her father's voice, and she knew that he was taunting the inspecteur. Buying her more time.

"You think that was your only crime?" the inspecteur lashed out, his circuitry blinking irritably. "Shall I enumerate your countless *other* offenses?"

Yes, Alouette thought hopefully. *Yes, please do.*

The inspecteur didn't wait for a reply. "You have escaped from a Ministère prison. Not once, but twice. You destroyed three droids and injured two of my men."

As the cyborg spoke, Alouette attempted to scoot closer to her father, wiggling her hips until the tool belt around her waist rotated. She knew precisely the moment her father caught on to what she was trying do. His hands brushed against her jacket, and she felt him tug at the pouch on her belt. And then, at last, the small wire cutters she'd taken from Sister Denise's workbench earlier were slipped into her hand.

Alouette didn't hesitate. With her wrists still bound, she attempted to turn the clippers around so that she could maneuver the handles. But with her limited mobility, her fingers felt fat and clumsy.

"Resisting arrest is not a crime punishable by death either," Hugo baited. "I thought cyborgs were programmed to follow the law."

"I *am* the law!" the inspecteur shouted. The sound was so startling, Alouette's hands fumbled and the wire cutters dropped into the dirt behind her. "I am the head of the Vallonay Policier. The general has entrusted *me* with keeping the peace in our capital city, and *you* are a disturbance to that peace."

Alouette panicked, her fingers roving desperately across the ground for the lost tool, but she was finding nothing except clumps of dirt and dried leaves. She stretched against the restraints, the wire digging painfully into her flesh, until finally her fingertips brushed the smooth surface of the handles sticking out of the mud.

She nearly yelped in relief as she navigated the tool toward Hugo's wrists.

"That is why you must be eliminated once and for all," Limier was saying. He seemed to have regained his composure as he lifted his weapon and aimed it directly at Hugo's chest.

When the cutters made contact with a solid surface, Alouette couldn't be certain whether she was about to cut wire or flesh, but she was out of time. She squeezed her fingers together, feeling the sharp blades latch on to something.

"Adieu, LeGrand," Limier said with a sneer as his finger pinched the trigger.

Alouette shut her eyes tight and squeezed harder. A moment later, she heard a snap, followed by the high-pitched *whoosh* of the rayonette.

Alouette opened her eyes to see Hugo rocketing forward as though he were a great and mighty flood being released from a dam. At the same instant, the tree at Alouette's back sizzled and blackened, shards of wood exploding outward as the pulse from Limier's rayonette buried itself into the bark, missing Alouette's cheek by a millimètre.

Alouette screamed as Hugo landed on top of Limier and the two men hit the ground with a thunderous clap. The rayonette flew from Limier's hand, before landing a few mètres away. Limier dove for it. Hugo pulled him back. Alouette could tell the paralyzeur in his blood was still slowing him down, softening his muscles. It seemed to give Limier an edge. The men grappled and tugged, Hugo using what was left of his brute strength, and Limier his unflagging tenacity.

Alouette tried to turn the cutters to the wire on her own wrists, but they kept slipping and sinking back into the dirt. She tried to yank her hands free instead, but the wire bit at her flesh, causing her to wince and yelp in pain.

Limier flipped onto his back and managed to wedge his knee under Hugo. The bottom of his boot connected with Hugo's stomach, and he kicked hard. Hugo was flung off him and Limier was free. He scrambled onto his hands and knees and reached for the weapon, his fingers wrapping around the handle.

Alouette whimpered and grappled for the wire cutters again. This time, she was able to prop the tool between her bound hands and the tree, holding it in place with one wrist, while she violently sawed the other back and forth against the small blade.

Hugo bounded to his feet and moved toward Limier, his left leg dragging awkwardly behind him. But Limier already had the weapon positioned in his hand.

"Papa! Watch out!" Alouette cried.

Limier took aim and fired. But with effort, Hugo managed to kick out his right leg, his boot slicing through the air, making contact with Limier's chest and knocking the inspecteur onto his back. The shot missed again, soaring too high and burying itself in a branch above Alouette's head. The tree sizzled and creaked in response.

Limier still had hold of the weapon. He tried to line up another shot, but Hugo was there, kicking again. This time the blow landed right on the rayonette, and Alouette watched the device fly through the air in a looping arc, disappearing deep into the trees. Limier let out a loud, robotic roar of frustration and took off after it.

Hugo leapt in front of him, blocking his path with his massive frame, and when the inspecteur tried to dodge him, Hugo grabbed Limier and hoisted him high off the ground. Limier's circuitry blinked furiously, lighting up the trees and branches around him. Then it was as though Hugo's strength suddenly returned in full force. His blood absorbed the last drop of paralyzeur in his system. The powerful and mighty Hugo Taureau was back. With a beastly roar, he flung the inspecteur over his head. Limier seemed to be airborne for minutes. When he finally hit the ground, there was the distinct sound of metal breaking.

The noise was sickening and unsettling. But not as unsettling as the noise Alouette was suddenly hearing above her. She glanced up and noticed the branch that had taken the second pulse from the rayonette was wavering. Crackling. Starting to come down.

And Alouette was sitting directly underneath it.

She sawed harder. But because she couldn't see what she was doing, her wrists constantly slipped, the sharp end of the wire cutters stabbing at her palm.

The branch above finally snapped. Hugo heard the sound and spun around, his eyes widening as he saw the giant piece of lumber hurtling toward Alouette. He lunged for her, presumably to push her out of harm's way. But just then, another branch seemed to come out of nowhere, smacking Hugo across the side of the face. With a grunt, he collapsed facedown onto the dirt.

Alouette yanked her wrists apart as hard as she could. The wire finally ripped, and she rolled out of the way just as the branch above her crashed against the base of the tree.

She shuddered out a breath and tried to run to her father. But her leg was still numb, and she immediately crashed to her knees. Hugo was moaning, struggling to get up.

Where did that other branch come from?

The answer came a split second later when Limier swung again and Alouette saw the massive wooden weapon in his hand.

"No!" Alouette screamed.

Limier brought the branch down hard across Hugo's back, and Hugo collapsed. The inspecteur pulled his weapon over his head, preparing to deliver another blow.

"No!" Alouette called again, just as the branch smashed onto Hugo's skull and her father crumpled.

This time, he didn't try to get up. He didn't move at all.

She opened her mouth to cry out, but then clamped it shut when she saw Limier rising up, wiping the blood and dirt from his mouth. His orange eye roved the grave site, looking for something.

Looking for *her*.

Alouette sprawled onto her belly, hiding herself in the tall grass, and started to slither toward the camp. She had to get out of there. And fast. If she didn't leave, that deranged cyborg would certainly kill her, too. She could hear his footsteps behind her. Each one like a clap of thunder. Alouette moved as fast as she could, but her leg was still numb from the pulse of the Renards' . . .

Alouette froze, an idea forming in her mind.

She peered up over the reeds, glancing quickly around to orient herself. She saw the lamp in the center of the clearing, directly behind her. It was a risky move, but she feared it might be her only option. Keeping herself low, she swiveled around and crawled in the direction of the light source, where she remembered Madame Renard dropping her rayonette as soon as the droids had arrived. Alouette's hands searched frantically through the damp grass. When her fingertips brushed up against cold, hard metal, she let out a quick gasp of relief.

But just as her hand curled around the weapon, a large black boot crunched down on her fingers. She screamed, but the boot only twisted and ground harder into the forest floor.

Alouette looked up to see Limier looming over her, his mechanical eye beaming down like a Sol on fire. The pain in her hand was excruciating. Her fingers could no longer clutch the rayonette. She felt it slowly slip from her grasp as the inspecteur's boot dug deeper into her skin.

He bent down to grab the weapon, lifting his boot from her hand. Alouette was free, but the pain was still blinding. She felt dizzy, like she might pass out. But then she heard a sickening sound. The sound of the rayonette clicking in the inspecteur's hand.

And something inexplicable rose up inside her.

Something very new and very familiar, all at the same time.

In a flash, Alouette was no longer facedown in the dirt. She was on her feet so quickly, Limier stumbled back in shock. Her arms swung gracefully, one hand arcing in front of the other as she moved swiftly toward the inspecteur.

She felt buoyant. Weightless. Like she no longer needed to pilot her body; her body knew exactly what to do. It remembered.

Every muscle and tendon knew these movements.

Her left hand curved up, making contact with Limier's nose, while her right sliced into his stomach with more strength than she knew she had. He doubled over and Alouette was already moving again, crouching down and thrusting her elbow up into his throat. The inspecteur let out a strange gurgle and went down, the rayonette falling into the grass.

It wasn't until Alouette pushed herself up from the squat that she fully recognized what she'd just done.

It was the fourth sequence.

The Darkest Night.

She had just performed Tranquil Forme in the middle of the woods! Except it wasn't Tranquil Forme. It was faster. More violent. Bloodier. Tranquil Forme wasn't supposed to be fast and violent and bloody, it was supposed to be gentle and slow and . . . *tranquil.*

Did the Sisters know you could do that?

Use their sacred meditation as a weapon?

Of course not.

She nearly laughed aloud at the idea of Sister Muriel fighting off a Ministère officer with her *Orbit of the Divine.*

And yet it had worked. Inspecteur Limier was on the ground at her feet, moaning in agony.

And somehow *she* was responsible.

She'd done this to him.

She'd incapacitated this terrifying inspecteur.

All on her own.

Suddenly a cold hand gripped her ankle and began to pull her down. Alouette shrieked and tried to leap back from the inspecteur's grasp, but she couldn't wrench herself free. He was too strong. The cyborg cackled a dark, chilling laugh and began to tug harder, using his grip on Alouette's leg to pull himself up.

Alouette felt herself slipping. She gave a furious kick, knocking the inspecteur back, and lunged for the rayonette on the ground. Limier scrambled to his feet again but halted when he saw Alouette holding the rayonette out in front of her, the weapon aimed directly at him.

"You think you can defeat me? You're a nobody. A worthless, silly girl. Just like your mother."

He lunged. She squeezed the trigger. The rayonette's pulse rippled through the wet air. It found its target in Limier's left temple, and for a moment, the entire forest was aglow. Everything turned bright and white as a shower of sparks erupted from the cyborg's circuitry. The inspecteur let out a gruesome cry, but the sound was cut short as his whole body seemed to immobilize. Like a powered-down droid. His mouth remained open in a silent scream. The circuitry on his flesh continued to sizzle as the inspecteur crumpled to the ground and landed in a heap.

Then, a moment later, Alouette heard a deep, wounded moan as someone in the clearing called out, "Little Lark?"

CHAPTER 70

CHATINE

CHATINE SHIVERED AS THE WIND DRIFTING OFF THE lake cut through her sorry excuse for a coat. She'd been waiting at the edge of the Forest Verdure for over twenty minutes for the general to arrive, and she had no idea what was taking him so long.

The words she'd said to him in her message were fluttering back through her mind like leaves trapped in a breeze.

I found the base. I know where they are.

The general had responded less than a minute later, telling her he'd pick her up shortly.

Chatine still couldn't believe the Vangarde had been hiding inside the city all this time. When she'd pictured a top secret base for an undercover revolutionary operation, she'd usually pictured something way out in the middle of the Terrain Perdu, maybe even a fortress carved into the ice, designed to blend in with the endless white land-scape. She'd imagined the general searching the entire planet. Search-ing for something that had been right under his nose the whole time.

The thought amused her. Chatine was impressed by anyone who could outsmart the Ministère. The location was clever. And gutsy as fric.

And it wasn't too dissimilar to the way Chatine had operated all these years.

Hiding in plain sight was often the best way to disappear.

The wind picked up. Chatine shivered again and pulled her coat tighter, but it did little to protect her against the furious gales that twisted and snaked around her.

The gusts were so strong, she didn't even hear the footsteps behind her until it was too late. Until she was already being hoisted off the ground.

She tried to scream, but a large hand clamped over her mouth, muffling the sound.

"Thought you could run away from us, did you?"

Chatine's eyes darted left and right, but she still couldn't see her attacker.

"Thought you could skip out on your debts to the Délabré and we wouldn't find you?"

Just then, a figure stepped in front of her. His slender, angular body cast eerie, misshapen shadows on the ground.

Chatine's eyes widened, and the hand over her mouth stifled another scream.

Claque reached out and gripped one of the metal rods that was holding Chatine's tattered pants together. He yanked hard and something tiny and metallic fell into his palm. "It's important to keep tabs on your resources." He held up the object, and Chatine felt her body go rigid.

It was a tracking device. He'd obviously hidden it on her when she was at the Grotte. She hadn't even bothered to check. How could she have been so stupid? He'd been tracking her ever since she'd left the docks that night.

And now she knew exactly what came next. There was no way she could escape it.

Claque wasted no more time. He reached into the pocket of his tattered sheepskin coat and pulled out his favorite tool. A pair of rusty bolt cutters.

Sheer terror coursed through Chatine's veins. She tried to speak, to reason with the man, but her words were muffled by what she now knew was Hercule's hand. Claque never went anywhere without his giant freightship of a bodyguard.

"What's that?" Claque asked, feigning interest. "I didn't get that."

Hercule dropped his massive hand from Chatine's mouth long enough for her to repeat herself. "I still have until tomorrow."

Claque clucked his tongue while he glanced down at his Skin. "That's true. You do still have until tomorrow." He paused, watching the clock. "57, 58, 59 . . . *and* now it's tomorrow."

He reached for her boot and easily slid it off, revealing her bare, blistered toes underneath.

Chatine struggled and kicked at the air, but Hercule tightened his grip around her waist, keeping her hoisted off the ground. Claque squeezed his fingers around the handles of the bolt cutters, giving them a quick trial run. The sharp *snap* sound that echoed across the lake made Chatine's heart leap into her throat.

"We'll start with the smallest and work our way in," Claque explained as he sauntered toward her, his gaze trained on her wriggling toes.

"Wait!" Chatine called out desperately. Her mind raced for a way to stall him, to buy herself more time. "I'm working on something even bigger now. I swear. I'll let you in on it. Fifty percent."

Claque pulled the bolt cutters apart and aimed the rusty blades at her pinky toe.

"Seventy-five percent!" she tried again, her voice trembling.

"Hmm. Now, why don't I believe you?" Claque said, pursing his lips. "Oh, right. Because you're a Renard. And your good-for-nothing parents already cheated me out of a big payout today. We were supposed to get LeGrand together and then they ditched me. So it looks like I'll be taking my cut from both that *and* the Bonnefaçon job tonight." He smirked, his bolt cutters splayed open like the mouth of a giant, snarling beast.

The wind spiked again, but there was something noticeably different about this breeze. It seemed to be localizing around them. Like a storm centered right over their heads. A violent gust swooped down and blew Chatine's hood straight off, ripping her hair from its bun. She tried to reach up to secure it back into place, but her arms were still pinned down in Hercule's grasp.

Claque barely had time to register Chatine's wild, swirling locks before a massive object descended from the sky right in front of them, whipping the wind into a frenzy.

"What on Laterre?" Claque uttered as he stared, slack-jawed, up at the strange craft.

Chatine's mouth hung open too. She'd never seen anything like it in her life. With its sleek silver body and wings cutting like razorblades through the air, it appeared to be a cross between a voyageur and a cruiseur. But voyageurs traveled through deep space and cruiseurs were designed to hover silently over terrain. This vehicle had just descended from the sky like a falling star.

The vessel hissed and juddered slightly as it came to a halt a mètre above the ground, and Chatine watched in awe as a door emerged from its seamless surface and wheezed open.

General Bonnefaçon's large frame appeared in the doorway. Chatine felt Hercule's grip around her body loosen just the slightest bit before the general hoisted up his rayonette, aimed, and fired two rapid pulses, back-to-back.

Whoosh.

Whoosh.

Chatine plummeted to the ground, landing on the shallow, reedy shore of the lake. Beside her, the bodies of Claque and Hercule slumped down in the water. Motionless. Dead. With smoking black holes in the center of each of their foreheads.

Speechless, Chatine stared up at her unlikely savior in disbelief, unsure what to do next.

General Bonnefaçon gestured to the doorway of the hovering craft. "Are you coming or not?"

CHAPTER 71

MARCELLUS

MARCELLUS NEEDED AIR.

He burst out of his room and rushed down the imperial staircase. Outside the Palais, the sculpted flower gardens shone under the artificial moon that hung in the sky.

It wasn't Bastille, of course. Sols forbid that the First and Second Estates have to look up and see a prison. It was some other moon. Some make-believe satellite where people weren't wrongfully imprisoned, freezing to death for crimes they didn't commit.

It was a lie.

Just like everything else under this protective dome. Just like every day of Marcellus's entire life.

One giant lie.

The entire planet thought Julien Bonnefaçon had bombed that exploit. The entire planet thought the Vangarde were responsible for killing hundreds of innocent people. But it had been his grandfather all along, doing the Patriarche's bidding like another loyal Palais dog.

General Bonnefaçon.

The man with whom Marcellus shared blood, a house, a future.

Marcellus stumbled over to the nearest rosebush and retched until his stomach was empty and his eyes teared.

But he still couldn't clear his head.

Not in here. Not with the Palais walls closing in on him. Not with this lie of a moon hanging over him. Those fake stars winking as though they were mocking him.

He couldn't think in here.

He couldn't *breathe* in here.

The TéléSky ceilings of Ledôme were too low. The air was too artificially sweet with the scent of power and privilege and corruption.

He needed *real* air. And he knew there was only one place he could go. Only one place he could ever go.

Marcellus scrambled over to the docking station and jumped onto his moto. He could be in the clearing soon. There, he would think. There, he would process. Figure out what on Laterre he was going to do next.

He initiated the engine and revved the throttle. The moto lurched into the air and zoomed forward. When he reached the west gate, the air lock opened automatically for him, sensing his arrival moments before he got there. He sped through and banked left, leaning into the turn. Once he was outside Ledôme, under the *real* sky, he thrust the moto into the next gear and gripped the handlebars tighter.

He swept downhill and raced alongside the rows and rows of hothouses in the lowlands. These giant buildings of plastique catered to the people in Ledôme, growing tropical fruits and summer vegetables that could never be grown in the outdoor fermes, where the Third Estate crops were harvested.

More lies, Marcellus thought. *More deception.*

The Third Estate starved not because there wasn't enough food. The Third Estate starved because the Ministère wanted them to.

Because it kept them weak.

It kept them cold.

It kept them obedient.

"A hungry working class is a productive working class," his grandfather had said.

And Marcellus, like the imbécile that he'd always been, had gobbled it up. It had gone down as easily as whatever decadent cream dish they'd been eating at the time.

Because his grandfather knew best. He always knew best. He was the ultimate strategist. He'd kept Laterre running for more than thirty years. While the Patriarche was out shooting pheasants and bedding women, and the Matrone was busy guzzling champagne and ordering new gowns from Samsara, his grandfather had been running a planet. Because that was his job.

The First Estate played.

The Second Estate governed.

The Third Estate worked.

That was how the planet operated. How it had always operated. Since the first freightships landed on Laterre. Since the last human beings left the First World.

I tried to teach you that everyone is equal under the Sols. That no one should be imprisoned or forced to live in squalor just because they were born on the wrong side of Ledôme walls."

That's what Mabelle had said in the Tourbay. Apparently that's what she'd been trying to tell him all along. But he had been too stupid and brainwashed to listen. He'd been so awestruck or intimidated—or *both*—by his grandfather, he'd failed to hear it.

Marcellus let out a roar of frustration and pushed his moto up to top speed.

Soon, he would be in the Forest Verdure at the Défecteur camp. Soon, he would be hidden from everyone.

"Disable tracker!" he commanded his TéléCom.

The map displayed on the inside of his visor blinked off. But just as it disappeared from view, Marcellus noticed ten new AirLink messages flickering at the corner of his vision. Every single one of them was from his grandfather.

Ten messages?

He suddenly remembered his grandfather trying to AirLink him earlier, when he was watching the microcam footage.

Marcellus cringed.

Was his grandfather angry that he'd declined the AirLink? Had he left him ten messages about duty and respect and loyalty to the Regime?

"You are so weak. Just like your father."

Marcellus gritted his teeth against the memory, and suddenly the ache in his ribs came back full force. As if they, too, were remembering.

No.

He was not a coward. Not anymore. His grandfather was the real coward. Killing innocent people and then pinning the blame on his own son. Just because the Patriarche told him to do it. Using the Vangarde as a mask. Afraid to expose himself as the villain he truly was.

Marcellus reconnected his TéléCom and played the first message.

The general's face appeared across the inside of his visor. His grandfather was sitting in his tall leather office chair. Just as he'd been seventeen years ago, when he'd agreed to bomb that copper exploit.

"Marcellus. Where are you? We're dealing with a very serious situation. There's been a break-in attempt at Warden Gallant's office in Ledôme. We believe Vangarde operatives were trying to infiltrate Bastille from within the Ministère headquarters. You must AirLink me immediately."

Marcellus jammed on the brakes and the moto careened to a halt. The general was still talking, but Marcellus was having trouble hearing him. Even though he'd stopped moving and was now idling a mètre off the ground, he still heard a deafening roar in his ears.

A break-in attempt?

Certain he must have misheard his grandfather, Marcellus rewound the message to the beginning and listened again, sucking in a breath.

He had not misunderstood. Someone had attempted to breach the office of the warden of Bastille.

The general continued. "Fortunately, we were able to intercept the two Vangarde operatives before any of our security systems could be compromised. The operatives are being brought to the Vallonay Policier Precinct for questioning. I'm AirLinking their images to you now."

Marcellus felt a jolt of something inside him, but he couldn't, for the life of him, identify the sensation.

Two Vangarde operatives had tried to bring down Bastille's security systems. Two Vangarde operatives had failed.

How did he *feel* about that? Afraid? Excited? Relieved? Disappointed? Maybe some strange, nauseating mix of all of them?

Then another thought struck Marcellus.

Could one of those operatives be Alouette?

"We believe," the general went on, "their larger objective was to ultimately break Citizen Rousseau out of Bastille. As you know, she would be *crucial* to the success of a second revolution attempt."

Marcellus swallowed. This was exactly what the Patriarche had been worried about. And Marcellus had to admit it was a clever move. The Vangarde's *only* move, really. If they hoped to launch a full-scale revolution—to finish what they started in 488—then they needed Citizen Rousseau. If she *ever* were to escape Bastille, the First and Second Estates would have much reason to be afraid.

"These captured Vangarde operatives must be questioned thoroughly," the general was now saying. "We need to get every last shred of information out of them. We need to know where their biggest cells are, who their biggest supporters are, and most important, where their base is located." The general leaned forward slightly, like he was trying to reach through the lens of the microcam and strangle Marcellus with his eyes. "Every force necessary will be taken to secure this information."

Marcellus instinctively leaned back, as though he could escape his grandfather's intimidating stare. But all he managed to do was knock himself off balance on his moto.

"I'm sending Inspecteur Limier to handle the interrogation," the general's message continued. "He's the best man for the job. But I can't seem to locate him. He, *too*, is not accepting my AirLink requests. I need you to track him down and send him immediately to the Policier Precinct. The apprehended Vangarde operatives are being transported there presently."

Adrenaline shot through him as an idea began to form. A bold idea. A reckless idea. Possibly the most stupide idea he'd ever had.

Two Vangarde operatives were on their way to the Precinct right this moment. They might even have arrived already.

If Marcellus ever had an opportunity to get answers about his father—*real* answers—this was it.

"Request AirLink to General Bonnefaçon," he commanded the TéléCom. On his visor, the connection initiated, and then, a moment later, his grandfather's face was back in front of him. Strangely, he was no longer in his office, where he'd sent the first message from. But Marcellus couldn't figure out where on Laterre he was. Behind him there was nothing but darkness, as though he were floating in the middle of the sky.

"It's about time!" the general barked. "Where have you been? Why haven't you—"

Marcellus cut him off. "I will interrogate the Vangarde operatives."

The general seemed momentarily stunned, and Marcellus wasn't sure if it was because this was the first time in his life that his grandson had *ever* interrupted him, or if it was the decisive, unwavering tone with which he'd done it.

His grandfather cocked a dark eyebrow, clearly pondering. "No," he finally replied. "Inspecteur Limier will question the operatives. This will certainly not be the Vangarde's last attempt to free Citizen Rousseau. They will try again. And we need to root them out before they do. This is too important to mess up."

For just a split second, Marcellus paused, feeling the sting. It was like lemon juice sprinkled on a wound that had been left open since he was a small child, constantly attempting to heal itself, but never quite managing to close up completely.

That sting had always debilitated Marcellus.

For as long as he could remember.

But today was different. The microcam footage had changed everything. Today, he was able to harness that sting. He let it spread through his entire body until it was fueling him. Until it turned from pain to power.

"No," Marcellus repeated with the exact same unfaltering inflection. "I said, I will take care of it."

And before his grandfather could utter another word, or cock another eyebrow, Marcellus disconnected the AirLink, turned his moto around, and headed back to the city.

- CHAPTER 72 -
CHATINE

THE INTERIOR OF THE GENERAL'S SHIP WAS EVEN
more remarkable than the exterior. There were monitors and con-
soles wall-to-wall. Lights flashed across rows and rows of control
panels. Two pilotes sat up front in a glowing cockpit.

And right in the center of it all, floating in midair was . . .

Well, *everything.*

The entire planet. All of Laterre stretched out before Chatine in
miniature form, emanating from a faint light projected from the ceiling. She'd heard of hologram maps before, but she'd never actually
seen one in person. It was truly spectacular. She marveled at the sight
of Laterre's single landmass surrounded by dark ocean. The two cities
of Vallonay and Montfer sparkled like little jewels on opposite coasts.
Chatine could make out endless rows of fermes and exploits and fabriques stretching out from the cities. And in the center of it all were
the barren and frozen moors of the Terrain Perdu.

"So," the general said, giving her an impatient look, "where is the
base?"

Chatine swallowed, her gaze falling once again to the hologram.

She pointed at the shimmering city on the cusp of a huge bay where the landmass of Laterre met the Secana Sea. "Vallonay," she said.

The general lifted a single eyebrow. He clearly was having the same reaction as she'd had.

Right under his nose the whole time.

"Vallonay," she repeated with a succinct nod.

The general barked out an order to the pilotes sitting in the cockpit. "Back to the capital."

The ship launched forward and banked into a sharp turn, knocking Chatine right off her feet. She fell onto a nearby jump seat and struggled to get the restraints clasped around her. "What is this thing?"

The general chuckled at her reaction. "It's a combatteur. We only fly them for battle."

"Battle?" Chatine repeated, hating the tremble in her voice.

But the general ignored her, pulling out his TéléCom to accept an AirLink request.

"It's about time!" he bellowed into the screen. "Where have you been? Why haven't you—"

Chatine leaned against her restraints to catch a glimpse at whom he was talking to. She could just make out the person's thick, dark hair.

Chatine inhaled sharply and leaned back, pressing her spine flush to the seat. It was Marcellus.

Her heart was suddenly pounding again. She did not want to see him. No, that wasn't true. She would have done anything to see him. That much, she couldn't deny anymore. She didn't want *him* to see her.

He already distrusted her. He already despised her. Seeing her in a Ministère battle ship with his grandfather would only prove that everything he'd accused her of back in the Fabrique District was true.

"You're poor. You're hungry. You're freezing. You'll do anything for a larg, isn't that right? Isn't that how your kind *operates?"*

Chatine tried to steady her breath, reminding herself that soon this would all be over. Soon she'd be on a cushy voyageur bound for Usonia, traveling at supervoyage speed across the System Divine, the stars reduced to an endless glow of light outside the window.

Soon Laterre would be nothing more than a vanishing gray sphere behind her.

And Marcellus would be an invisible spec on that sphere, as insignificant to her as she was to him.

Chatine turned and glanced out the window. They were high. So high, she even dared to peer up, thinking that maybe they had penetrated the cloud layer and she could catch a glimpse at the stars. But all she saw above her was murky gray darkness.

The ground below was whizzing by, and she could tell from the blinking red dot on the hologram map in front of her that they were rapidly approaching the city limits.

"No," the general said a moment later. "Inspecteur Limier will question the operatives. This will certainly not be the Vangarde's last attempt to free Citizen Rousseau. They will try again. And we need to root them out before they do. This is too important to mess up."

Free Citizen Rousseau? The Vangarde tried to infiltrate Bastille?

Chatine was now happier than ever that she would soon be getting off this Sol-forsaken planet. She had a feeling things were about to go from worse to catastrophic.

She braved another peek at the general's TéléCom to see that the screen was dark.

The AirLink had been severed.

Chatine couldn't believe it. Marcellus had *disconnected* the general of the Ministère.

Then, as though coming to some sort of decision, the general jabbed at the TéléCom and started speaking rapidly to an unseen recipient. "My grandson is on his way to the Precinct now. I don't want him anywhere near the operatives. Inspecteur Limier is the only person who has my permission to enter that interrogation room. Do you understand me?"

A moment later, the general released a breath and flung the TéléCom onto the seat next to him, letting out a huff. "Imbécile."

Chatine flushed with irritation, feeling the urge to defend Marcellus to his grandfather, but before she could utter a single word, her attention was suddenly pulled back to the window of the combatteur.

Outside, a cluster of silver crafts just like the one she was in had swooped in alongside them. Their knife-edge wings glinted in the darkness. Chatine's gaze whipped to the opposite window, where she saw even more combatteurs gliding into formation.

They were surrounded.

What is going on?

The general picked up his discarded TéléCom and spoke into the screen. "Thank you for arriving so quickly, pilotes. When we reach the base, I want every explosif on this fleet deployed. Full impact. Anything off target will be accounted for. The base must be annihilated. Obliterated. No survivors." He cricked his neck and added, "Vive Laterre."

Chatine felt the warmth drain from her face first, followed by her neck, her arms, until her fingers felt colder and number than they'd ever felt living in the freezing Frets.

"You're going to destroy it?" she asked, and she was honestly surprised at the surprise in her own voice. What had she thought the general was going to do when they got there? Knock on the door and ask for a chat?

The general flashed her a look of pure disbelief. Disbelief that she could be so stupid. So ignorant. "The Vangarde is the enemy of the Regime. They are an infestation. A disease. And the only way to deal with an infestation is to find the nest and destroy it." He nodded toward the glowing hologram in front of them. The map had refocused itself. It was now displaying the city of Vallonay. It glowed and sparkled like an actual paradise, not the dark, decaying cesspool that Chatine had spent the past ten years of her life in.

"Where is the base?" the general demanded from Chatine, and then into the TéléCom, he said, "Stand by for location."

Chatine couldn't breathe. She couldn't feel. The numbness continued to spread through her until she was paralyzed everywhere.

She stared, unblinking, at the map—at the pulsing red dot, which was now mere centimètres away from the city. In a matter of seconds, they would be right over the Frets. In a matter of seconds, the general and his entire Ministère army of combatteurs would be dropping explosifs from the sky, destroying everything below.

Chatine managed to find her tongue. "But, what if there are people nearby? Innocent people who have nothing to do with the Vangarde?"

The general shot her another look. He was growing impatient. "There are casualties in every war, Renard. It's called collateral damage. We are keeping the Regime safe. That's what matters. Now, do you want to get off this planet or not? Show me where the Sol-damn base is."

But Chatine could barely hear anything he was saying.

All she could hear was the screaming.

Thousands of voices screaming at once.

Calling for help. Begging for their lives to be spared. Crying out that they hadn't done anything. They didn't deserve this. They were innocent.

And then all she could hear was Azelle. Screaming as the ground gave way beneath her. Screaming as the world around her erupted into a storm cloud of metal and dust. Screaming until her scream was snuffed out forever.

Chatine glanced out the window at the fleet of combatteurs flanking them, waiting for the general's orders to annihilate the poor, defenseless Frets.

If she told him where the base was—if she told him it was buried under Fret 7—he wouldn't hesitate. He would wipe it *all* out. Fret 7 and maybe even parts of Frets 14 and 20, too. There was no way those crumbling structures would ever survive.

Tens of thousands of people.

Her people.

Dead.

Gone.

Collateral damage.

Fret rats just like her. Crocs just like her. Hungry mouths and empty stomachs just like hers. Diligent, hard workers just like her sister. Crying babies just like Henri.

Henri.

She could suddenly see his face at the window of the combatteur. His round gray eyes staring back at her. His beautiful gurgling laugh echoing through her mind. His chubby little hands pressed against the plastique, like he was reaching for her through time.

She'd always told herself he was better off dead.

Better off with the Sols than living on this wretched planet.

And maybe he was.

Maybe they all were.

Maybe there was nothing left on Laterre worth living for.

"Renard!" the general exploded. His voice cut through her thoughts and shattered the warm bubble around her. Chatine watched Henri's face disintegrate back into her memory.

She turned toward the glowing hologram in front of them. "There," she said quietly. Her finger shook as it landed on the crumbling structure that sat like a giant sore on the city. "That's where the base is. It's right there."

The general was immediately on his TéléCom, relaying the coordinates to the rest of the pilotes. Chatine felt her stomach lurch as the combatteur dipped into another sharp turn and then picked up speed, racing toward its destination.

There was no more doubt. No more uncertainty.

Chatine had made her choice, and there was no going back.

She forced herself to look out the window. To watch as the rusting monstrosity came into view on the horizon. To witness as it disappeared from existence in a blinding explosion of light.

CHAPTER 73

MARCELLUS

WORD OF THE CAPTURED OPERATIVES MUST HAVE spread quickly, because by the time Marcellus arrived at the Precinct, it was crawling with Policier. Countless more than the usual night shift. It seemed everyone wanted to get a look at flesh-and-blood members of the Vangarde. At these ghosts whom they'd heard rumors about for the past seventeen years.

Marcellus pushed past the swarm of deputies lingering in the hallway, making his way to the last interrogation room. The Truth Chamber, as it had been nicknamed in the Precinct. It was where the most stubborn of suspects were questioned. The ones who needed *extra* coercing. Marcellus knew, from checking the Communiqué before he'd arrived, that both operatives were being held there.

He had also been relieved to discover, when he'd looked at the pictures of the detained operatives, that Alouette was not one of them.

Two Policier droids were positioned in front of the door to the Truth Chamber. As Marcellus approached, both of their heads clicked toward him in perfect synchronization. It gave him the chills. Not only because droids always made him uneasy, but because he honestly didn't know *how* he was going to get through this.

Was he really going to interrogate two members of the Vangarde?

He cleared his throat and spoke to one of the droids. "Officer Bonnefaçon to interrogate the prisoners."

The droid's eyes flickered as it processed the incoming information. "Access denied."

"What do you mean 'access denied'?"

"We have been given instructions to grant access only to Inspecteur Limier."

Marcellus scoffed. "Instructions from who?"

"That would be me," said a voice behind Marcellus. He didn't need to turn around to know it belonged to Sergent Chacal. Marcellus clenched his fists. "The general called me directly. Said you weren't allowed anywhere near the prisoners. And that I should wait for Limier."

Marcellus spun around. When he saw the sergent, he knew the correct reaction was to wince. But all he could do was laugh. "What happened to your face?"

Chacal's glare seemed to make the enormous welt over his left eye pulse.

"You should probably go put some salve on that," he told Chacal. "It looks pretty bad." Then he turned back to the droids. "Officer Bonnefaçon overriding all previous directives."

The droid on the left jerked to attention at the command. Marcellus felt the orange light from its eyes flicker across his face as the droid scanned him.

"You can't do that," Chacal complained. "I have orders from the general."

"The general is not currently here," Marcellus pointed out, "which means local command of this building falls to the highest-ranking agent on premises."

The droid completed its scan and stepped away from the door, letting Marcellus pass.

As Marcellus opened the door, he turned back long enough to flash Chacal a smirk. "That would be me, now."

He dismissed the droids and stepped through the door, which sealed shut behind him. Marcellus stood motionless just inside the room as he took in the two women in front of him.

They were both wearing long gray tunics, similar to the one Alouette had worn. One of them had an unusual scar on the right side of her face, starting beneath her wiry dark hair and running down to her chin. She was sitting at the table, tapping her fingers rhythmically against the surface as though working an invisible TéléCom. She didn't even glance up at Marcellus.

But the other—the slighter, short-haired one, who was pacing the length of the room in a pair of red canvas shoes—stopped and stared at him, her lips tweaking into a knowing, almost *familiar* smile.

"My Sols," she said in a whisper, almost as though she were speaking to herself. "You look just like him."

Marcellus knew instantly that she was speaking of his father.

He'd been told throughout his life that he looked like Julien. It was one of the reasons, he'd convinced himself, that the general was often so distrusting of him.

"So you knew him," Marcellus confirmed.

The short-haired woman nodded. "He was a fine operative. A gentle man. He loved you very much."

Marcellus felt tears pool in his eyes and he blinked them away, suddenly remembering the microcams stationed throughout the room.

He schooled his expression and pointed to the chair next to the other woman. "Sit," he said, infusing strength into his voice.

"I like standing," the short-haired woman replied. It wasn't defiant or arrogant. It sounded more like she was reciting a well-known fact.

But Marcellus had no doubt that every deputy and officer who had been lingering in that hallway was now crammed into the monitoring room, watching them, listening to every word.

He had to make this look real.

Or he'd soon find himself on the other side of that table.

"I said, *sit*." His voice left no room for argument.

She sat.

The other woman still didn't look up. She continued tapping on her invisible screen, her mouth moving ever so slightly as though she were silently reciting something she didn't want to forget.

The woman with the cropped hair glanced at the wall behind Marcellus, which was covered, floor to ceiling, with steel lockers and compartments. Marcellus had a feeling that she knew exactly what was hidden inside those compartments. That she understood the kind of pain that could be—and often *was*—inflicted within these walls.

And yet, her expression remained eerily calm. Almost serene. As though she were imagining herself in a tranquil garden, not here in the Truth Chamber of the Policier Precinct. It reminded Marcellus of Alouette, and he found himself wondering if Alouette had learned her peaceful manner from this woman.

Marcellus motioned to the short-haired woman's left arm. "I guess there's no use in scanning you."

She pulled up the sleeve of her long gray tunic, revealing a scar similar to Alouette's. "No."

"So, do you have a name?" he asked, trying to keep his voice gruff and unrelenting.

"My friends call me Jacqui," the woman replied.

"Is that your real name?"

"Does it matter?"

Marcellus pulled out the chair opposite the women and sat down. He nodded toward the other woman. "Does she talk?"

Jacqui glanced at her fellow operative, and her lips quirked into a knowing smile. "Not much."

Marcellus pulled out his TéléCom and swiped at the screen until he reached the access panel that controlled the security feed. "I think you probably know why I'm here."

Jacqui cocked an eyebrow. "I have a few guesses."

"The general is not going to be happy until you tell us everything you know."

"Is the general *ever* happy?"

Marcellus nearly chuckled at that one but bit his tongue.

He hovered his fingertip over the screen of his TéléCom. "It'll be cleaner if there's no record of what goes on in here."

At that, the other woman finally looked up. But not at Marcellus. Her gaze was trained intensely on the device in front of him.

Jacqui let out a breath, as though she knew that whatever came next was inevitable.

Marcellus plunged his finger down on the screen. A moment later, a voice announced in his ear, "Security microcams disabled."

After that, the words rushed out of Marcellus so quickly, he wasn't even completely sure he was making sense. "I know about my father. Mabelle sent me a message to meet her in Montfer. She told me where she hid the microcam. I watched the footage. I know the Patriarche and my grandfather were behind the exploit bombing in 488. I know they pinned it on my father. I know Julien Bonnefaçon was innocent."

Sometime during his outburst, the silent operative had gone back to tapping on the table, no longer interested in the conversation.

Jacqui smiled at Marcellus again. This one, however, seemed sadder than the last. "That's right. He was."

"But if you knew that, why didn't you clear his name? Why didn't you clear your *own* name?" It was the question that had been bothering him ever since he'd torn out of Ledôme on his moto. "You had the proof. You had the footage from Mabelle. Why did you let him go down for it? You could have released it across the planet. You could have saved him. Saved his life."

"Because it wouldn't have done any good," Jacqui explained.

"But—"

Jacqui held up a gentle hand to stop him. "We had *inclinations* that the Patriarche and the general were behind the exploit attack, but we didn't know for sure. By the time Mabelle was able to get us the footage, it was too late. Your father was already in prison and so was Citizen Rousseau. The rebellion had fizzled out. Our numbers were too low to make another attempt. So we decided to hold on to the footage and wait for a more opportune time to release it. We needed to rebuild. Regroup. Bide our time. That's what we've been doing for the past seventeen years. We've been waiting for the right moment."

Marcellus's brow furrowed. "And *this* is that moment?"

Jacqui looked away, her tranquil expression faltering for just a second. "Not exactly. Things have gotten out of hand. We didn't expect any of this. We definitely didn't *plan* for any of this. The riots, the fights, the chaos. They forced our hand. We knew we had to act soon before things got really out of control. But it was a mistake to move forward before we were ready. We were ill prepared." She glanced around the interrogation room and sighed. "And now we're here."

Marcellus still wasn't following. "What do you mean, you didn't expect this? Didn't you *start* this?"

Jacqui shook her head. "No."

"So the Vangarde *didn't* kill the Premier Enfant to start another revolution?" It was a notion that had been blooming inside of Marcellus for the past few days. And now that he was saying it aloud for the first time, it felt oddly rational.

"We would never do such a thing," Jacqui insisted. "The entire philosophy behind the Vangarde is to bring about change with as little violence as possible. To awaken people. To make them realize we're all equal under the Sols. What has happened here over the past few days is just utter chaos. There's no organization. There's no structure. That's not how we work. It never has been. The death of the Premier Enfant proves that someone *else* is trying to overthrow the Regime. And they're using the Vangarde name to do it."

Marcellus swore he saw a twinkle in Jacqui's golden eyes. As though she were trying to tell him something. He'd known Jacqui for only a few minutes, and yet he already had the feeling that she was the kind of woman who liked to speak in riddles.

"You know who killed Marie," he said with sudden realization, his heart thumping in his chest.

"We do." She nodded once and held Marcellus's gaze as though she were attempting to cushion him from a fall. "And I think you do too."

Marcellus was suddenly sure he would retch again, all over the shiny floor of this interrogation room. He swallowed hard. "I'm sure I have no idea what you're talking about."

But she just smiled a small, cryptic smile that made Marcellus grateful he was already sitting down. He feared his knees would give out from the weight of the message hidden behind that smile.

Yes, you do.

In that very instant, Marcellus was certain he had known it all along.

He'd just been too cowardly to see it. Too cowardly to face it. Life was easier when you shoved things out of the way. When you lived a lie.

"He hates the new Patriarche," Marcellus said numbly, each word feeling like a tiny infidelity on his lips. "Ever since Lyon came to power two years ago, my grandfather has complained about how inept he is. And then the Patriarche decided to help the Usonian rebels. . . ." His mouth went dry as more and more pieces fell into place in his mind. "He sent Commandeur Vernay to Albion to be killed by the mad queen. He went against my grandfather's counsel." Suddenly, the footage from the hidden microcam flickered through Marcellus's mind again. "But even before that, Patriarche Claude forced him to sacrifice his own son."

Jacqui watched Marcellus intently but didn't say a word. Her steady gaze, however, was enough to encourage him to keep going. Keep searching. Keep unraveling.

"He's always talking about how perfect the Regime is. The envy of all of the System Divine."

But that was a lie too.

His grandfather hated the Regime. He hated being under the thumb of the Patriarche. He hated taking orders from a man just because he was born with the right blood in his veins. Doing all the work but getting none of the credit when things went right. And taking all the blame when things went wrong. He hated being stuck in the middle. In the Second Estate with no chance of ever ascending . . .

But is he really capable of murdering a child?

As soon as the question popped into his mind, Marcellus knew the answer. His grandfather was the ultimate strategist. He never did anything without the endgame in mind. And now the trail to that endgame was appearing in front of Marcellus like stepping-stones.

The murder of Marie had led to the cancellation of the Ascension, which had led to the riots in the Marsh. The public execution of Nadette and her alleged association with the Vangarde had escalated the tension. Over the past week, the planet had been plunged into chaos and was now on the brink of another rebellion.

And who better to swoop in and restore peace and order than a general? Who better to rule a planet than someone with his grandfather's experience?

His grandfather knew, just as Marcellus knew, that if you want to overthrow a regime, you have to take out the heir. If you want to bring down a monarchy, you have to make sure there's no one left to fight for it.

But there was something morbidly and disturbingly poetic about his grandfather's actions too.

Patriarche Claude had taken his son from him.

Patriarche Lyon had taken Commandeur Vernay from him.

And now his grandfather had taken something in return.

Marcellus looked into Jacqui's eyes and she nodded once, reading the painful comprehension on his face. But before he could utter another word, the room started to tremble.

Marcellus glanced to the door and knew exactly what was happening.

Chacal had managed to override Marcellus's orders.

The droids were coming back.

He glanced desperately between the two women, but neither of them was looking at him. They were looking at each other. They almost seemed to be speaking in some silent language.

"We're out of time," Jacqui said to the other woman.

The silent operative nodded, and before Marcellus could react, she had reached out and snatched his TéléCom right out from under him.

"Hey!" he said. He leaned across the table to grab it back but stopped abruptly when he saw that the operative was tapping furiously on the screen, accessing panels and programming screens that Marcellus had never even seen before. "What are you doing?" he asked, and then turned to Jacqui. "What is she doing?"

But neither of them answered his question. The thunderous footsteps grew closer. The silent woman continued to hastily tap on the screen of his TéléCom.

Jacqui caught Marcellus's gaze, speaking urgently. "Listen to me. She's ready, but she will need your help."

"What?" Marcellus asked, confused. "Who?"

The other operative suddenly thrust the TéléCom back at Marcellus, gripping his fingers in hers as she whispered in a gruff voice. "Find our Little Lark."

Then the door of the interrogation room unsealed, and two droids marched inside.

- CHAPTER 74 -
ALOUETTE

ALOUETTE PLANTED THE SHOVEL INTO THE WET
dirt and pushed down with her foot. Even in the cold night air, she
was sweating under her tunic and coat. She wiped her damp forehead and, with one hand, dumped another shovelful of dirt onto
the growing mound beside her.

"Should be just a little farther," her father said. "Here, let me help
you."

He started to push himself up but Alouette tossed him a glare. "No.
For the last time, you are in no condition to help me. I can do this."

"But you're hurt," he argued, gesturing to her right hand, which
hung limply at her side. It was still screaming in pain from the pressure of the inspecteur's boot.

"Not as hurt as you," she replied, putting an end to the argument.

Hugo collapsed back down against the tree. Through the light
of the nearby lamp, Alouette could see that even the small effort of
trying to stand up had pained him. He held his head in his hand and
pressed his lips together, as though fighting back a moan.

The inspecteur's final blow to his head had been enough to knock her father unconscious for a few minutes. He was awake and speaking now, but Alouette was still worried about him. She'd shone her flashlight into his eyes, just as Sister Laurel had taught her, and his pupils had reacted normally, but she knew he needed more help. She needed to get him back to the Refuge so Sister Laurel could examine him and perhaps give him one of her healing tinctures.

Alouette dug her shovel into the dirt again. With only one hand, it was slow going, but she was making progress. The hole was almost as deep as her knees now.

After her father had shown her where to find his shovel, hidden under a layer of soft dirt and wet leaves, he'd pointed to this spot, near a diamond-shaped grave. He'd sworn he'd buried something here, but she was starting to fear that someone had already gotten to it.

She was anxious to get out of this clearing. The eerie mist seemed to slink between the trees like phantoms, the strange sounds of the forest echoed around her, and of course, there was Inspecteur Limier.

He was still lying a few mètres away. He wasn't stirring, but he wasn't dead, either. His chest was moving steadily up and down, and every so often, his circuitry would fritz and spark, causing Alouette to jump.

She had no idea when or if the inspecteur would wake up and what condition he would be in if he did. The sooner they could dig up whatever her father had buried and get out of there, the better.

Alouette stepped on the top of the shovel blade, trying to force it farther into the dirt. But it didn't seem to want to move. It was blocked by something.

"That's it," Hugo said, wincing as he bent forward to peer into the hole. "That's the box."

Relieved, Alouette dropped the shovel, sank to her knees, and started pushing the dirt aside with her good hand until finally she could glimpse the surface of PermaSteel below. She fought to get a grip on the edge of the box and heaved it out of the hole, grunting from the effort.

Hugo let out a chuckle. "You definitely have my strength, Little Lark."

Alouette smiled at the compliment and carried the box over to Hugo. He dusted dirt from the top and sides, popped the latches, and opened the lid. Alouette felt the breath hitch in her chest.

The box was filled to the brim with titan. Blocs so shiny and smooth, they sparkled in the lamplight.

Despite the humidity in the air, Alouette's mouth went dry. She knew that titan was very valuable and that the First and Second Estates stored their wealth in blocs like these because they didn't trust digital currency. But she also knew it wasn't the kind of thing you'd normally find in the possession of a Third Estate convict.

She didn't want to ask. She didn't want to start another fight. She was done fighting. But she knew if she didn't ask, the question would always haunt her. "Papa. Did you steal all of this?"

Hugo's head bowed low and Alouette swallowed, preparing for the worst. "Not all of it."

His answer surprised her. "What?"

"Not this." Hugo reached deep into the bottom of the box and pulled out a long, tapered object that Alouette immediately recognized.

"Another candlestick?"

"They come in pairs," Hugo explained. "This one has the tracker." He tapped the top of the candlestick in his hand and then pointed at the matching one still lying on the ground nearby. "And that one has the map. They're designed to help you find your way back to something."

"And you didn't steal them?"

A far-off look passed over his face. "No. I didn't. They were given to me. As a gift."

She waited for her father to elaborate, but he didn't. Instead, he reached for his sac and began stuffing the titan blocs inside, retreating back into his usual silence.

Alouette was starting to wonder if she would ever know *all* of her father's secrets.

"Papa—" she began to say, but was cut off by the sound of leaves crunching.

They both looked toward the fallen inspecteur, only to find the ground empty where he once lay.

Alouette leapt to her feet and spun in a circle, her heart starting to pound again. "Where is he? Where did he go?"

"I don't know." Hugo hurriedly cinched up the sac and threw it over his shoulder. "But we need to get out of here."

Despite his condition, he was on his feet in a flash. He grabbed Alouette by the elbow and began to pull her toward the trees. "Let's go. We won't be able to outrun his transporteur in open terrain, but we can hide in the forest and wait until it's safe to escape."

Alouette stopped walking and tweaked her mouth into a knowing smile.

Hugo turned around. "What?"

"Outrun him?" she repeated playfully. "Silly Papa. We don't have to *run*."

Alouette pulled the stolen moto to a stop between Fret 7 and the entrance to the Marsh. It had been difficult to steer the bike with only one hand, but she'd somehow managed to get herself and her father home in one piece. Maybe she was finally starting to get a hang of this moto-driving thing. She climbed off the bike and beamed back at her father, who looked a little ruffled by the ride.

He clutched his sac tightly to his chest. "Where did you learn how to drive one of these?"

Alouette opened her mouth to explain, but her father held up a hand.

"You know what? I don't think I want to know."

Alouette let out a deep, full belly laugh. It felt so good to laugh with her father again. To *be* with him again. The notion that she'd almost lost him for good made her chest ache.

But then her laughter subsided as she took in her father's kind, familiar face with all its lines and creases and untold stories.

"I'm so sorry, Papa," Alouette blurted out. "I'm sorry for everything I said yesterday. You're a good man. I know that now. I've always known that. I just . . . I don't know. I guess I got confused. I found out about the prisoner tattoos and then I found your candlestick and those horrible people said you weren't my real father and then Limier said—"

Hugo pulled her to him and enveloped her in his huge arms. "Hush, Little Lark," he said again, and this time the words did calm her. She took deep breaths, inhaling the musty scent of his shirt. It reminded her of her childhood. It reminded her of the Refuge. It reminded her of home.

"I'm sorry to say, it's all true," Hugo said. His voice was so soft, Alouette was convinced she hadn't heard him correctly.

She pulled back and looked at him.

"It's true," he repeated. "I'm not your father. At least, not your real father. But I loved your mother. More than you'll ever know." He tapped at his temple and smiled. "More than this lowly brain can ever put into words. And when I met you, as soon as I saw you, I loved you with all of my heart."

Alouette felt a lump form in her throat. These were the words she'd been waiting for almost her entire life. The story she'd longed for her father to tell. The truth she'd craved more than anything.

Hugo reached out and touched Alouette's cheek. "A good man once gave me the gift of virtue. But you gave me the gift of love, Alouette. You were like the lark, singing in a new morning for me. My poor old heart, which had almost died in that prison, which went into hiding for too long, it came alive again. First with your mother, and then with you."

"Did she really give me to those horrible people?" Alouette asked, shuddering at the memory of that man and woman in the forest saying those dreadful things about her mother.

"Yes, but only because she couldn't afford to take care of you. She had every intention of coming back to get you. But then she fell very ill. I promised her I would find you and take care of you. I gave the Renards money only so that they would leave us alone. They are greedy, depraved people." He shook his head and rubbed at his eyes. "They treated you badly, Alouette. Very badly indeed. And I'll never forgive myself for not coming to find you sooner. I think that's why you don't remember any of it. You buried those years far away. Deep inside. And I let you, because I didn't want you to remember. When I came to get you in Montfer, I found you wandering alone in those creepy boglands, collecting reeds for them. You were terrified. Your skin was sore and blistered. You had bruises." His words hitched in his throat. "Sometimes when I look at you, I still see that child lost in the mist. Skin and bones. Frailer than a little bird."

A tear rolled down Hugo's weathered cheek. The sight of it caused the lump in Alouette's throat to rise up, and tears pooled in her own eyes as well.

And then, suddenly, she could see it. The inn. The place under the table where they made her sleep. The back of Madame Renard's hand before it would strike her cheek. The terrifying boglands where she would be sent with her pail. There were two other little girls there. She remembered them now. She remembered their bowls of food, always bigger and fuller than Alouette's. And yet, in their eyes, she could see they were hungry and frightened too.

The name from the forest suddenly came back to her.

Chatine.

Then another name.

Azelle.

And then . . .

"Madeline," she whispered. It sounded curious yet familiar on her lips.

Hugo nodded. "Your mother loved that name. I was so sad to have to change it. But I couldn't risk anyone finding us."

He reached for her hand and squeezed it. Alouette looked up into her father's tender brown eyes.

The same eyes that had come to take her away from there.

She could see that night now too.

His smile. The way he'd emerged like a ghost from the mist and helped her with her heavy pail. She remembered the kindness in his voice. A kindness that she'd never heard before. She remembered the doll that he'd brought her, Katrina. How she'd had to fight for it when one of the other girls—Chatine or Azelle?—had tried to steal it from her.

Then she remembered running.

Running so fast and for so long.

And even though she had no idea where they were going, somehow she'd known that they were running to safety.

To love.

To her own new morning.

She pulled on her father's hand and began to walk toward the entrance of Fret 7. "C'mon, Papa. We'll get you back home. Sister Laurel will clean you up and give you something for the pain."

But her father didn't move. And when Alouette turned back to look at him, she saw a heaviness in his eyes. "Little Lark, I'm not going back."

"What?" Alouette asked. "Why not?"

"I told you, it's not safe anymore. Inspecteur Limier is still out there somewhere. And as long as he's alive, he will continue to hunt me down. I will always be a fugitive here. I can't stay on Laterre."

Alouette swallowed hard and stood up taller, bracing herself for what she was about to say next. "Then we'll go to Reichenstat. *Together.*"

Her father shook his head as he pulled two titan blocs from his sac and slipped them into the pocket of Alouette's coat. "Laterre is your home." He lifted his hand to his chest. "I have a feeling, right here, that you will do great things. With your love and your trust and your intelligence, all the gifts the sisters have given you, you will do great things. You, Alouette, are needed here. This place," he said, motioning to the darkened Fret and murky skies. "This place needs you."

"But I want to be with you," she said, her voice desperate and shaking. "I can't lose you."

Hugo smiled. "I know. But I promised your mother I would keep you safe, and as we've both seen tonight, I can no longer do that if we are together. I have to make the right choice for you. And right now that choice is to leave you in the protection of the sisters. They will take care of you." Despite the tears still rolling down his cheeks, Hugo's lips curved into a smile. "They will teach you how to fly, Little Lark."

Alouette lunged for her father, crashing into his massive chest and wrapping her arms around him. She was crying now with huge, heaving sobs.

Because, suddenly, she knew.

She knew there was nothing she could say to make him stay. But she also knew—she knew deep in her sad, devastated heart—that she was going to let him go. She *had* to let him go.

Because *she* had to stay.

Hugo could take care of himself; she realized that now. He could protect himself like he'd always done. Like he'd always protected her, too. But now it was the sisters who needed protecting. Alouette had brought danger too close to their quiet and peaceful world. She'd brought danger too close to their sacred library.

And she knew she had to keep them both safe.

But to do that, she had to let her father go.

"I love you, Papa," she murmured as her warm tears soaked his shirt.

Hugo bent down and kissed the top of her head one last time. "I love you too, Little Lark."

CHAPTER 75

CHATINE

THE WRECKAGE CRACKLED AND HISSED AS CHATINE disembarked the combatteur behind the general. The view from above as the structure vaporized into a blazing ball of light before her eyes was nothing compared to the view right now. On solid ground. As the remaining strands of metal continued to burn and breathe smoke into the air.

Chatine had never seen fire before. It wasn't commonly used on Laterre. Except, she supposed, for things like this. For destruction. For death. But she felt oddly entranced by the flames. As though they were calling her, pulling her in, reminding her that they were one. She and the flames. They were the same. The Ministère might have brought about the destruction, but this was still their fault.

The pack of droids that had been sent into the wreckage to search for survivors was just now emerging from the smoking rubble.

"Well?" the general asked as they settled into formation in front of him. He actually sounded anxious. "What did you find?"

Chatine inhaled sharply, expecting the worst. She always expected the worst. It was how she'd lived her life. In constant preparation for the worst possible outcome.

And now it had come.

The only difference was, this time *she* had chosen it herself.

"No human remains found," one of the droids reported in that chilling robotic tone.

Chatine exhaled.

"What?!" the general thundered. "How is that possible? Did they escape? Were they somehow tipped off?" He tossed a scathing look toward Chatine.

"Unknown," the basher replied. "The structure appeared to be completely abandoned, apart from a storeroom filled with illegal bottles of weed wine, which were mostly destroyed. There was no evidence of Vangarde activity."

The general wheeled on Chatine. His face was no longer the stoic statue she had come to recognize from the Universal Alerts. It was now as angry as the fire raging behind him. "So you're saying this old bateau was *not* the Vangarde base?"

Chatine honestly couldn't tell if the general was speaking to her or to the droid. But it didn't matter. She curled her lips into her signature goading grin. It was probably the last time she would ever grin in her life. She had to make the most of it. "Oh, I'm sorry, General," she began, feigning confusion. "Did you want the *Vangarde* base? I thought you said the *Délabré* base. Oops. Wrong bad guys. My mistake."

The anger in the general's face deepened, and the storm in his eyes grew more violent, until Chatine was certain she was about to get slapped. Or worse. But she held her ground. She didn't stir. She didn't even flinch. She just stood there and, once again, prepared for the worst.

The general's hands balled into fists. The tendons in his neck swelled. But when he opened his mouth, all Chatine could hear was sadness. Sadness and disappointment. "Arrest her," he said with a shake of his head. "Get her out of my sight."

As the lead droid stalked toward her, Chatine noticed it arming its weapon and hoisting it up, in case she tried to run. And of course they would expect her to run. The old Chatine would have run. *Théo* would have run. But where was she going to go now? There was nowhere left to run.

So she let the basher bind her wrists. She let it lead her away from what was left of the Grotte, toward the awaiting Policier patroleur. She let herself be guided inside.

Because this was her fate.

This had always been her fate, since the day she was born. Since the moment the médecin had implanted the Skin in her arm and the audio chip in her ear, this had been decided as her final stop.

Regardless of all the dreams she'd built, all the trinkets she'd stolen, all the plans she'd made to one day make it to Usonia, somewhere deep inside, Chatine had always known she was destined to end up on the moon.

As the patroleur sped away from the run-down docks and the smoking remains of the Délabré headquarters, Chatine could see the colossal, shadowy outlines of the Frets looming in the distance. Still just as hideous. Still rotting away like corpses in the wet ground. But still standing.

And, for the first time in her life, the sight of them made her smile.

- CHAPTER 76 -
ALOUETTE

ALOUETTE GLANCED UP AT THE STARLESS BLACK SKY. Just in front of her, she could see the shadowy, jagged edges of the roof that had once covered the huge cargo freightship that now served as the marketplace for the Frets. The ceiling had almost completely rusted away.

Her heart, Alouette realized, was like that roof now, with a huge, irreparable hole right at its center.

He was gone.

Her father was gone.

And she had stayed.

In spite of the inconsolable ache in her chest, she knew she'd done the right thing. She *did* belong here. Her place wasn't on the foreign, frozen lands of Reichenstat. Her place was on Laterre with the sisters.

She pulled her devotion beads out from the front of her tunic and stared at the engraving on the metal tag, remembering Jacqui's words to her.

"You're one of us now and you're strong, Little Lark."

From this day forward, Alouette was going to be the sister she'd always dreamed of being. A good and diligent sister. A loyal and truthful sister. Just like the women who'd raised her. She would devote herself to a life of peace, contemplation, and study. And when she was considered ready, Alouette would help maintain and protect the Chronicles of the Sisterhood.

But most of all, she would protect *them*.

The sisters.

This would now be her most sacred task.

Alouette would make sure nothing disturbed their home or their safety. Nothing interfered with their simple life of thought and books and the written word.

Alouette glanced up again to see the color of the sky starting to turn from the darkest black to a soft, silvery gray. Dawn was here. The night was over. The sisters would soon be waking up. They would be hungry and needing a good meal before they went into Assemblée. And Alouette would be the one to give that to them now.

She laid a single kiss on her devotion beads and dropped them against the front of her coat. Then she continued into Fret 7 and navigated down the long hallways and dark corners that had once seemed like an endless maze. Her feet were already starting to remember the way. Her mind was starting to understand the pattern. She could sense when the mechanical room was getting closer.

And she could also sense the footsteps behind her.

Rhythmic and mindful. Like a hunter stalking prey.

Limier.

Her pulse quickened.

She knew she had to lose him. Alouette picked up her pace until she was running. She turned corners at random, climbed stairwells she'd never been in before, and dashed down corridors that all started to blend together.

But she could still hear those footsteps behind her at every turn, on every step. They were echoing the sound of her own pounding heart. *Thump. Thump. Thump.* They were getting closer.

Alouette berated herself for leaving the Renards' rayonette back at the graveyard. She could have used it again now. She reached into her tool belt and fumbled for the first thing she could find. Her screwdriver.

She stopped in her tracks.

The footsteps halted an instant later.

She spun around, wielding the screwdriver like a weapon, before dropping it to the floor.

"Marcellus."

His name slipped out like a whisper, and for a moment, the briefest of moments, Alouette felt as if the hole in her heart had closed over just a little. But then something unsettling occurred to her. He seemed to have been waiting for her near the mechanical room. But she'd never told him where she lived.

"How did you find me?" she asked.

He walked toward her. But there was something hesitant and guarded about his step, as though *he* were the one afraid of *her*.

"I followed the blood," he replied vacantly.

"The blood?"

"That first time we met in the hallway. You told me you'd followed my drops of blood. That's how you'd found me. They're mostly gone now. Dried up. But I could still make out traces."

Alouette's heart started to race again as she remembered the little crimson droplets leading out from the mechanical room. Had she already failed in her new sacred task? Had he already found the Refuge? Were the sisters in danger?

Sister Jacqui had said something earlier about Marcellus not being a threat to them, but how could she possibly know that? She didn't even know him.

Alouette desperately studied Marcellus's face, searching for clues.

But his expression was soft, almost pensive. As though he were in some kind of trance.

He stopped in front of her, reached out, and gently scooped the end of her devotion beads into his palm. He stared down at the metal tag. "Little Lark," he said aloud, like he was piecing something together.

Alouette swallowed, now certain there was something wrong. Suspicion flashed in his eyes.

"Marcellus, are you all right?"

He blinked and finally looked at her. "You were afraid of me," he said flatly.

"What?"

"Back at the Défecteur camp, when you found out my grandfather was General Bonnefaçon, you looked genuinely afraid. I thought it was because you were a Défecteur and you were scared I would report you and bring you in."

"A Défecteur?"

Marcellus shook his head. "But it turns out you're not a Défecteur, are you? You're something *else*." He spat out the last word. "So why? Why were you scared back there at the camp? That was the only part that didn't make sense to me."

The same fear he was talking about was suddenly back inside of her, tearing and knotting its way through her chest.

"I don't underst—" Alouette began.

"And this," he said, nodding toward her string of devotion beads. "You showed it to me. You made me read it. You revealed your nickname willingly."

Alouette's brow furrowed. "Marcellus. What are you talking about?"

Marcellus latched on to her gaze and stared at her with such a deep intensity that, for a moment, Alouette felt light-headed. "You really don't know, do you?" he said.

"Don't know what?"

Then something else flashed in his eyes. It looked like anger. "Don't mess around with me! I can't stand to have anyone else lie to me. Especially not you. I can't . . ." His voice broke and Alouette saw moisture spring to his eyes. He dropped her devotion beads and swatted at his tears with the back of his hand.

"Hey. Shhh. It's okay." She reached up and rested a palm on his cheek. At first he startled at her touch, but then he seemed to shudder into it. Like her small, delicate palm was the only thing holding him up.

"What's going on?" she asked.

"I just came from the Precinct. Where we've detained two Vangarde operatives." His voice was hesitant, halting. As he spoke, he watched her face with vigilance, as though waiting for her to give him permission to continue.

"Yes," she prompted.

His eyes narrowed. "The Vangarde is a long-time enemy of the Regime." He paused again, scrutinizing her. "They are the ones responsible for the Rebellion of 488. Seventeen years ago. You know, the one led by Citizen Rousseau?"

Questions bubble and churned inside Alouette. Had the boy lost his mind? What on Laterre was he talking about? A rebellion? The Vangarde? Citizen who? She'd never read anything in the Chronicles about that. If there had been a rebellion on Laterre, the sisters would have told her about it. Principale Francine would have made her study it to exhaustion. Analyze all the angles. The politics, the economics, the strategy. Just like she did for all those wars on the First World.

Marcellus sighed, reached into his pocket, and pulled out a strange object. To Alouette, it looked like a folded-up piece of paper. But when he unfurled it, swiped against the surface, and made it glow to life, Alouette realized it was a TéléCom, the device the Second Estate used to communicate.

He tapped the screen a few times and turned it around to face Alouette.

"Do you recognize these women?"

Alouette took one look and sucked in a sharp breath. Sister Jacqui and Sister Denise were staring back at her from the screen. Except they didn't look like themselves. Their faces were stony and grim. Jacqui's twinkly smile was gone.

Alouette shot a scathing look at Marcellus. "What is going on? What did you do with the sisters? Why do you have pictures of them on your TéléCom?" Then she felt a lump form in her throat. "Was it me? Did you find them because of me?"

"Alouette," Marcellus said in a sharp tone that felt like a slap. "These are the operatives that we detained. They were captured last night, trying to break into the warden's office at the Ministère. They were attempting to hack Bastille's security systems." He nodded down at the screen and then stared back at Alouette. "There's no doubt. These women are members of the Vangarde."

Break into the warden's office?

At the Ministère?

To hack into Bastille's security systems?

But that was nonsense! Sister Jacqui and Sister Denise couldn't go to the Ministère. That was in Ledôme, and only the First and Second Estates and authorized members of the Third Estate could enter Ledôme. The sisters didn't even have Skins. How would they ever have gotten past the Policier and droids at the checkpoints, let alone the ones posted at the Ministère?

But then, for a moment, Alouette flashed back to the last time she saw Jacqui and Denise. It was only yesterday. Alouette was sitting on Jacqui's bed, watching the two sisters leave, asking to know where they were going.

"That, I'm afraid, I'm not allowed to tell you," Sister Jacqui had said.

Alouette shook her head. No. She would not believe it. She refused to believe it. The sisters were . . . *sisters*. They read and studied and ate meals in Grateful Silence.

They weren't *operatives* of this Vangarde whatever.

They didn't try to hack security systems or lead rebellions.

"Give me that," Alouette blurted out.

But as she grabbed the TéléCom from Marcellus to get a better look, the device vibrated in her hand and suddenly the two pictures of the sisters disappeared into a haze of pixels.

"Where did they—"

The words caught in her throat because, just then, like a puff of steam from her father's kettle, the pixels rearranged themselves and a message blinked onto the screen.

When the lark flies home, the Regime will fall.

Alouette's disbelieving eyes darted across the bright white letters.

"What is that?" Marcellus asked, and before Alouette could even start to comprehend what the message meant, Marcellus had grabbed the TéléCom back.

But as soon as it was in his hands again, the letters evaporated.

Marcellus shook and prodded the device. "Where did it go? What *was* that?" His eyes darted up to meet Alouette's. "It was some sort of message, wasn't it? What did it say?"

Frustration bloomed in Alouette's chest. Frustration and fear and confusion. "I'm the one who can read"—she yanked the TéléCom back from him—"so give it to me."

The TéléCom vibrated again, and then there it was.

That same cryptic message.

When the lark flies home, the Regime will fall.

What did it mean? Was she the "lark" it was referencing? Alouette's mind whirled with questions as her gaze roved back and forth over the words.

The meaningless words.

"The operative," Marcellus blurted out, as if a realization had suddenly dawned on him. "The one with the scars on her face. *She* did this. She did something to my TéléCom back in the interrogation room. She must have hacked it. She told me to find you. She was sending you that message. Let me see that."

Marcellus lunged forward and yanked the TéléCom back from Alouette. The words evaporated yet again. Curiously, Marcellus moved the TéléCom toward Alouette. The message returned.

"Your beads," Marcellus said absently.

Alouette's gaze snapped up, her fingers reaching protectively toward her devotion beads. "What?"

"They're triggering the message somehow. Look."

Both of them watched silently as Marcellus continued to move the TéléCom back and forth. Each time the device got closer to Alouette, the mysterious words would appear, only to disintegrate into a mist of pixels again when he pulled it away.

Marcellus shook his head. "The metal tag must have some kind of sensor implanted or—"

"Stop!" Alouette jumped back, away from the TéléCom. "Arrête. You don't know what you're talking about."

"Alouette," Marcellus said, trying to take a step toward her, but she retreated farther. "I'm sorry. I thought you knew. I thought you were working with them. I thought you were sent to—"

"No! Please stop! This is just some big mistake."

"Alouette, there's no mistake. I—"

But Alouette didn't wait for him to finish. She pushed past him and took off down the hallway. Suddenly it was like a force from somewhere else was moving her. She had to get away from him. Away from his piercing eyes and ridiculous accusations.

"Alouette. Wait!" she heard Marcellus shout behind her. "Please. Stop!"

But she didn't stop. Not for a second. She kept running. Back down the corridors and stairwells that had led her here. It was like the mechanical room—the Refuge, her home—was a target and she was a beam of light heading straight toward it.

She unlocked the air vent and shot down the ladder, barging into the Refuge. She knew exactly where she was going. She knew exactly what she needed to do to prove Marcellus wrong.

The main hallway of the Refuge was empty. The sisters must still be asleep. She charged forward, toward the heavy wooden door at the end. The one that had always remained closed to her. The one she'd never been allowed to pass through.

"Not until you're a sister," she'd always been told.

Well, she was a sister now. She'd been given the beads. She had every right to enter the Assemblée room. She passed by the hallway that led to the sisters' bedrooms. She passed by the entrance to the common room. She passed by the kitchen.

But her gaze never left that door.

Principale Francine suddenly appeared from the dining room, her eyes red-rimmed and fatigued. As though she'd been up all night.

"Alouette," she said in her usual stern tone that left no room for negotiations. "Please, come with me."

But Alouette kept going.

She was done talking.

She was done following orders.

She was done being lied to.

She reached the door to the Assemblée room, grabbed the handle, and flung it open, practically leaping back at the sight of what was on the other side.

A second door.

This one made of thick, riveted steel. Just like the door that led to the entrance of the Refuge.

Another door?

For a moment Alouette hesitated. But then her determination returned full force. She reached out and twisted the large, circular handle.

"Alouette!" Principale Francine's voice was even sharper now. She was closing in behind her. "Stop."

That word. It fueled Alouette. It gave her strength.

She was done stopping.

She took a deep breath, steeled herself, and pushed against the door with all her might. The door flew open, and Alouette stumbled into the room.

Into a dream.

Into another world.

Everywhere she looked there were screens. Screens embedded into the walls. Screens spread across desktops. Screens stacked high to the ceiling. They all looked like the monitor that Alouette used to watch in the vestibule, except these screens didn't show just the dingy, wet, boring mechanical room outside the Refuge. They showed everything.

Everything.

The hallways of the Frets. The stalls of the Marsh. The ominous cube-shaped building of the Precinct. There even appeared to be flickering images from inside Ledôme. There were towns Alouette had never seen before. Landscapes she'd only ever read about in the Chronicles.

And sitting among all those screens were the sisters.

The sisters whom Alouette had known for almost her entire life.

The sisters she had thought were *sleeping.* Waiting to eat breakfast in silence so they could begin their day of peaceful contemplation.

Now they were all staring at her.

Alouette turned in a slow, stunned circle, attempting to take it all in. Wires and cables crisscrossed the floor, strange lights blinked across complicated circuit boards, invisible speakers hummed and chattered. Above a tall shelf filled to the brim with books and papers, an enormous clock displayed the time to the millisecond. By the door, there was a giant pinboard covered with scribbled notes and hand-sketched drawings. And in the dead center of the room, hovering above a solid black pedestal, a hologram map glowed bright and luminous.

But unlike the hologram Alouette had found inside her father's candlestick, this map was not displaying the planet of Laterre.

It was displaying the great, spinning orb of Bastille.

Laterre's only moon.

"They were attempting to hack Bastille's security systems."

"Little Lark," came a voice behind her. Alouette startled and turned to see Principale Francine standing there. But she wasn't looking disapprovingly over her glasses at Alouette, the way she usually did. Instead, Alouette saw something gentle in her eyes. Almost sympathetic. "Sit down. We need to talk."

- CHAPTER 77 -
MARCELLUS

THE GRAND BOULEVARD RUNNING THROUGH THE center of Ledôme the next morning was a sea of red.

Red hats, red dresses, red suits, red shoes and shawls. Marcellus himself was dressed head to toe in the color, as was every other aide, advisor, and Ministère official sitting around him on the stage that had been erected at the end of the boulevard. Spectators had gathered from across Ledôme, filling the wide avenue all the way to the Paresse Tower, with its latticed metalwork and soaring antennae glinting in the early Sol-light.

Looking out over the somber, scarlet crowds, Marcellus thought of Sol 2 and how its vivid red glow had become *this*.

Laterre's official color of mourning.

The color of death.

Marcellus's gaze slipped over to the small coffin that had been placed in the center of the stage. It was so impossibly tiny. Just big enough for the body of a little girl. A little girl who would have been three years old today.

The Premier Enfant.

Marcellus still couldn't believe it. Only last week, little Marie Paresse had been so alive. Squealing and babbling through brunch. Watching him fold a napkin into a tiny bird.

Her smile so bright. Her dark curls so exuberant.

And now this.

A sleek, bloodred coffin.

A sudden drumroll interrupted his thoughts. The Paresse family and their entourage had arrived. Marcellus stood with the rest of the officials as the Patriarche, the Matrone, and their top advisors, including General Bonnefaçon, exited their fleet of cruiseurs and ascended the steps to the stage.

The Patriarche, like Marcellus and his grandfather, wore the red funeral uniform with its double rows of titan buttons and ceremonial epaulets, while the Matrone was dressed in a floor-length, pure-silk gown of deep scarlet. Her matching veil fluttered gently in Ledôme's artificial breeze.

As the entourage filed past, the Matrone wept into a red silk handkerchief and the Patriarche stopped to receive condolences from the officials onstage.

"I'm deeply sorry for your loss, Monsieur Patriarche," Marcellus said as he shook the man's hand, bowing his head in respect.

The Patriarche nodded and spoke in a low, throaty voice. "Your grandfather informs me that two of the governess's conspirators were apprehended."

"Yes, Monsieur Patriarche."

"Good work." He gripped Marcellus's hand tighter. "Do whatever it takes to make them talk. I want *every* one of those Vangarde murderers found."

Marcellus swallowed hard and repeated, "Yes, Monsieur Patriarche."

Lyon Paresse released his hand and swept onward, taking his position between the Matrone and the pedestal that held his daughter's tiny casket.

Marcellus looked up to see his grandfather making his way toward him. He stiffened, knowing he would have to sit next to him for the entire ceremony.

His left hand instinctively reached for his right little finger. For the spot where his mother's ring used to be. The ring was still gone, but he rubbed the bare skin there anyway, trying to summon strength.

"A sad day," the general whispered as he took his place next to Marcellus.

Marcellus felt dizzy. Nauseous. The heavy wool of his scarlet uniform itched and grasped at his neck. How could his grandfather even show his face at this funeral when he was the one responsible for it? Did his evil truly run that deep?

"*I said* sad day," the general repeated, an edge of irritation in his tone.

"Yes, sir. Very sad."

It made Marcellus sick to say these words, sick to the very pit of his stomach to call his grandfather "sir."

To speak to him at all.

But he couldn't let on what he knew.

He needed the general to trust him.

"Inspecteur Limier is still missing in action," the general informed Marcellus in a low tone so no one around them could hear. "His TéléCom is not responding to any connection attempts. His last known location was just outside the Forest Verdure. I'm sending out a search party this afternoon."

Marcellus nodded. "Very good." Then, upon feeling his grandfather's scrutinizing gaze on the side of his face, he forced himself to add, "I hope they find the inspecteur soon."

The drumroll built to a spectacular finale and everyone onstage took their seats. The red crowd of mourners on the boulevard hushed and stilled.

An officiant in a billowing scarlet robe stepped up to a titan-plated lectern at the front of the stage. "We are gathered here today to pay our last respects to Marie Violette Justine Paresse, our dearly beloved and now tragically departed Premier Enfant." His voice boomed out across the stage, down the boulevard, and into every audio chip across Laterre. The Third Estate were all watching the funeral live on their Skins. "She was taken from us far too soon, but her effervescent light will live on in our System Divine."

After the officiant concluded his eulogy, First Estate family members and other officials stepped up to the lectern, one after another, to offer their tributes. The Matrone was too overcome with tears to speak, but the Patriarche delivered a few somber words, praising his daughter's "sparkle and joy" and everything she'd brought to the Paresse family in her short time on Laterre.

Marcellus did not look at his grandfather once through the whole ceremony.

He couldn't.

He wouldn't.

Finally, the eulogies came to a close, and Marie's casket was slowly raised until it was standing upright on the pedestal. A sound, which started as a low hum, crescendoed into a thundering roar as the coffin began to shake.

"Vive Laterre and vive the Premier Enfant," the officiant said in closing. "May she rest with the Sols."

There was a bright orange flash as the accélérateurs under the casket ignited and the stabilizeurs initiated. Then the stage beneath Marcellus began to shudder. Everyone looked up, and an entranced hush fell over the crowd as the roof of Ledôme eased open.

Mètre by mètre, the vibrant blue TéléSky gave way to the dreary cloud cover of Laterre. A blast of cold, damp air shot downward onto the Grand Boulevard, blowing and blustering at all the red dresses and scarlet veils below.

Finally, there was a deafening boom and the Premier Enfant's coffin took flight.

It launched like a missile through the warm air of Ledôme and out through the gash in the artificial sky.

On its direct trajectory to Sol 2.

Marcellus watched as the dazzling trails from the accélérateurs disappeared into the clouds, leaving behind a faint and ghostly orange glow.

After the light had faded, the roof slowly shuddered back into place, and once again Ledôme was encapsulated in the blinding blue of the TéléSky.

As Marcellus gazed up at the three artificial Sols, he thought about the Premier Enfant.

He thought about her murder.

He thought about the Vangarde, the riots and mayhem that had erupted since Marie's death, the two operatives still being held in the Precinct, where they would be relentlessly interrogated until they gave up the location of their base.

He thought about Alouette.

She hadn't known that she'd been living with the Vangarde. That much Marcellus was certain of now. And yet, they had clearly been preparing her for something.

"She's ready, but she will need your help."

Ready for what? What was Marcellus supposed to do? What help did they want him to offer? And what had that message on his TéléCom said?

They obviously already had at least some level of access to the Ministère. He was confident that was why Alouette didn't have a profile in the Communiqué. Because the Vangarde had erased it.

If the Vangarde could delete files from a Ministère database, Marcellus wondered what else they could do. What else did they have access to? Was it possible they were watching them all right now?

And then, just as had been happening all morning, his thoughts finally drifted back to Laterre.

Its fate, much like his own, seemed so uncertain now.

How would he ever go on living the same way? How would he ever be able to look his grandfather in the eye again? What would happen if the Vangarde made another attempt to break Citizen Rousseau out of Bastille? And what would that mean for the Regime, if they somehow managed to succeed?

The officials on the stage rose to their feet and followed the Paresse family off the stage. Marcellus walked slowly behind his grandfather, keeping his gaze trained on the heels of the general's shiny black boots.

It was the place he'd always known. The footsteps that had always guided him.

Before his world had shattered.

Before he'd learned the truth.

But, as he followed the procession down the Grand Boulevard and his gaze drifted over the red sea of mourners, for the first time in his life, Marcellus felt an invigorating rush of certainty.

He might not know what was going to happen to this planet, or how he fit into that uncertain future, but he did know one thing.

He knew which side he was on.

CHAPTER 78

CHATINE

CHATINE BIT BACK A SCREAM AS THE ORANGE LASER sliced into her skin, sending a bolt of hot, searing pain through her. The clamp crushed around her arm. She heard a sizzle and smelled burning flesh, and then it was over.

The machine withdrew and Chatine looked down at the five metallic bumps it had left behind. She tried to run her fingertips over them but pulled back when her skin cried out in agony.

"Prisoner 51562," came the voice of a droid behind her. "This way."

She shuffled away from the machine and followed the droid's voice down the hallway, walking as well as she could with the cuffs around her ankles. She silently took her place at the end of the long line of people waiting to board the voyageur bound for Bastille.

Prisoner 5.1.5.6.2.

That was who she was now. That was who she'd become. Théo was gone. Chatine was gone. They'd both died in that explosion. They'd both died saving the Frets. Prisoner 5.1.5.6.2. was who had crawled out of the smoky remains.

It was better this way.

Her parents had never loved Chatine.

Roche thought Théo was a traitor.

And Marcellus despised them both.

Why not start over with a brand-new identity? One that was tattooed right into her arm so she never forgot. Never forgot where she'd come from. Where she belonged. What she'd done.

Earlier this morning, she'd been brought into the prisoner transport center. She'd been stripped of her normal clothes. Her hooded coat and black pants—with their chain links and metal stitches— were replaced with a threadbare blue uniform. The same uniform she'd seen on Marcellus's father in the morgue all those days ago.

Her hair had been ripped from its knot at the base of her neck and shorn off. As she'd watched her long, light brown locks fall to the floor and wash down a nearby drain, she'd thought about how long it had taken her to grow them. Two hundred largs gone. Just like that.

Not that she needed largs where she was going.

All she needed was this tattoo.

"OWWWWWW!" she heard a voice cry, and she turned around to see Roche standing next to the machine, his arm outstretched, angry tears in his eyes.

She felt the uncontrollable urge to run to him, to shove the device away, to hold him until he stopped crying. But of course, she didn't. She'd sealed both of their fates. There was nothing she could do about that now.

At least, she thought, *I can do my best to protect him up there.*

When the machine was finished and the scrawny boy was forever marked, he brushed the tears away with the back of his hand as the droid led him—prisoner 5.1.5.6.3.—to stand behind Chatine. She turned to look at him. It was the first time they'd been face-to-face since she'd betrayed him at the Precinct.

"Roche," she whispered, "listen to me. I'm sorry for what happened. I thought you were just playing around when you talked about working for the Vangarde. I never thought—"

Roche shuffled his bound feet until his body was turned away from her. He wouldn't look at her. He wouldn't even acknowledge her.

"Roche, please. I—"

"No talking," a nearby droid thundered. "Face forward."

Chatine sighed and turned. But she was not giving up. She would make it up to Roche. That much, she promised herself. And she certainly had plenty of time to do it. Her sentencing had been pronounced the moment she'd arrived at the prisoner transport center this morning.

Twenty-five years.

Twenty-five years in those freezing-cold exploits. Twenty-five years in those dark, dirty cells. She'd heard stories about those cells. They made the couchettes sound like the Grand Palais. Some people even claimed that they were haunted. That when you died on the moon, your spirit couldn't get to the Sols. So it just stayed there forever. Roaming the halls.

"All prisoners walk forward!" the basher commanded.

The line in front of her started to move. Chatine scuffled her feet along the floor, trying to keep pace with the person in front of her.

As she walked, her thumb drifted to the index finger of her right hand, rubbing at the smooth metal of Marcellus's ring. She'd managed to sneak it past the droids by hiding it under her tongue during her processing.

Behind her, she could hear soft whimpers. Roche was crying again.

"Hey," she whispered over her shoulder. "Didn't you say your parents were revolutionary spies?"

The whimpers stopped, but Roche made no reply.

Chatine passed by a droid whose glowing orange eyes seemed to follow her. When she'd moved far enough away, she went on, "And didn't you say they were captured in the line of duty?"

Still no response. Just the quiet shuffling of feet.

"Maybe you'll see them up there," Chatine said.

Chatine heard Roche sniffle, and she allowed herself the tiniest of smiles.

The hallway spilled out onto a loading dock where a voyageur awaited them, its huge body and sleek silver wings hovered just above the ground. Chatine glanced up at the morning mist that had settled around the city. She felt a single drop of rain on the tip of her nose. For some reason, it made her feel hopeful.

She boarded the vessel into the passenger hold, a dim chamber with two rows of PermaSteel jump seats. As the restraints were fastened around her chest, Chatine remarked on how, before this week, she'd never ridden in any sort of transportation, apart from the bateau that had brought her family from Montfer to Vallonay ten years ago. And now, in only the past few days, she'd ridden in a patroleur, a cruiseur, a moto, a combatteur, and now a voyageur.

Not bad for your last week on Laterre.

The ship rumbled beneath her, and Chatine felt herself thrust against the bottom of her seat. Her stomach lurched, and for a few moments, there was nothing but the strange sensation of falling upward.

Chatine turned her head toward the window just in time to see the voyageur plunge into the permanent layer of clouds that surrounded Laterre. The view from the window went from murky gray—the color that had shadowed her entire life—to a pure, perfect white. It was so bright and clean and soothing, Chatine felt as though she were staring not into a color, but into the absence of color. The absence of everything. Dirt, grime, pain, suffering, hunger, cold.

Then, weightlessness.

The juddering beneath her stopped, and they were floating. She was floating. Her body was still restrained to the seat, but Chatine no longer felt as though she were inside of it.

She was empty. She was made of nothing but air. She was free.

Outside the window, the white had vanished and the sky was dark. There were no stars. There was no light. But it was nothing like the dark she'd experienced on Laterre. This one didn't feel heavy and hovering and crushing. It felt infinite and vast and hopeful. Like it was filled with endless possibility.

The ship banked left, heading toward its final destination.

And that's when Chatine saw them.

Three Sols hanging in the darkness, like jewels in the sky. A massive glowing white orb flanked by two smaller stars—one red, one with the slightest tinge of blue.

She pressed her face to the plastique of the window and blinked against the light. It was the most beautiful sight she'd ever seen. They were just as magnificent and breathtaking as she'd imagined. Brighter and bolder and more exquisite than anything anyone could ever hope to replicate in Ledôme.

But the thing that surprised Chatine the most about the Sols was that they were there at all.

She'd spent so many hours lying in darkness or walking under rain-soaked clouds, doubting that the Sols even existed. Convinced it was all just another ruse conjured up by the Ministère to give them false hope.

And yet, there they were.

Brilliant. Strong. Unwavering.

Like sentinels in the sky. Watching over the whole System Divine.

The ship veered into another sharp turn, and at once Chatine could see the shadowy, colorless sphere of Bastille coming into view on the horizon in front of them and the spinning globe of Laterre growing smaller and smaller behind them.

As she watched the only home she'd ever known vanish outside her window, Chatine couldn't help but laugh at the irony of it all.

She'd finally gotten off that miserable planet.

ACKNOWLEDGMENTS

Thank you, Nicole Ellul, our editor *magnifique*! *Sky Without Stars* owes so much to your smart, insightful, and diligent guidance. You helped us go deeper and ask questions we'd never thought to ask, and your enthusiasm, kindness, and friendship helped us every step of the way.

Jim McCarthy! *Merci merci merci* for believing in this book from the very beginning. From the moment you said, "You had me at '*Les Mis* in Space,'" you have been such a brilliant and passionate cheerleader for this book, and we couldn't have done this without your support.

Everyone at Simon & Schuster, you are the dream team and our shining bright Sols in the sky. Mara Anastas, Liesa Abrams, Chriscynethia Floyd, Ruqayyah Daud, Julie Jarema, Emily Hutton, Jessica Handelman, Michael Rosamilia, Heather Palisi-Reyes, Nicole Overton, Elizabeth Mims, Sara Berko, Samantha Benson, Nicole Russo, Caitlin Sweeny, and Anna Jarzab. And a huge shout-out to Mary Nubla and Christine Foye, sales rep extraordinaires! Thank you for getting behind this book before there was even a book to get behind!

Copyeditors don't always get the credit they deserve but Clare McGlade deserves all the kudos and all the thanks in the whole System Divine. (Just look at the size of this book!?) We nicknamed you Athena, goddess of copyedits, because of your wisdom and shrewd eye, and because at times it seemed you understood the world and history of Laterre even better than we did!

Extra sparkly, star-filled cheers for Billelis! We hardly know where to begin thanking you for the most beautiful, dazzling, and perfect cover. And thank you to the insanely talented Francesca Baerald who brought Laterre to life in your gorgeously stunning maps that we are *still* drooling over!

Our first EVER reader was Kristin Bair, who, out of the goodness of her heart, read a work-in-progress by two authors she'd never met before. Thank you for your comments, your incisive reading, and your excitement about the world and story we created. Your enthusiasm spurred us on right when we needed it most.

Thank you to Nini Kauffman-O'Hehir and Fae Leonard-Mann, our fabulous teen beta readers. We're not sure how you both read *Sky Without Stars* so fast (again, have you seen the size of this book!?), but we were delighted you ate up the story. Your feedback was invaluable! And to the utterly *fantastique* and impossibly brilliant Jessica Khoury. Thank you for your comments, ideas, sci-fi genius, and, most of all, for your patient ear as we griped incessantly about plot holes and word counts.

For two authors who know very little about solar orbits, Goldilocks Zones, or cloud coverage on distant planets, Marguerite Syvertson . . . you saved us! Thank you for taking the time to answer our many, often *stupide*, questions. And thank you, Joel Skinner, for your energy expertise and enthusiasm for helping us bring a distant imaginary world to life.

We were fortunate to have some wonderful booksellers read advance copies of this book. Kristen Gilligan (at Tattered Cover), Emily Hall (at Main Street Books), Julie Poling (at Red Balloon Bookshop), and Madeline Dorman (at Blue Willow Books), your support for *Sky Without Stars* and passion for getting it out into the world is deeply appreciated. Thank you!

And of course, *merci* to Monsieur Hugo for lending us Eponine, Marius, and Cosette (among others) so we could reimagine them on a far-off planet in a far-off future.

JOANNE:
Thank you to my mum, Kate Matthews, for being my first reader and my first true fan. Jana, Alan, and Janine Lewis, for your love, songs, and endless support. My dad, Frank Rendell, who introduced me to great literature and my brother, Jim Rendell, who was Luke Skywalker to my Leia back in the day!

Many thanks to my friends, especially my hard-working and creative mama friends who know the juggle like I do: Katia Belousova, Luisa Giugliano, Emma Iacono-Mannings, Dina Jordan, Leslie Kauffman, Caroline Roland-Levy, Stephanie Schragger, and Julie Von. Lesley Sawhill, Ron Aja, and Brandon Sawhill-Aja, thank you for your wonderful friendship and for bringing Shakespeare so deeply into our lives. And, of course, Pamela Mann for your beautiful poems and Donna Lewis for being my best Welshie—I love you always forever!

Jess Brody! You are the most incredible teacher, inspiration, coauthor, and most of all friend. Thank you for letting me play *Les-Mis*-in-Space dolls with you!! You are the capitaine of this voyageur, and you and your endless talent keep us up in the sky, flying in the right direction, and making sure we're not losing characters or vital plot points along the way. May the fun continue and the tea never run out. And thank you to Charlie Fink for putting up with our endless chat and the dumb questions about science and how to fix things.

And finally, Brad Lewis and Benny Rendell. Every day I learn from you and laugh with you. Benny, you shine on stage and behind the camera and make me so proud to be your mum (plus, your knowledge of all things *Star Wars* and sci-fi has been exceedingly useful for this book!). Brad, you're my own personal Krishna and Foucault rolled into one. Thank you for your unending wisdom and love. *Je t'adore!*

JESSICA:
I would be nothing without my amazing author clan: Jessica Khoury, Jennifer Wolfe, Marie Lu, Stephanie Garber, Marissa Meyer, Leigh Bardugo, Beth Revis, Danielle Paige,

Laini Taylor, Brendan Reichs, Morgan Matson, Kami Garcia, Andrea Cremer, Suzanne Young, Len Vlahos, J. R. Johansson, Alexandra Monir, Tamara Stone, Anna Banks, Emmy Laybourne, B. T. Gottfred, Carolina Munhóz, Raphael Draccon, Robin Benway, and Mary Pearson. Thank you, all you beautiful souls, for your support, encouragement, and constant reassurances that I'm not crazy . . . it's just part of the process.

And special thanks to Christina Farley and Vivi Barnes. Five years ago, you two taught a retelling class that I sat in on, and you asked us to write down classic stories that we loved in one column and possible alternate settings in another. By the end of that class, I had written *"Les Misérables"* and "space" in my two columns and had drawn a line between them. A line that would eventually become this novel. Thank you for your inspiration.

But this book certainly would not exist without you, Jo. I will never forget that dinner where you said, *"Les Misérables* is one of my favorite books!" and I said, "Do you want to retell it in space with me!?" The three-year process that has resulted from that fateful night has been some of the best years of my life. From the delirious late-night chocolate-fueled revisions, to your hilarious comments in the manuscript, to our epic brainstorming sessions (we really should invest in Skype), I'm quite certain I've never laughed so much in my life, and I've definitely never had this much fun writing a book. Thank you for being there to lift me up, delete my unnecessary adverbs, and replace every instance of [Jo! Help! This needs one of your epic descriptions!] with another one of your epic descriptions. The best part about writing with a partner is there's always someone who's not freaking out about the book. So far . . .

Thank you to Jo's family—Brad and Benny—for lending me your superstar for hours and days on end. I'm not sure how any of us would survive without her, am I right? And thank you to my own family—my parents, Laura and Michael Brody, my sister Terra Brody, my brother-in-law, Pier, and of course, *always*, Charlie. The sky is never starless when you're around. I love you and would live anywhere with you: even the Frets.

And last but never, *ever* least, thank you to my readers around the world, who have followed me from book to book, across cities, centuries, dimensions, and now galaxies. Thank you for indulging me in every creative whim that strikes my fancy—from spoiled heiresses, snowed-in airports, and magic jewelry boxes to mysterious plane crashes, time loops, and now Laterre. I would never be able to travel to any of these magical places without you. Even in my darkest nights, you are the light that keeps me going.

Merci beaucoup.